A WIDOW'S HOPE

EVELYN HOOD

Boldwood

First published in 2006 as *Voices from the Sea*. This edition published in Great Britain in 2025 by Boldwood Books Ltd.

Copyright © Evelyn Hood, 2006

Cover Design by Colin Thomas

Cover Images: Colin Thomas

A CIP catalogue record for this book is available from the British Library.

Paperback ISBN 978-1-80600-197-2

Large Print ISBN 978-1-80600-196-5

Hardback ISBN 978-1-80600-195-8

Ebook ISBN 978-1-80600-198-9

Kindle ISBN 978-1-80600-199-6

Audio CD ISBN 978-1-80600-190-3

MP3 CD ISBN 978-1-80600-191-0

Digital audio download ISBN 978-1-80600-193-4

This book is printed on certified sustainable paper. Boldwood Books is dedicated to putting sustainability at the heart of our business. For more information please visit https://www.boldwoodbooks.com/about-us/sustainability/

Boldwood Books Ltd, 23 Bowerdean Street, London, SW6 3TN

www.boldwoodbooks.com

This book is for Ruth, Nigel and Robert – former neighbours, and friends for always.

GLOSSARY

Farlins – Large troughs in which herrings are gutted
Hoosie – A small house, such as a fisherman's cottage
Hoose – A larger house
Whiley – A short while
Quine – A term of affection for a girl or woman
Loon – A term for affection for a boy or man
Fit – What

Glossary

1

PORTSOY, AUGUST 1865

Most of the villages strung along the Moray Firth coastline were built to a neat plan, with their sturdy stone-built houses in orderly rows, their windowless gable walls facing the sea in order to withstand the winter storms. But in Portsoy the houses were at all angles, as though the builders had simply set them up wherever they happened to find a piece of spare land.

Walking down towards the harbour after tramping round the surrounding villages, selling fish from door to door, Eppie wondered, as she often did, whether the village was rushing eagerly towards the sea, or clambering uphill, panic-stricken and desperate to get away from the rocks not far offshore, waiting with their sharp black wave-lashed fangs bared in the hope of one day being able to swallow up the entire village.

The first time she had voiced these thoughts aloud, Murdo had laughed the easy deep laugh that seemed to come from the very centre of him and made his sea-green eyes crinkle and his mouth stretch almost from one side of his brown face to the other. When Murdo laughed everyone within hearing could not resist breaking into broad smiles. It was his glowing zest for life that had made Eppie fall in love with him. He had teased her, telling her that only a lassie from Fordyce could think up such an idea.

'It's a' that education they fed you wi' instead o' porridge and good herrin',' he had teased, 'and dinnae try tae deny it, you that comes from a family o' schoolteachers. Education makes the brain work too hard.' And when she had tried to protest: 'It's hooses an' rocks ye're talking o', lass, no' livin' creatures. Hooses dinnae run and rocks dinnae eat folk!'

Even though the conversation had been more than eight years earlier, she remembered it vividly. The two of them, newly-weds and still joyful at having found one another, had been walking hand in hand on the grassy hill near to the marble quarry at the time. When Eppie, determined to explain, started to point out the way the sharp rocks protruding from the green, spray-flecked water below looked just like teeth, he had tickled her until she squealed for mercy, then tumbled the two of them on to the springy grass and kissed her squeals into a happy, submissive silence.

She didn't even realise that she was smiling at the memory of it until an elderly fisherman passing by her as she went through the town square squinted at her beneath thick grey eyebrows and remarked, 'Ye're fairly content wi' yer ain company, m'quine.'

Eppie blushed. 'It's just – it's been a good day for the fish,' she stumbled to explain, but he had already gone on his way, his own face wreathed in a smile.

It had indeed been a good day; the creel on her back was almost empty though her shoulders were tender where the straps had been rubbing them for hours. Eppie tried to ease the creel into a different position as she left the square and began to walk down North High Street towards the harbour.

She had been right on that day after all – the rocks did eat folk. They had eaten her Murdo a scant two years after he had laughed at her fancies. As the boat he and his father crewed on struggled back to harbour one dark and stormy night, weighed down in the water by the fish filling the holds, the rocks lurking beneath the surface had torn a great hole in the hull. They had scooped her precious man out as easily as the women baiting the hooks for line fishing scooped the mussels from their shells, and had chewed his bones and flesh so thoroughly that no matter how much she had screamed and wept and begged the next day, the grim-faced men who had found what remained of Murdo on the beach refused to let her see him.

'It's yersel', Eppie. Have ye had a good journey?' Barbary McGeoch, calling from her open cottage door, shattered the bitter memory. Eppie smiled at her friend, grateful for the inter-ruption.

'Aye, well enough. No' much fish left.'

'I'll take a hauf-dizzen if ye've got them.' Going by local custom Barbary's name would normally have been shortened to Babs, or Babbie, but her father, who had crossed and recrossed the world's seas and oceans in his youth, had insisted on naming his only daughter after the wild and beautiful Barbary Coast, and had never allowed anyone to alter it. Barbary, tall and straight-backed, with smooth olive skin, long black hair and high cheekbones, suited the name; although Portsoy born and bred, there was a striking look about her.

'Have ye no' got a' the fish ye need?' Eppie asked now. Barbary's husband Tolly was a fisherman and the young woman, as well as being a friend and neighbour, was one of the two gutters in Eppie's crew at the farlins. Fishing families always had a barrel of salted fish available.

'Aye, but there's no' much left an' some friends are comin'

over from Sandend for their dinner the night.' Barbary gave the
neighbouring town its local pronunciation of 'San'ine'. 'They
like a dish o' herrin' and they've got terrible bellies tae fill. The
way they eat ye'd think they never had a meal except when they
come tae us. I'll fetch the money.' She disappeared, to return
swiftly with a dish in one hand and a small child tucked beneath
her other arm. As Eppie transferred the fish from creel to plate,
the afternoon sun made the silver scales glitter and the baby
immediately removed his fingers from his mouth in order to
reach out towards the new pretty playthings.

'Na na, my wee loon, we'll no' have that.' Barbary deftly
swung her body round so that the herring was beyond wee
George's reach. 'He'd have a' six o' them in his mouth afore I
could stop him if he got the chance. He's teethin', so everythin'
he can get hold of gets pushed intae his mouth.' She kissed the
thwarted child, who had started to grizzle. 'Ye'll like it better
when it's cooked,' she assured him.

'He's comin' on,' Eppie said as the other girl put the dish
down on a table just inside the door and dipped a hand into her
pocket.

Barbary's dark eyes shone with maternal pride. 'Aye, they
grow fast, do they no'?'

'They do.' It was all Eppie could do to keep from snatching
the child into arms that ached to hold a solid squirming little
body again. Her Charlotte was seven years old now, but every
time Eppie saw a mother with her children her heart ached for
her own bairn.

'Come an' eat wi' us the night, ye'd be more than welcome,'
Barbary said warmly, but Eppie shook her head.

'I've got work tae do in the hoosie.' Part of her would have
welcomed the company, for there was little pleasure in eating
alone, but on the other hand she knew that being with a family

would only make her feel all the more lonely when she returned to her own cottage afterwards.

When she left Barbary another dozen or so steps brought her to the small cottage where she lived. As the door closed behind her, shutting out the noise and bustle of the street, the silence seemed louder than anything she had heard all day.

The coals in the range were still glowing, and the hob was hot. Slowly, wearily, she set a shallow iron pan in place and dropped a knob of butter into it. While it melted, she took the two remaining herring from the creel, splitting and gutting them with practised ease. Then she dipped them in oatmeal from an earthenware crock and dropped them into the butter, which immediately began to sizzle. While the herring cooked she sliced the potatoes she had boiled that morning.

Once the meal was eaten she cleaned pan, plate and cutlery before going to bed. It was still daylight, but the boats would start coming home early in the morning, which meant that she and the other fisher lassies would have to be at the farlins before dawn.

There was little comfort in going to bed. Eppie had always been used to sleeping close to others. Once she was old enough to leave the cradle in her parents' room she had shared a bed with her elder sister Marion, and after her wedding she had slept soundly in Murdo's strong, warm arms, or lain awake, thinking of him, on the nights when he was at sea. On the terrible night of his death she had huddled in a chair until, unable to bear the wild keening of Mag, her mother-in-law, she had slipped into bed with the older woman, holding her close and trying to soothe her, when all the time her own heart was breaking. And every night after that she had slept with Mag, trying to ease the terrible nightmares that tormented the woman during the dark, silent hours.

Mag had never recovered from the shock of losing both her husband and her son on the same night. A strong, active woman all her life, she had taken to sitting in a chair by the fire all day, scarcely speaking, leaving the housework and cooking and shopping to Eppie. The only person who could coax a smile to her grey face was wee Charlotte, then two years old. When she was with the little girl, Mag was more like her old self, which was fortunate because it meant that Eppie could leave her daughter in Mag's care while she worked long hours at the farlins.

When the barrels of herring were covered and stacked and the other fisher lassies were free to go back to their homes and families, Eppie then started on her second job – tramping inland with a full creel on her back, selling herring from door to door. Every penny she could earn was needed to keep herself, her mother-in-law and her daughter fed and housed and clothed.

She would return home at the end of the day to find Mag singing to Charlotte, or telling her a story, or playing a game with the little one while the housework and cooking awaited Eppie. The only work the elder woman stirred herself to do was to keep the fire going so that Charlotte was warm, and to set out the cold midday meal that Eppie had prepared for them both before setting out with her creel. Bone-weary, Eppie would cook an evening meal, put Charlotte to bed, then spend the evening cleaning and washing and darning.

At least in those days the house was occupied. Charlotte, too young to be touched by tragedy, bustled about the place like a tiny whirlwind, playing with her rag dolls and chattering and laughing. Neighbours called frequently to keep Mag company, and as often as not, one or another of them would bring a little soup or a few scones to add to the midday meal. But when, eighteen months after Murdo drowned, Mag was laid to rest beside her husband and their son, Charlotte had to go to Fordyce so that Eppie's parents could look after her. And then, for the first time in her life, Eppie was alone.

Being on her own in the cottage carried no physical fears for her. Nothing that might happen to her could ever be as bad as losing Murdo, and in any case, this was Portsoy, where the folk were decent and law-abiding, and neighbour looked out for neighbour. But she had never realised until she experienced it that being truly alone was like falling into a deep black void, with not a glimmer of light in it, and no hope of ever reaching the bottom. Every night in bed she curled up into a ball, shut her eyes tight and said her prayers, then filled her mind with pictures of Charlotte, sleeping soundly in her little bed in Fordyce, with her long, silken lashes brushing her round, rosy cheeks and her hands tucked beneath her dimpled chin.

She thought of Charlotte awake, laughing and talkative and always busy at something, be it standing on a stool, swathed in a pinny as she helped her grandmother to bake, or sitting at the table, drawing a picture with the tip of her tongue poking out between her lips and her hazel eyes squinting in concentration.

Tonight, though, she had something to look forward to, for tomorrow was Saturday. As the fishermen kept the Sabbath, their boats never went out on Saturday nights, which meant that once she had finished work Eppie was free to walk to Fordyce. She would get there in time to play with Charlotte and put her to bed, then in the morning after the family attended church she would have the rest of the day with her daughter. She wouldn't have to leave until the evening.

She held on to that thought, clutching it to her like one of the lucky charms the gypsy women sold from door to door in the summer, until, finally, she slept.

* * *

A quick knock at the door brought Eppie out of a dream that she knew was happy, but had flown the instant her eyes opened. 'Time tae get up, quine!' Will Lomond, the cooper who employed the fisher lassies, shouted, and even before she had time to respond with, 'Aye, Will, I'm wakened,' she heard his boots clattering on down the brae towards the harbour, and his fist hammering on another door.

She lay for a moment, trying to recapture the dream – trying with such determination that fragments of it floated back up from the depths of her subconscious. Murdo had been in it, alive and well, and they had been walking on the shore together, with Charlotte, a wee bairn again, riding high on his shoulders with her two fists buried in his thick fair hair. They had been talking together, but the words refused to come back, though the happiness of the dream ran through her like a golden river, giving her the strength to get out of bed and pull on her clothes.

It was still dark outside, and the air was cold against her bare arms. She had forgotten to steep oats for porridge the night before, so she hacked a thick slice of bread from the loaf and spread it with butter and the last of her mother's home-made raspberry jam, then poured out a mug of strong, black tea from the pot that had been stewing on the stove all night. The jam tasted of summer and sunshine, and the almost-perfumed flavour of the fruit painted a picture of her parents' back garden where, in season, the raspberry bushes were weighed down with large, soft berries that melted in the mouth.

Before going out she pulled on an extra skirt and a sturdy fisherman's jersey. She had been knitting it for Murdo when he died, and although he had never worn it, she felt, each time she put it on, as though he were holding her close. As she hauled on her thick-soled boots she could hear the women passing by on their way to the farlins, their voices hushed in the chill morning air.

Eppie tied her long, stiff oilskin apron around her waist before hurrying out to join the steady stream of women on their way to work.

* * *

When selling fish, her first call on a Saturday was always at the three-storey house owned by Alexander Geddes. Jean Gilbert, his housekeeper, had been a friend of Mag's, and Eppie could usually be sure of a cup of tea, a home-made pancake, and a chance to sit down for ten minutes before starting the walk up through town, stopping at doors along the way, then out into the surrounding countryside.

Today, Jean's usual smiling calm had a faint edge to it. 'Come away in, lass,' she instructed as soon as she opened the door. 'The tea's ready and waitin' for ye.'

'D'ye no' want tae look at the fish first?'

'And why should I bother my head wi' that? I know they'll be fine. I can trust ye. Just put a dizzen o' them in the pantry,' Jean said from the range where she was pouring tea into two thick cups, 'then sit yersel' down. I've somethin' important tae say tae ye.'

Eppie always felt a sense of awe when she went into the Geddes pantry, the same awe she felt in church. The cool room with its stone flags and scrubbed shelving was almost as large as her kitchen, the main room in her cottage. One long shelf held crocks filled with flour, rice, currants, raisins, lentils, barley and goodness knew what else, while another shelf held cheeses. Hams and cuts of beef had a shelf of their own, as did jars and bottles of preserved fruit, home-made jams and jellies and pickles and chutneys. The cupboards below held an amazing collection of cooking utensils including stewing pans, saucepans, frying pans and baking tins.

She selected a dozen of the best fish from her creel, laid them carefully on the marble slab awaiting them and then covered them with a white earthenware lid before tiptoeing back into the kitchen.

'There's the money, m'quine.' Jean was sitting at the table, sipping at her tea. 'Sit yersel' down now and listen tae what I've tae tell ye.' She cast a glance over her shoulder, as though making sure that the door leading to the rest of the house was firmly closed, then leaned forwards, lowering her voice. 'I've decided it's time for me tae stop workin' here.'

'Leave here? Why?' Eppie was dismayed; since Mag's death she had come to look on Jean as the nearest she had to family in Portsoy.

'Och, it's a' these stairs – my poor auld knees are tired of carryin' me up and down them day in and day out. Look at them...' Jean got up from her stool and hoisted her skirt up to her thighs, displaying puffy ankles, calves lumpy with varicose veins, and knees that were clearly swollen far beyond their normal size.

'They look awful sore!'

'They are, lass, they are. I doubt,' Jean said, shaking her skirts into place and lowering herself carefully back onto her chair, 'if I could manage anither winter in this hoose.'

'But where will you go?' Even as she asked the question, Eppie recalled that Jean had a married daughter who lived not far along the coast.

'Tae Lizzie's in San'ine',' the older woman confirmed. 'Now that her eldest's got a good position as kitchen maid in a big hoose in Aberdeen there's room for me. And I can earn my keep by helpin' oot with the younger bairns.'

'Mr Geddes'll be sorry tae lose ye.' Eppie knew that Jean had started working as a kitchen maid for the present owner's parents when she was twelve years old, left when she got married, and returned as housekeeper after she was widowed. By then, Alexander Geddes, the only son of the house, had married and inherited his father's business interests.

'I've no' told him yet,' Jean said now. 'I wanted tae speak tae ye first. Eppie, lass, I want ye tae apply for the position.'

'Me?' Eppie sat bolt upright suddenly, and tea almost slopped over the rim of the cup in her hands.

'Aye, you. Why no'?'

'What would I ken about bein' a hoosekeeper? I'm a fisher lassie, an' a fishwife.'

'Ye look after a hoosie, dae ye no'? And ye keep it spotless. Ye can cook an' bake – I know that from when I used tae veesit wi' poor Mag.'

'There's a difference between seein' tae a wee cottage and lookin' after a place this size!' Eppie waved a hand at the ceiling to indicate the two floors above. 'And cookin' for gentry's nothin' like cookin' for mysel'!'

'I've got some very good recipe books ye can have, and there's two lassies that come tae help with the hoosework. An' if I stay on here for another few weeks after it's decided you could come in every day tae work alongside me and get tae know the way o' the hoose. That's why I've no' said anythin' tae the master as yet. I wanted tae talk it over wi' you first an' make certain ye're willin'.'

'That's another thing – it's no' just Mr Geddes that'll make the decision. What about his mither?' Eppie had heard often enough from the other fisher lassies that old Mrs Geddes, who had moved back into the house to be with her son when his wife died, was a strong-willed woman.

'If I can get him tae go along wi' the idea o' hirin' you in my place, then she'll have tae go along wi' it tae. She doesnae always get her own way, and he's no' a man that takes kindly tae domestic worries. He'll want the matter settled and the new hoosekeeper in place as soon as it can be done.' Jean leaned forwards, her eyes fixed on Eppie's. 'Listen tae me, lass. If you worked here ye'd get bed and board as well as a decent-enough wage. Ye wouldnae have tae find rent for the cottage, an' lookin' after this hoose'd be easier than the hard work ye're at now.'

There was no denying that. Eppie was a packer, and working at the farlins for long hours in all weathers, filling the big barrels with layer upon layer of herring, was sore on the back. Constant immersion in cold brine meant that her hands were red and swollen, the skin chapped by cold working conditions and salty brine, and scarred by cuts from sharp fish bones. In some cases, helping to lift barrels full of fish and pickle had caused internal damage to fisher lassies, resulting in difficult childbirth and early ageing.

Jean was watching her closely. 'Ye'll soon have tae follow the boats doon tae England, will ye no'?'

'Aye, that's right.' The herring were beginning to swim south and already the catches brought in by the local boats were shrinking. In another few weeks the autumn season would show its face and the fleet would start preparing for the day when it would set sail for the English ports. The gutters and packers would have to follow them. It was hard enough having to go for a whole week without seeing Charlotte; every year Eppie had come to hate being away from her child for up to two months.

'If ye take the post o' hoosekeeper here ye'd no' have tae go south,' Jean pointed out. 'Give it a try, lassie. Let me tell the master that I've found someone tae take my place. Ye'll no' regret it, I'm sure o' that.'

Eppie drained her tea and got to her feet, scooping up the money for the fish, which had been put out, as always, on the table by her cup.

'I'll have tae be on my way. But I'll think about it, and let ye know my answer on Monday,' she promised.

2

Eppie loved the walk from Portsoy to Fordyce. Although she had almost three miles to cover it was a pleasant journey, and she enjoyed the peace and quiet as well as the freedom of walking without the weight of a creel on her back.

Leaving Portsoy behind, she strode out along the road leading to the town of Cullen, then took a right turn that led her between fields where flocks of sheep grazed. Ahead of her the fields sloped up towards Durn Hill, a great rounded mound where, her father had told her when she was a little girl, there had once been an ancient Celtic settlement protected by a series of ditches to deter invaders. The narrow road took a turn to the left and began to climb, passing a stand of tall trees, their leaves beginning to show the first yellow and red tints of autumn, before levelling out. Again, there were fields to either side, with several small farmsteads to be seen in the distance. Ahead, she could see the wooded slopes of another hill – Fordyce Hill.

Striding along, breathing in deep lungfuls of the country air, she reached the triangular field known as the Feein' Market, where the local farmers and those looking for farm work came together twice a year to strike work contracts. Tinkers used another triangular area of rough ground on the opposite side of the road as a makeshift camp when they came to the area to sell their wares.

To Eppie's relief, the camp area was empty of the tarpaulin and cloth shelters that the tinker folk could set up in no time; she had never had any problems with these people and was always happy to deal with the women when they came to her door to sell their goods, but at the same time she was uneasy whenever she passed along that road while a clan was in residence. The women and children tended to disappear silently and swiftly into their makeshift homes when she or any other stranger approached, while the men watched warily, and their lean dogs curled their tails between their legs and flattened their ears back, narrowing their eyes at her. Her father, who maintained that all folk were equal and nobody should fear anyone else, always passed the camp with a cheery word and a friendly wave of his walking stick, but to Eppie there was something unfamiliar and vaguely menacing about the men when they were gathered together in groups.

Almost as soon as the Feein' Market and the tinkers' ground fell away behind her she was in Fordyce itself, passing the Free Kirk schoolhouse with the one-roomed school behind it, then the church itself and on down the sloping street to where the small castle stood in the middle of the village. From there it was only a minute's walk to the lane where her parents' cottage stood.

Charlotte, as always, was waiting at the garden gate. 'Mother!' she cried as soon as Eppie came into view. She came rushing out of the gate, her golden brown curls flying about her round little face. 'Mother!'

Laughing, Eppie dropped the basket she carried and held

her arms open. Charlotte flew into them and as Eppie hugged her daughter she saw that her own mother, alerted by Charlotte's excited screams, had come out to the gate and was waiting there, beaming.

Eppie was home.

* * *

'You should apply for the position,' Marion McNaught told her sister in her usual decisive way. 'It's a sight better than working on the farlins and selling fish door to door.'

'But what if Mr Geddes doesn't consider me good enough to be his housekeeper?' Eppie had become almost bilingual since marrying Murdo and moving to his village – in Portsoy she spoke as the other fisher lassies did, but when she was home in Fordyce she reverted to the more formal speech her family used.

'Of course you're good enough – more than good enough. You're the daughter of a schoolteacher and the sister of a schoolteacher, aren't you? You've been educated in Fordyce – that alone should be sufficient to make the man's mind up.'

'But in Portsoy I'm a fisher lassie and a fishwife,' Eppie protested.

'Is that what they call folk that smell of fish?' Charlotte asked. She was sitting at her mother's feet, playing with the little doll that Eppie had brought for her. 'You always smell of fish, Mother.'

'Everybody in Portsoy,' Marion told her little niece, her nose wrinkling, 'smells of fish.'

'And some of the folk in Fordyce smell of chalk,' Peter McNaught put in, smiling at his younger daughter in an effort to take the sting out of Marion's hectoring tone. 'Charlotte, most of the folk in Portsoy earn their living by catching fish, just as your father did, God rest his soul, or by cleaning them and selling them as your mother does. It's only natural that they should always carry the scent of the sea about them.'

Grateful for his intervention, Eppie returned his smile, then said defensively to her sister, 'Nobody down in Portsoy knows or cares about what I did afore I married Murdo.'

'"Before",' Marion corrected her without thinking, and then, as Eppie flushed and bit her lip, 'I can write a recommendation for you if you like.' Marion taught at the village's infant school, while her father taught at Fordyce Academy.

'That'll no' – not – be necessary,' Eppie said hurriedly. On occasion, especially when she was tired, she found it difficult to make the transition from her Portsoy voice to her Fordyce voice. 'Jean Gilbert's recommendation'll be good enough. What do you think I should do, Mother?'

Annie McNaught was sitting in her rocking chair by the window, listening to the conversation but keeping her own counsel. Annie tended to leave the talking to her husband and her elder daughter, both well read and with strong opinions of their own. But when she did choose to speak she was worth listening to, as Eppie knew. Now she said, 'I think you should listen to this Jean Gilbert, lass. If she thinks you good enough to fill the position, then you must be. There's nothing wrong wi' being in service.'

'I'm not saying that there is anything wrong with being a servant, Mother,' Marion protested. 'I know fine well that you were in service yourself, but you didn't have Eppie's education. She should have been a teacher, like Father and me. She's got the brains for it.'

'But not the will.' Eppie decided that it was time to speak up on her own behalf. 'I'm grateful to all of you for your advice, but I'll wait till I get back to Portsoy tomorrow before I make up my mind. In the meantime, I'm off to take a walk round the garden.'

'I'm coming too,' Charlotte said at once. A placid, contented child, she was happy enough during the week with her grand-parents and Marion, but when Eppie was there the little girl stayed close to her side all the time. 'I'm going to call her Peggy,' she said as the two of them went into the walled garden at the side of the cottage. She held up the doll, made from a clothes peg and dressed from scraps of material stitched into a frock. Eppie had drawn smiling features on the peg's round top and glued on some yellow wool to give the illusion of hair. A tiny bonnet was tied over the little head. 'She's a very pretty lady and she lives in a castle.'

'Like the one in Fordyce?' Fordyce Castle was a tiny fairy-tale building nestling in the centre of the village. Mary Beaton, one of Queen Mary Stuart's four ladies-in-waiting, had married an Ogilvie of Boyne and lived in the castle. She was buried in the local graveyard.

'Much, much bigger,' Charlotte said. 'A castle like King Arthur's, with knights and horses in it and a big table. We got told about that at school. Lady Peggy has a big white horse with silver reins and a golden saddle, and she rides all over the castle grounds on it.' She skipped off down the garden between the fruit bushes, clicking her tongue to simulate the sound of horses' hooves and dancing the little peg doll up and down, as though she were rising and falling on a saddle.

'She's doing fine, lass.' Peter fell into step with his daughter. 'She's enjoying the school and she's a clever bairn.'

'Like Marion.' Eppie, the younger by three years, had always lived in her sister's shadow.

'Och, you're just as clever as your sister.'

'That's why I pack herring, then sell it door to door,' Eppie said drily.

'What sort of talk is that?' Peter took his daughter by the shoulders and turned her to face him. 'We both know that you could have been teaching alongside Marion in the infant school if you'd wanted to. And what stopped you?'

'I met Murdo.'

'Exactly. You put your heart before your head and there's nothing wrong with that,' Peter said firmly. Then, closing one eye in a huge wink and lowering his voice until only Eppie could hear the words: 'You take after me, for I did the same thing myself. When I fell slave to a bonny face and a sweet smile my father was raging because the lass I wanted was a servant and they had me marked down for marriage to another teacher, or mebbe even a gentleman's daughter. But I went ahead and married your mother, and I've never regretted it, just the way you'll never regret choosing your Murdo, God rest him.'

They had reached the end of the garden, where the three bee skeps stood close by a wall of rose-coloured bricks. Bees flew in and out of the entrances and a low contented buzz could be heard from inside each skep. One or two bees came to investigate the visitors, and when they landed on Eppie's hands she made no move to brush them off. If startled, the tiny creatures might sting, and that would be a tragedy, for Eppie had learned almost before she could walk that honeybees had a barbed sting that stayed in the wound, and once bereft of its sting the bee then died. Peter, like his father before him, had always had skeps, and even as a small child Eppie had learned to work with them. Bees held no fears for her.

She watched the bees crawl over her hands and then, curiosity satisfied once they had flown away, she asked, 'How are they doing?'

'It's been a good summer and they've worked hard. Now they're beginning to settle down for the winter. Your mother'll have a few jars of honey and some beeswax for you to take back with you,' her father said. And then, rubbing his hands together in eager anticipation, 'Now then, it's time to go indoors, for even at this distance I can smell that herring you brought sizzling away in the pan, and it's fair making my mouth water.'

* * *

As always, Eppie's visit to Fordyce passed too quickly. She and Charlotte always shared a bed, and she lay awake most of the night, listening to her daughter's slow soft breathing and making the most of the child's nearness.

On Sunday morning the family, all members of the Church of Scotland, attended morning service in the sturdy little church where her parents and she herself had been married, and where she and Marion and Charlotte had been christened, then as evening approached it was time to return to Portsoy and what she looked on as her other life.

As always, the parting from Charlotte was heartbreaking, and the walk back to the fishing village had none of the pleasure she had known the day before.

* * *

When she came back from selling fish on the following Wednesday, Eppie fetched the hip bath kept in the lean-to at the side of the cottage and filled it with water that had been heating on top of the range all day. She sank into its comfort with a sigh of relief, and would have stayed there contentedly until the water cooled if she had had the time.

Instead, she reached for the small stiff-bristled brush and the cake of washing soap laid out on an adjacent chair and scrubbed herself all over, taking special care to run the bristles of the brush right under her fingernails until the tender skin began to tingle.

Then she washed her long brown hair, rinsing it again and again in an attempt to rid herself of the smell of herring that clung to all the fishermen and fisher lassies. Charlotte sometimes referred to her 'Fish Mam', and although it was meant as an endearment, the name, coupled with Marion's barbed remarks, embarrassed Eppie.

When she had dried herself, and dried her hair as best she could with the towel, she pinned it up before putting on her best clothes. Finally, she opened the cottage door and took a long, deep breath to calm her nerves before setting off for the Geddes house. It was located at the harbour, a handsome three-storey building on the corner of Low Road and Shorehead. The house faced onto Low Road, with two narrow flights of stairs set flush against the house wall, running up from the street to meet on a landing before the main door, which was on the first floor. A door set in the Shorehead side of the building led to the kitchen and servants' quarters on the ground floor.

'Ye look grand, m'quine,' Jean said as she opened the kitchen door.

'Ye think so?'

'That I do. The master'll see for himsel' that you're a clean, decent quine. And mind,' Jean said as she opened the door leading to the rest of the house, 'that he's the one ye want tae please, and nob'dy else.'

Eppie had never been further than the kitchen; venturing beyond it and up into the area where the family lived was like travelling into a hitherto unknown land. She followed Jean

along a flagged passage with doors to either side, then up a flight
of stone steps to a wide hallway where the doors were polished,
panelled and decorated with fine brass handles. Large paintings
hung on the walls between each door. To Eppie, who had never
been in such an imposing house before, it looked like a palace.

'The ground floor's got the kitchen an' pantry, an' a store
room an' my own wee room,' the older woman explained as she
bustled along. 'Up here's the room where they eat their meals,
an' the big parlour, an' the master's library an' a wee room that
Mrs Geddes uses as her own parlour. The four bedrooms are on
the next floor. Now then...' She paused before one of the doors
and turned to face Eppie. 'Are ye ready tae meet yer new master,
lass?'

'I-I don't know if I'll be suitable...'

'Of course ye will. He's no' an ogre, even though he's no' what
ye'd cry a man wi' a keen sense o' humour. No' that he's got
much tae laugh about, poor soul.' Jean lowered her voice to a
whisper, though Eppie was doubtful that anything louder than a
shout could penetrate the solid panels of the door before her.
'And I've given ye a bonny reference,' she added briskly, 'so that
should go a long way tae makin' him look on ye wi' favour.' And
without further ado, she tapped on the door.

Butterflies began to flutter so hard in Eppie's stomach that
she clutched her waist with both hands. She thought of turning
and fleeing back down the stairs and out of the kitchen door, but
almost at once a man's voice barked out a command and Jean
opened the door and stepped into the room beyond.

'Eppie Watt's here, sir, tae apply for the post of hoosekeeper,'
she said, and then, opening the door wider: 'Come on in, then,
lass, an' let Mr Geddes take a look at ye.'

Everyone in Portsoy knew who Alexander Geddes was, for

the man was involved in several of the local industries. Eppie knew that he was part owner of the fishing boat that Tolly McGeoch crewed on as well as the small marble quarry to the south of the harbour. She had heard that he also had an interest in the salmon bothy, where salmon caught locally was prepared and packed. He shipped goods in and out of Portsoy, and she had seen him often enough striding about the place or riding through the streets on his horse. But she had never been as close to him as she was now, or been the subject of his piercing gaze.

'So – Mrs Watt.' He had been seated on the far side of a large desk, but now, to her surprise, he rose to his feet, for all the world as though she was gentry like himself.

'Sir.' Not quite sure what she should do, Eppie dipped a hasty curtsey.

'Jean tells me that you've got experience of housework.'

'Just in my mother's house, and then my own. Not in a big place like this, sir.' Eppie kept her gaze fixed on the desk. It was as large as her kitchen table, with piles of paper stacked neatly on its polished surface. One pile was held in place by a large lump of polished marble, the light from the window striking green glints in its glossy surface.

'I'm sure one house is much like another. Mebbe this one's larger than those you've known, but it's got furniture to polish and floors to wash and stairs to sweep like most other homes. You'll have daily help with the heavier work, of course. And you know about how to do laundry, and cooking and baking?'

'She kens a' these duties, Mr Geddes,' Jean said firmly. He was still on his feet, and now a few steps carried him around the desk to the long window that looked out over the harbour. He stood gazing out for a moment, framed by the graceful sweeps of the heavy curtains, which were caught back with cords. Eppie

glanced at Jean, who smiled and nodded encouragingly. While
she waited for Alexander Geddes to resume the interview she
glanced round the room. It was easy to see why the room was
known as the library, for three of its walls were hidden by
shelves of books, from the floor to the high ceiling. The fourth
wall held a handsome wooden fireplace flanked by two dark
brown leather armchairs, and two portraits. One, directly above
the fireplace, was of a very beautiful dark-haired, green-eyed
young woman, her soft rosy lips slightly parted as though about
to curve into an amused smile. The other, slightly smaller
portrait was set to one side of the fireplace, and was of an older
woman with dark brown hair drawn smoothly back from an
oval, serious face.

'I understand that you are a widow, Mrs Watt, and that you
work at the moment as a fisher lassie.' Alexander Geddes had
turned away from the window to face into the room, hands
clasped behind his back. With the light behind him, Eppie could
see little of his features; all she could make out was that he was
quite tall, and lean-built.

'Aye, sir, I'm a packer, and when we're done at the farlins I
take my creel round the doors an' sell fish tae the housewives.'

'A fishwife as well as a fisher lassie? You must work long
hours.'

'Needs must, sir.'

'I suppose they do. At least it proves that you're hardy, and
not afraid of work. Since you come from Fordyce I take it that
you've had a good education? The place is well known for its fine
school and academy.'

'My father teaches at the academy.' Pride in the declaration
helped Eppie to lift her head and look squarely at the dark
outline against the windowpanes. 'And my sister teaches too, at
the infant school.'

'Indeed? But you chose to turn to the sea for your living.'

'I chose marriage, sir.'

'And as I understand it, you were widowed young. That,' he said, his voice suddenly bleak, 'happens all too often. Jean tells me that you have a child.'

'A daughter who lives in Fordyce with my parents. She's content there,' Eppie said swiftly, suddenly worried in case he thought that she expected him to take Charlotte in as well.

'How old is she?'

'Seven years, sir.'

'The same age as my own daughter. I asked about your child, Mrs Watt, because I would not want a housekeeper with no experience of children. I have a son too, but he's a good few years older than his sister. I don't suppose you would object to working in a house where young folk live?'

'Of course not, sir!' Eppie was shocked at the very thought.

'In that case...' Geddes was saying when the door, which Jean had closed, opened and a querulous voice said, 'Alexander, I really must speak to you about— Who's this?'

Eppie turned so sharply that she almost stumbled. Her first impression of the woman confronting her was of a pair of piercing eyes as blue as a summer sky, but with none of its warmth. Cold and hard, they were set in a strong, lined face with a long, straight nose and a thin mouth. The newcomer had a head of snowy white hair; once, she must have been breathtakingly beautiful but now, in the winter of her life, she was striking. Eppie had glimpsed her in the village, looking out of the window of the small carriage she used to travel even short distances.

'Who are you?' the newcomer wanted to know, though the tone of her voice was really asking, *And what do you think you are doing here?*

'Mother, this is Mrs Watt, come to discuss the post of housekeeper. As you know, Jean has decided to move to Sandend...'

'I know that very well, and I have been setting my mind to finding another...' the terrifying blue eyes raked Eppie from the top of her head to the toes of her boots, then travelled back again '...*suitable* housekeeper,' Mrs Geddes finished.

'I believe that I may have found one,' Geddes said calmly, while Eppie wanted nothing more than to sink through the thick carpet beneath her feet and fall right out of sight.

'What households has she worked in before?'

'Mrs Watt works at the moment as a fisher lassie and a fishwife.'

'I could have told you that, for the room reeks of fish,' Mrs Geddes snapped, and Eppie took a step back, one hand flying to her mouth. She felt as though she had just been slapped hard.

'I was not aware of it – and even if it is so, almost every soul living in Portsoy and along the entire Moray Firth smells of fish, since catching, preparing, selling and cooking fish is the main industry in these parts,' Alexander Geddes said calmly. 'It is honourable work and there is a lot to be said for anyone involved in it. You can't deny, Mother, that you enjoy eating fish as much as the next person.'

The woman's already thin lips tightened even more, and Eppie saw a splash of crimson appear on each high cheekbone.

'If you insist on interviewing prospective servants – though I believe that you have better things to do with your time than that – then I should be present in order to advise you. Hiring servants is not a man's work.'

Alexander Geddes began to move, and as he passed Eppie he ceased to be a shadowy outline and she saw that his hair was thick and dark, greying at the temples. His eyes were dark and heavy-lidded, while he had his mother's long nose and straight mouth.

'Perhaps, Jean...' he reached the door and opened it '...you could take Mrs Watt to the kitchen and offer her some tea. I'll be with you shortly.'

3

'Now then, ye might as well start learnin' where things are,' Jean said when they were back in the kitchen, 'so we'll just start with a fresh pot o' tea. The tea caddy's on that shelf, and there's the pot. There's oatcakes in that tin and butter on yer left hand as ye go intae the pantry. I'll put the plates out.'

'There's no sense in me learnin' where everythin' is, since I'll no' be gettin' the position.' Eppie's hands shook as she lifted the caddy down, and there were tears behind her eyes and in the tremor of her voice.

'Fit makes ye think that, m'quine?'

'Och, Jean, Mrs Geddes would never have me in the hoose. You heard her – I'm no' good enough an' I smell of f-fish.' Eppie scrubbed at her eyes with her free hand and sniffed loudly.

'Ach, that old woman doesnae like anyb'dy. It's nothin' against you,' Jean said airily. 'She's vexed because the master didnae ask her tae see ye along wi' him – or instead o' him. An' he didnae ask her because he kens fine that she'd scare ye off. The final word'll rest wi' him – and he listens tae me, does Mr Geddes, for he kens I've got a good head on my shoulders.'

'I wish she didnae bide here!'

'So does Mr Geddes, I'm thinkin',' Jean said drily. 'Oatcakes – and butter.'

'I'm gettin' them.' Eppie put the tin of oatcakes on the table and then located the butter.

'Ye just have tae be polite tae the woman and get on wi' yer own work,' Jean said, buttering oatcakes. Eppie, used to making every scrap of food go a long way, watched in astonishment as the rich yellow butter was spread thickly. 'She invited hersel' here when young Mrs Geddes died and the maister was left wi' two bairns tae raise, one o' them newborn. I could have managed fine wi' the help o' a sensible lassie tae nurse wee Lydia, but Mrs Geddes was inside the hoose before me or the maister got time tae sort ourselves oot. An' she's had her feet well lodged under his table for the seven years since, lookin' after her son and his bairns, by her way o' it.' Jean poured some tea into her cup and studied it. 'Ye make a good strong cup o' tea, lassie,' she said approvingly, then went on as she filled both cups. 'If the truth be known, she's stayin' here tae make certain that the man doesnae get the opportunity tae make another bad marriage.'

'A bad marriage?'

'Eat up, lassie.' Jean buttered another oatcake for herself. 'An unfortunate marriage, I should have said, for there was nothin' wrong wi' both the lassies he married, other than bad fortune. The maister's her only child and his first wife was the daughter o' a friend o' his parents – that was Duncan's mither. She brought a dowry with her, enough tae let Mr Geddes expand his business interests. Then she died, and for a good few years he was too busy tae consider marryin' again. Then one day he met up wi' a young lady visitin' the place wi' her faither, who'd a share in the marble quarry here. Mr Geddes fell head o'er heels for her, and afore his mither realised what was happenin' he'd followed her back tae Glasgow an' asked her tae be his wife. Mrs Geddes never took tae the poor lass, though she was a lovely lady and she made the man very happy. Then did she no' pass away when wee Lydia was born. It was awfu' sad—'

She broke off abruptly as the door opened and Alexander Geddes came in.

'You're still here, Mrs Watt.'

'Aye, sir.' Eppie scrambled to her feet, almost knocking her cup over in her agitation. 'I was just about tae leave, sir.'

'Take your time. You thought, Jean, that Mrs Watt could come in every day for a month to work with you and get to know her duties?'

'Aye, sir. I'd no' leave ye without makin' sure that ye're a' bein' well cared for.'

He smiled at the housekeeper – a warm smile that lit up his dark eyes. 'I know you'd never leave us in need, Jean,' he said, and then, to Eppie: 'So perhaps you could start next Monday, and arrange to move in once Jean feels that you are ready to take over as housekeeper?'

'But what about—?' Eppie began, then as Jean's booted foot sent pain flaring through her ankle, she said meekly, 'Aye, sir. Thank you, sir.'

* * *

'I'll miss ye,' Barbary said as she helped Eppie to clean out the cottage and make it ready for its new tenants.

'I'm only goin' as far as the harbour.'

'You're goin' further than that.' Barbary, who had been scrubbing the floor, sat back on her heels and used her strong, rounded forearm to sweep a lock of thick black hair from her face. 'You're goin' up in the world. You'll be livin' in a big hoose.'

'In a room next tae the kitchen, just.'

'Even so – who'd have thought when we were workin' thegither at the farlins that you were goin' tae be livin' in the same hoose as the man that's got a share in the *Grace-Ellen*?' Barbary said, referring to the vessel her husband sailed on. 'An' he's got an interest in the cooperage that employs us tae gut and pack the herrin' too. I'm tellin' ye, Eppie Watt – ye've gone up in the world!'

'It won't make any difference tae me – or tae you,' Eppie said, suddenly worried in case she lost her closest friend. 'We can still see each other, can we no'?'

'Aye, but you'll have tae come tae my wee cottage, for I'd no' feel right in that big place.' Barbary plunged the scrubbing brush back into the pail of soapy water, spattering her apron.

A hand seemed to catch at Eppie's stomach and squeeze it painfully. 'Ye don't think I'm makin' a mistake, do ye, Barbary?'

'I do not.' The other girl was working so vigorously that the water sprayed from her brush with each sweep forward and back. 'Ye deserve a better life, and it's hard work ye've been doin' for the past few years, slavin' at the farlins and then walkin' for miles wi' a heavy creel on yer back. You're doin' the right thing, m'quine!'

* * *

At first Eppie doubted her friend's faith in the move from the farlins and her tiny cottage to Alexander Geddes's big house. Despite the fact that three other people lived there – she had not yet seen Duncan, her employer's son, since he was boarding in Aberdeen, where he attended school – the house was unnervingly quiet. Although she had often felt lonely in her little cottage she had always heard boots and horses' hooves and wagon wheels clattering and rumbling along the narrow cobbled street just outside her windows. The farlins, too, were noisy, with the fisher lassies talking and singing, seagulls screaming, the coopers hammering at their barrels and the voices of the fishermen, buyers and spectators all about the place. But even the noise from the nearby harbour failed to penetrate the Geddes house's thick walls, and its occupants were silent most of the time – Mr Geddes working at the big desk in the library when he was not out and about on business, and his mother in her own small parlour, or prowling about silently in order to spy on the servants.

Even seven-year-old Lydia made little noise, spending most of her time in her own room or with her governess in her grand-mother's parlour, which was used as a schoolroom in the morn-ings. Eppie, used to her Charlotte's constant chatter, found the little girl's adult behaviour quite worrying. It wasn't natural in a child of that age.

Throughout her first week in the house she lived in constant terror of doing or saying something wrong, or of breaking one of the lovely, delicate glass and china ornaments. 'It's Mrs Geddes,' she told Jean nervously. 'She moves about the hoose so quietly that I never hear her comin', and then I get such a fright when she speaks, or when I turn round an' see her standin' there, starin' at me. Can I no' work in the kitchen just now an' leave the rest o' the house tae you?'

'An' fit use wid that be? When I'm gone tae San'ine tae bide wi' my faim'ly you'll be in charge o' the whole hoose. I know ye'll have Sarah an' Chrissie comin' in tae dae the heavy work, but you'll be responsible for where they go an' what they do. Ye cannae hide in the kitchen an' leave them tae run aboot upstairs on their own, especially Chrissie. She's a grand strong worker, and nob'dy can scrub stairs or polish furniture like her, but ye darenae leave her on her ain, for she gets so carried away wi' what she's doin' that she's apt tae send one o' those wee ornaments flyin' aboot the room.'

'Mebbe I'm no' the right one for this position...'

'Aye, ye are, an' I've already told the maister that, so ye cannae let me down now,' Jean said calmly. 'Ye'll be fine. Just treat Mrs Geddes wi' respect – she likes that – an' give yersel' time tae settle in.'

As the days passed and Eppie became more accustomed to the big house, her nervousness eased – just as Jean had predicted. Mrs Geddes still frightened her, but she learned to hide her nerves behind a calm face and quiet voice, and the woman began to accept her, albeit grudgingly.

'Though I don't know how I'll be when Jean leaves and I'm on my own,' Eppie told her parents and Marion on her next visit to Fordyce.

'You'll be fine,' her father said comfortingly. 'You've got a good sensible head on your shoulders.'

While her mother added, 'An' ye're a grand cook, so they'll no' hae any worries on that score.'

'You're just as good as they are,' Marion added almost fiercely. 'They're fortunate to have you working for them. Keep telling yourself that.'

It was easy for Marion to say that, Eppie thought ruefully. Her elder sister had always had a good opinion of herself, and neighbours had been known to say in amusement when Marion was little more than a toddler that she behaved as though God had created the world just for her benefit. It sometimes seemed to Eppie that Marion had enough confidence for both sisters, while she herself had almost none.

But a month later, when Jean had gone off to live with her family in Sandend and Eppie had moved into the small room next to the Geddes kitchen, she was surprised at how well she was settling in.

Each time Eppie visited Fordyce, Charlotte insisted on hearing all about Lydia's nursery. 'Tell me again,' she begged whenever she could get her mother's attention. 'Tell me about that girl and her toys.' And then her hazel eyes and neat little mouth rounded into three almost-perfect O's as Eppie described the big dappled rocking horse with its bright-red harness studded with tinkling bells, the enormous doll's house with every room furnished in perfect detail, and the shelf of dolls and teddy bears. Charlotte's favourite doll, formerly Prudence, was now known as Lydia.

'Now tell me about her clothes.'

'We'll keep that for after church tomorrow,' Eppie said, but Charlotte was already bouncing with impatience.

'Now, now!' she insisted, and when Eppie had described the tallboy filled with vests and petticoats and stockings and drawers, and the wardrobe holding handmade dresses and skirts and blouses, she said, 'That girl must go to a lot of parties.'

'No, she doesn't,' Eppie said in surprise. It was something she had not thought of before. 'In fact, she doesn't go out much at all unless she's in her grandmother's carriage.'

'Why doesn't she go out every day?'

It was a question that Eppie was beginning to ask herself. 'Mrs Geddes says she's too delicate to go out,' she said, and then, as Charlotte's brow furrowed: 'That means that she isn't very strong and she has to be careful in case she catches a chill from the cold wind, or gets her feet wet.'

'De-li-cate,' Charlotte said thoughtfully. 'Write it down.'

Words fascinated her, and since starting school she had

taken to carrying a bundle of paper and a stubby little pencil in the pocket of her smock. Now she laid them on the table and watched as her mother wrote down the word 'delicate'.

'Now me.' She took the pencil and copied the letters one by one, the tip of her pink tongue protruding from one corner of her mouth and her eyes narrowed in concentration. 'De-li-cate,' she said with satisfaction, stuffing the papers back into her pocket. 'I'm not delicate, am I?'

'No, you're not. You're a very healthy lass, and I'm glad of that.'

'Does Lydia go to school in the carriage?'

'She doesn't go to school at all. A teacher comes in every day to do lessons with her.'

'A teacher like Aunt Marion?'

Delighted by her niece's natural enthusiasm for learning, Marion had taken to giving Charlotte extra lessons at home. It troubled Eppie, who wondered at times if the little girl was being worked too hard, but dependent as she was on her parents and sister to look after Charlotte on her behalf, she could say little. When she did mention her concerns to her father he told her soothingly that Charlotte enjoyed the sessions with her aunt, and that he would not allow Marion's zeal to give the child more work than she could cope with.

'Yes,' she said now. 'A teacher like Aunt Marion.'

'But if she doesn't go to the school, and she doesn't go out to play, how can she see her friends?' Charlotte persisted.

'She doesn't have many friends,' Eppie admitted. 'I think Mrs Geddes takes her to houses sometimes where there are little girls to play with.'

'I could be her friend. You could take me back to Portsoy with you, and I could play with her. I'd like fine to see that

rocking horse with the bells that ring when it's rocking, and the
bonnie hoosie that her dolls live in.'

'One day, mebbe,' Eppie said, knowing full well that old Mrs
Geddes would be horrified at the very idea of her precious
granddaughter having anything to do with the housekeeper's
child.

As she set off for Portsoy the next day Charlotte's *'How can
she see her friends?'* rang in her head. It had seemed to Eppie from
the very beginning that Lydia Geddes was a lonely little girl.
Missing Charlotte as she did, Eppie would have liked to take
Lydia for walks, or down to the water's edge to show her the
wonders of the seashore with its shells and pebbles and rock
pools. But when she suggested such an outing to Helen Geddes
the woman was shocked.

'My granddaughter is not a strong child and I will not have
her exposed to the bad elements that float in the air.'

'But the sea air's good for bairns, surely?'

'For bairns from the cottages, maybe, but not for the likes of
Lydia. We'll have no more talk of her going out with you, if you
please,' she said sharply. 'Perhaps you should bear in mind that
you're employed here as the housekeeper and nothing more
than that. There's plenty of work indoors to keep you occupied,
and Lydia's welfare is none of your business.'

There was such a difference between Charlotte and Lydia,
Eppie thought as she walked along the road between Fordyce and
Portsoy. Charlotte was brown from the summer sun, and her cheeks
were rosy, whereas Lydia's oval face was milk-pale and her beautiful
green eyes and black hair, inherited, Jean had said, from her
mother, made her skin seem even whiter. Her only outings were
when she went with her grandmother in the carriage to visit Mrs
Geddes's friends, but she seemed content to spend the rest of her

life either at lessons in her grandmother's little parlour, or playing in her room. Although it was clear from the way Alexander Geddes looked at his daughter that he adored her, her upbringing was left to her grandmother, who spoiled her and indulged her every whim.

It was Eppie who had to bear the brunt of the little girl's spoiling. Following Mrs Geddes's example, Lydia never put anything away when she had finished with it. On the few occasions when she returned from an outing her hat, coat and gloves were left discarded on the floor, and her bedroom was littered with toys every day. To tell the truth, Eppie quite enjoyed tidying the child's room, for it gave her the opportunity to handle silks and satins and muslins and velvet, as well as toys she had never even known existed before – pretty dolls with real, silky hair, and delicate china faces – along with miniature furniture from the doll's house, perfect in every way.

Unfortunately, Lydia knew where everything should go, even though she herself did not see the need to put it there. No matter how careful Eppie was, she could never get it right. 'Not there,' Lydia would snap if she happened to come into the room when Eppie was settling a doll into a doll-sized chair, or carefully putting a piece of furniture back into the large, exquisite house that stood on its own table to ensure that it was just the right height for Lydia to play with. 'It goes there, can't you see?' And she would snatch whatever it was from Eppie's hand and put it in its rightful place, sighing loudly or tutting over the housekeeper's stupidity.

'It would be better if you just put them in the right place when you finished with them,' Eppie suggested one day, her tone deliberately mild. To her astonishment the child turned to gaze at her with cold green eyes and said, 'Why should I, when my father pays you to keep the house tidy?'

'If my own wee lassie had said that to me,' Eppie said in the kitchen later that day, 'I would have put her over my knee.'

'That's the trouble,' Chrissie grunted. 'That bairn's never been taught right from wrong.'

'It's the way rich folk do things,' Sarah chimed in. It was Tuesday, and the two women had come to help with the ironing and floor scrubbing. 'Why should she lift a finger when we're paid tae dae everythin' for her? But ye're right, Eppie – if one o' my bairns spoke tae me like that I'd warm her arse for her.'

'It's that Mrs Geddes.' Chrissie nodded. 'She's ruinin' the lassie, and Mr Geddes is that caught up wi' makin' money that he never notices it. No' that it matters a' that much, for Lydia'll be bonny enough tae find hersel' a rich husband when the time comes, and he'll supply enough servants tae run aboot after her for the rest o' her days.' She drained the last of the strong tea and laid the mug on the table. 'Well, I suppose we'd best get back tae work.'

Lydia had her sweet moments too. Sometimes when she had nothing else to do she would seek Eppie out, following her around the house or sitting at the kitchen table while Eppie baked or darned or prepared the next meal, talking about the lessons she had been doing earlier that day, or about her brother.

'He'll be home for Christmas and Ne'erday,' she said, her eyes shining at the thought. 'I've got a calendar on the wall in my bedroom and I'm putting a big cross on it every night before I go to bed. Duncan will be here in...' she paused, her face screwed up in intense concentration, her pursed mouth moving silently as she calculated '...ten weeks. Seven days a week equals seventy days. Seventy days isn't as long as ten weeks, is it?'

'It doesn't sound as long,' Eppie agreed tactfully.

'Do you know my brother Duncan?'

'No, I don't.'

'He's very nice and kind. He laughs a lot and he plays games with me.' Lydia's normally sulky little face glowed with hero worship. 'He's the best brother in the whole world and I wish he could stay here all the time. I like it when he's here.'

'Do you not have any wee friends who could visit you when your brother's not here?'

Lydia's dark curls bounced as she shook her head. 'There's nobody for me to play with,' she said, adding as Eppie thought of the many children running around Portsoy, 'nobody good enough. I sometimes play with two girls I meet when I visit grandmother's friend Mrs Bailey, but I don't like them very much. They're nasty to me when grandmother's not looking. My brother Duncan's nearly grown up and he has to work very hard at school. His school's in Aberdeen. Have you ever been there?'

'No, never.'

'Duncan says he'll take me there when I'm older.'

Difficult though she could be, the child's loneliness made Eppie's heart ache, especially when she visited Fordyce and saw Charlotte playing with the friends she had made since going to school. But there was little she could do for Lydia, apart from welcoming the child any time she chose to seek Eppie out. She did, once, let Lydia help her with the baking, but unfortunately Helen Geddes chose that day to make one of her rare visits to the kitchen, and when she discovered her granddaughter happily rolling out a round of dough at the table, her face tightened with rage.

'Lydia, what do you think you're doing?'

'Making a tart for Father's tea.' The little girl folded the dough over and attacked it with the roller. 'Look, Grandma, look what I can do!'

'Put that down at once and come here,' Helen ordered, and

when the child obeyed: 'Look at you – you've got flour all over your face, and in your hair!'

'It'll brush out, Mrs Geddes,' Eppie hurried to assure her, but was ignored.

'On your pretty velvet dress too. And me expecting visitors! What'll they think when they see my granddaughter looking like a child from the gutter?'

'I'll put her to rights...' Eppie began, then fell silent as the woman turned to survey her with eyes as blue and as hard as sapphires.

'You,' said Helen Geddes, 'have done enough damage. I will see to my granddaughter myself, and I will certainly speak to her father about this disgraceful episode. Come along, Lydia.' She held out her hand, then drew it back sharply as Lydia went to clutch it. 'Walk in front of me. I don't want flour all over my clothes, thank you. I am expecting two visitors in one hour's time,' she added icily to Eppie as she followed the little girl out. 'See that tea is ready to be served in my parlour as soon as they arrive. And make sure that you have a clean apron on when you open the door to them.'

Then she and Lydia were gone, and Eppie was on her own, struggling to hold back her tears. She was convinced that she would be dismissed before the day was out, and even though nothing was said, she went about in fear for a whole week before realising that either Mrs Geddes had kept silent, or her son had decided to take no action. Eppie doubted, given the outrage in the woman's eyes and voice as she swept Lydia from the kitchen, that she had been able to hold her tongue, but she found it even more difficult to believe that Mr Geddes had let the matter pass without comment.

Just when she had begun to believe that she was safe from

any further reprisals he came into the dining room one morning as she was clearing the plates from the table.

'I'm sorry, Mr Geddes,' she stammered as she looked up and saw him standing in the doorway, 'I thought you'd finished in here...'

'I have. Eppie, I hope you're settling in here.'

'I am, sir, I like it very much. I'm just not sure...' she suddenly faltered, recalling his mother's rage when she found Lydia in the kitchen, covered with flour '...if I'm suitable.'

'You're very suitable. At any rate, you suit me, and if you have any worries I hope that you will bring them to me so that they can be dealt with.'

'I will, sir. Thank you, sir,' she said, and escaped to the kitchen, realising that she was fortunate to be working for such a kind and decent man.

4

Even though she was in the kitchen two floors down, Eppie heard Lydia's high-pitched squeal, followed by the thud of feet rushing down the stairs from the nursery.

Startled, thinking at first that something had frightened the child, or that she was hurt, Eppie rushed along the flagged passage and up the flight of stairs to the hall. She had just arrived when Lydia reached the final step, screaming, 'Duncan! Duncan's here!' and dashed to open the front door.

Eppie stopped short, one hand clutching at her thudding heart, as Alexander Geddes and his mother appeared, he from the library and she from her parlour. By that time Lydia had lifted the latch and rushed out, heedless of her grandmother's cry of: 'Lydia, you'll catch a chill, get back in here at once!'

'Duncan!' the child screamed again, and Eppie saw her launch herself off the doorstep, arms spread out as though she were flying. For a terrifying moment it seemed that she was doomed to fall to the pavement with a bone-shattering crash, but instead, a tall figure came striding up the steps and into the hall, Lydia's arms wound tightly around his neck and her stockinged legs wrapped about his waist.

'Lydia Geddes!' Helen screeched, reaching out to tug her granddaughter's skirt over her legs. 'You're making an exhibition of yourself! Duncan, set her down this moment!'

Laughing, the newcomer did as he was told, rumpling his half-sister's hair as he straightened. 'It's grand to get such a warm welcome home,' he said, and then, leaning forwards to kiss Helen's proffered cheek, 'How are you, Grandmother?'

'All the better for seeing you.' For once, her face was wreathed in smiles. 'Did you have a good journey from Aberdeen?'

'Well enough. Father, how are you?'

'In fine form, as you can see. Welcome home, Duncan.' Alexander Geddes shook his son by the hand. 'There's a fire burning in the parlour and your room's ready for you. You'll be eager for some food, I've no doubt?'

'Laddies of his age are always eager for food,' Helen said warmly, and her grandson's ready laugh rang out again.

'I'm starving. I've not had a proper meal since I was last here. Let me just get my boxes upstairs.'

'And while you're doing that I'll ask Eppie to bring the food from the kitchen.'

Alexander was turning to go along the hall when Eppie said timidly from the shadows, 'I'm here, sir. I'll see tae it at once.'

* * *

Suddenly the house was filled for the first time with sound and movement. As Eppie made tea and heated broth and arranged plates and cups on the big tray, she could hear Duncan Geddes running upstairs and then back down again almost immediately. Lydia was chattering as she never had before and her father and grandmother also sounded unusually animated. It was as though the young man's arrival had wakened the house from a deep sleep.

She was ladling the steaming broth into a large bowl when Lydia burst into the kitchen, followed, to Eppie's surprise and embarrassment, by her brother.

'This is Duncan,' the little girl announced importantly. 'This is Eppie, Duncan. She works here.'

'How do you do, Mrs...?' Duncan Geddes, with his dark hair and long straight nose, was very like his father apart from two distinctions; his eyes, heavy-lidded like his father's, were a warm brown, and his smile, as he held out a large hand, was surprisingly quick and warm.

'Just Eppie,' Lydia insisted.

'It's Eppie Watt, but Eppie's fine, sir.' She wiped her hand on her apron and, blushing, put it into his for a brief moment.

'Then Eppie it shall be.'

'Duncan's going to be a physician,' Lydia said proudly.

'I don't know about that. I doubt if I'm clever enough.'

'Father says you are, and he should know. So you will be,' Lydia insisted, but her brother was brushing past her to take the tray from Eppie.

'I'll see to that. Open the door, Lydia,' he ordered, and they set off in procession, Lydia skipping ahead while Eppie brought up the rear.

* * *

Both of the Geddes womenfolk seemed to Eppie to blossom during Duncan's brief visit home. Lydia bloomed like a sunflower, stretching and growing almost overnight to welcome the sun's warmth, while her grandmother was more like a rose with its tightly packed petals relaxing, while at the same time remaining formal. There was a change in Alexander Geddes too; Eppie, quietly going about her duties, noticed the warmth in the man's dark eyes as he watched his son, thinking himself unobserved. And yet when he and Duncan spoke to each other there was always a stiff formality between them. It was as if they were both afraid to show their true feelings.

It was a great pity, Eppie thought, that they should be so careful with each other; she put it down to the way the gentry behaved, and, having been raised in a home where affection was a natural way of life, she pitied both the father and son, but particularly Duncan, who was at his happiest when alone with his young half-sister. Only with her, it seemed, could he be himself, letting his natural, warm affection take over. Eppie hoped that one day, when he was grown to manhood, he would find a young woman who would understand and return his need for affection.

When his father and grandmother were out of the house, or busy with their own pursuits, Duncan took to coming into the kitchen where he sat watching Eppie about her work, asking her about herself and her family, telling her about his school life, and eating anything that was to hand. He had a healthy appetite, and no amount of eating between meals prevented him from clearing his plate at every opportunity.

One day he wandered into the library when she was dusting. Alexander Geddes was a man who liked order in his life, and so his large desk was always tidy and the many books he possessed stood in ordered rows on their shelves. 'The master cannae abide tae have his things moved out o' their proper places,' Jean had told Eppie, 'and if anythin' goes missin' you'll be held responsible, even if it wasnae you tae blame at all. The only answer is tae always attend tae his possessions yersel'.'

Today, the desk was empty but for a neat pile of papers and the marble paperweight standing, as always, near the right-hand corner. Eppie dusted beneath the papers and then replaced them just as she had found them. Then she picked up the paper-weight and gave it a good rub. It fitted her hand easily, its cool smoothness comforting against her palm. Before setting it back down she turned to the window and marvelled at the way the light made the green marble glow. She stared into it, seeing black whorls and flecks deep within, and marvelling at the beauty of it. Then she almost dropped it as Duncan said from the doorway, 'It's a miracle of nature, is it not?'

He came forwards and took it from her, then used his free hand to draw her closer to the window. 'D'ye see how the colours seem to move as you turn it about?'

She nodded, fascinated. 'It's like the sea on a summer's day, with the big green waves comin' in.'

'Well described. Imagine such beauty,' the youth said, 'hidden from sight in ordinary rock, waiting to be released by the quarrymen.'

'What makes it look like that?'

'It takes millions of years.'

'Millions?' she asked, and he laughed at the way astonish-ment made her voice rise to a squeak.

'More years than your brain, or mine, or anyone else's can even begin to imagine. I've read a lot about it; it's made up of calcium carbonate – that's the bones of tiny sea creatures that lived millions of years ago. It takes layers and layers of those wee skeletons. Then over those millions of years, volcanoes that used to be all over the earth heated them, and they were under tremendous pressure from the movement of the mountains.

That's another thing that's hard to believe – that mountains can move, but they do, very slowly. That's how we get coal and diamonds and emeralds – and marble. We're blessed to have all that beauty at our feet, just waiting to be released.' He ran a finger lovingly over the surface. 'Its real name's serpentine – that's a form of marble. Look...' He laid the marble down and pulled open one of the desk drawers. From it he took a small stone that he placed in her hand. 'That's what marble looks like before it's released from the rock and treated.'

'But it's just like any other stone you'd find on the beach. How do you know there's marble in there?'

Duncan laughed, delighted by her interest. 'The quarrymen know all right. They can read the rocks.' He put the stone back into the drawer, then caught at her hand. 'Come with me.'

She had no option but to follow him along the hall to the family parlour, blushing to think of how rough her fingers must feel against his. 'This came from our own quarry,' he said proudly, indicating the room's fine mantelpiece. 'Well, it's not entirely ours. The Ramsays in Glasgow have leased the right to quarry the area from the Earl of Seafield – you'll know that he owns all this area – and my father has shares in it and works it for the Ramsays. So that nearly makes it ours.'

'This is from Portsoy?' She had always admired the mantelpiece, which, like the paperweight, was a translucent green, marked with black and white streaks and patterns.

'Indeed it is. And there are two mantelpieces in the Palace of Versailles, shipped all the way there from our Portsoy quarry. The palace I'm talking about is in—'

'France,' Eppie said without thinking, and then, seeing surprise in his expressive brown eyes: 'My father's a school-teacher,' she said, and watched the quick colour rise to his cheeks. He hadn't thought that a mere housekeeper would know such a thing, she thought with a mixture of amusement and resentment.

'Oh – I see. Have you ever been to the marble quarry?'

'No, never.'

'I could take you there if you like.'

'I'd like it fine, but what would your father say?'

'I doubt if he would mind, but we could go when he's elsewhere on business if you like. And when my grandmother's out,' he added, one eye closing in a swift, amused wink. 'Tomorrow afternoon. I know that they're both going to be away from the house then.'

'I'm not sure that I should, Master Duncan.'

'Nonsense, there's no harm to it. We'll go tomorrow.'

'Go where?' Lydia asked from the doorway.

'I'm taking Eppie to see the marble quarry and you must keep your mouth shut tight and not tell on us.'

'Can I come?'

'Mrs Geddes wouldn't want me to take you out in this cold weather,' Eppie began, but the little girl stamped her foot.

'If you're going then so am I! And if you leave me behind I shall tell Father and Grandmother!'

'You're a little minx,' Duncan said, a mock scowl on his face and laughter in his voice.

'You'll take me too? Oh, please, Duncan! I'm never allowed to go anywhere interesting!'

'I don't see why you shouldn't come too. Nobody will ever know,' Duncan went on as Eppie began to protest. 'I'll tell the men at the quarry to keep quiet about it, and we needn't be away for long. But one word out of place, madam,' he added to Lydia, 'and I shall pick you up and swim out to the black rocks and leave you there for the fishes to eat.'

And Lydia squealed with laughter and promised that she would never ever tell a living soul about their adventure.

* * *

A brisk wind blew in from the sea on the following day, and on the horizon the heavy grey clouds seemed to be bearing down on the tossing, white-capped waves.

'Can we not wait until the weather's better?' Eppie asked nervously as Duncan and Lydia arrived in her kitchen only moments after the front door had closed behind Helen's straight, narrow back.

'It's not raining, and I'm going back to school tomorrow,' Duncan reminded her, while Lydia chimed in with: 'You promised!'

'You must wear your warmest clothes then.'

'I will, I will! Come on.' Lydia grabbed Eppie's hand and rushed her upstairs. 'Let's get ready and go before they come back!'

* * *

As they left the streets and began to climb to the headland Lydia skipped ahead, revelling in the pleasure of being able to run without being told to behave like a young lady.

'How did Mr Geddes come tae be in charge of the quarry?' Eppie asked Duncan as they followed the child.

'Through Lydia's mother, Celia Ramsay. Her portrait hangs over the fireplace in the library.'

Eppie had often looked at the portrait when she was cleaning the library. The woman in it, little more than a girl, was dark and vivacious, and very beautiful.

'My stepmother,' Duncan was saying, 'came from Glasgow. Her father owned several quarries and was a shareholder here – that's how she met my father; her own father came here on business and brought her with him. When they married, Mr Ramsay asked Father to look after the Ramsay interests here. When he died he left his share in the quarry to my father. Eventually, it'll be Lydia's.'

He eyed the small figure bustling along ahead of them, now jumping from one clump of grass to another, and sighed.

'Lydia's the fortunate one – I love the quarry, but my grandfather on my mother's side was a physician and I'm told that my mother had set her heart on me following him into the profession.'

'Physicians are highly regarded,' Eppie said.

'I know they are, but I've no interest in being highly regarded, and it's hard to be good at something if your heart's not in it.' Then he stopped and lifted his head to the wind, which was getting stronger as they climbed. 'Listen – can you hear it?'

She listened intently and caught an irregular chinking sound. 'It's like a lot of bells that are ringing flat.'

'That's the men splitting the rock. You can't use explosives to get to marble because it's too fragile,' Duncan said, jamming his hat down on his head more firmly lest the wind take it. 'We've arrived. Lydia, come back here.'

A moment later the small quarry lay beneath them, with men dotted here and there on its slope, working on the rock face. A few were gathered round a large slab of rock on the beach below.

'How do we get down?' Eppie asked nervously, and Duncan nodded at a pathway running down the side of the quarry.

'We use that.' He grasped Lydia's hand. 'It's easy as long as you take it slowly.'

By the time the three of them had scrambled down to the beach they were breathless and almost too hot in their warm clothing. The quarrymen, intent on their work, threw swift glances at the newcomers, and some nodded to Duncan before turning back to their work.

'They're shaping the marble, probably for a mantelpiece,' Duncan explained as Eppie studied the pulley-operated machinery the men were working with. 'They use a template with the shape cut out of it, and a mixture of slurry and rough sand. By hauling on the pulley they can pull the template back and forth to wear the marble down into the shape they need. They have to keep washing the sand out and replacing it.'

Eppie was so intent on watching the men work and listening to Duncan's explanations that she became quite oblivious to the cold until Lydia, who had wandered off along the beach in search of pebbles, returned to tug at her sleeve.

'Can we go home now? I want to go home!'

Eppie glanced down at the little girl and saw to her horror that Lydia's eyes were watering and her face chalk-white, apart from her nose, which was like a little red button. Her hands were bare, and blue with cold. When Eppie pulled her own glove off and caught at one of the child's hands it was as cold as ice.

'Where are your gloves?'

'There, s-somewhere.' Lydia indicated the beach behind them. 'I took them off to pick up some nice stones and I c-can't find them. I w-want to go home!' Her teeth were chattering and the words were stuttered out.

Eppie pushed her own gloves on to the little hands and then called to Duncan, who turned at once, his eyes darkening as he saw the little girl's ashen face. 'Come on,' he scooped his half-sister into his arms and settled her on his shoulders. 'I didn't realise we'd been here for so long. Can you link your arms about my neck, Lydia? That's the lass. Off we go.'

Eppie followed him up the path, her heart in her mouth. It wasn't fear of the climb or knowing that behind them a steep slope fell to the stony beach that frightened her, but the realisation that they had spent longer than they should have at the quarry, and now they would be fortunate if they got back to the house before Mrs Geddes.

At the top of the hill Duncan swung Lydia from his shoulders and then gathered her into his arms as though she were a baby, and set off at a run, Eppie panting along by his side.

'I'll take her straight up to her room,' he said as they sped along, 'and you bring some hot water to warm her. She'll be fine – you'll see.'

By the time they had reached the house Lydia was beginning to enjoy the journey and laughing at the way Eppie's gloves flapped at the ends of her short arms.

'There, home and dry,' Duncan said as Eppie opened the back door and stood back to let him in. 'Now then, young lady, it's upstairs with you—'

He stopped so abruptly that Eppie, turning after closing the door against the cold grey day, almost walked into him. Peering round his arm, she saw Helen Geddes, still in her outdoor clothes, standing at the inner door.

'So you're back at last,' the woman said. 'And where have the three of you been?'

'I promised not to tell,' Lydia piped up, while at the same time her brother said, 'Just out for a breath of fresh air.'

'On a day like this? You took the bairn out into that cold wind when you both know very well that she's got a delicate chest? And what's that she's got on her hands?' Helen swept forwards and snatched the gloves off. 'My goodness, lassie, your hands are like ice. And so's your wee face! Give her to me at once!'

She dragged her granddaughter from Duncan's grasp. Lydia, sensing trouble, burst into tears, throwing her arms around Helen's neck and burying her cold face into her while Helen ignored Duncan, concentrating instead on Eppie's stricken face.

'I blame you for this,' she said, and then, raising her voice to drown out Lydia's sobs and Duncan's attempt to speak, 'You're paid to look after this bairn, not drag her out on a bitter day like today. You'll suffer for this – make no mistake about it!'

5

It had never been Alexander Geddes's intention, or his wish, that his mother move into his house after the death of his wife, Celia. Indeed, he had been too stunned at the time by the shocking unexpectedness of his loss to think clearly about anything.

Celia had been well throughout her pregnancy, and unlike Alexander's first wife, a timid young woman with a chronic fear of pain, she had looked forward to the birth of her first child with eager anticipation. He would never, as long as he lived, forget his last sight of her: propped against a mound of pillows, her dark hair spilling over her shoulders, her cheeks flushed and her eyes bright with excitement.

'It won't be long, my love,' she had said as the midwife shooed him towards the bedroom door. 'And just think – when we next meet, Duncan will have a brother or sister of his very own!'

On the way downstairs Alexander had passed the doctor, who slapped him on the shoulder and said jocularly, 'Sit yourself down and have a tumbler of whisky, man. She's a healthy young woman and I warrant she'll not keep you waiting long.'

Six hours later, sometime after the sound of a newborn child's mewling had drifted down the stairs to where Alexander paced in the hall, he was finally allowed into the bedroom. This time, despite the whimpers of the child in the cradle, there was a terrible sense of stillness about the room. As before, Celia lay back against her pillows, but now she was silent, her lovely green eyes hidden by blue-shaded lids, her mouth with a slight downturn at the corners as though she had died blaming herself for the sudden haemorrhage that had taken her from him.

'No rhyme nor reason to it... did all we could, Geddes, but...' The doctor's words fluttered like intrusive birds about Alexander's head as he took his young wife's hand in his. It was still warm, but limp and unresponsive, and no matter how hard he tried to will her back to him her eyes remained closed, the dark lashes smudged against snow-white skin.

'God's will, man, and there's little any of us can do against that,' the doctor said, and then, in an attempt to give some comfort to the man who finally turned to look at him, his own eyes dead in a bone-white face, 'The bairn's well, though. Ye've got a bonny wee daughter, Geddes.'

He nodded at the midwife, who stepped forwards and waited beside Alexander. At first he paid her no heed, for all he wanted to do was to stay with Celia, holding her cooling hand, until death found the kindness to take him as it had taken her.

When the bundle in the woman's arms let out an angry yell he turned, frowning at the interruption. The nurse had drawn the blanket back from the baby's face and Alexander stared down at the tiny red features and flailing fists, so wrapped in his own misery that at first he was not sure why the little creature was there at all. Then his daughter's screwed-up face suddenly smoothed itself out and she opened her eyes, her mother's beautiful green eyes, and looked directly at him.

And in that moment Alexander Geddes knew that his Celia had not deserted him entirely; she had left this little part of her to comfort him and give him reason to continue with his own life.

When Faith – Alexander's first wife and the mother of Duncan – died of pneumonia, Jean Gilbert had taken over the running of the house and care of Duncan, then seven years old – the age Lydia was now. Alexander and Jean were so used by then to each other's ways that the arrangement suited them both.

When he married Celia she and Jean got on well together, and when fate decreed that he become a widower for the second time Alexander – and Jean herself – had taken it for granted that she would continue to look after the house, and the baby as well, with some help from a wet nurse.

But Helen Geddes had no intention of leaving her son to his own devices for a second time. An ambitious and possessive woman, she had chosen for her own partner a man some ten years older than herself, a fisherman who owned his boat. With his young wife's active encouragement and assistance Duncan Geddes had invested in another boat, and then a third. The proceeds from the boats' catches soon enabled him to stay on land while his crews risked their lives, and when he died of a heart attack it was in his own comfortable house and in the knowledge that he had left his widow and young son well provided for.

Helen had then turned her attention to Alexander himself. Like his father, he was willing to work hard, and with his mother's encouragement he began to invest money earned from the fishing boats. Before he reached his mid-twenties he had shares in the rope works, limestone quarries and the salmon bothy, as well as the three boats he had inherited from his father. Realising that he might well turn his mind to thoughts of marriage,

Helen had chosen a suitable wife for him – the daughter of a doctor who lived in Roseneath, a nearby town. Alexander, who had been raised to do as his mother wished, had married Faith and used the dowry she had brought with her to buy some property in the area. One of the houses, by the harbour, became home for him and his bride, while the other properties were rented out.

Alexander was more interested in business than in relationships, and although there was no passion or fire in his marriage, he was content enough, and delighted when Faith presented him with a son and heir named after Alexander's father. The boy, they agreed within days of his arrival, would receive the best education money could buy, and would become a physician.

To his mother's relief, Alexander showed no interest in marrying again after Faith died. He had his son, and Jean Gilbert looked after them well. Helen decided that she need have no fear of having to share her son with another woman, and was therefore taken by surprise when Alexander, in his thirties, fell passionately in love, for the first time in his life, with Celia Ramsay.

When James Ramsay came to Portsoy to inspect the quarry the wealthier residents in the area, excited at having strangers in their midst, set themselves out to entertain the man, who had brought with him his wife, son and daughter. Alexander and his mother were invited to a social evening held in the Ramsays' honour, and it took only one smile from Celia and one glance from her sparkling green eyes, to tell Alexander that, at last, he had found his soulmate.

By the time the Ramsay family were due to return to Glasgow Alexander had managed to win Celia's heart. His sharp-eyed mother had noticed what was going on, but felt, when the visitors left, that the danger was over. She had no idea that Alexander and Celia were writing to each other, and that the young woman's letters made him hunger for her so much that he soon found a reason to go off to Glasgow on business. By the time he returned, with a spring in his step and a glow in his eyes, he and Celia were engaged to be married.

Helen was furious, although she made a good job of hiding it. Alexander had made up his mind and there was little she could do about it. A few months later he and Celia were man and wife. From Helen's point of view, the only saving grace about the entire business was that she would not lose her son and grandson entirely. Celia was more than happy to move to Portsoy, and Alexander was given the task of making sure that his new father-in-law's investment in the marble quarry brought good financial results.

Alexander Geddes had never been so happy or so fulfilled. For the first time in his life he knew what it was to love and to be loved. The house, which had simply been somewhere to live until Celia came to it as his wife, now overflowed with light and happiness, and his only comfort when he had to be out and about on business was the pleasure of returning to it, and to Celia.

One short year later she was dead and as soon as she had been laid to rest Helen announced that she was going to move into her son's house.

'There's no need,' Alexander had protested.

'There's every need. How can you look after a tiny bairn yourself – and then there's Duncan, coming home from school for the holidays. We must put your children first, Alexander.'

'Jean's going to look after them – after all of us.'

'Jean's a housekeeper, not one of the family. You need family about you at a time like this,' Helen said. 'And where's the sense in me living at one end of the town and you at the other, in this big place? I'll sell the house I've been living in, and you can be comfortable in the knowledge that I'm here for you and your children.'

Alexander had never been able to win an argument with his mother, and at that moment, so soon after Celia's death, he was too dispirited to try. So Helen moved in and took over the running of the house and its inhabitants. The little happiness left to Alexander came from Lydia, growing up to be the image of her mother, and Duncan, who was doing well at school. Alexander had never lost sight of his determination to see his son become a successful physician, and each year brought the prospect a little nearer.

A year after Celia's death her father was killed in an explosion at one of the stone quarries he part-owned. To Alexander's surprise and Helen's delight, the man left his share in the Portsoy marble quarry to his son-in-law with the proviso that it would pass to Lydia. The main share in that particular quarry belonged to Celia's brother, Edward Ramsay, who was content to leave the running of it to Alexander.

At least having the quarry to think of as well as all his other business interests kept Alexander's mind occupied, although Celia was never far from his thoughts. He had been dismayed at Jean Gilbert's decision to give up her duties as housekeeper, but the young woman she had found as her replacement was eminently suitable. Lydia was thriving and Duncan doing well at school, and Alexander's only problem, he well knew, though he would never admit it even to himself, was his mother.

Riding home at the end of a busy day, his face chilled by the cold wind blowing in from the sea, he wished, guiltily, that he could be returning to a house where it was just him and his children, with Eppie Watt presiding over the kitchen and looking after the three of them.

As he neared the harbour opening, his son stepped forwards, and Alexander drew his sturdy horse to a halt.

'Duncan? What's amiss?'

'I wanted to speak with you before you got to the house.' The boy came to stand by Alexander's stirrup, one hand smoothing the horse's neck. 'Grandmother's vexed with Eppie, but it was my idea entirely.'

Alexander sighed; more family problems! 'What was your idea?'

'To take Eppie and Lydia to the marble quarry.'

'Dear God, there's not been an accident, has there? Lydia...!'

'Nothing like that. It's just that we meant to be back at the house before Grandmother, since she doesn't like Lydia to go out in the cold. But she was well happed up, Father. It's just that...' the boy bit his lip '...we stayed longer than we meant to and Lydia got cold, and when we reached the house Grandmother was waiting for us. Now she blames Eppie, the way she always does. But it was my fault. I wanted you to know before you spoke to Grandmother—'

Alexander held up a hand. 'All right, I'll deal with it.'

'You'll not let her turn Eppie out of the house, will you?'

'No, I'll not do that. Run on, now,' Alexander said sharply, seeing that his son's face was almost blue with cold. The boy must have been waiting for him for some time. 'Get indoors, out of this wind.'

His heart was heavy as he rode to the stables not far from the house. He had had a busy day and all he wanted was a good hot meal and some peace in which to enjoy it. But it seemed that he was going to be denied even that simple pleasure. 'You're fortunate,' he murmured as he dismounted and stroked the horse's velvety nose, 'to be staying in this nice quiet stable.'

Leaving the animal with the stable hand, he walked the

short distance to the house, wishing as he went that he'd had the strength and the sense to stop his mother from moving in after Celia's death. But he had never in his life been able to deny her, and even though he was a man now, and a successful man at that, the child he had once been, the child nurtured and trained by Helen Geddes, was still locked into the core of his being, rendering him powerless to defy her. It was a wonder to Alexander that women were thought of as the weaker sex, when mothers had such terrifying power over their children.

Normally he entered his home by the front door, but this evening he walked round to the side and found Eppie working in the kitchen. She whipped round when the door opened, ladle in hand.

'Mr Geddes...' Her eyes were wide in a pale face and Alexander, who well knew how his mother's tongue could sting like the lash of a whip, found himself feeling sorry for the poor young woman.

'I met Duncan on my way home.' He put his hat and gloves on the table and began to unbutton his coat, relishing the kitchen's warmth. 'I understand he took you and Lydia to the marble quarry this afternoon.'

'It was my fault, sir. He saw me admiring the bonny marble stone on your desk and offered to let me see the quarry for myself. I thought it would be a nice outing for Lydia, but we stayed overlong and she got awful cold...'

He went over to stand by her at the range, holding his hands out to the heat. 'Where is Lydia?'

'In her room. I gave her a hot drink, and she's fine and warm now...'

'Then no harm's been done. Did you enjoy the quarry, Eppie?'

'It was very interesting, sir,' she faltered, taken aback.

'I think so too. It's a cold day, as you said. I'm looking forward to a good hot dinner when it's ready.'

'I can have it on the table in ten minutes, Mr Geddes.'

'I'm glad to hear it,' Alexander said, picking up his outdoor clothes.

As he had expected, his mother appeared at the door of her small parlour as soon as she heard his step in the upper hall. 'Alexander, I have something serious to discuss with you. In spite of my orders, Eppie took wee Lydia out today, and to that marble quarry, of all places!'

'I understand that it was Duncan's idea.'

'You've spoken to him?'

'We met in the town. He wanted to give his sister a treat before leaving for Aberdeen.'

'Even so, Eppie should have known better than to let him take Lydia out on a day like this. She knows fine that the bairn has a delicate chest. She was blue with the cold when they got back!'

'Mother, every child living in Aberdeenshire has to get used to cold weather. Cosseting Lydia might do her more harm than good, and in any case,' Alexander went on firmly as his mother opened her mouth to protest, 'Duncan had my permission to take his sister out.'

Her face went red. 'You knew about this? And you didn't tell me?'

'I didn't see the need to tell you. It was an arrangement between me, my son and my daughter. Now if you'll excuse me, I'm going upstairs to wash before dinner's on the table.'

Mounting the stairs, he wished passionately that Celia had lived. If she were only here, she would have known right from wrong; as it was, he'd had to tell a lie to his mother, and the knowledge of it sat uncomfortably in his mind, for he was an honest man.

He took time to look in on his daughter before going back downstairs. She was sitting on the floor playing with her dolls, looking bright-eyed and cheerful. 'Duncan took me and Eppie to the quarry,' she said as soon as he entered. 'I got stones there – look!'

She picked up the box at her side, and Alexander peered in at the collection of pebbles and agreed that they were very bonny.

'It must have been very cold at the quarry today,' he remarked, and she gave a shiver at the memory of it.

'It was freezing cold, and Duncan said my nose was all red.'

'But you're warm now?' He put the back of one hand to her soft cheek as she nodded. He would have liked to pick her up and hold her close in his arms, but he had never been cuddled as a child and now he felt awkward with the strong affection he felt for his own children.

That, he thought as he went back downstairs, was something else that Celia might have helped him with if she had lived.

If only she had lived!

6

Lydia survived the outing to the quarry with no ill effects, much to her grandmother's secret annoyance, but in March, despite being zealously protected from the bitter winds, she took a fever and lay in her bed, flushed and irritable, with both Eppie and Helen fussing over her and Alexander returning home at intervals during the day to find out how she was.

The doctor advised bland food and plenty of liquids, and Eppie, returning from a visit to Fordyce with several jars of her parents' honey, proceeded to administer some to the little girl in hot milk, and as a spread on tiny little doll-sized scones specially baked for Lydia.

The child summoned up a smile at sight of the scones, but eyed the pale golden spread with some misgiving. 'What's that?'

'Honey. Have you never tasted it before?'

'No.' Lydia's flushed face screwed itself into an expression that said that she had no desire to taste it at all.

'It's very good for sore throats. It will ease the pain,' Eppie coaxed, and eventually Lydia consented to lick a little of the honey from a scone. She liked it, and although the scones, small as they were, annoyed her throat, she ended up licking the honey from most of them, then taking a little from a tiny silver spoon that Eppie had found in a kitchen drawer. 'A special little spoon for a special little girl,' she flattered as she popped honey into Lydia's mouth.

That night the little girl managed to drink a cup of warm milk with honey stirred into it, and in the morning, she declared that her throat felt a little easier.

Eppie sweetened her breakfast porridge with more honey and as she fed it to Lydia she told her about the bees that lived in their skeps in her parents' garden, and how they made honey, and about how a bee that had found a good crop of flowers could tell its companions about it by performing a special dance.

'But they're nasty and they sting people,' Lydia objected. 'They stung me once, on my hand.' She held out a small hand. 'Right there, on my middle finger. And it *hurt*!'

'What were you doing when you got stung?'

'Picking flowers in the garden.'

'And the poor little bee must have been inside one of the flowers, trying to gather pollen to make honey to feed the other bees in its hive. It must have got a terrible fright when a big hand suddenly picked it up. It was only trying to tell you not to hurt it. They don't want to sting you,' Eppie went on as Lydia's face puckered up into the threat of tears at the memory, 'because once a bee stings, it dies.'

'Does it?' Lydia's eyes rounded in astonishment. 'Has a bee ever stung you?'

'No, but that's because my father taught me when I was smaller than you to treat them gently, and not to get frightened when they settled on me. They just want to know if you're a flower, and they fly away soon enough if you just let them alone. Some folk say that you can talk to the bees,' she went on.

'Do they talk back to you?'

'No, but they listen, and they're very good at keeping secrets. Sometimes if you have a very special secret that you mustn't tell anyone, or if you're unhappy about something and you can't talk about it, you can tell the bees instead.'

'Have you ever told anything to the bees?'

'Lots of times,' Eppie said. The bees had been the first to know when she fell in love with Murdo, and when he asked her to marry him. They were the first to know that she was carrying Charlotte, and they were witness to her tears and her despair after the sea took Murdo from her. 'Lots of times,' she said again. 'It helps to talk to the bees.'

'When I'm better, will you take me to see the bees in your father's garden?'

'I don't think your own father would allow that. My parents live quite far away.' Eppie knew that Mrs Geddes would not be pleased at the idea of her granddaughter visiting the housekeeper's family.

'I don't mind walking – or we could go in my grandmother's carriage.'

'Wait until you're better before we think of anything like that,' Eppie said evasively, and Lydia put a hand to her throat and swallowed carefully.

'I think I'm getting better already,' she said cheerfully.

* * *

'Father,' she wheedled that evening when Alexander went upstairs to say goodnight to her, 'can we have bees in our garden?'

'We can't avoid having bees in the garden during the summer. Do you not remember the time one stung your hand?'

'But that was because I frightened it. They won't sting you if you talk to them,' his daughter explained earnestly. Alarm shot through him, but close inspection showed that the feverish flush of the past few days was less hectic than before and the brightness in her eyes owed more to enthusiasm than sickness.

'You want to talk to bees?' he was asking cautiously when his mother came into the room.

'Ach, this is just some nonsense Eppie's filled the bairn's head with! Would you believe that she wants to go to Fordyce when she's better, to visit the woman's family?'

'To see the bees,' Lydia corrected her. 'Eppie's father has bee skeps in his garden and her mother makes beeswax that she uses to polish the furniture, and honey too. Eppie gave me some of the honey and now my throat feels much better. Can I go and see the bees, Father?'

'Of course not,' Helen said sharply, before her son had the chance to reply.

'Then can I get a bee skep of my own in our garden? Please, Father?'

'I've already said no, Alexander, so don't go telling her otherwise!'

But in her enthusiasm Lydia was so like her mother that Alexander Geddes shut his mother's voice out, and smiled down at his small daughter.

'Let me think about it,' he said, and she lay back on her pillow, satisfied.

'You're just confusing the bairn,' Helen nagged at him as the two of them left Lydia, already half asleep, and made their way back downstairs. 'I'm going to have to speak to Eppie, for she's got no right to go filling the child's head with such nonsense. And as for taking her to Fordyce – that's just sheer impertinence!'

'Leave Eppie to me. She's a good housekeeper and I'm sure her intentions are always good. It seems that the honey she gave Lydia has helped her to feel better,' he went on, ignoring his mother's loud sniff. 'In any case, the wee one'll soon forget this nonsense about having bees of her own.'

* * *

But Lydia, whose busy little brain normally danced from one thought to another, never lingering for long, had been enchanted by the housekeeper's talk of bees who loved flowers and danced and listened to folk and made honey to eat, and beeswax to keep furniture gleaming. Once she was up and about again she began to pester her father until at last he sought out Eppie, finding her polishing the big dining table.

For a moment he stood in the doorway, unnoticed. There was something soothing about watching a woman go about her domestic duties, he thought. Eppie's sleeves were rolled up to above her elbows, and her rounded arm moved swiftly and firmly to and fro as she swept the cloth over the glossy table. The frill on her white cloth cap bounced in time to the hymn she was singing beneath her breath. Every part of her body moved to the rhythm of her work, he noticed, then was suddenly embarrassed at watching her unawares.

He cleared his throat and she immediately swung around, her face, flushed from her work, reddening even more. 'Do you want to be in here, sir? I can come back later...'

'No, Eppie, not at all. I wanted to talk to you.' He went to the table, looking down at it to see his face, and hers, reflected in its rich tawny surface. 'That polish you're using – would it be beeswax?'

'Aye, sir, from my father's bees. It's the best thing for furniture.'

'There's a pleasant smell to it,' Alexander acknowledged. 'My daughter tells me that your father keeps bees in his garden.'

'Yes, sir.'

'And she also claims that the honey they make has eased her sore throat considerably.'

'It's very good for painful throats, and for the chest too, if it's constricted.'

'She wants me to set up a skep in our garden, but I admit to being apprehensive about that. I wouldn't want to see her or her grandmother suffering from bee stings.'

'They wouldn't be, sir, not if the skep was put right at the back, where the bees would be undisturbed. There are some nice flowering bushes there,' Eppie said enthusiastically, 'that the bees would like fine.'

'And where would I get a skep, or the bees to occupy it, come to that?'

'My father could help you there. The young queens swarm in the summer in search of a home of their own, and that's when the beekeepers have to find somewhere for them to live.'

'Hmmm.' He pulled at his lower lip, frowning, then said, 'And you know how to look after these bees and keep them under control?'

'Aye, sir. I always helped my father with the bees, even when I was younger than Lydia is now.'

'In that case,' said Alexander Geddes in the full knowledge that as well as pleasing his daughter, the decision would infuriate his mother, 'I believe that it would be in order for you to ask your father if he could let us have some bees when the time is right.'

After all, he thought when the housekeeper had returned to

her kitchen and he was alone, pleasing Lydia was far more
important than keeping his mother contented.

* * *

When Duncan came home for summer Lydia was able to lead
him proudly to the far end of the garden to show him the bee
skep, with some of its inmates flying around and hurrying in and
out of the entrance.

'They make good honey,' she told him importantly, 'and they
talk to each other by dancing.'

'Not by buzzing, then?'

'I suppose they can buzz to each other too,' Lydia said seriously. 'If you go close enough to the skep you can hear them all
buzzing because that's the way they keep the skep aired, by
using their wings like ladies with their fans. But we mustn't go
near the skep unless Eppie's with us because she knows the bees
and they know her. You can talk to them too. You can even ask
them to do things for you, if they're really important things that
you want very much.'

'And do they grant your wishes?' her brother teased her,
amused by the little girl's air of self-importance.

'No, that's what fairies do, and magic folk. Bees aren't magic.
You can talk to them and they listen. They just... help folk sometimes. And the best part is that they don't tell anyone what
you've said, so you can tell them anything at all, even the things
you shouldn't even be thinking. They're my very best friends.'

Lydia had taken to sitting on an old tree stump within sight
of the skep but at a safe distance, with one of her dolls in her
arms, talking to the bees in a low monotone. Eppie, gathering in
vegetables for dinner or pegging out washing on the clothes line,
did so on pleasant, warm days to the sound of the little girl's

voice droning on for up to half an hour at a time. She never went near enough to hear what Lydia was saying though, for she knew from her own personal experience how important it was to know that only the bees heard what was being said.

Lydia had been stung once since the skep was brought from Fordyce. A bee had landed on her wrist, and before Eppie could do or say anything the child had brushed it away automatically, then let out a shrill scream and clutched at her wrist.

Eppie caught her up and ran with her into the kitchen, where she snatched the pantry door key from its lock then sat the little girl on a chair and pressed the head of the key against the red area. 'Hold that for me,' she instructed as the tiny dark sting appeared at the surface of the skin, 'and push it down hard.' Lydia, curiosity beginning to win over pain and fright, did as she was told, and by the time Eppie had fetched tweezers and drawn the sting, the patient was becoming interested in the operation.

'Now then...' Eppie fetched an onion and cut off a generous slice, which she rubbed gently over Lydia's arm. 'That'll take the pain away.'

It did, but not before the pungent smell of the vegetable had set Eppie to sniffing and blinking her tear-filled eyes. Lydia laughed at the sight, then as Eppie removed the onion and said, 'There, has it stopped hurting yet?' the child's mouth suddenly turned down at the corners and her own eyes filled with fresh tears.

'What is it, my wee quine? It is still hurting?' Eppie asked anxiously, and the girl shook her dark curly head.

'No,' she sobbed. 'I'm not c-crying for me, I'm crying for the poor wee b-bee. I k-killed it and I didn't mean to!'

It was fortunate that Mrs Geddes was out of the house at the time, but as soon as she returned Lydia was anxious to spill out the story of her latest adventure and proudly display the tiny red mark on her arm. The woman wasted no time in seeking out Eppie and giving her a tongue-lashing that ended with: 'And what my son is going to say when he hears of this latest mishap I dare not think. But I do know that he will wish that he had listened to me when I advised him to hire an older and more responsible person as his housekeeper!'

Eppie could only agree, and when she heard Alexander Geddes's firm tread on the passageway outside the kitchen door that night her heart started to thump faster. As soon as he came in she started to stammer out an apology, but he held up one hand to stop her.

'I have heard my mother's opinion, and my daughter's story of what happened today, and now I would like to hear yours,' he said, and stood listening without interruption, his dark eyes steady on hers, until she had come to a breathless stop.

'A cut onion, you say?'

'Aye, sir. Or vinegar, or mebbe bicarbonate of soda in a little water. The important thing is to get the sting out first. But I should never have let Lydia get too close to the bees...'

'We have to learn all through life, and Lydia tells me that if she had done as you told her and stayed calm when one of the creatures decided to alight on her, she would not have been stung. In fact, she is quite eager to be given another chance, so that she can behave properly next time. No harm was done, and her pleasure in having the bee skep outweighs her chance of being stung again. The matter is closed,' he said, and left the kitchen.

* * *

As had happened over Ne'erday, the house seemed to come alive when Duncan returned for his summer holiday. His doting grandmother made no objection when he took Lydia down to the harbour to watch the boats come in, each one followed by a fluttering banner of screeching seagulls.

They saw the silver scales flashing in the sunlight as the herring were brought ashore, listened as the quayside auctioneers sold the catches to waiting merchants and watched the fisher lassies slit, clean and pack the fish so quickly that it was impossible to make out each moment of their deft hands. They squatted over rock pools to study the tiny crabs scuttling about their business, and peered into the lobster pots, where great sharp-edged claws snapped and clashed in panic and baffled frustration inside skilfully woven prisons.

Duncan also took his young half-sister to the hills beyond the village, where they gathered flowers and played games and rolled down grassy hills. Lydia came home from each of their outings pink-cheeked and glowing with excitement. Her appetite improved noticeably, and so did her temper, for Duncan would not allow the tantrums that Eppie often had to tolerate.

There were also some occasions when he went out on his own, refusing to take the little girl with him. When she discovered that no amount of pleading or coaxing would sway him, she would draw her breath in sharply and bottle it up in her lungs until her face turned first red, then purple; or she would throw herself down and scream at the top of her voice, going rigid and drumming her heels on the floor. But each time she tried one of the ploys that generally brought her whatever it was she wanted, her brother merely looked at her with dislike and said, 'You're much too old to behave like a baby, Lydia. You look ridiculous.' And then he would turn on his heel and leave her to her tantrum.

At first, Eppie suspected that Duncan's long outings were to do with a young lass. He was almost sixteen years of age, and a good-looking youth – the fisher lassies were always quick to flirt with him when he went to the harbour to watch them at work – and she was sure that plenty of girls would be more than happy to be his sweetheart. Then she realised that he never wore his good clothes when he went out, and that when he came to the kitchen in search of something to eat between meals, and stayed to talk to her as she worked about the kitchen, almost all of his conversation was about the marble quarry. Without even realising it she was learning a lot about the process of mining the beautiful patterned marble from the dull rocks near the harbour.

When he realised that she shared his fascination, Duncan loaned her some of the books he had in his room, and even helped her to choose a little marble pendant for Charlotte from one of the local shops – a chip of ruby-red marble set in a silver frame. It cost more money than Eppie could afford, but her daughter's birthday was approaching, and she wanted to buy something special to mark the event.

'Did she like it?' he asked when she returned from her weekly visit to Fordyce, and grinned with pleasure when she described Charlotte's delight.

'She says that she'll wear it all her life.'

'Even if she grows up to marry a rich man who can give her gemstones every day of the week, she'll never have anything bonnier that her Portsoy marble,' he said.

'You know, Duncan, I've never met anyone who likes stones as you do. Most folk are only interested in marble and the like after it's all been quarried and turned into something nice, like a vase or a mantelshelf or a bit of jewellery, but it seems to me that you like it best before it gets to that.'

He was sitting at the kitchen table, eating scraps of dough that she had trimmed from an apple pie in the making. 'It's the thought of it changing slowly, then lying all those hundreds of years within the stone, waiting to be discovered,' he said enthusiastically. 'It's like those stories Lydia likes, about the princess sleeping for a hundred years, waiting for her prince to come and find her. Marble has to wait a lot longer than that.'

'I can't for the life of me see those big dusty quarrymen as princes, and you're sure to get a bellyache if you eat much more of that raw dough, laddie.'

'Not me,' Duncan said cheerfully. 'I never get a bellyache.' Then as they heard the door from upstairs bang against the wall and Lydia come hurrying down the stairs, newly released from her lessons and anxious to seek out her brother, he swept the last of the dough from the table, popped it into his mouth and stood up, ready to catch her as she came rushing into the kitchen and threw herself at him.

7

As the time came near for him to return to Aberdeen and his studies, Duncan grew quieter and spent more time out on his own, or in his room. Eppie worried about him, wondering if he was sickening for something, but his appetite remained as hearty as ever. It was only his mind that seemed to be out of sorts.

A week before her grandson was due to leave Portsoy, Helen Geddes went to her bed early, complaining of a headache.

'I'll have a cup of hot milk in my room at nine o'clock, Eppie,' she ordered as she left the dinner table. 'Mebbe an early night will ease the pain.' Eppie delivered the drink as the grandfather clock in the hall was chiming the hour, then looked in on Lydia, who was sleeping soundly. She was passing the study door on her way back to her kitchen when she heard Duncan say passionately from behind the library door, 'It's my future, Father – not yours to use as you wish!'

'I am your father!' Alexander Geddes snapped in reply. 'And it is my duty to set your feet on the right road!'

'There's no need for that, since I've found my own road. It

would be wrong of you to try to force me in another direction against my will – surely you can see that?' Duncan's voice was almost as deep as his father's now.

'And surely you can see that it's a son's duty to heed his father? I followed in my own father's footsteps—'

'Then let me follow in yours!' Duncan said. 'Is that too much to ask?'

'I didn't have the brains to do otherwise, but you do. You can make something of yourself, boy, can you not see that?'

'I have every intention of making something of myself; you may have no concerns as to that. But I will do it in my way, not yours.'

There was a pause, and Eppie found herself imagining the two of them facing each other across the big desk, faces flushed, neither willing to give way. Then her employer's voice came again, almost pleading this time. 'It was your mother's wish, boy. Would you deny her?'

'Over a matter as important this, aye, I would – to her face if she were here.'

'You dare to say such a thing about your own mother?' Alexander Geddes barked out the words, and Eppie's heart began to beat faster.

'Perhaps if she was here in this room with us, she would listen to what I'm trying to say to you, and perhaps she would understand that I must follow my own inclination. What sort of a physician will I be if my heart's not in the work?'

'A disciplined one, benefiting from the need to deny your own needs for the sake of the poor sick folk you'll be helping. I'll hear no more,' Alexander said as the boy began to argue. 'I have work to do and you'd better go to your room now and think long and hard on what I've said to you, for I won't change my mind!'

'I think best out in the night air,' Duncan snapped back, his voice getting louder as he headed for the door. Eppie fled, and only just managed to get herself on the other side of the door opening on to the kitchen stairs before he emerged.

It was fortunate that the young man didn't choose to leave the house by the back door as he often did, for he would have run into her before she had time to scurry to the kitchen. As it was, he left by the front door, closing it just as his father called him back. Standing at the top of the back stairs, clutching the door handle, she heard her employer's hiss of anger and frustration, then the study door closing again.

Then, and only then, did she dare move quietly, as guilty as a thief in the night, to the safety of her kitchen.

* * *

As far as Eppie could tell, no more was said about the quarrel she had overheard between father and son, although there was a strain between them. They spoke to each other as little as possible, and when they had to it was in brief, formal sentences. She was certain that neither of them had mentioned their disagreement to Helen, for the woman was her usual self, continuing to make a fuss of her grandson as though nothing amiss had happened. Had she known the truth, she would almost certainly have taken one side or the other and thus managed to fan the flames of the disagreement between father and son. Eppie wondered which of them Helen Geddes would have supported – the grandson she adored and spoiled as much as he allowed her to spoil him, or the son who had been taught to do as she wished.

Duncan divided his time between Lydia and his solitary walks, but rarely came to the kitchen. At first, Eppie's guilt at eavesdropping on her employer and his son made her suspect that Duncan knew what she had done, but then she decided that the lad had a lot on his mind and was in no mood to chatter and laugh as he usually did when he spent time with her. Throwing swift glances at him as she served at table she saw that when he was not talking to his half-sister or his grandmother his face, usually open to the world, was closed and his eyes darkened by inner thoughts. He was deeply unhappy, and she longed to be able to comfort and help him, but she could not say a word.

His father too, was quiet and spent more time than usual, certainly more time than he had since Duncan's arrival, away from the house. At night he sat in the library long after the rest of the household had retired. Eppie, lying in her bed below stairs, would hear the library door open and the tread of his feet along the hall long after the grandfather clock had struck midnight.

It hurt her to see father and son estranged like that, and when she next went to Fordyce she confided in her father when the two of them were alone in the back garden. 'Duncan's going back to Aberdeen in a few days' time, and it wouldn't be right for the two of them to part on bad terms. I'm sure they both want to make it up – I can tell by the way Mr Geddes looks at the lad that he wants to make his peace – but it seems to me that making up their differences would mean that one or other of them would have to give in, and neither wants to do that.'

'It's a sore thing when father and son fall out, right enough, but it happens. We're so used to guiding our sons and daughters when they're small that sometimes we don't notice they're close to becoming adults themselves. We still want to do what's best for them. And all too often, what's best is what we want, not what they want. That's when the tempers start to rise.'

'You never tried to push me and Marion into doing something against our wills, not even when I said I wanted to marry

Murdo,' Eppie said, and then, as he suddenly became interested in picking a dead leaf from a nearby bush, understanding dawned. 'Father, were you and Mother against it?'

'Never against it, for Murdo was a decent hard-working loon, and God rest his soul, he'd still be a good husband and father if the Lord had seen fit to spare him...'

'But marrying a fisherman was never what you wanted for me, was it?'

Peter McNaught stooped and pulled off a sprig of mint, rolling it between his palms and then breathing in its sharp aroma before he said, 'You'd have made a fine teacher, Eppie. I always knew it, and I never made a secret of it. But you had to choose your own way in life, lass, and besides...' he turned and gave his younger daughter the slightly mischievous grin that always made him look years younger than he was '...our Marion was so against the idea of you giving up the classroom that she said more than enough for the three of us at the time. You'd enough opposition from her without your mother and I chiming in as well. In any case, I know you, Eppie – opposition just strengthens your mind. If we'd all gone on at you, you'd have proposed marriage to every eligible fisherman on the Moray coast just to spite us.'

'I only wanted the one and I'll never regret marrying him, even though we only had a short time together.'

'How can anyone regret it, lassie, when the two of you brought Charlotte into our lives?'

'I'm not sure that Mr Geddes is as wise as you are. And even if he did agree to let Duncan go his own way, old Mrs Geddes might well be against it. Duncan's own mother was daughter to a physician, and seemingly she'd her heart set on him following his grandfather.'

'Poor laddie, to have to carry such responsibility on his

shoulders. Still, it'll work itself out,' Peter assured his daughter. 'Life always does, though sometimes it takes a few strange turns along the way.'

* * *

As the date of Duncan's departure approached he spent more time away from the house. When he was in his father's presence, the two of them continued to be formally polite to each other, and it seemed to Eppie that they were not going to make up their differences before the boy left for Aberdeen.

Unfortunately, Duncan's grandmother had also become aware of the tension, and her sharp mind must have worked out what was amiss, for one day Eppie overheard the woman telling Duncan how proud she would be of him when he was a fine, successful physician, with his own grand house and a bonny carriage for his wife to ride in.

'I've not given much thought to taking a wife, Grandmother,' the boy said with a laugh in his voice.

'Not yet, of course, for you'll have years of study to get through first. But when you're finished with all that—'

'Grandmother, I don't see myself as a physician. It's my father's idea entirely,' Duncan said in a rush of words, 'not my wish at all. Could you not—'

'You'll make a grand physician,' Helen said swiftly, raising her own voice to drown his out. 'And I'll be proud of you, so proud of you.'

'Yes, Grandmother,' he said, and the resigned, hopeless way he said it wrenched at Eppie's heart.

During the week before he left she was kept busy washing and ironing all his clothes, and making sure that everything was ready. She baked too, making extra supplies of his favourite pancakes and scones so that he could take them with him to Aberdeen. She would have happily packed his box for him, but he refused her help.

'I like to do it for myself, then I know where everything is,' he insisted.

The day before he was due to leave she took the last armful of carefully ironed and folded linen to his room and put it on his bed. The trunk he was packing stood in one corner, and one of the shirts he wore while at home had been thrown casually across a chair. She picked it up and went to hang it in his large wardrobe. Opening the door, she stared in surprise at the interior, where all the shirts she had prepared for Aberdeen still hung, cheek by jowl with his jackets and trousers and waistcoats.

Puzzled, Eppie went to the chest of drawers only find that it too was still full of the clothes prepared for Duncan's return to school; then she moved over to the trunk in the corner of the room. She raised the lid and was staring down at the pile of books and the few neatly packed clothes inside when Duncan asked from the doorway, 'What are you doing?'

She jumped, feeling the heat rush to her face as she turned to face him. 'I... I was putting the ironing away when I saw that your good school clothes are still in the wardrobe. And in the chest of drawers too.' Then, as he said nothing, she opened the lid of the trunk. 'You've packed old clothes in here – clothes you don't need at school.'

He closed the door and came into the room. 'You've no right to go snooping through my possessions!' His voice was low and tight with anger, and his normally friendly face had darkened. His brows were drawn together and in that moment Eppie saw him as he would look when fully grown to manhood. He was the image of his father and, like his father, would not suffer fools gladly.

Her mouth had gone dry, and when she swallowed in an attempt to relieve it, the gulping sound she made was ridiculously loud. 'You're right, I shouldn't have looked in the trunk,' she said, almost in a whisper. 'But I did, and the harm's done now. Why are you packing the wrong clothes?'

'That's my business.' He opened the door and moved to one side of it in a clear, unspoken command for her to leave the room. But when she started to obey he closed the door before she had time to walk round the narrow bed.

'You'll not speak to my father, or my grandmother, of what you've seen.'

It was meant as an order – she knew that – but halfway through the sentence his voice wavered, and it ended up as a question – almost a plea.

'Duncan, I work for your father. I can't keep secrets from him – you must see that.'

'You might if you knew why it had to be a secret. Sit down, Eppie – please,' he added as he closed the door.

As she sank onto the edge of the bed, he drew up the only chair in the room, a wooden kitchen chair that stood against the table he used as a desk for studying, and placed it so that when he sat down they were facing each other, their knees almost touching.

'You must know that my father and I have been having our differences this summer. He wants me to be a physician like my grandfather, but I've no heart for it. I want to work in the marble quarry and learn to manage it and make it prosper. There are many improvements in quarrying now,' he rushed on, his eyes beginning to glow. 'Improvements that would help us to get more benefit from the quarry without having to increase manpower. And less dangerous ways too – if he would just let me go to college to learn about these things, I could do so much!

But he can't see past doing what my mother wanted. I was only a baby in swaddling clothes when they planned my whole future, Eppie. Surely that can't be fair!'

'He's your father,' she tried to argue. 'He has the right.'

'He might have sired me, but that doesn't mean that he owns me. I'm a person, Eppie – flesh and blood and with a brain in my noddle.' He thumped a frustrated fist against his temple. 'Don't *I* have any rights?' Then as she stared at him, trying to find the right words, he said, 'Look at you – your father's a schoolteacher, isn't he? And your sister too. Didn't he want the same for you?'

'Aye, but...'

'But you married a fisherman. I mind you telling me about it. Did your father try to stop you?'

'No, he didn't.'

'Then you're fortunate, Eppie Watt, and I wish to God I had a father like yours. But even if I had,' Duncan said, his voice bitter again, 'even if he were willing to let me have some say in my future, my grandmother would talk him out of it. She doesn't mind living in this fine house and spending the money the quarry and his other businesses bring in, but she'd not want to see me working the marble myself. No matter how hard I might study geology and engineering, she'd still see it as demeaning work for her grandson! And he'd listen to her, for he always does. And that's another thing, Eppie. I don't want to be hag-ridden the way he is.'

'Duncan!'

'Don't make that face at me – it's the truth and you know it. He's been raised to think that he has a duty toward her and he can't break free of it, much as he'd like to. She spoiled me when I was a bairn, but I was fortunate to be a boy, so I was sent off to school where I had the spoiling knocked out of me. Now she's doing the same to Lydia. The poor quine's going to grow up fit for nothing but marriage to a man soft enough to let her have her own way for the rest of her life. Well,' he ended savagely, getting up and pacing about the room, 'not me. I'm going to break free, Eppie.'

'What d'ye mean?'

'I'm going to Glasgow, to Lydia's uncle.'

'Does he know this? Is he plotting with you behind your own father's back?'

'He knows nothing – it was all my own idea. Mr Ramsay owns several quarries, and I'm hoping that he'll agree to take me on so that I can earn my way and learn how to be a quarryman. I'm not asking to be sent to college or the university – I can learn just as well, mebbe a sight better, by working my way up.'

'You're running away?'

'I suppose I am.'

'But how will you get to Glasgow?'

'I'll leave from Aberdeen. I've got some money, mebbe enough to get me there. And I've got a good Scots tongue in my head – I'll find ways and means. I've packed all my schoolbooks so that I can sell them to raise money if I need to, and all my books on quarrying and geology too, though I'd never sell *them*.'

'Lydia's uncle might send you back to Aberdeen.'

'I'll take my chance,' Duncan said grimly. 'If he does, I'll just run away again. Mebbe to sea the next time – I could work my passage to the Americas; they have a lot of quarries there and I could learn as well there as in Scotland, mebbe better. But you have to hold your tongue, Eppie, at least until I get well away.'

'If your father ever found out that I knew, and said nothing, I'd be put out of the house.'

'How could he find out? I swear to you that I'll never tell him. We must trust each other, Eppie – God knows I've nobody else to trust!'

'He'll go out of his mind with worry when he discovers that you've not gone back to the school. And your grandmother too...'

'I'll write to him as soon as I get to Glasgow, I promise. Just let me get away without them knowing,' he begged.

There was a long silence, during which Eppie's mind circled wildly, seeking a way out of the dilemma she had been forced into. Duncan had returned to his chair and now he watched her closely, his brown eyes anxious.

'If you promise to write to your father as soon as you reach Glasgow...' she said at last, and he jumped to his feet, plucking her from the bed and into a hug that almost bruised her ribs.

'Thank you, Eppie, and bless you!' he said, and planted a hearty kiss on her cheek.

When she returned to her kitchen five minutes later it was with a heavy heart. Mr Geddes trusted her. She could not let Duncan down, but the knowledge that she had betrayed his father's trust was a burden she could scarcely cope with.

8

The only person Eppie could spill out her worries to was Barbary. She took time, the next day, to visit her friend while she was shopping.

'There's one thing for certain – ye cannae tell on the loon,' her friend said decisively. 'I've seen him around the farlins, and he's a pleasant lad, with no badness in him. Tae tell ye the truth, Eppie, if I'd a grandmother like that old Mrs Geddes, I'd want tae run away mysel'. And his father's a cold man too.'

'Mr Geddes is a good, kind employer,' Eppie hurried to defend him. 'It's just that he's too busy tae think much about his children.'

'He should, instead of leavin' it tae that mother of his,' Barbary said firmly. 'They're only given tae us for a wee while, then they grow up and go off – just as that lad is. We need tae make the most o' them while we have them.'

'Aye,' Eppie agreed, glancing down at three-month-old Martha, who was slumbering in her arms. The back door was open and George sat just outside, happily sorting out buttons from a large tin box.

Sunlight splashed through the doorway and window, lighting up a great fistful of large, bright-red paper poppies jammed into a jug and placed on the broad stone sill. Every spring the travelling folk came round the area selling clothes pegs, lucky heather and paper poppies; Eppie's mother had always bought some to brighten the house after the long, dark winter, and she had done the same when she'd had her own home. She had also bought poppies during her first spring in the Geddes house, and had arranged them carefully in a pretty vase and put them in the family parlour – only to have them ridiculed and then thrown out by Helen Geddes.

Suddenly she felt homesick for the small cottage where she had lived with Murdo and his mother and little Charlotte.

* * *

On the day of his departure, Duncan came to the kitchen to say goodbye to Eppie.

'Are you still determined?' she asked, low-voiced.

'I've never been more determined. I'm standing on the threshold of the rest of my life, and I'm happy, Eppie.' He looked happy – surprisingly happy for someone returning to school. When she pointed this out he grinned at her before putting on a mock-sad face.

'What would I do without you?'

'What will your father and Lydia do without you?' she parried, and for a moment the amusement was gone and his sadness was genuine.

'I'll be home again – next year, probably, once the fuss has died down. In the meantime, have a last look at me as a young gentleman. The next time you see me I'll be a working man.' The grin returned, and he circled slowly around, arms held out so that she could admire his fashionably short twill jacket and slightly flared trousers, which were becoming more popular than the formal fashion for narrow trousers strapped beneath the feet. A blue cravat was tucked into the collar of his pale grey shirt.

A lump suddenly formed in Eppie's throat and her eyes stung. She hadn't known this lad for long but she was already fond of him. 'I made this for you, for the journey.' She held out a packet and then, as he took it, she dipped into her apron's deep pocket. 'And take this as well.'

He opened the purse, looked inside, then shook his head and tried to hand it back to her. 'No, Eppie. I told you that I had some money saved. I'll not take your earnings.'

'Aye, you will.'

'You've got a wee lass to think of,' he insisted.

'She doesn't have to go without. Take it, Duncan, then I'll not have to lie awake imagining you sleeping under a hedge because you've not got the price of a bed for the night.'

He hesitated, then stowed the purse away in his pocket. 'You'll get it back,' he promised, 'with more to keep it company.' Then, holding his hand out: 'Wish me good fortune, Eppie.'

'You know I'll always wish you that. Goodbye, Duncan.' She gave him her hand and to her astonishment and embarrassment he lifted it to his lips.

'What's your wee girl's name?' he asked as he released her fingers.

'Charlotte.'

'Charlotte.' He savoured the name, rolling it around his mouth. 'A bonny name – and she's fortunate to have you for a mother,' he said, and then he was gone, and Eppie was left to scrub back the tears that threatened to overflow.

* * *

The house was like a mausoleum without Duncan in it. Lydia wept inconsolably for two days and her grandmother was even more irritable and waspish than usual. Alexander Geddes spent most of his time out on business, and when he was at home he was more likely to be found in his study than anywhere else.

For her part, Eppie kept to her kitchen as much as possible, waiting for the storm that she knew would erupt when her employer discovered that his son was not, as he thought, back at his studies in Aberdeen.

It took some time, for Geddes went off to Edinburgh on business for the best part of two weeks, and it was not until he returned and began to deal with the post that had gathered during his absence that he discovered that Duncan had absconded.

The first Eppie knew of it was a full-throated roar of 'Mother!' from above. She was baking at the time, and she jumped and dropped the roller onto the newly floured board. A puff of white flour rose up to cover her blouse while the roller itself hit the ball of dough she had been flattening and ran along the table before dropping off over the edge. Eppie clapped her hands to her face, then hurried noiselessly from the kitchen and into the corridor. She stood, trembling, at the foot of the stairs leading to the doorway to the upper hall; there was no need to go any further, for Alexander Geddes's voice was loud enough to be heard all over the house.

'Mother!' he roared again, and Eppie calculated that he was standing just outside the library door, which was not far from the kitchen stairs.

'I'm coming!' Helen screeched in return, then her voice grew louder as she came down the stairs from her room. 'God save us,

Alexander, do you have to make such a noise? Is the house on fire?'

'Have you heard from Duncan?'

'Not since he went back to school, but I wasn't expecting to hear from him. He's never been one to write letters, even to his grandmother...' Helen started to complain.

'Well, he's written to me, and you'll not believe where he is!'

'In Aberdeen, surely.'

Alexander made a sound that was half bark, half laugh. 'You think so?' he began, then Lydia's piping voice suddenly cut in.

'What's wrong? Has something happened to Duncan?' she demanded to know, while in the background Eppie could just make out a questioning murmur from the little girl's governess.

'There's nothing wrong with Duncan,' Alexander Geddes said curtly. 'Miss Galbraith, kindly take Lydia back to her lessons. Mother—'

The door to the small sitting room closed, and a moment later, the door of the study also closed. Now there was nothing to hear – not even the murmur of voices.

Eppie returned to her work, her hands shaking.

* * *

That afternoon Alexander Geddes packed the bag he had only just unpacked, and went off on another business trip.

During his stay in Edinburgh his mother had insisted on having the entire house scrubbed, polished and cleaned from top to bottom; Eppie, with help from Sarah and Chrissie, was kept hard at work from the time she rose early in the morning until she collapsed thankfully into her bed late at night.

On several occasions she had had difficulty in preventing Sarah and Chrissie from throwing their aprons off and walking out. 'Who does that old woman think she is?' Chrissie had asked furiously. 'My mither minds when Helen Geddes went tae the school wi' her and lived in a wee hoosie just the same as everybody else. Tae hear the airs and graces she puts on ye'd think she'd been born tae money, when the truth is that she's no' any better nor me!'

'I'd as soon go and work in the rope factory,' Sarah agreed. 'At least we'd be among our own sort, and we'd no' have tae put up with the cheek that woman gives us.'

'It'll not be for long,' Eppie had pleaded, and although they grumbled they had stayed by her side until the work was done. Even when the two women had returned, thankfully, to devoting just one day a week to the Geddes house, Eppie was forever having to stop what she was doing to dust a picture frame or sweep up a few cinders from a hearth at Mrs Geddes's bidding. She would have given anything to walk out of the place herself, but instead she nipped her lower lip between her teeth in order to control her rising anger and meekly did as she was told, praying as she did that Mr Geddes would come home soon.

When he did get back, his arrival was unannounced and unexpected. Eppie was shaking the dust out of the mats at the back door and revelling in the mellow sunshine; when she went back into the dim passageway the sun still dazzled her eyes and she could see nothing. As a result, she jumped when a voice said, 'Good morning, Eppie.'

'Who...?' She blinked, and as her eyes became accustomed to the interior she saw her employer standing before her. 'Ye're back, Mr Geddes.'

'Aye, it would seem so,' he agreed with tired irony. 'Unless I'm a ghost. Is my mother in?'

'She's gone into the town, sir.'

'And my daughter?'

'Miss Galbraith has the toothache, so Mrs Geddes took Lydia with her, since it's such a pleasant day.'

'Good. I've been travelling all night and I'd appreciate the chance to rest. And have a wash,' he added. His face was drawn and lined and his clothing dusty. 'Can you bring some hot water to my room? No...' he went into the kitchen '...just pour it into a jug and I'll take it up myself.'

She hurried to obey. 'You'll be hungry – I'll set some food out in the dining room.'

'Don't bother yourself, I'll have it in here. Some broth, and cheese and bread would do. But first, a wash and a change of clothes.' He was still carrying the bag he had taken with him, and now he picked up the ewer of hot water with his free hand and went out.

The food was ready when he returned. 'I'll just go and tidy the parlour,' Eppie said, but he stopped her as she was about to hurry out.

'Sit down and keep me company.'

'I'd best get on, sir. Mrs Geddes—'

'Mrs Geddes doesn't pay your wages, and I'm in the mood for company.' He tore a thick slice of bread apart and dipped it into the broth, then stuffed it in his mouth. 'Have some tea,' he mumbled through it.

She sipped at the tea as he ate hungrily. When he had emptied the soup bowl he spread two slices of bread with butter, then sandwiched a wedge of cheese between them while Eppie poured his tea.

'I've missed your cooking,' he said, leaning back in his chair with a contented sigh. 'Tell me, how are those bees of yours?'

'Settlin' in well, sir. You've a good garden for bees.'

'I look forward to enjoying their honey. Are you happy here, Eppie?'

The question was unexpected, and she stammered slightly as she said, 'Aye, s-sir.'

'It must be hard for you to be away from your child. A daughter, isn't it?'

'Charlotte.'

'Much the same age as my own daughter, I believe. You should bring her to play with Lydia,' he went on as she nodded.

'I don't think Mrs Geddes would approve, sir.'

'I suppose she wouldn't,' he agreed, a flicker of annoyance crossing his face. 'Tell me, Eppie, do you worry about your daughter when you're not with her?'

'I think of her, sir, but I've no need to worry, for I know she's in safe hands.'

Alexander Geddes picked up the mug she had set before him and took a deep draught of hot tea. 'Ah yes, with your family in Fordyce,' he said. 'Did you not tell me that your father is a schoolteacher?'

'Yes, sir, and my sister too.'

He raised an eyebrow. 'Did you have no wish to go into the same profession yourself?'

'I'm not as clever as my sister, and in any case, I wanted to marry.'

'And now, like me, you're alone. Fondness for other folk can be a curse at times,' he said, 'especially when they take our hearts and then leave us too soon. It must be a blessing to go through life without knowing that loss.'

For a moment, Eppie thought of Marion, who had never loved and never lost and who lived her life on her own terms. For a moment, she almost agreed with the man sitting opposite, then she heard herself saying, 'It's not a blessing I'd have wanted, sir. If I'd not met Murdo Watt my Charlotte would never have been born, and I'd not deny her life, or deny myself the blessing of knowing her.'

For a moment he stared at her, startled, then said bitterly, 'You may find out for yourself one day that children can bring sorrows as well as blessings.'

'I may, sir, but that's a chance that I must take.'

He paused, eyeing her closely as though wondering if she could be trusted, then he leaned forwards and was about to speak when they heard the front door open and the sound of Lydia's feet racing along the hall floor overhead.

'Damn!' Alexander Geddes said beneath his breath, then went to meet his family.

* * *

Helen Geddes usually insisted on putting her granddaughter to bed at night, but that night it fell to Eppie. Lydia, unsettled by the faint but unmistakable air of tension that hung around the house, took some time to settle, insisting that she could not sleep without a certain doll, then changing her mind as soon as Eppie brought it to her and wanting another doll instead. Then she demanded a story, but rejected all the books lined up on the shelf in her room. Finally, in desperation, Eppie discarded the books and started on a story that she made up as she went along. Lydia, who had been bouncing around the bed and showing no signs of going to sleep, began to listen, wide-eyed, and then as the tale wound on, with more and more characters coming into it, her lids began to droop. Not long after that she was fast asleep and Eppie was free at last to hurry downstairs to serve the evening meal, which had been left to simmer on the kitchen range.

As she went quietly down the stairs she could hear voices

from the study, where Alexander Geddes and his mother were closeted. Helen Geddes's sharp voice came to her as she reached the final step. 'But you should have brought him back here, where he belongs!'

Alexander's voice was low, his reply little more than a mumble, and his mother snapped, 'Nonsense, man! When my uncle ran away to London to become a soldier my grandfather went after him on horseback and made him walk every step of the way home at his stirrup. That cured him of running away, I can tell you! It's not as if the quarry has anything to do with him – Lydia's the one who will benefit from it.'

Again, the reply was too low for Eppie to catch it.

'You're too soft on that lad, always have been.'

For the first time, Alexander Geddes raised his voice. 'And you, Mother, have ruined him.'

'*I'm* not the one who's allowing him to do as he wishes instead of getting on with his studies. I've a good mind to go to Glasgow myself to fetch him back.'

'You'll do no such thing!' Alexander's voice was like the crack of a whip, and Eppie, creeping silently past the door, shivered at the cold anger in it. 'He's made his mind up and I'll have no more to do with him.'

'But he's your son!'

'If he wants to come back to beg my forgiveness he will have it, but the move must come from him. And I'll not have you interfering, Mother, so take heed of what I'm telling you!'

The last thing that Eppie heard before she hurried through the door leading to her own part of the house, was Helen's gasp of outrage. And when she served supper to the two of them in the dining room half an hour later they sat at either end of the table, backs ramrod straight, never once looking at each other or speaking to each other.

When they had left the room, Helen Geddes going her own bedroom and her son to the library, Eppie cleared the table, tutting over the scarcely touched food, then set it again, this time in readiness for the morning meal.

She left a covered bowl of oatmeal steeping in the kitchen, made sure that all was in readiness for the morning, then went upstairs to tap timidly on the library door.

'Aye, what is it?'

She slipped into the room, staying close by the door. 'Is there anythin' else I can bring you, Mr Geddes?'

He was sitting at his desk, a decanter and glass by his hand. 'No, nothing. Go to bed, Eppie.'

'Aye, sir,' she said and retreated.

9

PORTSOY, FEBRUARY 1870

Someone was thumping on the side door with a fist, or possibly, given the noise, a lump of wood. Eppie, drowsing in her chair by the fire, awoke with a start. Her knitting wires had slipped from her hands to her lap, and as she hurried to the door they fell to the floor, trailing blue wool.

A man she knew as one of the coopers stood outside, rain plastering his hair to his skull while the wind that had been gathering strength all day tugged at the hem of his jacket.

'Is Mr Geddes at home?'

'Aye, but I think he's gone to his bed.'

'Then he'll have tae get out of it quick, for he's needed at the harbour.'

'What's wrong?' But she knew already, for she could hear the slap of swift feet on the pavement. Looking beyond the caller she could see dark shapes hurrying by, all heading towards the harbour. It could only mean one thing.

'One of the boats...?'

All afternoon the weather had grown worse. Most of the boats had returned early from the fishing grounds; any stragglers would have to cope not only with the rising seas and the darkness as they approached the harbour, but also the hungry rocks, hidden beneath the tossing waves.

'It's no' a wreck – at least, no' as far as we can tell. It's the *Grace-Ellen*,' the man said. 'The other boats are safe in harbour but she's no' come in yet. Ye'd best tell Mr Geddes, since it's one o' his vessels.'

He turned and disappeared into the darkness, and Eppie, now wide awake, and chilled by more than the cold damp air that had swirled into the house, closed the door and hurried upstairs. The *Grace-Ellen*, missing. The boat that Barbary's husband, Tolly McGeoch, crewed on. Missing…

She glanced into the library and finding it empty, carried on upstairs to the bedrooms, where she tapped gently on Alexander Geddes's door, not wanting to waken Lydia or her grandmother.

The door opened almost immediately. She could tell by the tousled state of her employer's dark hair that he had been in bed, but he was wearing a shirt and trousers and pushing one arm into his jacket sleeve. 'I heard the noise of the folk outside.' Most of the houses in a fishing community turned windowless walls to the sea for added protection against the worst of the weather, but the Geddes house had two windows facing the harbour; the lower one belonged to the library, the upper window to his bedroom. 'What's amiss?' he wanted to know now, thrusting his arm into the other sleeve of his jacket.

'The *Grace-Ellen*, sir. She's not come in yet and it seems that nobody knows where she is. You're wanted down at the harbour.'

He was shrugging the jacket into place over his shoulders when his mother's door opened and she came onto the landing, her slender figure clothed from top to toe in a woollen robe and her hair hidden beneath a white cap. 'What's happening?' Her eyes were puffy with sleep.

'One of the fishing boats has failed to come home.'

'And what can you do about it at this time of night?' Then, alarm sharpening her voice, Helen Geddes said, 'You're not going out on one of the wee boats to look for them in this weather, are you? Alexander, I forbid it!'

'Nobody's going out on the water, Mother. From what Eppie says the vessel could be anywhere. It doesn't seem as if she's foundered just outside the harbour walls. But I must find out what's going on. Get back to your bed, Mother; there's nothing you can do.'

'If you'd any sense, you'd go back to your own bed.'

Alexander was already on his way down the stairs. 'Not while there's a boat out there mebbe needing help.' He threw the words back over his shoulder in an exasperated whisper. 'Go back to bed before you wake Lydia!'

Muttering to herself, the woman did as she was advised while her son, followed by Eppie, continued on down the stairs and then down the back stairs to the side door.

'You might as well go to your own bed, Eppie,' he said as he lifted the latch. 'There's nothing you can do either.' The wind swirled in as he opened the door, bringing with it a smattering of rain. Eppie's apron immediately blew up over her face and, when she had pulled it down, the door frame held nothing but black night.

For the second time she pushed the sturdy timber door shut against the elements. The kitchen was safe and warm, but its comfort only made her more aware of the missing boat and its crew, somewhere out on the storm-tossed waves. Her mind raced over the dangers facing them. Perhaps a heavy sea had broached them while the hatch covers were off, and the weight of tons of water crashing into the very centre of the vessel had caused it to go down like a stone. Perhaps the wind had torn the big red dipping lugsail away; without it, she knew, they could be drifting, helpless. Or the mast may have snapped off... Or they had been blown by the gale on to a submerged rock and holed. There were so many dangers...

The fishing boats were built to cope with all that the sea and the weather could do to them and the crews were all experienced, but even so, every time men up and down the coast, or even all over the world, raised sail and took their boats to sea they were gambling with their very lives. Every fisherman's wife knew that, but they also knew that their menfolk knew no other way of earning a living, and so the gamble had to be made, time after time.

Eppie thought of Barbary, and decided that she could not stay indoors, safe and sound, while Tolly McGeoch and the others aboard the *Grace-Ellen* were missing. She fetched her warm cloak and pulled it closely about her shoulders, pulling the hood over her head before letting herself out into the wild night.

She went first to the cottage; as she had half expected, there was nobody there. The door had not been latched properly and now it swung creakingly with every gust of wind. Eppie secured it before hurrying down to the harbour.

It was thronged with folk; women and men huddled in segregated groups, many of the women carrying infants and with older children, half asleep and bewildered, catching the air of fear from their elders but not knowing why they were afraid, clinging to their wet skirts. Men and women alike spoke, if they spoke at all, in low murmurs, their heads close together to give the gale less chance to snatch the words from their lips and carry them in unheard fragments into the dark. In the light from the oil lamps that many of the men carried their sombre faces looked waxy and almost unreal. Rain lanced down, falling faster and heavier than it had been when Eppie first arrived from the Geddes house.

Normally most of these men would still have been out on the water, their nets overboard and filling with the 'silver darlings' – the herring that swam in huge shoals in the calm beneath churning, foaming waves. But the advent of the storm had caused the fishermen to bring their nets in before they were full in order to raise sail and hasten back to the shelter of their harbours.

It would be a poor catch, and the farlins would only be half full, if that, when morning's light finally arrived. As she searched for Barbary, Eppie could hear above the keening of the wind the boats in harbour grating against each other. Falling rain gleamed like silver and gold threads in the lamplight, which gave glimpses of swaying masts and made the men's wet oilskin coats and hats gleam like the scales of the fish they sought year in and year out.

'What happened?' Eppie thrust herself into one of the huddled groups of women.

'It's the *Grace-Ellen*,' someone told her. 'She's never come in.' While another added, 'The *Homefarin*' was fishin' alongside her when they had tae bring in the nets. My man's wi' her. He says that when the first squall came up they lost sight o' the *Grace-Ellen*, but they'd seen her ahead o' them before that, and thought she was well on her way home. But when they got here there was no sign o' her. They've gone back oot tae look for her,' she added, her face tight with the terror she felt for her own man's safety.

'Barbary McGeoch – has anyone seen her?'

'She's here somewhere. I saw her a wee while since,' someone said vaguely.

Eppie struggled on, with the wind continually trying to pull the hood from her head. It took some time to find Barbary, who was standing against a warehouse wall, the rain streaming over her black hair and down her face. Her two oldest children, five-year-old George, who had been a babe in arms when Eppie first went to work for Alexander Geddes, and Martha, close to her fourth birthday, clung to her legs while the baby, Thomas, whimpered in her arms.

'Barbary?' Eppie touched her friend's arm; it felt as cold as marble. There was no response. 'Barbary!' she said again, raising her voice, and this time the other woman turned to look at her.

'His boat's no' come in yet, Eppie.' Her voice was flat.

'I know. It'll come soon. Barbary, you cannae stay out in this weather. The bairns are cold and wet. We'll take them home, eh?'

'Aye, m'quine, you take your bairns home, awa' frae this place.' Agnes McBrayne, an elderly woman who lived opposite Barbary's cottage with her widowed daughter and grandchildren, stepped forwards from the huddle of shadowy figures close by. 'You go wi' Eppie, and get the wee ones intae shelter.'

'I have tae be here when Tolly comes back,' Barbary said in the same flat, toneless voice. 'He'll be lookin' for me as the boat comes intae the harbour.'

Agnes and Eppie looked at each other helplessly, worried for Barbary, the three children, and the bairn she was expecting in the summer. 'He'd no' want ye tae make the bairns ill, though,' Agnes persisted, while Eppie held out her arms.

'Give the wee one tae me, Barbary; he's too heavy for you. We'll take the three of them home. They can wait there for their daddy.'

For a moment it seemed that Barbary was going to cling on to the baby, then her grip on him relaxed and Eppie was able to take him.

'I cannae leave till the boat gets back,' Barbary insisted.

'Then I'll stay wi' ye and we'll let Eppie take the bairns home,' Agnes suggested. 'Go on, Eppie, an' we'll follow ye in a wee while. Eh, Barbary?'

'As soon as Tolly comes intae harbour,' the woman agreed as Eppie, clutching Thomas close in an effort to warm him with the heat of her body, persuaded the other two to let go of their mother and go with her.

When they reached the cottage and she lit the lamp in the kitchen, she saw that all three of the children were blue with cold. As usual in every cottage, the kettle was steaming gently on the range, and Eppie, working as fast as she could, stripped and bathed them before drying them vigorously with a rough towel.

Mute with exhaustion and bewilderment, they submitted without protest, and after dressing them in dry clothes she sat the two oldest down beside the warmth of the range and laid the baby in his crib so that she could heat up a pan of milk. Breaking bread into bowls, she poured the warmed milk over it, then added generous spoonfuls of sugar.

One by one the children fell asleep before they had finished eating; George, determined to stay awake until his mam and da came home, held out the longest before suddenly collapsing into his half-empty bowl. If Eppie had not been there to lift his face clear and wipe the milk from it, he might have drowned. She tucked George and Martha into the truckle bed that, by day, was pushed under the wall bed. Then she heated more water and washed the bowls they had used.

Barbary and Agnes were still not back from the harbour. Eppie longed to go back out into the night again to look for them, but the children could not be left on their own, so after emptying the basin she sat down to wait as patiently as she could. The wind moaned around the house walls and the rain beat against the windows. The fire spat and crackled now and again in response to rainwater seeking entrance by way of the chimney, and once or twice one of the children coughed or whimpered or thrashed restlessly for a moment, though thankfully without wakening.

Another hour crawled by before Barbary arrived home, leaning heavily on Agnes's arm.

'There's no news comin' tonight, an' if the *Homefarin*' gets back afore the mornin' someone'll come tae tell Barbary,' the older woman said. 'So I've persuaded her tae come home tae her bairns.'

Barbary checked all three of her children carefully, as though finding it hard to believe that they were safe, then she sat down by the fire, staring vacantly into its red glow, oblivious to the water dripping from her clothes and her hair and her chin to form a puddle on the floor. She looked, Eppie thought with an inward shiver, as though she herself had been drowned and returned from the sea.

She was deaf to suggestions that she might be more comfortable if she were to change into dry clothing, and finally Eppie and Agnes had to strip, dry and dress her. She lifted her arms when told to, submitting to being turned this way and that and to having her damp hair brushed out and tied back with a piece of string, without a murmur. At one point, looking into her friend's face, Eppie realised that Barbary's beautiful dark eyes, with their unusual upward tilt at the outer corners, were looking at her without seeing her. It was as though Barbary's mind and her body had come adrift from each other. Her body was in Portsoy, being tended to by her friends, but her mind was far away.

Eppie, having lost her own man to the deep, knew well enough that inside her head Barbary was searching for Tolly, calling across the water to him in the hope that she could unite in his struggle against whatever was keeping him from reaching the shore, and home, and her empty, hungry arms.

She refused to lie down on her bed, so they settled her back in the chair. Agnes made tea, and they wrapped Barbary's long slender fingers around the cup and coaxed her through the process of lifting it to her lips and taking little sips of the hot, sweet liquid.

By then, half the night had gone by. 'I'll have to go,' Eppie murmured. 'Mr Geddes'll be expectin' me tae have the breakfast ready in the mornin'.' She looked hopefully at Agnes. 'Could you...?'

'I'll sit wi' her till the mornin', for I'm no' needed at hame. Ye'd mebbe knock on the door an' tell my Margaret where I am, m'quine.'

'I will, and I'll be back as soon as I can in the morning,' Eppie promised, then went out into the night.

The wind had abated and the rain, too, had eased off. She could hear voices from the harbour, and as she reached the side door to the Geddes house she could see that there were still folk crowded there, staring out into the darkness. There was nothing they could do, but as happened when tragedy hit any community that depended on the sea, they needed to keep vigil until – one way or another – the crisis was over.

She went into the house quietly, wondering if her employer was still at the harbour with the others, or had come home before her. Perhaps he was looking for her to make food, or tea. But he was in the kitchen, sitting at the table, a glass in his hand and a bottle close by.

'Mr Geddes! I was just seein' tae Barbary McGeoch. Her

man's on the *Grace-Ellen*. I didnae realise you were lookin' for me. Can I make ye some tea?'

'I'd not mind some, as strong as you want to make it.' He looked bone-weary. 'It's a terrible thing, Eppie, when a boat goes missing – but you'd know that yourself.'

'Aye, sir.' She busied herself with the kettle. 'Is there any news?'

'None – and I doubt if there will be any until daylight. The *Homefaring* won't be back before then. We can only pray to God that they've found the other vessel.'

When the tea was put before him he drank it down swiftly although it was scalding hot. Then he emptied his glass before getting up from the table.

'I'm going back out. You get to your bed, Eppie,' he said, picking up his coat, which was still wet.

* * *

By the morning the storm had blown itself out and the sea drifted, quiet and innocent, beneath blue skies. The *Homefaring* returned with nothing to report. There had been no sighting or sign of the *Grace-Ellen*, not even a piece of driftwood. As the day dragged on, hopes that she had been crippled and taken shelter elsewhere along the coast began to fade.

It was not until the afternoon that the mystery of what had happened to the *Grace-Ellen* and her crew became clear. Word ran along the coast, eventually reaching Portsoy, that a cargo ship putting into Aberdeen that morning had reported a collision some thirty miles off Kinnaird Head on the previous night. No other boat had been sighted in the vicinity before the collision, and after it, thinking that they heard voices crying out in the darkness, the captain of the cargo boat had ordered it to be put about. But after remaining in the area for some time without receiving any replies to their shouts and whistles, they had continued on their way.

A swift check up and down the coast showed that the only boat missing was the *Grace-Ellen*, which had been fishing in the area earlier. It could only be assumed that the collision with the larger vessel had caused such damage to the fishing boat that it sank within minutes, giving the crew of eight little time to save themselves.

A collection was raised for the bereaved families, and Alexander Geddes pledged to pay them a small pension and to seek a Board of Trade inquiry into the worst disaster that Portsoy had ever known.

In the days and weeks after Tolly and his fellow crewmen were lost, Barbary retreated into a world of her own. She was still able to care for her children and to work at the farlins, but she had become a mere shadow of her former self, her once-glossy black hair lank and her dark eyes lifeless.

Agnes, the elderly neighbour who had brought her home on the night Tolly went missing, did all she could to help the young mother look after the children, and Eppie went to the cottage as often as she could. They both believed that eventually Barbary must accept what had happened, if only for the sake of her children, but time went on with no sign of this happening.

It seemed that bereavement had dealt Barbary McGeoch a blow so hard that somewhere inside her head, or her heart, or perhaps the very soul of her, she was injured beyond healing.

10

The basket on Eppie's arm had grown steadily heavier during her long walk. She paused at the square, taking a moment to set it down and ease her stiff shoulders.

'Aye, Eppie,' a woman passing by greeted her. And then, nodding at the laden basket, 'Ye'll have been visitin' hame?'

'My mither seems tae think that nobody can make jam or scones like herself, and my faither's certain that his bees make better honey than my own.'

'Well, they're Fordyce folk.' The woman's voice sharpened slightly while her smile tightened. 'Fordyce folk are always of the opinion that anythin' they do's better than anyone else.'

Eppie, used to such remarks about her home village, held her tongue and picked the basket up again before setting off down North High Street on the last leg of her journey.

Passing the double flight of steps that led up to the front door of the Geddes house, then rounding the corner into Shorehead, she reached the entrance to the kitchen quarters and was thankful when she was finally able to set her heavy basket on the table. She started to unpack it and then paused, head to one side as she heard a noise from overhead.

It came again – a high-pitched screech. Eppie's spirits, which had begun to rise at the thought of a cup of tea and a rest in the comfortable chair by the range, sank as she realised that, once again, Lydia and her grandmother were at loggerheads.

She went out into the passageway and up the stairs leading to the upper hall. Now she could hear Lydia shouting from behind her bedroom door, which was slightly ajar, 'It's not fair – you hate to see me enjoying myself!'

'You are a selfish, spoiled girl and you can enjoy yourself when you have earned the right!' Helen Geddes's voice was clear and cold.

'I am not spoiled! You're so old that you've forgotten what it's like to be young like me,' Lydia retorted, and Eppie, realising that the two of them must be separated before things got out of hand, began to mount the next flight of stairs. 'That's why you're so mean to me,' she heard Lydia shout as she hurried upwards. 'It's because you hate being an old woman who—'

There was a sudden sound, as though someone had clapped their hands together loudly, and Lydia's voice was cut off in mid-sentence. Eppie, realising that there was no time for niceties, pushed the door wide open.

Lydia stood by the window, one hand to her face, while her grandmother stood in the middle of the room. The two figures were immobile, and as Eppie looked from one to the other, she saw the same look of shock mirrored in the girl's green eyes and the older woman's clear blue eyes. Then, as they became aware of Eppie standing in the doorway, Lydia's face crumpled and her eyes flooded with tears.

'She hit me!'

'I chastised you,' Helen Geddes snapped, 'because you were

being disobedient, and you know very well that you deserved to be punished!'

'You hit me!' Lydia said again, her voice beginning to rise towards hysteria.

Eppie took a step forwards, frantically trying to think of a way to calm them both without drawing the older woman's sharp-tongued fury down on her own head. Then she spun round as Alexander Geddes's voice thundered, almost into her ear, 'What is going on here?'

Eppie immediately stepped aside, while Lydia's sobs redoubled at the sight of her father.

'She hit me!' she roared.

'I chastised her,' Helen Geddes repeated, the two bright-red spots already over her cheekbones deepening. 'She was being impertinent, Alexander, and I will not have it. You don't want to see your daughter behaving like a common village girl, do you?'

'She slapped my face and it hurts.' Lydia threw herself at her father and wept into his chest. 'I was only dancing and she came in and hit me!'

'Dancing, you call it? She was crashing around the room, making a terrible noise.' Helen put a hand to her forehead. 'I was about to lie down because I have a headache. Is a little consideration too much to request?'

'I was only dancing! Father—'

'Be quiet, Lydia.' Alexander's voice was low, but firm enough to make both of his womenfolk fall silent for the moment. 'How can I find out the truth of this – this unseemly brawl if the two of you keep screeching at me?'

'The truth?' His mother almost choked the words out. 'You dare to doubt what I'm telling you?' Then, pointing at Eppie: 'And must we discuss our private family affairs in front of the servant?'

'For pity's sake!' he suddenly burst out, making them all jump. 'Can a man not even get peace in his own home now? Eppie, take Lydia down to the kitchen and bathe her face. Then, Lydia, you can return to your room and wait until I come to speak with you. Mother, we will continue this conversation in the library, if you please.'

There was no denying that Lydia's face had been slapped, and slapped quite hard. Her left cheek glowed fiery red, and finger marks could be seen clearly against the smooth skin. At first she refused to be attended to, insisting that her father should see the damage first, but when Eppie pointed out that he had already seen her, and that without swift treatment she might end up with swelling or even bruising, she gave in.

'It's not fair,' she stormed as Eppie sat her down on a stool and began to bathe her face with water and vinegar. 'I was only dancing to the music on my music box when Grandmother came in and started shouting at me to stop it at once.'

'And did you?'

'Why should I? I like dancing – you know that I do.'

'So you answered her back instead.'

'She deserved it,' Lydia said obstinately. 'She knows I like dancing, and she never lets me do anything now. She hates me!'

'Of course she doesn't hate you.'

'She does – she *does*,' the girl insisted. 'I can't please her no matter what I do!'

'Lydia, she's your grandmother and she loves you.'

'She used to love me. She used to give me sweets and brush my hair and tell me stories and take me visiting with her, but now she only finds fault with me. She hates me and I hate her!'

'But she's your grandmother,' Eppie said again, and the girl twisted round, almost getting the vinegar-and-water sponge in her mouth.

'That doesn't mean that she can treat me cruelly, and I still have to be polite. I don't like her because she doesn't like me and she's mean to me – you know she is. At least I've got a reason,' she said, her eyes dark with hurt and anger.

When her face had been dried she slipped from the stool and went to examine her cheek in the wall mirror. 'Does it look all right?' she asked anxiously.

'Of course it does. You'd not know that anything had happened. Where are you going?' Eppie asked as the girl headed for the door.

'I'm going to tell the bees.'

'Your father told you to wait for him in your room – and that's where you're going, young lady,' Eppie said as the girl opened her mouth to argue. 'You don't want to make him any angrier than he is already, do you? You can talk to the bees later,' she added as Lydia's shoulder's slumped.

At the door, the girl turned. 'I wish Duncan would come home,' she said, her voice suddenly very young and forlorn. 'I miss him, Eppie.'

'I know you do, m'quine.' Without thinking, Eppie opened her arms – then held her breath. Sometimes, unused to affection, Lydia rejected her when she tried to hug her. But at other times, her need overcame her reticence. And this, to Eppie's relief, was one of those occasions. She came across the room and let her tense body relax into the housekeeper's arms.

'Do you think he'll come back soon?' she asked, her face buried in Eppie's shoulder.

'Only Duncan knows the answer to that question.'

'I pray every night that he'll come back,' Lydia confessed, 'but I sometimes wonder if I'll ever see him again in my whole life. Ever.'

'I'm sure you will. You're his wee sister, and he'd never desert you.'

She had said the wrong thing. Lydia immediately pulled herself free. Her eyes were filled with tears and her face flushed with the effort of holding them back. The pale imprint of her grandmother's hand stood out against the red.

'But he has,' she cried. 'He already has!' Then she turned and deliberately swept her arm across a corner of the table as she rushed to the door. Before going through it she turned and shouted, 'I don't pray for Grandmother any more!' Then with a whisk of her skirts she was gone.

Fortunately the only object that had been within her reach was a small, empty pot. It crashed noisily to the floor while its lid flew off and came to rest beneath the dresser.

Eppie rescued it, and the pot, and put them away, her heart aching for Lydia. She had now been housekeeper to Alexander Geddes for almost five years, and during recent years she had watched the once-close relationship between his mother and his daughter deteriorate steadily. When Lydia was small, her grandmother had treated her like a little doll, spoiling and indulging her, but as the girl grew older and began to form her own character, Helen Geddes proved to be incapable of realising that her once-loved granddaughter could not be an obedient, loving child forever. She had begun to demand Lydia's love, with no thought of earning it, and even used it as a form of punishment. On more than one occasion Eppie had had to watch helplessly, unable to intercede, as Lydia's attempts to hug her grandmother were spurned because of some small, often imagined, piece of bad behaviour.

'Why should I let you kiss me when you refused to play dominoes with me last Wednesday?' she would say in a hurt tone. 'You wanted to go and watch your precious bees instead of spending time with me. Why should I hug you now, just because you want me to?'

Lydia, hurt and confused, made to feel guilty over something she couldn't recall doing, had begun to withdraw from the woman for fear of yet another rebuff while, for her part, Helen interpreted the withdrawal as yet another indication of her granddaughter's lack of respect and affection.

Comparing Lydia with her Charlotte, and Mrs Geddes with her own parents, Eppie had come to realise that she and her daughter were blessed. Annie and Peter McNaught had had the wisdom to give Charlotte room to grow and develop. She was able to speak her mind without fear when she felt the need, and even Marion, with her inclination to dominate, had had the sense to recognise that Charlotte was moving towards woman-hood, and to guide, rather than dictate.

But Lydia had nobody to consider her needs. Alexander Geddes, wrapped up in his various business interests, was completely unaware of what was happening, and much as Eppie would have liked to warn him, she was a mere servant and so it was impossible for her to do so.

She had done her best to show affection towards the child; at first, when Eppie hugged her Lydia froze and tried to struggle free, but there were times when, knowing how hurt the girl felt, Eppie clung on, even though it was like hugging a stone pillar. And eventually, Lydia's rigid body would relax slightly, though she never returned the hug. Sometimes she tore herself free, but Eppie kept on trying, for she could not bear to think of Lydia growing up to be as cold and uncaring towards others as her grandmother was.

At least once a month she made a point of walking to Sandend to visit Jean Gilbert, now enjoying a well-earned rest with her family. Apart from the fact that she enjoyed Jean's company, the former housekeeper was the only person she could talk to about the Geddes family, in the knowledge that not a word spoken between them would go any further. Only the week before, she had spoken of her growing concern for Lydia.

'I've always had a feelin' that somethin' of the sort might happen,' Jean confessed. 'Lydia was the bonniest wee bairn ye could ever imagine, the image o' her mither. It was easy tae spoil her, 'specially since the poor lass never had a mither o' her own. Mrs Geddes doted on her, but there were times when I wondered what the old lady would do once Lydia began tae find her own mind. That's when spoilin' starts tae turn, jist like curdled milk. Mebbe ye'll have tae take your courage in both hands and tell Mr Geddes what's goin' on, since he cannae seem tae see it for himsel'.'

'How can I say such things about his own mother tae his face? If Duncan was still comin' home for the holidays I'm sure he'd see what's happenin' and do something about it, but...' Eppie threw her hands out helplessly '...nob'dy seems tae care about him, either.'

'That's what happens when folk are rattlin' about in a big hoose. When ye live in wee places like this...' Jean indicated her own humble but comfortable surroundings '...ye're so close tae each other that if one sneezes the other wipes his nose. Ye have tae learn tae get on thegether. But wi' the Geddes's, ye've got him sittin' alone in his library an' his mother in her wee parlour – and the bairn on her own too, most of the time, in that nursery o' hers. All blood kin, yet they never seem tae spend time in each other's company. They might as well be complete strangers. If ye ask me, that woman was behind the door when the good Lord was dolin' out kindness and understandin'. She used tae sweep about Portsoy with her nose in the air, with never a word or even a nod tae folk she grew up with. The only person she really cares about is hersel'. It's a wonder her eyes werenae put intae her head the wrong way round so's they could look in instead o' out.'

* * *

Alexander Geddes dined alone that night. Lydia, as was the custom, had eaten earlier and retired for the night, while Helen Geddes had decided to have her dinner in her room, on a tray. When Eppie took it in, the woman was sitting reading her Bible. Without deigning to lift her eyes, she had said, 'Set it out on the table by the window. I'll ring the bell when I want you to collect it.'

When Eppie went to clear the table in the dining room she was surprised to see that her employer was still sitting at the head of the table, staring down at his empty plate.

'I'm sorry, sir, I thought you had finished.' She hesitated at the door, not sure whether to go in or back out. Normally he retired to the library after his meal and had a glass of brandy while working at his desk.

'I am finished, if you want to clear the dishes away. I don't suppose you drink brandy, Eppie?'

'No, sir, I don't.'

'Have you ever tasted it?'

'No, sir. I'd a wee sip of ale given to me once by my father, but I didn't like it at all. I'm happy enough with tea.'

'Then perhaps you would be good enough to make some tea and bring it here.'

'Of course, sir,' she said, puzzled. In all her time as house-keeper to the man, she had rarely seen him drink tea after his dinner.

When she returned to the room with teapot, milk jug, sugar bowl and cup and saucer on a tray, he was still seated at the head of the table, but he must have visited the library during her absence, for the brandy decanter normally kept there was now on the dining table, and the fingers of one hand curved lightly round a full glass of the spirit.

'Your tea, sir.'

'No, Eppie, it's your tea. Sit down and pour yourself a cup.' He indicated a chair close to his own, adding when she began to protest, 'I want to talk to you about this afternoon.'

It felt strange to be sitting at the handsome table, looking down at her own reflection in the surface she polished regularly. It was even more strange to be pouring tea and sipping it carefully from one of the fine cups reserved for the Geddes family and the few guests who had come to the house in the five years she had worked there. And it was unnerving to be sitting, dressed in her usual blouse, skirt and apron, so close to her employer. At least, she thought, taking a sip of tea in an attempt to calm herself, her apron was clean on.

'About this afternoon,' Geddes was saying. 'What's your account of it?'

'I don't know much more than you do yourself, sir. I had just come back from Fordyce when I heard the voices upstairs. I went up to Lydia's room to see what was amiss, and you came in just after that.'

'My daughter's face looked quite sore.'

'It's fine, sir. The bathing took the heat out of it.'

He leaned forwards, holding her gaze with his own so intently that much as she would have liked to look away, she could not. 'These... disagreements... between my daughter and my mother are happening more regularly, are they not?'

'I wouldn't know about that, sir,' Eppie pleaded. He had been absent when most of the sudden rows erupted, and she had no wish to make things worse by telling him the truth.

'But I would,' he said firmly. 'Just because I'm not here it doesn't mean that I'm unaware of what's happening under my own roof.' Then, as she stared at him, puzzled: 'My mother makes sure of that, by reporting every happening and misdemeanour – be it real or imagined,' he added, 'that takes place. So you'll not be telling tales, if that's what you're thinking. They've already been told.'

He took a sip from his glass, set it down, and then got to his feet and paced to the window, then back again. 'The question is, what am I to do about it?'

'I wouldn't know, sir.'

'Your daughter's much the same age as mine, I believe.'

'Twelve years old, sir. Lydia's the elder by three months.'

'Then you understand girls of that age.'

'I don't know about that, since my parents have brought up my daughter. I've been working all her life.'

'Yes, of course; I'd forgotten. It must have been hard for you, being away from her during her growing years.'

'I know that she's been well cared for, and she's happy. And I see her every week.'

'Even so – does your daughter have tempers like mine does?'

'Not that I know of, sir.'

'And why would that be? Eppie,' he said, a slightly impatient note coming into his voice as she hesitated, 'I am trying to make sense of the ridiculous scene I came home to this afternoon. If I can't understand it then I can't cure it. I have had my mother's story, and my daughter's, and all the two of them do is blame each other. You are the only person who can tell me the truth, and perhaps advise me on this matter.'

'But I'm only your housekeeper, Mr—'

'For pity's sake, woman, will you stop trying to hide behind excuses and help me? D'you think I haven't noticed that there's something far wrong between my mother and Lydia? D'you think that I am not concerned for both of them – for all three of us? I swear that if I don't get this business settled once and for all I will send Lydia to a boarding school and then set off to see the world on one of the ships that come into our harbour to take cargo aboard!'

There was a short silence, during which she stared up at him, astonished; then he gave an abrupt bark of laughter and sat down again. 'Poor Eppie, your face speaks volumes. I'm sorry if I've startled or offended you, but you must see that I can't go on like this – none of us can. I need advice from a friend, and I would appreciate it if you could bring yourself to talk freely to me. I promise that not a word you say will be repeated, nor will it be held against you in the future. Now, drink your tea before it gets cold, and then explain to me exactly what is going on in this house.'

11

'We'll start with Lydia,' Alexander Geddes said when Eppie, having finished her tea and refilled the cup at his urging, still found herself tongue-tied. 'You surely have some idea of what's in her mind, from watching your own daughter. It's difficult, trying to raise children without the benefit of a woman's assistance. I have tried to do the right thing, but it seems that I've gone wrong – first with my son,' he added in a harsh, bitter aside, 'and now with Lydia.' He sat down behind his desk and asked quietly, 'Why have I gone wrong, Eppie?'

'You haven't, sir – you mustn't think that,' she said, upset by the despair in his dark eyes. 'It's just... well, she's mebbe a wee bit spoiled...'

Far from being offended, he nodded slowly, considering her words. 'I've often wondered if trying to make up for her not having a mother's love meant that I indulged her too much. But I care for her, Eppie, with all my heart. It's difficult not to spoil such a sweet, bonny lassie. At least, she used to be sweet...'

'She still is, sir, but – it's not you,' Eppie burst out, throwing caution to the wind. The man had said that he wanted the truth, and if giving it to him was the only way to escape from the embarrassment of sitting at his grand table in her working clothes, drinking tea out of a china cup so delicate and fragile that she was frightened out of her wits in case she set it down too hard on its fluted saucer and broke it, then the truth he would have.

'It's Mrs Geddes, sir. She spoiled Lydia far more than you ever did, and that's understandable since she was such a lovely wee thing. But she's growing up, sir. She'll soon be a young woman. Mrs Geddes says she's become difficult and rebellious, but I don't believe that. I think she just has a mind of her own now, and that's only to be expected with bairns as they grow older. Mrs Geddes wants to keep Lydia the way she was, and because that's not possible she blames the lassie for growing up. And then Lydia blames her for not understanding and – that's what it's all about, Mr Geddes.'

She stopped, exhausted by the unexpected torrent of words and horrified by her own impertinence. When she set the cup back on its saucer they rattled against each other, sending a faint, melodic chime into the silent room. Then she folded her hands tightly together in her lap and waited for her employer's reaction.

She had counted a full ten ticks of the clock on the mantelshelf before he said, 'I see. Thank you for telling me the truth, Eppie.'

'I'm not saying that it's the truth, sir. It's just the way I see it.'

'And you put it clearly. I appreciate that.' He got to his feet, picking up his glass and the brandy decanter. 'I have work to do,' he said, and went out of the room. When she carried the tray to the kitchen, the china chiming softly because she was still shaking, the library door was closed.

* * *

It was the hardest thing Alexander Geddes had ever had to do in his entire life. As a businessman he had developed a thick skin when it came to dismissing bad employees, or dealing with surly behaviour – he had even been cursed to his face. Once he had managed to give a good account of himself when attacked by a particularly resentful former employee. He had dealt with everything that came his way and in the process he had earned the name of being a fair, but strict man who would brook no idleness or dishonesty from anyone, including himself.

But he had never before had to tell his own mother that she was no longer welcome under his roof.

It took him two days to work up the courage to face her, and two wakeful nights, during which he rehearsed speech after speech. He had decided, by the third day, that his best method would be to turn the situation to her own advantage. Lydia was growing older, he explained to her when he finally faced her in the small parlour that she had made her own, and she was beginning to test the patience of the adults who looked after her. This natural phenomenon was something that he would have to handle himself, but, he said earnestly, it was not fair on his mother, who had reached a time in her life when she was entitled to – indeed, had earned – a life of peace and quiet. It was for this reason, he explained, that he had decided to buy a house in the town where Helen could live in comfort, with her every need attended to by a good, respectable housekeeper of her own.

'I, of course, will pay the woman's wages,' he went on while Helen Geddes sat bolt upright opposite, her blue eyes impaling him in a way that reminded him of a tray of butterflies, each pinned down securely, that he had once seen in the home of an acquaintance. He had not enjoyed the sight, and he liked it even less now that he felt he had become one of the poor insects.

'So,' he finished, 'what do you think to my proposal, Mother?'

'I'm surprised that you bother to ask my opinion, Alexander.' Her hands gripped the arms of her chair so tightly that her knuckles looked as though there were no skin over the white bone. 'It seems to me that you've already made up your mind. The only surprise to me is that you have found the time to tell me of your plan instead of just bundling me into a carriage and rushing me off to whatever cottage you might deem suitable for me. Or, indeed, to the workhouse. That's where most old folk go when they've outlived their usefulness and they're no longer wanted by the children they gave their lives to raise.'

'There's no question of the workhouse, or of you not being wanted...'

'Indeed? You surprise me. Are you or are you not telling me that you no longer wish me to live under your roof?'

'I am saying that I know you have found Lydia difficult of late, and you would surely be happier if you had a place of your own.'

'I would be happier if you would learn to control your daughter, Alexander, and teach her to treat her grandmother with civility. I have devoted the last twelve years,' Helen Geddes said passionately, 'to looking after your motherless children, and how do the three of you repay me? Duncan runs off without a word and you just let him go, when you should have done as I told you and made him walk every step of the way back to Aberdeen to continue his studies.'

'I told you, Mother—'

'I have given Lydia the love that her own mother, God rest her soul, was unable to give her, and when she thanks me by sulking and storming and behaving like a... a spoiled brat, you find fault with me, instead of giving her the whipping she deserves. Mark my words, Alexander...' her eyes blazed into his and her voice lashed him like a whip '...you've already lost Duncan, and you will soon regret that you did not take a stronger line with Lydia.'

He drew in a deep breath to steady himself before saying, 'I would ask you to remember, Mother, that they are my children and not yours. I have the final word on the way they are raised, and I will most certainly not subject my daughter to a whipping or to any other punishment. If anyone has spoiled her or indulged her, it's you.'

'How dare you accuse me of such a thing!'

'I am just as much to blame. I believed that you could give my daughter the womanly love that a man can't understand. But I should not have allowed you to make such a pet of the child.'

'To think,' Helen almost choked in her fury, 'that I gave up a comfortable home in order to look after you and your two young children...'

'There was no need of that, for Jean Gilbert was perfectly willing to help me care for them.'

'Jean Gilbert was only the housekeeper. I will not have my flesh and blood raised by a mere servant!'

'Jean had already raised a family of her own, and they have all given a good account of themselves. Eppie has a daughter of Lydia's age. Both women have had experience of caring for children.'

'And I have not? Did I not raise you on my own after your father died?'

'Yes, you did,' he conceded, remembering his cold, lonely upbringing.

'There is a difference,' Helen Geddes swept on, 'between

being raised by someone from the lower classes and being raised by your own blood kin. Housekeepers cannot prepare Lydia for the life she will lead. As you and I both know, Alexander, discipline plays a large part in the lives that people of our station lead, and as far as Lydia is concerned that discipline is sorely lacking. I don't consider Eppie Watt to be a suitable housekeeper and I never have. She does not know her place.'

'I disagree. She is fond of Lydia and I believe that the child has grown to trust her.'

'That,' his mother said, 'is all the more reason why you must replace her with someone more... aware of her position in your household. Because Lydia has never known what it is to have a mother she has a regrettable tendency to attach herself to every woman she meets. As a result, she is easily drawn to the wrong sort of woman. It is a great pity, Alexander, that both your wives died young, before they could fulfil their duties towards your children. That's probably what went wrong with Duncan too...'

'That is quite enough!' Alexander, unable to bear her taunts any longer, jumped to his feet and glared down at her. 'I will not listen to such nonsense. Now that we have settled the matter, I would be grateful if you could find a new home for yourself, Mother. Or, if you wish, I will find one for you.'

She started to speak, but he glanced at the pretty little clock on the chest of drawers then said swiftly, 'Now I must go down to the harbour; a boat is coming in shortly to unload some goods and I want to make sure that everything goes well.'

As he strode the short distance to the harbour, he drew in deep lungfuls of air in an attempt to calm himself. The first step had been taken and now, having heard what his mother had to say, he was all the more determined to remove her from his house. He was well aware that the fight had only just begun, but it was a fight that he would win, he promised himself grimly, nodding to a group of fishermen mending their nets. He *would* win it, even if it meant leaving his mother where she was and moving himself, Lydia and Eppie to a new home.

* * *

The next few weeks were a trial to the entire household. Helen Geddes made life almost impossible for Eppie, and she treated Lydia with a distant frostiness that confused and troubled the girl. The few friends she had, women of her own age and temperament, visited her more often than usual, and each time Alexander happened to meet one or other of them on their way in or out of her little parlour they stared at him coldly. One or two hesitated, clearly on the verge of taking him to task for his cruel treatment towards his own mother, his flesh and blood, but each time he steeled himself to meet their eyes with his own steady gaze, and had watched their resolve crumble into a sharp lift of the head or a slight, but audible, sniff as they walked by him.

Helen herself, whenever she found the opportunity to be alone with him, tried sulking, arguing, and even reverted on one occasion to weeping pathetically and accusing him of deliberate cruelty to a woman too old and feeble to defend herself. But for the first time in his life, her son stood firm.

'Mother, I am sure that once you are settled in your own home you will agree that this move is best for all of us. Lydia will no longer annoy you as she has been doing for some time, and I will of course visit you regularly. So will Lydia – I will see to that. You will always be welcome in my home – as a guest,' he added firmly. 'Now – shall I start to look for a suitable house?'

'I would prefer to do that myself, rather than end up in one of the fisher cottages, cheek by jowl with my neighbours and with no peace or privacy,' she said huffily, and rather than protest that he would not dream of sending her to a cottage, he merely smiled, bowed and left the room.

When she eventually found a house that she deemed suitable, he was taken aback by her choice – a villa on the outskirts of the town. Like his own home, the house consisted of three floors. A large kitchen, a laundry room and a servant's bedroom, as well as a pantry, scullery and coal cellar made up the ground floor, while the well-appointed dining room and drawing room were on the next floor, together with the main bedroom, which had its own dressing room. Three more bedrooms were on the top floor.

'It's a large place for one person, is it not?' he said when he went to inspect it.

'I am used to large rooms. I would feel that I were suffocating in anything smaller.' Helen surveyed her son through narrowed eyes. She and her friends were all agreed that if she must be ousted from the place she had come to look on as her own, she should make the move as heavy on Alexander's purse as possible. 'If I must leave your house I am surely entitled to my comfort. But if this house is too much for your purse, then no doubt one of my dear friends would be willing to take me in...'

'That will not be necessary, Mother. I am perfectly willing to buy this house if it's what you want.'

'As you can see, one servant would not be able to keep this place as it should be, as well as attending to my own personal needs. I shall require at least two.'

'Very well,' Alexander agreed, while pounds, shillings and pence started running through his brain. Business had been somewhat sluggish of late and until the Board of Trade met to investigate the loss of the *Grace-Ellen* he was also paying out small pensions to the families of the men who had drowned when the fishing vessel went down. The fine family house that his mother insisted on, and the staff he would have to pay to run it, would eat into his savings. But it would be worth it to resolve the matter.

'And I shall need a gardener, and an assistant gardener,' Helen added, nodding out of the dining room window at the pleasant flower garden in front of the house. There was also a large kitchen garden at the rear – Alexander noted that he must find a cook who knew how to make the most of homegrown vegetables. That, at least, would save a little money every week.

'Of course. I will visit the lawyer this very afternoon and make an offer for the house. I am sure that you will be very comfortable in it – and very happy.' Alexander turned to face his mother and saw, with guilty pleasure, the frustration in her cold blue eyes.

He had never been a gambling man, but now he felt that he had ventured on one of the greatest gambles of his life, and had won. He had won his freedom, and his beloved daughter's future, and although it was going to cost him dear, it would be worth every penny.

* * *

'Mrs Geddes is goin' tae live in a hoose of her own,' Eppie said, and then, as Barbary said nothing: 'A fine place, by all accounts. It'll certainly make life easier for me once she's gone. And mebbe for Lydia too. Her grandmother was always nippin' at her and complainin' about her bein' sulky or difficult. What growin' lass isnae difficult at times? I mind my own mother despairin' of me...'

She could hear her own voice going on and on in an attempt to connect with her friend, but when she turned from the sink, where she had been washing clothes, Barbary was still sitting by the range, the baby in her lap, staring vacantly at the steam dribbling from the kettle's spout.

Eppie put the clothes through the big mangle that stood in a wooden lean-to Tolly had built at the back door when he first brought his bride to the house, and then took them outside to the clothes line. George and Martha were playing in the backyard; when she spoke to them, they both looked up at her, George with his mother's dark eyes and Martha with her father's clear blue gaze. Their little faces were solemn, as though they carried the weight of the world on their small shoulders.

And so they did, Eppie thought as she pegged the clothes onto the line. She could see by the way they watched Barbary, the way one or other of them tended to put a small hand on top of hers as she sat dreaming, that their mother's depression had seeped into their own minds.

Barbary was rising to her feet as Eppie returned to the kitchen. 'He's sleepin',' she said. 'I'll put him tae his bed.'

'And I'll pour away this tea, for it's cold, and put in some hot.' Eppie emptied the untouched cup into the sink and refilled it, knowing that it too would probably be left to cool.

When she had laid the baby in his cot, Barbary put both hands to the small of her back and stretched in an attempt to relieve the pain of stiff muscles. Her once-rounded body was thin and her seven-month pregnancy showed as a huge bulge protruding between her hipbones.

'I have tae go now, but I've left some soup, and some stew, enough for all of you. Mind and take your own share. You've the new bairn tae think of,' Eppie urged.

Barbary gave her a sweet, absent-minded smile. 'I'm no' hungry these days.'

'Ye have tae keep yer strength up,' Eppie pleaded, and then, as the other woman drifted over to the window, where she stood watching her children: 'They need you, Barbary. Never forget that.'

'Everyone needs someone. I need Tolly,' Barbary said, and looked at her friend with eyes suddenly awash with tears.

* * *

Once he had settled his mother into her new home, Alexander Geddes made up his mind to pay more attention to his daughter. She was growing fast and it was time, he realised, that he took more of an interest in her life and her well-being.

First of all he turned his attention to her schooling and was horrified to find that it consisted of little more than the basic elementary education that he himself recalled mastering when he was about seven years old. When he questioned her carefully about the books he had bought through the years and which were lined up on a shelf in her room, he realised that Lydia had not opened any of them other than, perhaps, to look at the pictures. He suggested one evening that she might like to read to him, but the ruse turned out to be a disaster. After stumbling slowly through half a page, Lydia burst into tears, threw the book down on the floor, accused him of laughing at her, and ran to her room.

Her father, distraught, hurried to the kitchen to beg Eppie to soothe her. It was not an easy task.

'Why can't he leave me alone?' Lydia wailed, casting herself down on the bedroom floor and banging her fists on the carpet.

'He's never wanted me to r-read to him before, so why must he d-do it now?'

'I'm sure that he just thought that it would be pleasant to be read to. You have such a pretty voice...'

'But he chose a book that was too h-hard! He looked at me as if I was daft just b-because I couldn't understand some of the words!'

'Does Miss Galbraith ever ask you to read to her?'

'Of course not. It's her fault,' Lydia said, suddenly realising that she had found a scapegoat. 'She never asks me to r-read, so how do I know if I can do it?'

'I'm sure your father feels very sorry that he upset you when he didn't mean to. Come along, Lydia, there's no need to behave like a baby. You're twelve years old now. Sit up and let me dry your eyes, then you can wash your face and get into bed while I fetch you some hot milk and a biscuit. Then I'll read to you, if you like,' Eppie suggested. 'My daughter Charlotte likes to be read to before she goes to sleep.'

'Does she?'

'Oh yes.' It had been years since she had been allowed to read to Charlotte, who had insisted on doing all her own reading as soon as she had learned a sufficient number of words, but Eppie kept that information to herself.

A suspicious green eye peered up at her from beneath a tumble of black hair. 'You won't make me read to you instead, will you?'

'Of course not. Choose a book while I'm away,' Eppie said, and went back to the kitchen.

Her employer met her in the downstairs hall. 'How is she?'

'She'll be all right. I'm going to take her some hot milk and a biscuit. Mr Geddes, what book did you ask Lydia to read to you?'

He held it out to her. 'Surely she should have been able to read that?'

Eppie glanced at it, and nodded. Charlotte had long since left that sort of story behind. When she looked up at her employer, his face was grim.

'I must go out early tomorrow,' he said, 'but perhaps you would ask Miss Galbraith to wait behind after lessons? Tell her that I will be sure to come back as soon as I can. I can see that I shall have to have a word with her.'

12

'But Mrs Geddes was satisfied with my work,' Miss Galbraith protested.

Alexander Geddes took the brightly coloured book from his desk and held it out to her. 'I asked my daughter to read this to me last night and she could scarcely pronounce any word of more than four letters. I don't consider that satisfying, given that she is twelve years old.'

'Mrs Geddes—'

'Mrs Geddes does not pay your salary, Miss Galbraith. I do, and I am not satisfied with the standard of my daughter's education.'

'I understood that she was to be taught the ways in which a young lady is expected to behave.'

'I'm not even sure that she has succeeded in that respect,' Alexander said drily, thinking of Lydia's temper tantrum on the previous evening.

Bright crimson flared over the governess's cheekbones. 'You may not recall this, Mr Geddes, but it was your mother who interviewed me for this position, and your mother who watched over my work. She was content with me, and if you are not, then clearly we have come to a parting of ways.'

'Clearly,' he agreed, 'we have. I will pay your salary for the rest of this week, but I think it best that we look on today as your last visit.'

* * *

When the woman had gone, he gathered up the work he found in the schoolroom and took it to the principal of the girls' school in Durn Street, who happened to be an acquaintance. The man frowned as he looked through the small pile of lesson books and exercise books.

'How old did you say your girl is?'

'Just turned twelve. I was thinking of enrolling her in your school in the autumn.'

'She's got a way to go before she's ready to join a class of her own age. I'd advise you to find yourself a good governess to bring her up to the proper level first.'

Alexander sighed. 'Do you happen to know of a suitable woman?' he asked wearily.

* * *

Miss Hastie, an elderly woman who had previously taught at the girls' school in Portsoy, came with excellent references. When Alexander explained that he wanted to see his daughter's education brought up to the standard accepted by the school, the woman bobbed her head in a series of swift movements that reminded him of a bird pecking through grass in search of insects.

'I quite understand, Mr Geddes.'

'But at the same time,' he added, 'Lydia needs to be treated with understanding. She never knew her mother, and was more or less raised by her grandmother, who recently moved into her own house. My daughter has been somewhat upset by the changes in this household, and you may find her a little difficult until she gets used to you.'

'I lost my own mother when I was very young,' Miss Hastie told him, 'but I was fortunate in that an aunt took me in. A God-fearing woman who understood that education is the greatest gift a girl can have. I can assure you that your daughter is in safe hands.'

It took some time for Eppie to realise that with Helen Geddes out of the house, she could get on with her work without fear of being criticised and lectured. For the first time she began to feel like the mistress of her own kitchen – and a very pleasant sensation it was too.

At her employer's insistence she began to take her evening meal with him and his daughter. 'But what will folk say if they hear about it?' she asked, dismayed, when he first suggested it. 'Servants don't sit at the same table as their masters.'

'You've been with us for almost five years now, Eppie, and to my mind, you've become more than a mere servant. In any case, it will be good for Lydia. Now that my mother has her own home, you are the only woman in my daughter's daily life. You will eat with us every evening,' he said firmly, and she had no option but to obey.

Lydia found it harder than anyone to accept that her grandmother was no longer dictating her every move. If anything, she became more difficult, as though testing her father and the housekeeper, challenging them to lose their tempers with her. It was hard on both of them, but since Alexander was out of the house for most of each day, the burden tended to land on Eppie. She bit back her exasperation and managed to develop a system based on allowing the girl to win the small battles while Eppie herself doggedly held out for victory in the larger issues.

With her employer's permission, she began to take Lydia with her when she went to the shops, or down to the harbour. Although the girl affected disinterest, standing back from the people Eppie stopped to talk to and sighing loudly to indicate how tedious she found everything, she sometimes forgot herself and allowed a look of interest to creep through.

'I don't know if you realise,' Eppie said one day as they walked back to the house after one of their shopping expeditions, 'that with your grandmother gone, you're mistress of the house now.'

'Me? But what about you?'

'I'm the housekeeper.' When she was with Lydia, Eppie made a point of reverting to the way she and her family spoke at home. 'You're the lady of the house. That means that you need to learn about things like what food to buy, and what meals to order. So you have to learn all about your father's favourite foods. And at the same time, you'll be learning how to run your own hoose – house – when you're a grown married woman.'

'I'm not sure that I want to marry,' Lydia sniffed.

'You will if you meet the right man. But there's plenty of time for that,' Eppie went on briskly, 'and a lot to learn. I can teach you how to plan menus for each day. Every morning before Miss Hastie arrives, we will discuss the meals for the following day, and then after your lessons we can go to the shops together. You need to learn how to choose fresh vegetables, and the best fish and meat.'

From then on each morning she and Lydia gravely pored over the recipe books that Jean Gilbert had accumulated during her time as housekeeper, and in the afternoons the two of them went round the shops. The shopkeepers and people they met in the streets started to know the girl, and to greet her civilly. She nodded and occasionally smiled, but being unused to speaking to strangers, she was reluctant to say too much.

Her shyness concerned Eppie. She didn't want Lydia to grow up with no friends and no experience of dealing with folk outside her own home. She was summoning the courage to speak to Alexander Geddes about her concerns when he asked her, for the second time, to bring a pot of tea to the dining room after they had finished the evening meal.

'I called in on my mother this morning, Eppie, and she tells me that my daughter has not yet visited her.'

'I suggested it to her the other day, but she paid no heed to me.'

'Perhaps you need to do more than suggest it.'

'If you don't mind me sayin', sir, it's not my place to make her do anything she doesn't want to do.'

He raised an eyebrow at her. 'My mother seems to think that the blame lies with you – that you are discouraging Lydia from visiting.'

Eppie felt colour rush to her face, and the hand holding the teacup began to tremble so much that she had to lower the cup to its saucer, the tea untested. 'I'd never do such a thing, Mr Geddes! How could Mrs Geddes think that of me? I've asked Lydia every day if she should not walk up to see her grand-mother but she's refused every—'

He held up a hand to stop the agitated flow of words. 'I know my daughter, and I never for a moment thought that you were responsible for her dereliction of duty. Do you know why she won't visit my mother?' he asked, and then, as she remained silent, staring down at the cup and saucer on the table: 'You're right, that is an unfair question. The matter is between Lydia and myself. Tomorrow morning I will order her to visit her grandmother, and you will accompany her. And that...' he emptied his glass and poured a little more brandy into it '...will be an end to the matter.'

'And if she refuses, sir?'

His face and tone hardened. 'Then perhaps I will have to assume that my mother was right all along, and Lydia needs to be taught a lesson about the need for courtesy towards her family.'

'Mr Geddes, Lydia's only a child as yet. You can't expect her to—'

'A child fast approaching womanhood and old enough to know how to conduct herself.'

'I'm not so sure about that,' Eppie said, and could have bitten her tongue out as soon as she had spoken as he set his glass down and stared at her.

'Indeed? And why would that be?'

She had let her foolish tongue lead her into a difficult situation and now, she knew, she had to justify her impertinence towards this man who paid her wages and owned the roof over her head and the food she put into her mouth. She drew in a deep breath and said, her voice trembling slightly, 'Lydia has little confidence in herself, Mr Geddes.'

'It's my mother's opinion, and mine at times, that she has overmuch confidence in herself.'

'That's just a pretence that she wears like a cloak to cover up her uncertainty. She's spent most of her life inside this house. She's never had the chance to meet other children because she's never gone to school – and that's because Mrs Geddes kept her home for fear of her catching some disease or other. I take her to the shops with me now, and I can see how shy she is when she's with folk she doesn't know. She needs to learn to be comfortable among strangers. I was thinking, sir,' she rushed on, raising an idea that she had wanted to discuss with him for some time, 'Lydia enjoys dancing and I often hear her in her room, playing that wee music box of hers.'

'Really?' he asked in surprise, and then began to say something else before biting his lip and staring down at his glass again. His fingers reached out to grip it so tightly that she saw his knuckles whiten, and feared that the glass might crack under their pressure. Then at last he said, 'Her mother was very fond of music, and of dancing.'

'Then that may be where the bairn gets her sense of movement. I've seen her dance, and she's very graceful. So I was wondering – if you don't mind me being so outspoken...'

His brows began to draw together over his straight, longish nose. 'My dear woman, I would have hoped that by now you would know I'm not an ogre. Whatever you want to say to me, get on with it.'

'There's a man in the High Street who runs a wee dancing class, and I was wondering if you'd consider letting Lydia have proper lessons.'

'Dancing lessons? Would that be – seemly?'

'Oh yes, sir, I've been asking around and some of the young gentlemen and ladies from the big houses around the town go there. You'll probably know their fathers, sir.'

'I may. I can't say that I've ever discussed dancing lessons with any of my business colleagues though.'

'It would help her to meet up with folk of her own age – and her own class too,' Eppie hastened to add. 'She's growing up and she needs to learn the art of conversation. It's not something that I can teach her.'

He deliberated for a long moment, then shrugged his shoulders. 'Very well then, perhaps you should suggest this notion of yours to my daughter and see what she makes of it.'

'If you don't mind me saying, Mr Geddes, I believe that it would be better coming from you. You're her father,' Eppie pleaded on as his frown reappeared. 'She'd be pleased if she thought it was your idea, and she'd mebbe consider it seriously.'

'You really think that she would care for it?'

'I think she would.'

'Then I shall strike a bargain with my daughter. I will send her to this dancing class if she will visit her grandmother on one afternoon a week. If she agrees, you will take her there to make sure that she keeps her word.'

'Very well, Mr Geddes.' Eppie picked up her cup and saucer and, as she prepared to leave the room, she added with quiet dignity, 'But I'm confident that if your daughter agrees to anything, she will keep her word.'

* * *

Alexander had hoped that now they were free of his mother's presence he and his daughter might become more at ease with each other, but to his disappointment Lydia had continued to be moody and temperamental.

It was not easy, therefore, to bring up the subject of dance lessons, but after two days of deliberation and false starts, he decided to plunge in and get it over with.

'I heard someone in the street the other day, talking about a dancing master who's set up in High Street,' he said when he and his daughter were at breakfast together. 'Would you like to take classes with him?'

'Me?' Lydia had been staring down at her plate, making circles in her porridge with her spoon and then watching them fill with milk to form a pattern. 'Why should I want to learn to dance?'

'Lassies like to dance, do they not?'

Lydia eyed him warily, suspecting a trap of some sort.

Alexander cleared his throat. 'Your mother enjoyed dancing, very much. She was good at it – very graceful on her feet. And that trouble between you and your grandmother not long before she moved to her own house – was that not because of you dancing in your room?'

Her face reddened and she ducked her head down and concentrated on the porridge again. She loved music and she loved dancing, and she desperately wanted to take the lessons her father now offered, but over the past few years, confused by her grandmother's gradual change from doting on her to criticising her every action, and expecting her to earn praise where once it had been given freely, she had become suspicious of all adults. She loved her father more than anyone, other than Duncan, but she resented the fact that when her grandmother's attitude had hardened towards her, her father had been too involved in business to defend or protect her.

'I just thought...' he persisted now, painfully '...that learning how to dance might be a good thing. You're growing fast, Lydia, and you need to meet more young folk of your own age.'

Glancing up from beneath her thick dark lashes, Lydia caught him looking past her to the mantelshelf, and the clock upon it. In his mind, he was already slipping away from her, beginning to plan the day ahead – plans that did not include her.

If she made things too difficult for him, she might miss the opportunity he was offering her.

'I wouldn't mind trying,' she admitted, adding swiftly, 'but if I don't like it, I'll not go back.'

Relief flooded over Alexander Geddes. He had not expected her to agree so easily. 'That's fair enough. I'll not hold you to anything you don't want to do. I'll ask Eppie to find out when you can start.' He smiled across the table at her, and she smiled back, tentatively. Then her smile wavered and disappeared as he went on, 'I visited your grandmother yesterday. She's settled in well, and is looking forward to seeing you. She says you've not visited her as yet.'

An all-too-familiar, mulish expression settled on her pretty face. 'If she wants to see me, then let her visit me here.'

'She's your grandmother, Lydia, and it's your place to call on her.'

'But she doesn't like me!' Lydia's voice took on the childish whine he had begun to dread. 'She's happier without me – and I'm happier without her!'

'That's nonsense. She likes you very much – you're her only granddaughter.'

'And you both think that I should love her just because of that? It's not fair!' Her lower lip began to protrude. 'Why do we have to like folk just because we're related to them?'

'Because we're flesh and blood kin, and because it's your duty.'

He began to get angry. 'You should be grateful that you have a grandmother who cares about you and wants to see you.'

'But she doesn't care, Father! She thinks that I should earn her love and yet she doesn't think that she should earn mine, just because she's old and I'm still a child.' The girl pushed her plate away and clenched both hands on the table. Her face was flushed and her eyes sparkled with unshed tears of anger; a glance at her told Alexander that he was in danger of moving into the sort of unpleasant scene he had witnessed between his daughter and his mother the day he found them, and Eppie, in Lydia's bedroom.

He took a deep breath and tried to subdue his own growing exasperation. The last thing he wanted was to alienate her. His mother had done that, and had lost her. 'Lydia, we all have to do our duty towards others, particularly towards older people. Your grandmother may not seem to care for you, but she does, in her own way. She misses you. The trouble is that she has forgotten what it's like to be your age. You must try to understand that, and learn to forgive her for it. If you punish her by staying away, you'll only hurt her, and since she's my mother, you'll hurt me as well. And one day when you're her age you might remember this, and wish that you had been kinder to her. If that happens you'll feel the same hurt, only it will be too late to make it up to her.'

There was a long silence, during which the grandfather clock in the hall chimed the hour. Alexander resisted the urge to look at his watch; he was expected at the quarry shortly, but he could not afford to leave this discussion with his daughter unfinished. The men awaiting him would just have to wait, even though it would hold up the work in progress.

'Do you remember what it was like to be my age?' she asked at last.

'I do indeed.' He would never forget his lonely childhood; school had been the only place where he felt free to be himself, among his friends. He recalled how hard it had been, and how painful, having to spend day in and day out earning his mother's approval and her cold idea of affection. Lydia, he realised, didn't even have school friends, and he himself had not defended and protected her as he should have done. He had let her down, and in doing so, he had also let down his beloved Celia, who had given her own life in order to give him his daughter.

Recalling his decision to use the dance classes as a bribe to make her visit his mother, he felt bitterly ashamed. If Eppie was right – if Lydia loved to dance – then she would go to the classes and have the chance to meet other young people while she was indulging in something she cared for. And he would no longer insist on her being a dutiful granddaughter. He felt that having let her down when she most needed his protection, he had no right to bargain with her.

He opened his mouth to say so and then closed it again as, to his astonishment, Lydia said, 'If it's what you want, Father, I'll visit Grandmother tomorrow afternoon – if Eppie can come with me.'

'Of course she can. And now you can go downstairs and tell her to find out when the next dance class is held.' In his relief, and his shame at being so close to blackmailing this child whom he loved more than anyone else in the world, he rose and went round the table to take her flushed face in his hands and kiss her forehead.

The gesture was so unexpected that they were both embarrassed, and both relieved when Alexander stepped back.

'You'd best be off, Father,' Lydia said primly, 'you must be late, surely.'

'I am,' he said, and then paused at the door. 'Eppie tells me that you are helping to plan the meals and do the shopping now.'

'I must be the mistress of the house now that Grandmother's no longer here.' She tilted her chin at him, as though defying him to object.

With every year that passed, he thought with a sudden ache in his heart, she looked more like her mother.

'Of course you must,' he said, and went out, the memory of her soft face imprinted on his lips.

When she was alone, Lydia got up from the table and skipped around the room, twirling and swooping to the music in her mind. Then she sped downstairs to tell Eppie the good news, and to insist that the two of them went into the town at once, to find out when she could start her dancing lessons.

Halfway down the kitchen stairs, she stopped so suddenly that she almost tipped forwards. Her father had kissed her – for the first time in her life, he had kissed her. She closed her eyes for a moment, hugging herself with both arms as she recalled the moment. Then, smiling, she ran on down the steps and burst into the kitchen.

13

Helen Geddes's new home looked down over Portsoy's jumbled roofs to the Moray Firth beyond. As Eppie and Lydia neared it the girl's steps began to slow, and by the time they had reached the gate she was clinging to Eppie.

'You'll come in with me, won't you? And stay with me?'

'Of course I will. The time'll pass quickly, you'll see. Just think of the pleasure you're giving to your grandmother. She's very fond of you, Lydia, and it's only natural that she wants to see you,' Eppie coaxed. She freed her arm from Lydia's grip and took hold of the door knocker, her own heart fluttering nervously.

A maidservant, neat in her white apron and with a small starched cap on her head, escorted them upstairs to the parlour, where Helen waited in the narrow, tall-backed chair she had brought with her from Shorehead.

'Lydia – you've decided to visit me at last.' She waited, then frowned as Lydia stayed close to Eppie's side. Eppie gave her a nudge and whispered, 'Kiss your grandma,' and the girl went forwards slowly.

Helen tipped her chin up and inclined her head slightly to one side to receive the kiss, then said, 'Sit in that chair, child, near me.' Then, to Eppie: 'You may go.'

Lydia, about to sit down, looked panic-stricken. 'But Eppie said she'd stay...'

'I'm not in the habit of entertaining servants in my parlour, Lydia. Sit down,' Helen ordered. 'You may return in one and a half hours' time to take my granddaughter home,' she told Eppie coldly. She picked up a small brass bell from the table by her chair and rang it, adding, 'Not a minute before and not a minute after. Maisie, you may show this person out – by the back door, of course.'

'Eppie—'

'I'll be back, don't fret,' Eppie said, then she was back in the hall, being led away from the front door and towards the kitchen. 'Come an' have a cup o' tea while you're waitin',' Maisie said once the kitchen door was closed behind them and there was no chance of her mistress overhearing. 'You dinnae mind, do ye, Anne?'

The cook, rolling dough at the kitchen table, glanced up and nodded at Eppie. 'O' course no'. Sit down, lass.'

'Mrs Geddes might not like it.'

'Mrs Geddes doesnae like anythin',' the woman said, adding with heartfelt sincerity, 'She's an auld bitch, that one. Have ye ever worked for her?'

'For five years.'

'Five years!' Maisie almost screeched. 'I doubt if I'll last near as long as that. Five weeks, mebbe. And Anne's lookin' for another place already.'

'I am that.' Anne set her work aside while Maisie poured three mugs of tea.

'She'll ring the bell for her own tea in half an hour,' she said, nodding at the tray, set and covered with a muslin cloth. 'We'll no' be bothered till then.'

'Aye, we're safe till then,' Anne said, her face bright with anticipation of a good gossip. 'Was that auld yin up there always so difficult tae please?'

* * *

One and a half hours and two cups of strong black tea later, Eppie was led back into the hall. 'Ye'd best wait here,' Maisie advised before she took Lydia's coat and hat up to the parlour. The girl herself came hurrying down the stairs almost at once, marching past Eppie without a glance and hauling the front door open before Maisie could reach it.

'It looks tae me like that one's as bad as her gran,' the maid murmured out of the side of her mouth as Lydia stalked down the path. She was stepping along the road so fast that her skirts tangled around her legs, and Eppie had to run to catch up with her.

'Will you slow down? We're not running a race!'

'You promised to stay with me!' The girl rounded on her, tears of sheer fury in her eyes. 'You said you'd stay and then you went away and left me!'

'How could I stay when I wasn't wanted?'

'But you promised!'

'Lydia!' Eppie caught hold of the child's wrist, dragging her to a standstill. 'You're behaving like a spoiled wee bairn instead of a lassie who's almost grown. D'you know what the maidservant said to me when you walked out the door without as much as looking at her? She said that you were just like your grandmother.'

Sheer shock dried Lydia's tears in an instant. 'I am not like her! I'll never be like her!'

'You will if you don't learn to stop this nonsense. Now listen to me – Mrs Geddes is alone now, apart from her servants, and you've got me and your father – and the bees. And as far as I'm concerned you can dance all over the house, in and out of all the rooms and up and down the stairs from now on, and there won't be a word of complaint – as long as you spend just a wee while every week bein' a dutiful granddaughter.'

'All over the house?'

'On the roof, if you want,' Eppie said. 'D'you know what I hated most at school? Latin. I never could get my mind round it, so when we were being taught Latin, I used to sit and say my favourite nursery rhymes in my head all the time, to keep from showing how much I hated it. If visiting your grandmother gets to be difficult, you could always dance in your head.'

'In my head?'

'You can do anything in your head and nob'dy knows about it – as long as you keep a pleasant smile on your face,' Eppie said, and to her relief, Lydia's temper was gone, replaced by a huge and delighted grin.

* * *

Mr Forbes, the dance teacher, had turned the top floor of his house in the High Street into a studio with a sturdy wooden floor and seats around the walls for the adults – most, like Eppie, were maidservants accompanying his young students.

The class on Lydia's first afternoon was for beginners, a group that ranged from five-year-olds to several girls and two lads around Lydia's age. It took some coaxing to get Lydia on to the dance floor, where the other beginners were already huddled together, looking for all the world like a herd of cows seeking shelter and comfort on a wet day. But once the teacher's daughter had seated herself at the old piano in the corner and began to play something made up of rippling notes that seemed to Eppie to flow like the Soy Burn hurrying to the sea, the girl's tense body noticeably relaxed. It was almost, Eppie marvelled, as though the music took Lydia over. When the class was urged by the teacher to move about the floor in time to the music, she was one of the first to step to the rhythm. While most of the others were still walking about self-consciously, her shoulders and arms and hands began to move easily. She even tried a tentative, graceful swirl that lifted her skirts about her ankles, and then, encouraged by the teacher's: 'That's grand, lassie, you've got the idea. Just think about enjoyin' yourself...' she began to move faster, with an easy, assured grace. Eppie watched, astonished, reminded of the way the fishing boats, once they had been nursed between the harbour walls and out into open waters, unfurled their big, dark-red sails to the wind and began to dance through the waves, dipping gracefully from one wave to the next.

They went on to learn some basic steps, and in every case, Lydia was the first to grasp what the teacher wanted them to do. When the lesson ended the others scurried from the floor at once, in a hurry to retrieve their coats and hats and get out into the fresh air, while Lydia stood alone in the middle of the floor for a moment, her face dazed, as though she were still listening to some inner music. When Eppie touched her arm she blinked, awakening from her trance to look around, surprised to find herself alone.

'You did well – the best in the class,' Eppie said proudly as they walked home. Lydia, still in a daze, said nothing, but as soon as they returned to the house she went straight to her room, and Eppie, passing the door on her way to put the laundry away, heard her singing to herself, and knew that she was dancing, lost once more in a world of her own.

Lydia had awakened from her trance by the time her father came home, and throughout the entire meal that evening she described every moment of the lesson to her father. 'It was as if I've always known what to do, but this was the first time anybody had ever told me to do it,' she tried to explain to him.

He listened intently, smiling, asking questions and, watching them, Eppie thought that she had never seen them so close.

* * *

'D'ye ken that there's things bein' said in the town about you?' Maisie asked on the following week. Again, Eppie was being given tea in the kitchen.

'What sort of things would anyone find tae say about me?'

'Ach, it's just daft nonsense about you and Mr Geddes bein' alone together in that big house now that the old one's moved out.'

'We're not alone at all – Lydia's there, and her governess is in every mornin' but Sundays.'

'Aye, but the only other one in the hoose at nights is the lassie, and she's no' what ye'd call a – what is it?' Maisie sought for the word and finally found it. 'A chaperone.'

'But they cannae be gossipin' about me and Mr Geddes bein' – surely not!' Eppie said, horrified. 'Who would start nasty gossip like that?'

'You've said more than ye should, Maisie,' the cook broke in. 'D'ye want tae lose yer place here?'

Maisie shrugged. 'I'm not that bothered. In fact, it would be a blessin'.'

'Wait until ye've got somewhere else tae go afore ye take chances.'

Maisie said nothing more, but as her eyes met Eppie's over the rim of her cup they widened, then rolled in the direction of the door.

'Mrs Geddes?' Eppie said.

'Maisie, I'll no' have ye sayin' another word about the mistress in my kitchen!' the cook snapped, quite unaware that she had answered the question herself.

'No' anither word,' the maidservant agreed meekly, winking and nodding at Eppie. 'Except that, wherever the slander comes from, it's runnin' a' round the place.'

'But it's nonsense!' Eppie said angrily.

'Ye know what folk are like when they get their teeth intae a bit o' gossip – they go after it like a dog after a rat, and they dinnae let go until another good piece o' scandal comes along tae take its place,' Maisie said, then subsided as Anne snapped, 'Maisie – one mair word an' I'm goin' tae tell the mistress aboot you makin' eyes at the gardener!'

Eppie tried to dismiss the maid's idle gossip, but as she and Lydia returned to Shorehead she found herself looking with suspicion at the women she passed in the street, and fancying that one or two of them looked back at her in a strange way and then murmured something to their companions behind her back.

She was trying to tell herself that it was her imagination when Lydia, skipping along by her side, relieved that the ordeal of visiting her grandmother was over for another week, said, 'Why is it wrong for you to eat your dinner with us?'

'It's not wrong at all.'

'That's what I thought, but Grandmother had on one of her grumpy faces when she asked me if it was true.'

'It was your father's idea, so that I can teach you how to behave at the table.'

'I knew that it was Father's idea – I said that to Grandmother. But I didn't know why,' the girl said casually.

Over the next few days Eppie tried hard to tell herself that she was imagining the sudden interest being shown towards her when she went about the town, but there was no denying that conversation faltered every time she went into shops, then picked up again as she left. This, she knew, had never happened before.

As it happened, Lydia's next visit to her grandmother fell on the cook's day off, which meant that Eppie could ask Maisie outright about the gossip in the town.

The girl spread her work-reddened hands on her knees and leaned forwards, her eyes alight with the pleasure that only a good gossip could bring. 'It's the mistress that's behind it all right – her an' her friends that visit tae take tea wi' her. They like nothin' better than tae pull folk's reputations tae shreds – it doesnae matter who, rich or poor. They've been talkin' about you gettin' Mr Geddes tae put his mither out of his hoose so's the two o' you can be together in peace.'

'That's not true!'

Maisie shrugged. 'They're no' bothered about whether it's true or no'. That doesnae stop them sayin' it. And I know for certain that the auld bitch up there...' she jerked her head towards the upper floor '...is still ragin' at her son for makin' her move intae this place. She wants tae blame someone, and it's you.'

'How do you know this?'

'Because they talk aboot it openly in front o' me when I'm servin' their tea. Ye know what the gentry are like,' Maisie said contemptuously, 'they seem tae think that servants are born deaf tae anythin' but orders. Though I sometimes think there's a deliberate way to it as well – they talk gossip in front of the likes o' you an' me so's we can repeat it tae folk they'd no' lower themselves tae gossip wi'. Whatever the way o' it, I can promise ye that it's a' roond Portsoy that you and Mr Geddes have a fondness for each other.'

'If Mr Geddes gets tae hear this, he'll—'

'I doubt if he will, for men dinnae enjoy gossip the way women dae. It's you she's out tae hurt, an' if ye take my advice...' Maisie reached for the teapot and replenished their cups '...ye'll pay no heed. Somethin' else'll come along soon enough tae take up their attention.'

Eppie tried to do as the girl suggested, but it was impossible. When folk smiled at her in the street and wished her a good day, or when a shopkeeper thanked her for her custom, she was convinced that there was an element of malice or amusement behind every word and look.

She said nothing to her family when she visited Fordyce. For one thing, although she knew that she and her employer were innocent of any wrongdoing, the very fact that they were being talked about made her feel ashamed and embarrassed, and for another, she knew that this was something she had to resolve for herself. Finally, unable to bear the situation any longer, she made her decision, waiting until Lydia had gone to her room for the night before making her way upstairs to tap on the door of the library.

Alexander Geddes's normally neat desk was strewn with papers and he was scribbling busily when she went in. 'I'll not be a minute, Eppie,' he said without lifting his head from his work. 'Sit yourself down.'

She stayed on her feet, looking up at the two portraits on the fireplace wall, going hot with shame at the thought of what those two gentlefolk who had been wed to her employer would think of his name being linked with that of his housekeeper.

When he looked up a few moments later and saw that she was still standing on the other side of the desk, her hands gripping each other tightly, his eyes darkened and his shoulders tensed. 'It's not something Lydia's done, is it? I thought that she was much happier with her life now.'

'It's not Lydia, Mr Geddes. I've come to tell you that I must leave your employment.'

'What?' He looked stunned. 'Leave us? But why?'

'I've been here for five years now and it's time to move on. I'll not leave you until I've found a suitable replacement – you've no need to worry about that.'

'Is it the wage I pay you? When did I last increase it?' He ran a hand through his greying hair. 'I'll pay you more, of course I will. You deserve it. Or do you need more help about the house?'

'It's nothing to do with the money, or more help – you've always been a generous employer and Sarah and Chrissie aren't afraid of hard work. I just feel that it's time to go elsewhere.'

'Someone's offered you more money, or more time off.' He got to his feet and began to come round the desk. 'Eppie, I thought that you were content here, and I know that Lydia's happier now, and she likes you. It was your idea to send her to those dance lessons, and there's such a difference in her since she started. She feels safe with you—' He broke off, glancing back at the cluttered desk. 'I can't be doing with this sort of upheaval just now,' he said. 'I have enough to worry about without more domestic problems. Whatever you've been offered, I can better it. You only need to tell me what I can do to keep you with us.'

'There's nothing you can do – I just need to go!' She had not realised that it would be so difficult. 'I'll find you another house-keeper, and then I must leave.'

She took a step towards the door, then another, but before she could take a third Alexander Geddes caught her by the shoulders, whisked her about, and sat her down in a chair. Then he propped himself on the edge of the desk and said in a steely voice he kept for the men who worked for him in the marble quarry and his other businesses, 'I will not accept this, Eppie. You're lying to me and you will not leave this room until I have the truth out of you.' Then, as she gaped up at him, fear in her eyes, he modified his tone a little as he added, 'If I can do anything about whatever troubles you, then I will. If not, then I must accept your decision. But surely we've known each other for long enough – there should always be truth between us, even if it means you criticising me or my daughter.'

'It's nothing to do with Lydia, sir, or with you.'

'I'm glad to hear that, at least.'

'It's...' She gulped nervously, then said in a rush, 'It's the folk in Portsoy.'

'All of them?' He looked startled. 'I doubt if even I can make a difference to every soul who lives in this town, but if you would explain just why they are troubling you, I'll try...'

'It's the gossip, sir. The gossip about me and...' the final word stuck in her throat like a fish bone, but as he said nothing, waiting for her to find the courage, she finally did '...me and you.'

'What?' He shot upright, coming off the edge of the desk to stand over her, staring down at her in disbelief. 'What have we done to cause gossip?'

'Nothing, sir – we've done nothing at all, but that doesn't stop folk's tongues wagging and I can't be doing with it, so I must go.'

'Wait!' He held up a hand. 'Let me get the sense of this. What is it that folk are saying about you and me?'

'That I persuaded you to send your mother away so that we could be... because I want to become mistress of this house.' Just saying the final words shamed her so much that she could only mumble, staring down at her lap.

There was a pause, then: 'Dear God!' Alexander Geddes said. 'What is it that makes folk so eager to malign their neighbours? To think that we sit shoulder to shoulder with them every Sunday morning in the kirk, and shake hands with them afterwards and we all wish each other well – and then they return to their homes and their malicious tattle.' His voice began to deepen with anger, and he started to pace the floor. Glancing up timidly, Eppie saw that he was scowling and that his fists had begun to clench.

'It's just the way folk are, sir. The best thing is usually to ignore their nonsense, but this time I can't do it, so I've decided tae go back to Fordyce.'

'You're letting them drive you away?'

'Mebbe it's time I went back to my own folk. I've not had the raising of my own daughter – she'll soon be full-grown and I'd like fine to spend time with her before it's too late.'

'Who would spread such scandal?' Geddes asked. 'I've never heard a whisper of it, but if I had I would have put a stop to it at once – you must know that. Not that it would trouble me as much as it's troubling you. But who would want to drive you out of the town like—' He stopped suddenly and swung round to face her.

'I don't know, sir,' Eppie said swiftly. 'Gossip can just start from a chance remark in a shop or on the street...' But she knew, by the stunned anger in his face, that he had already realised the truth.

'Whoever it was,' she hurried on, rising from the chair, 'that doesn't matter now. Now that you understand why I must go, I'll start looking round for a suitable housekeeper tomorrow. I'm sure I'll find one soon. Mr Geddes?' she ended timidly as he stared past her, lost in his own thoughts.

He blinked, and looked at her. 'Lydia is well settled with you, and so am I. If I put a stop to this nonsense – and I promise you that I *will* put a stop to it – then you'll stay with us?'

'No, sir. Once an idea's put into folk's heads they hold on to it, and I can't bear that. And as I said, I want to spend more time with my own bairn before it's too late. Goodnight, Mr Geddes,' she said, and hurried from the room before he could stop her.

14

Alexander's first reaction was to face his mother, make her admit to her malicious troublemaking, and demand that she end it at once. But on the following morning he realised that he would only be playing into her hands.

He was still a child when he first realised that Helen Geddes had an amazing ability to erase wrongdoing from her mind as soon as it was uncovered. She would only deny her involvement in this latest business, then go on to discuss it in the guise of concerned mother and grandmother. She would advise him, in a sweet and reasonable voice, that should such gossip be allowed to spread through the town, it would damage his reputation and upset his daughter.

And she would then suggest that the only way to put a stop to it was for him to dismiss Eppie Watt and find a more suitable housekeeper – someone older and beyond reproach. She would, of course, offer to undertake the task of appointing a new house-keeper – someone who would be answerable to her and who would keep her informed of all that went on in his household. He had no illusions as to the lengths she could go to.

He groaned as he recalled the number of times that her gentle, reasonable voice and those sincere blue eyes had turned him in a direction he had not intended to take. And the number of times he had come to regret listening to her.

No, there must be some other way to retain the harmony that had only recently come to bless his home, while at the same time putting paid to his mother's mischief-making. A way that he must find for himself.

And find it he did, after three days of searching. He examined it carefully from all angles, and decided that it was sound and acceptable.

* * *

Lydia had taken her new duties as mistress of the establishment very seriously. Instead of spending most of her time in her room when she was not with her governess, she had taken to flitting about the house and garden during her free time, planning meals in the kitchen with Eppie, overseeing the housework, or tending to her beloved bees, now beginning to stir from their winter sloth. Every time her father entered the house she was there, waiting to greet him and to make sure of his comfort.

This new and quite delightful Lydia pleased him, but at the same time it made it difficult for him to speak to Eppie in private. The only time he could be certain of being on his own with the housekeeper was when Lydia was asleep.

Three evenings after Eppie had handed in her notice, he pulled the little-used bell rope that hung by the library fireplace. When Eppie arrived he nodded to her to sit down, then began to pace the floor, his hands tucked behind his back.

'I want to talk to you about your decision to leave my employment.'

'Yes, sir. I've heard of a woman who lives in Fochabers – a widow with her family all up and married. She has very good references and she expects to leave her present employment in three or four weeks' time.'

'I don't believe that that will be necessary. Lydia is well settled now, and I feel that bringing in a new housekeeper at this time would not be good for her.'

'I'm willing to stay on for a week or two, to see the woman settled in and make certain that you and Lydia are content with her.'

'Even so – you've encouraged my daughter to take an interest in the running of this house, which pleases me as it's time she began to learn these skills. And she's enjoying her dance classes more than I thought she would. They give her the chance to meet young folk – a chance that I now realise has been denied her,' he added guiltily. 'She needs more young company, and since one of your reasons for leaving us is that you want to be with your own daughter, it seemed to me that we could solve the problem by inviting her to come, as a friend and companion to Lydia.'

'Bring Charlotte to Portsoy?' Eppie blinked at him, startled.

'Why not? I can assure you that she will lack for nothing. I would provide for her as I provide for Lydia. She could share Lydia's governess, or if you prefer it, she can attend the girls' school. I believe that it is very good; I am considering sending Lydia there after the summer.'

Eppie was trying to collect her scattered thoughts. Her first reaction to the suggestion that she could have Charlotte close by was delight, but it would not, she realised, solve the problem. When Alexander finished speaking and pacing, and turned to look at her, his eyebrows raised, she shook her head.

'It's very kind of you, Mr Geddes, and generous too. But it

wouldn't stop the gossips. We'd still be the only adults in the house, and my Charlotte coming to bide here would only make them all the more certain that you and I are...' she stopped, her face burning, then said in a low voice '...living in sin. I can't do that to my daughter, or to yours.'

He heaved a long sigh, and began to pace again. Eventually he came to another stop before her and said, 'Then we must resolve the problem in another way. Face the gossips – let them think that they were right, if it pleases them – and stop them in their tracks once and for all.'

'But how do you propose to do that?'

'A simple solution,' said Alexander Geddes. 'You and I will be wed.'

Looking back on the scene, Eppie was shamed by the fact that sheer astonishment brought on a choking fit. She had no option but to snatch up her apron and bury her crimson face in it while she coughed and coughed again, each breath she struggled for resulting in yet another bout.

When she finally got herself under control again, her eyes streaming and her heart thumping, her employer was standing before her, offering a glass of water.

'I put a little brandy in it,' she heard him say above her own whooping and gasping. 'Try to drink it.'

Mercifully, the brandy was not strong enough to make the water unpalatable, or to send her into another paroxysm of coughing. She sipped cautiously and let the cool liquid trickle down her raw throat. While she drank, Alexander Geddes returned to his own side of the desk and sat down, his dark eyes fixed on her face.

'My apologies, Eppie – I had no idea that my proposal would alarm you so much.'

'It was the suddenness of it,' she finally managed to say.

'I suppose I could have put it better. I'm more used to business than to – other things. Would you like some time to consider my suggestion?' he asked.

'No, Mr Geddes, I would not, for there's no way I could agree to it.'

'Oh,' he said, then, 'am I such a bad catch?'

'It's got nothing tae do with that, Mr Geddes. When I wed Murdo Watt it was because I loved the man, and I still do. I'm not saying that I'd never marry again, but if I do, it'll be for love, not for convenience.'

'Not even for your daughter's sake?'

'She's happy enough where she is. I've no need to wed for her benefit.'

'But you're still apart – marriage to me would have allowed you to bring her here, and to still the gossips' tongues. In fact,' Geddes said, 'I would still be happy for you to bring your daughter to this house. It would be of benefit to Lydia to have a close friend.'

'It's kind of you, sir, but it would be no help to the situation I find myself in. The gossiping would probably get worse if I brought Charlotte here.' Eppie got to her feet. 'Will there be anything else, Mr Geddes?'

'No, there won't,' he said.

By the time he went to his own room for the night Alexander was beginning to see the humour of the situation. If his mother only knew that the housekeeper she had treated with such disdain had turned down his offer of marriage! He startled himself by laughing aloud at the thought, and then slapped a palm against the bedpost.

'By God!' he said. 'I'll do it. I'll see her expression for myself. It's the least she deserves for her meddling!'

* * *

On the following morning he was on his way to his mother's house astride his sturdy gelding when he recalled that in his haste, he had forgotten to take papers needed for a meeting that afternoon in the town of Elgin, several miles away. He muttered a curse under his breath; he would not have time to return for them after leaving his mother's. There was nothing for it but to turn the horse about, and hurry home.

When he let himself in at the front door, the house was silent apart from the murmur of voices from the small parlour, where Lydia was at her lessons with Miss Hastie. Hurriedly, Geddes collected his papers and was on his way out when he heard the governess's voice say, 'You are a very stupid girl!'

He stopped in his tracks, unable for a moment to believe that he had heard correctly. Then the voice came again. 'I've a good mind to make you sit in the corner with a dunce's cap on your head.'

'I'm not stupid – I'm not!' Lydia shouted. 'You're a liar!'

'How dare you speak to me in that fashion! Your father will hear about this, madam, make no mistake about it. He'll punish you for your impertinence!'

Two strides took Alexander Geddes to the door of the small parlour. He threw it open to see Lydia, her face crimson with rage and mortification, glaring up at the governess, who was looming over her. The two of them swung round as the door opened.

'Ah, there you are, Mr Geddes. I'm afraid that Lydia has just been very rude to me!'

'I heard her, Miss Hastie. I heard you both. Lydia, go downstairs and ask Eppie to give you some milk and a biscuit. I have something to discuss with Miss Hastie.' Alexander stood aside and as his daughter passed him and he saw the way her teeth were clamped into her lower lip to stop its trembling, he felt such a wave of love go through him that it left him shaking.

'I scarcely think,' the governess said sharply as he closed the door, 'that your daughter should be rewarded. Bad behaviour should always be punished.'

'Miss Hastie, my daughter is not stupid, and I will not allow anyone to tell her that she is.'

The woman had the grace to look slightly ashamed, but only for a moment. 'No, she is not stupid, I agree with you there. But she has an unfortunate attitude towards authority. She resents being told what to do, and she refuses to accept chastisement, even when it is well deserved. If you ask me, Mr Geddes, she is a perfect example of the old adage. Spare the rod, Mr Geddes, and you will certainly spoil the child.'

'When I first interviewed you for the post of governess to my daughter, did I not explain to you that she had been unsettled by recent changes in the household? I had hoped that you would understand my meaning, and treat her gently.'

The woman's sparse eyebrows rose. 'Gently? Did you not tell me, Mr Geddes, that you wanted the child's education to be brought up to an acceptable standard for admission to the girls' school?'

'I did, but telling her that she is stupid does not seem to me to be the right way to achieve that standard.'

'If you will forgive me for saying so, sir, I am a trained school-teacher. I know how to get the best out of children.'

'By treating them harshly?'

'By instilling discipline. It was the way I was raised, and I am grateful to those adults who taught me to listen and to obey without argument.'

'I have a feeling, Miss Hastie, that you must have been a most unhappy child,' Alexander said. 'But I will not have my daughter treated as, clearly, you were. I think it best that I find another governess for her – one who can follow my instructions.'

The woman's pale face suddenly flooded with hot blood. 'You're dismissing me?'

'Sadly, I must, for my daughter's sake. You may leave now, and I will make sure that you are paid until the end of the month. Goodbye, Miss Hastie,' Alexander said, and went down to the kitchen, where Eppie and Lydia sat close together at the table. As soon as he went in, the two of them stood up; Lydia's mouth was set in familiar, mutinous lines that were at odds with the tears glistening on her cheeks, while Eppie had an arm about the child, so that they were both confronting Alexander. It looked, for all the world, he thought, half amused, half exasperated, as though he were the enemy, rather than that unpleasant bully of a woman he had just dismissed.

'She's leaving the house,' he said abruptly, 'and she will not be back.'

'Miss Hastie?' Suddenly Lydia's face was radiant. 'Oh, Father!'

To his astonishment she broke away from Eppie and ran round the table to throw her arms about his waist. He looked down at the dark head against his chest, and was shaken by a second wave of fierce, protective love. Awkwardly, he patted her soft shining hair. 'There there,' he said, and then, over her head to Eppie, 'And now I must find another governess.'

* * *

Another governess – and another housekeeper, he thought a few minutes later, on his way to his mother's house once more. Would he never be free of the problems that beset him?

Arriving at the house, he paid a lad to take charge of his mount before rapping on the front door with such determination that he could hear the maid running through the hall in her haste to answer the summons.

'Your mistress is in?' he asked abruptly as soon as the door opened.

'Aye, sir. She's in the parlour. Will I take yer hat an'—'

'There's no need for that,' Alexander said crisply. 'I'll not be staying.' And then, tossing the words over his shoulder as he marched across the hall and began to mount the stairs: 'I'll announce myself.'

Helen Geddes was reading her newspaper, sitting with her back to the window to catch the light, and holding the paper at arm's length. Her fine blue eyes had been dimming slightly over the past year, but she was so proud of their beauty that she was doing her best to delay the day when she would have to hide them behind spectacles. Now, she looked up with a start as the door was thrown open and her son strode in, whipping off his hat as he entered.

'Alexander – I didn't expect you this morning.' Her eyes swept over him. 'You might have left your coat in the hall, my dear. I'll tell Maisie to bring tea—'

'I don't need tea, Mother, for I'll not be staying for long. I'm on my way to Elgin, but first, I have a matter of business to discuss with you, if you have a moment?'

'Yes, of course.' She folded her newspaper and put it aside, motioning him to a chair. He glanced at it, but did not sit down, choosing instead to force her to look up at him.

'I have a problem, Mother, so I have come to talk it over with you.'

'Naturally.' Helen was delighted – she had known that sooner or later her son would have to turn to her for advice instead of dealing with everything on his own. 'Is it to do with Lydia?'

'Not at all. As a matter of fact, her sulkiness has much improved now that she's going to these dance classes. She enjoys them greatly and I'm told that she's a fine dancer. I should have sent her years ago.'

A frown creased the soft fine skin on her forehead. 'Are you sure that you're right in encouraging this fancy of hers, Alexander? Is it wise? You don't know who she's mixing with, or what diseases she might pick up. She's always been a delicate child—'

'She seems sturdy enough to me, and if learning to dance makes her happy then I'm contented with it. No, Mother, I'm here on another matter entirely. A daft thing, but annoying all the same. I've been told that some foolish tales are sweeping through the town; tales concerning me and my housekeeper.'

'Really?' Now Helen's eyebrows arched carefully. 'What sort of gossip?'

'You don't know, Mother?'

'I make it a rule never to listen to tittle-tattle,' she said primly.

'Of course not. That would be beneath you, would it not? Well, then, I must tell you, unsavoury though it is for me to tell and for you to hear. It seems that some vindictive woman – it must surely be a woman,' he added scathingly, 'since men have more to do with their time than meddle in matters that don't concern them – some vindictive woman is busy telling folk that Eppie Watt and I are living in sin.'

'My goodness! That's terrible, Alexander. Has Lydia heard this?'

'Not as far as I know, and I intend to make sure that it never reaches her ears.'

'This must have come about since I left your house. The

gossips, whoever they are, must have assumed that I was removed in order to leave the way clear for the housekeeper to make a good marriage.'

'That,' Alexander said, 'is exactly what I heard. Strange that it should come into your mind word for word, when you say you've not heard it for yourself.'

Colour flooded his mother's face, and she fanned her flushed cheeks with one hand. 'The very thought of it has upset me. Would you open that window, please? I need some air.' Then, as he did as asked, she hurried on, 'I can see why you need my advice. Alexander, you have no choice but to dismiss Eppie Watt. You and I are well known in this area, and well respected; we cannot afford to be tainted by scandal. What your father would say if he were still with us I do not know. I will find a good elderly woman to take her place.'

'But Lydia likes Eppie, Mother, and she trusts her. Changing housekeepers now will only upset her.'

'And discovering – almost certainly from one of the children she meets at this dance class of hers,' Helen said pointedly, 'that her father is the subject of gossip will do her no good either!'

'Exactly. That is why I have decided,' Alexander said, relishing every word, 'that the best way out of this unpleasant business and at the same time beat the scandal-mongers at their own game, is for me to marry Eppie.'

15

Alexander Geddes had not meant to upset Eppie with his proposal of marriage on the previous evening, and he had been quite concerned by her reaction. Now, though, he watched with secret pleasure as his mother, with a shrill scream of 'What?' shot out of her chair and then almost immediately collapsed back into it as though her knees refused to bear her weight. The telltale flush ebbed swiftly from her cheeks, leaving them ashen.

'You cannot be serious!' Her voice was little more than a whisper, and one hand went up to clutch at her throat as though she were defending herself against a physical attack.

'I am perfectly serious. My main concern is for Lydia – as, I am sure, is yours. She needs a mother, and she has come to trust Eppie. Eppie has a daughter of the same age, which means that Lydia would have a sister. And by making Eppie my wife,' Alexander finished cheerfully, 'I would silence the malicious gossips once and for all. As you can see, my decision would deal with several problems at one stroke.'

'I won't allow it!'

'I'm a grown man, Mother, and I have already buried two

wives. I don't see that you can have any say in whether or not I should take a third.'

'But she's a servant! And a fisher lassie before you took her into your kitchen. Alexander, do you not realise that if you marry this woman you will make me a laughing stock? My friends will refuse to speak to me – they will whisper and point behind my back. You cannot marry that woman!'

Helen Geddes seemed to have aged a good ten years in the past few minutes. She sat huddled in the chair she had filled comfortably when he first entered her parlour, her white face shrunken and her eyes huge. And filled with genuine pain, he suddenly noticed. It was time to relent and end the farce before he frightened her into a fit of apoplexy.

'No, Mother, I cannot marry her.' He sat on the edge of a chair close to hers. 'I already know that because last night I asked her to be my wife, and she turned me down.'

'She refused you?'

'Sadly, she did. Eppie Watt is a woman of greater integrity than I realised. She would rather be widow to her dead husband than mistress of my home. The loss,' Alexander said, 'is mine.' And then, as the clock in the hall chimed the half hour: 'I must go.'

He got to his feet and looked down at his mother, who was still struggling to come to terms with what she had just heard.

'But I intend to retain Eppie as my housekeeper – in fact, I am determined on it. As I said, she is a woman of great integrity; this vicious and uncalled-for scandal-mongering has upset her so deeply that she is talking of leaving my employment. But I'm just as determined that she shall stay where she is. So, Mother, I would appreciate it if you could put a stop to any further gossip – should it happen to reach your ears. If it doesn't end very soon, I will be forced to make it known – through the pages of the

Banffshire Advertiser if needs be,' he added, stooping to pick up the newspaper from the floor, where it had fallen when Helen leaped from her chair, 'that I offered to make Eppie my wife, and she refused me. That, if all else fails, should stop the chattering. Or at least turn it on me, and not on my blameless housekeeper. Good day, Mother.'

On his way out he took time to look in at the kitchen door. 'I believe that your mistress would like a hot cup of tea,' he told the servant, 'and perhaps some smelling salts.'

Claiming his horse, which was cropping grass by the roadside, he tossed an additional coin to the lad who had been tending it and then leaped up into the saddle. As he went on his way to the distant town of Elgin, he began to whistle a cheerful tune.

* * *

It was a pleasant day, though with a stiff wind that chased the clouds across the sky before they had time to think of releasing rain onto the ground below, and whipped the tops of the high waves on the firth into white lace. Alexander's thick coat and the scarf about his throat kept him snug. He always enjoyed this journey to Elgin; the road he had to travel took him past the turn-off to Fordyce on the left, then Sandend on the right, and through farming country for a few miles before reaching Cullen, home of the wealthy Seafield family, feudal lords of Portsoy.

The wide main street fell away before him steeply, so that it seemed as if he and his horse were going to ride straight into the sea, which was framed in a stone archway, part of the great viaduct that ran above the town. On the other side of the arch the road swung to the left; following it, he looked down on his right to the roofs of the fisher cottages squeezed between the road and the shore, then he was riding uphill again, back to the green fields.

One of the reasons why he preferred to travel on horseback rather than by coach was that Alexander Geddes was a man who felt more comfortable in his own company than in the company of others. He enjoyed looking about him at the fields where sheep and cattle grazed, or up at the birds wheeling and calling overhead, or out to the Moray Firth which, whatever the weather, was one of the bonniest sights he knew.

But today, once the euphoria of besting his mother had eased, his mind was claimed by more sombre thoughts. Freeing himself and his household of Helen Geddes's domination had come at a cost. At the time, he had thought to buy her a small but pleasant house in its own little garden, with one live-in servant and extra help for the heavy work brought in on a part-time basis. His plans had included a part-time gardener as well. He could afford to run both households, but even so, the large house his mother had chosen had cost him dear. He had assumed that she would take the furniture from her bedroom and her private parlour with her, but with maddening perverseness she had decided that she would leave most of that furniture behind, and furnish her new home afresh throughout. This meant that he had been forced to spend a lot of money on the expensive pieces she'd selected, not to mention the wages for more servants than he had first expected, and a full-time gardener, with a boy to help him.

He may have won his freedom, but his mother had made sure that he paid a heavy price.

And then there was the loss of the *Grace-Ellen*. A date had not as yet been set for the Board of Trade investigation into the tragedy, but when it did take place Alexander was determined to get as much compensation for the families of the crew as he could – the widows, the young children, and the elderly parents who had lost the sons they relied on to help them through the enforced poverty of helpless old age. In the meantime, he was paying each family a small monthly pension from his own purse, which seemed to emptying before his very eyes.

A century ago Portsoy had been a major trading port, but tariffs imposed on wines, silks and other imports during the Napoleonic Wars in the early part of nineteenth century had caused a decline in trading. Alexander did well enough, and the two cargo ships he owned took fish, grain, serpentine from the marble quarry and soapstone to Europe, bringing back coal, bones, flax and anything else that could be sold at a profit. In the early part of the year one of them had been badly damaged in a storm, only just managing to limp into Calais, and was then forced to remain there for some time while costly repairs were carried out. Then there was the marble quarry. A week earlier he had received a letter from Edward Ramsay, the principal share-holder, informing him that with the advent of modern machinery it was felt that the time had come to consider making changes to the small Portsoy quarry. Someone would be travelling north within the next few months to assess the quarry and discuss future business projects with him. Alexander groaned, so preoccupied in his thoughts that the turn-offs to the fishing villages of Portknockie, Findochty, Portessie and the town of Buckie fell away behind him unnoticed.

Riding down the narrow main street of Fochabers and crossing the bridge over the waters of the River Spey, Alexander wished that Ramsay would either leave him in peace to continue as things were at present, or take responsibility for the quarry off his hands altogether.

Then, riding out along the final stretch to Elgin, he fell to thinking of Lydia. She had benefited from her dancing classes, though from what he gathered from the things she did not say rather than what she did say, she was not finding it easy to make friends among the other young people who attended the class. This, he felt, was because she had had a lonely childhood, with only his mother and the governess for company. Perhaps he should find a girls' school that took in boarders – if the fees were reasonable, he could manage them. But he was not certain that her education to date had equipped her well enough. It would be madness to send her to a school where she was unable to compete academically with her fellow pupils.

It was almost a relief when he realised that he was riding into the handsome and elegant cathedral town of Elgin, and was finally free to concentrate his mind on the day's business, instead of fretting over domestic problems.

The fresh air had whetted his appetite and there was time, before his meeting, to eat in one of the town's inns. Handing his mount over to the stable boy, he stretched his limbs before going indoors to wash the road's dust from his hands and face.

One of the men he was to meet with later was already seated at a table, so Alexander joined him, relieved for once to have someone else to talk to instead of having to deal with the thoughts that were still chasing round in his brain – Lydia's future, Eppie's imminent departure and the business of trying to get accustomed to a new housekeeper, not to mention his mother and her expensive lifestyle and vinegar tongue.

'Did ye ride in?' his companion asked when they had ordered their food. And then, when Alexander nodded: 'So did I, since it's a pleasant enough day. I've no' long arrived – I must have come down the road frae Fordyce as you were leavin' Portsoy. A few minutes either way and we could have ridden in together.'

'You live in Fordyce?'

'Born and bred, and weel content tae die there when my time comes. It's a bonny wee place. Have ye ever visited it?'

'No, but my housekeeper comes from there. Eppie Watt – that's her married name; she's the widow of a Portsoy fisherman. I've no knowledge of her own name.'

His companion frowned over the name for a moment, then said, 'I think ye'll find that she was born a McNaught. Her faither's a schoolmaster.'

'I believe I've heard that.'

'A good one, tae. I could have sworn that my lad was beyond learnin', for he'd never sit on his rump long enough tae let anythin' stick tae his shoes, let alone stick in his noddle, but Peter McNaught has the patience o' a saint an' the ability tae hold a youngster's interest. I don't ken how he did it, but by the time my son came out of the academy he was able tae add and subtract and make a good fist at writin' too. And he knew his geography. He's in Leith now – he owns a ships' chandlery and does well out o' it. Aye, the McNaughts are well thought of in Fordyce,' the man went on as the waiter arrived with two plate-fuls of food. He tucked a large handkerchief into his shirt collar and then picked up his knife and fork and began to saw busily at the large chop set before him. 'He's got two lassies of his own. I think your hoosekeeper's the younger. The other one's as clever as her father – she teaches in the infant school and I've heard good reports of her too.'

The conversation turned to talk of the forthcoming meeting, but on the way home later that afternoon Alexander returned to fretting over what to do about Lydia, and how to find a way of retaining his housekeeper. And then, as he passed the end of the Fordyce road, the answer came to him.

* * *

He wasted no time when he got back home, entering the house by the side door that took him straight to the kitchen.

Eppie, rolling out dough on the big kitchen table, her sleeves tucked up above her elbows to keep them clean, was startled when he walked in, still in his outdoor clothes. 'I didn't hear you come in, Mr Geddes...' she began to dust flour from her hands and roll her sleeves down.

'Where's Lydia?'

'At her dancing. I'm off in another five minutes tae fetch her home.' Now that Lydia had settled into the dance class Eppie only needed to take her and then bring her home again. 'Can I get you some food before I go?'

'Nothing at all. Go on with your work.' Alexander pulled a chair out from the table and sat down. 'I've been thinking that mebbe I should send Lydia to the girls' school after the summer. She needs to meet folk of her own age. What d'you say?'

'I think it would be the right thing, Mr Geddes.'

'What school does your own daughter attend?'

'She did well in the infant school, but now that she's getting older, she's in the girls' school. My sister's tutoring her at home too.'

'Is she clever – your daughter?'

'So they say,' Eppie admitted, unable to prevent a note of pride creeping into her voice. 'Marion – my sister – says she takes in knowledge like a cloth soaking up water.'

'I don't believe that any of Lydia's governesses have made a good job of teaching her. It was all very well when she was small, but she should know more than sums and lettering and reading by now.' Alexander settled his spine more comfortably against the chair's wooden back and stretched his booted legs across the flagstones. It was pleasant to be sitting in this warm, fragrant kitchen, watching Eppie's rounded arms send the roller across the dough with smooth, easy sweeps. Every few seconds she put the roller down and turned the dough, shaping it with quick, deft pats of her floured hands before picking up the roller again.

'I was thinking,' he said, 'that she could do with special tuition over the summer to prepare her for the school. Would your sister be willing to take on the position?'

'Marion? I don't know, sir. Mebbe she would.'

'You'll ask her for me, then, next time you go to Fordyce?'

'If you're sure. But it would mean Marion coming here every day, or Lydia going to Fordyce. There's surely someone nearer here than Fordyce.'

'I need a good governess. If your sister's willing, she could spend the summer here. We've got plenty of room, and if your own daughter would like to come as well, I'd be willing to pay your sister to tutor both of them. Your girl would be company for Lydia, and—' he played his trump card with the carefully casual expression of a gambler displaying his winning hand '—with your own sister here to keep watch over the two of us, the gossips will surely be silenced once and for all.'

* * *

To Eppie's surprise, Marion did not turn down the offer of employment as soon as she heard it. She narrowed her pale blue eyes and pursed her neat firm mouth in deliberation, then said, 'And Charlotte and I would both live as guests of Mr Geddes?'

'Bed and board would be included, of course, but you'd be paid a wage for your work as governess to his daughter – and to Charlotte.'

'Please, Aunt Marion,' Charlotte beseeched, hopping up and down. She had never tired of asking Eppie all about Lydia during her visits home, and the thought of actually meeting the girl, and seeing her fine home, thrilled her. 'Please say yes!'

'I'll think about it,' Marion decided, 'and tell you before you go back tomorrow.'

'Just think,' Charlotte whispered in the dark of the night, when she and her mother were in bed together. 'We're going to spend the whole summer together, you and me!'

'Only if your Aunt Marion decides to accept Mr Geddes's invitation,' Eppie warned, terrified in case the girl built her hopes up too high and had to cope with disappointment.

'She will! I'm sure she's as eager as I am to see the fine big house where you work. Anyway, I told the bees about it this afternoon, and I explained to them that it is very important for you and me to be together,' Charlotte said. 'And I told the good Lord too, when I said my prayers. Aunt Marion will say yes – I know she will!'

* * *

A few days after the school term ended Marion McNaught and her niece travelled to Portsoy in a hired carriage sent by Alexander Geddes to convey them and their luggage. The heaviest item was a large box containing the textbooks that Marion deemed necessary for the task that lay before her.

They arrived, as arranged, at the front door, and stood in the hall, gazing in awe at the handsome panelling and the large paintings, while the driver, with the aid of a man hired by Alexander Geddes, carried their luggage to the upper bedroom the two were to share.

Lydia, as excited as Charlotte at the prospect of a meeting, had been watching out of the parlour window for the new arrivals for over an hour. When the carriage drew to a standstill below, she rushed along the hall and down the back stairs shrieking, 'They're here, Eppie – they're here!' and then, suddenly struck by an attack of shyness when Eppie opened the front door, she hovered at the rear of the hall.

'Lydia...' Eppie, suddenly remembering the girl, turned and held a hand out to her '...come and meet your new governess, Miss McNaught, and Charlotte, your fellow student.'

The girl came forwards slowly, and then at a firm nod from Eppie, she dropped a curtsey to Marion before holding out a hand to Charlotte. 'How do you do?' she said in a stilted little voice. Charlotte, overcome with a sudden shyness of her own, shrank back against Marion – choosing her aunt, and not her mother as a refuge, Eppie noted with a pang – and then, urged forwards by Marion, she put her hand into Lydia's.

'How do you do?' Her voice was little more than a whisper.

'Lydia, show Charlotte the room that she and Miss McNaught will share, and then I'm sure she would like to see your dolls. I will take Miss McNaught to the schoolroom.'

* * *

'This was used by Mrs Geddes as her private parlour,' she explained to Marion as they went into the room, 'but it was also used by Lydia and her governess. Mr Geddes has decided that for the summer, at least, it is to be known as the schoolroom, and at other times you will use it as your own parlour.'

'That's very civil of him.' Marion, trying hard to behave as though she were used to visiting grand houses, looked around the small, well-furnished room with approval. 'When do I meet my new employer?'

'This evening. He'll be back in time for dinner. I do hope that you're going to be happy here, Marion.' Eppie knew that if her sister decided to return to Fordyce, Charlotte would have to go with her.

Marion gazed with rapture at the pretty little writing bureau where Helen Geddes had whiled away many hours penning notes to her friends. She imagined herself sitting there, planning out the next day's schoolwork. It would be such a delight to live like a lady for the next three months.

Aloud, she said casually, 'I'm sure that it will be a pleasant diversion, and in any case, it's only for the summer.'

16

In the bedroom that Charlotte was to share with her aunt, she and Lydia eyed each other in a wary silence.

'It's a nice room,' Charlotte ventured at last. And then, as Lydia pursed her mouth into a rosebud but said nothing, 'May I see your dolls now?'

Lydia considered the question for a moment before leaving the room. Charlotte followed her across the hallway, her eyes widening as she walked into an Aladdin's cave of toys. They were piled along the bottom of the bed, with its pretty rose-sprigged white counterpane and its pile of pillows, and lined up on a shelf running the length of the room. There were delicate Eastern dolls with perfect porcelain faces, wooden dolls with painted smiles, rag dolls and dolls with wax faces and real hair. There were baby dolls in long robes, girl dolls and boy dolls, and elegant lady dolls dressed in silks and lace.

A handsome dappled rocking horse decked out with an elaborate leather saddle and a deep-scarlet harness was mounted on a wooden frame that allowed him to move back and forth. When

Lydia saw Charlotte's face soften with desire at sight of it she immediately climbed into the saddle and set the horse in motion, the tiny silver bells attached to the reins tinkling with each movement. The animal had flared nostrils and large dark eyes, and Charlotte could see that the thick tail, as well as the mane on its proudly arched neck, was made of real horsehair.

A puppet theatre was set out on a table by the window, and another shelf held a long row of books. Charlotte's fingers itched to take them down and open them to see what wonders they held within their stiff covers, but she resisted the urge, aware that it was too early for her to presume.

The front of the large doll's house lay open, and its interior was far beyond anything that Charlotte had ever seen, or even dreamed of. Again, her fingers yearned to touch, so she tucked her hands behind her back to keep them well away from temptation while her eyes feasted on every detail.

The ground floor held a large kitchen with an adjacent pantry, both complete with everything that would be found in real kitchen premises. Above was a parlour with paintings and tiny vases of flowers and miniature plants on long-legged occasional tables. There was a marble fireplace and velvet curtains, and plush chairs and sofas where the master and mistress of the house reclined. The dining room table was set for a meal, with elegant glasses and dishes, a delicate candelabra in the middle, and even cutlery laid out at each place.

The floor above held a nursery with its own doll's house, rocking horse and tiny toys, as well as a baby in its lace-bedecked cradle and a small child playing on the rug, supervised by a uniformed nursery maid in a rocking chair by the fire. There were two bedrooms on that floor, one with a four-poster bed, and the very top floor held a servants' dormitory.

The rocking horse's silver bells tinkled faster and faster as Lydia threw her body back and forth, urging her mount to greater speeds. Finally, she let it slow down, then slid from its back.

'You have lovely toys,' Charlotte ventured, and Lydia tossed her head in acknowledgement of the compliment.

'My father gave them to me, and my grandmother too. Some of them came from other countries in my father's ships,' she said, taking a delicate little Japanese lady, in full traditional costume, from the shelf. 'This one,' she said, and then, putting the doll back and lifting a little Dutch doll, 'and this one. They're all mine. I have bees too, in the garden.'

'I know. They came from my grandfather's garden. He has bees.'

'The ones in our garden are mine,' Lydia said swiftly. And then, with a sidelong glance. 'Are you clever?'

'I don't know. Are you?'

'My father asked Miss McNaught to be my governess over the summer because he thinks I've outgrown Miss Hastie. I'm glad, because she wasn't a nice person.'

'My Aunt Marion is a very good teacher,' Charlotte said quickly. Unfortunately, her attempt to defend her aunt was construed by Lydia as a strong hint that, having already had the benefit of Marion's teaching, she was cleverer than Lydia.

'I,' she said coolly, 'am the mistress of this house. Eppie says so. I plan out the meals with her every evening before I go to bed.'

'You're very fortunate to live in such a beautiful house. And very pretty,' Charlotte added with genuine admiration. Lydia's green eyes widened slightly, and her delicate oval face flushed with pleasure at the unexpected compliment.

'Do you think so?'

'Oh yes, indeed. I wish I had black hair like yours.' Charlotte caught up a handful of her own brown curly hair and gave it a good tug. 'Mine is so ordinary.'

'My father says that I look like my mother.' Lydia opened a beautifully enamelled box on one of the nursery shelves and brought out a little silver-framed portrait. She brought it to Charlotte and the two girls studied it, their heads close together.

'She's beautiful too,' Charlotte said. 'And you do look very like her.'

'She died on the day I was born, so every birthday I have is sad for my father because it's also the day she died,' Lydia explained. 'I wish she were still here.'

'I wish my father were still here. He drowned when I was little and I don't remember him.'

'We're both orphans then.'

'Half-orphans,' Charlotte corrected. 'You still have a father and I still have a mother.' She had always been a generous child, and for a moment she was tempted to suggest that perhaps they could share each other's living parents, then she realised that it was too early in their new and somewhat fragile acquaintance-ship to suggest such a thing.

'Half-orphans,' Lydia agreed. And then, fetching her least favourite doll from the shelf, 'You can hold her if you want.'

* * *

After investigating her sleeping quarters and unpacking her things, Marion descended the kitchen stairs and settled herself at the table to watch her sister prepare the evening meal.

'Don't you think that it will be difficult for the two of us – me upstairs as the governess and a guest in the house while you're the housekeeper, living below stairs?'

'Not at all.' Eppie herself had been worrying over the situation, but she was determined that spending the summer with Charlotte was worth any embarrassment. She chopped carrots briskly. 'I'm not in the least troubled, and neither is Mr Geddes. It will do Lydia the world of good to have a companion of her own age. Her grandmother spoiled her and discouraged her from playing with other children. I'm fond of her, but I warn you, Marion, you may find her a bit of a handful at first.'

'Hardly – you forget that I'm used to dealing with children.'

'Be careful with her, Marion,' Eppie said anxiously. 'I doubt she's of the same standard as Charlotte.'

'I doubt it very much, since Charlotte's had the benefit of my teaching since before she was old enough to start formal schooling.' Marion's voice was smug, and Eppie had to bite her lip and take her frustration out on the carrots instead. It hurt her to think that due to her circumstances Marion had had more to do with her beloved daughter than she had herself for so many years.

'I believe that Charlotte herself has more natural academic ability than poor Lydia ever had,' she pointed out, unable to keep a slight edge from her voice.

But Marion was not to be bested. 'Of course,' she agreed. 'After all, she comes from an academic family.' And then, mercifully changing the subject: 'This is a very handsome house. And very comfortable too. I looked into the dining room before coming downstairs and I see that the table is set for five. Is there to be a guest this evening?'

'No, it's for the household – Mr Geddes and Lydia, who is allowed to dine downstairs in the evenings now – and you, me and Charlotte.'

'You dine at the same table as your employer?'

'Only for the evening meal, and only since his mother moved into her own house. Mrs Geddes would never have allowed it when she was mistress of this place, but Mr Geddes felt that it was better for Lydia to have the two of us with her at the dinner table.'

'I see. Going by what I hear of him, he seems to be quite a modern employer.'

'I suppose he is,' Eppie agreed blandly, adding the carrots to the casserole she was making.

'When will be he home?'

'At around seven, I believe. We will eat at eight, and Lydia and Charlotte will go to bed immediately afterwards. I will come back downstairs, and you will be able to use the small parlour. I'm sure that you have a lot of preparation for your first lesson tomorrow.'

* * *

Alexander Geddes returned home at two minutes after seven. As he mounted the stairs to his room, Lydia came rushing from her nursery.

'They're here!' she mouthed elaborately, and would have tugged him into her room if he had not held back.

'Come in here, you can talk to me while I shave.'

His shaving things had been laid out, and a jug of hot water had been placed in the room only minutes before his arrival. While he shaved, Lydia perched on the edge of a chair, telling him all about the newcomers.

'She – Charlotte – says that I'm very pretty!'

'Indeed? She's quite right.'

'Do you think so?'

'I've always thought so.'

'But you never said,' she pouted.

'Only because I don't want you to become too proud.' He cast a sidelong glance at her and was amused by her scowl. 'So... I hope you made Charlotte feel at home?'

'Yes, of course. Father...' she lowered her voice to a confidential murmur '...I believe that she's very clever.'

'Did she say so?'

'No, but she seemed interested in my books. And she looks clever.'

'Is she as pretty as you?'

'I don't think so, and she doesn't think so.'

'Then she can envy your looks, and you can envy her brain. And just think – if you work hard at your lessons over the summer, you can become just as clever as she is. But she might not be able to become as pretty as you are.'

'Oh yes!' Lydia was clearly charmed by the thought.

'And what of your new governess – Miss McNaught?'

'She seems quite nice.'

'Good.' Alexander patted his face dry. 'I'm sure that we are all going to get along very well. And now you can return to your own room, for I must change into fresh clothes before dinner. You don't want me to disgrace you before your new companion and your new governess, do you?'

Twenty minutes before dinner was due to be served, he went to his library and rang the bell. When Eppie arrived he said, 'I hope that your sister and daughter have settled in?'

'Oh yes, thank you, sir. They're very pleased with their room, and Marion is delighted with the classroom.'

'Do you think that Miss McNaught would be willing to take a glass of sherry with me before dinner, Eppie? I would like to discuss Lydia's lessons with her.'

'She's in the small parlour, Mr Geddes. I'll fetch her.' Eppie whisked off and returned in under a minute to usher her sister into the room. She introduced the two of them swiftly before excusing herself and hurrying back to her pots and pans.

'Welcome to my home, Miss McNaught. I hope that you enjoy your stay with us. Will you have a glass of sherry?'

'Thank you, Mr Geddes.' Marion, suddenly and most unexpectedly shy, kept her gaze lowered.

He motioned her to a chair by the fire, and after bringing the wine to her – in a very handsome crystal glass, she noted with pleasure – he seated himself in the chair opposite. 'I understand that your niece, Charlotte, does well at her lessons.'

'She's a clever child,' Marion acknowledged, 'with a quick, enquiring mind. But then, she's had the benefit of being raised in a household that can boast two teachers.'

'While Lydia seems to have had little success with her governesses – unless, of course, she is simply not very academic. That is what I need to find out. Unfortunately I am a busy man, and so a great deal of her upbringing has been left to my mother, who lived with us until recently. No doubt,' he added, giving her a level look, 'Eppie has told you something of our family life.'

'A little – but nothing of a private nature.' For the first time Marion met his glance fully, and was surprised to realise that her heart had begun to skip like a lamb in the spring sunshine, and her face was beginning to feel quite warm. As soon as she could, she glanced away and took a steadying sip of wine.

'I am quite sure of that. I have always found your sister to be discreet. But I must speak openly to you about Lydia, if you are to be of any help to her. Her own mother died when she was born, and my mother spoiled and indulged her more than I realised at the time. She would never allow Lydia to mix with other children and had little interest in the child's formal education. When Lydia reached the age where she developed a mind of her own, her grandmother saw that natural development as bad behaviour. When she was chastised, the child became rebellious. Finally, more for Lydia's sake than hers, I admit, I realised that my mother would be happier in a house of her own. I feel quite ashamed of all those years when I put business affairs before my own child,' he admitted.

'But you had a duty to provide for her.' Marion found herself rushing to defend him. 'You had little choice but to make sure that your business prospered, and it was natural to believe that your daughter was safe in the hands of her grandmother and a governess.'

'That may be so, but as a result of her upbringing I fear that you will find quite a difference between Lydia and Charlotte in academic terms. And you may also find that my daughter can be quite rebellious.'

'From what you've told me, I would say that she's been confused by her grandmother's move from indulging her to criticising her. She needs to feel secure again, and to settle into a proper routine. I can promise you that I will do all I can to build up her confidence. And as for her academic skills – I will assess her carefully, without her knowing it, and if it is necessary I will work out a way of bringing her up to the standard of others in her age group. As for Charlotte – she is a pleasant, agreeable child and I think that she will make a good companion for Lydia. Do I have your permission to take your daughter out and about, Mr Geddes?'

'Indeed you do – I plan to send her to the girls' school in town when you judge her to be ready for it, and I want her to learn how to mix with other children. Thanks to Eppie, she's now taking dance classes and enjoying them more than I had believed possible. It seems that she has a natural talent for dance – something that I had to learn from your sister since I did not realise it myself,' he added ruefully.

'Perhaps Charlotte should also be enrolled in that class.'

'I will be happy to pay her fees. Does she also have a natural talent for dancing?'

'Not at all.' A smile turned up the corners of Marion's mouth, and twinkled in her eyes. 'Although she has a quick mind, in the physical sense she can be quite clumsy at times. But I believe that it will be good for Lydia to see that while Charlotte may outdo her in one way, she can outdo Charlotte in another.'

As he watched the new governess leave the room Alexander Geddes felt that, at last, he had done the right thing by his daughter. He had already formed a good opinion of Marion McNaught, with her calm, forthright manner and her neat appearance. Her hair was a darker brown than Eppie's, and drawn tightly back from an oval face. During the few occasions when her gaze had met his for an instant he had noted that her eyes were blue and her features more classic than her sister's. He felt more cheerful than he had for some time, and confident that this latest governess would be an excellent mentor for his daughter.

* * *

For her part, Marion had hurried upstairs from the study to the room she was sharing with Charlotte. It was empty, so there was nobody to see her pour cold water from the pretty jug into the matching china basin and then proceed to splash her hot face again and again, until it began to cool down.

Drying herself, she looked over the top of the towel, meeting her own wide, somewhat dismayed blue eyes in the mirror. She was going to find it hard to sit meekly at the dinner table with her normal serenity, because for the first time in her well-ordered, controlled and eminently sensible life, Marion McNaught had fallen, suddenly and entirely unexpectedly, in love.

17

'The way Mrs Geddes sees it, Lydia will eventually marry a man with money, and the only things she needs to know is how to run a house and how to behave in social circles – not that the poor wee thing's had much practice in that way either,' Eppie had explained to her sister when she first spoke about Marion and Charlotte spending the summer in the Geddes household. Even so, Marion was shocked when she realised just how little the child knew.

'She's scarcely been taught more than her letters and the very beginnings of numbering,' she told Eppie. 'Charlotte's away ahead of her!'

'You'll not let Charlotte get a swelled head over it, will you?' Eppie asked anxiously. She knew, although Charlotte had not said a word to her, that there was awkwardness between the two girls, mainly due to Lydia's insecurity and nervousness with other children. The last thing she wanted was for the poor girl to feel inadequate in the schoolroom.

'Of course not – and she's got more sense than to crow in any case. But at the same time, we can't allow her own education to be harmed. I must find a way of encouraging Lydia and opening up her mind, while continuing to work with Charlotte at her level. It won't be easy,' Marion said, and then, enthusiasm beginning to sparkle in her eyes and put steel into her voice: 'but I shall do it!'

At first her attempts met with little success; it was as though Lydia had erected a stone wall around herself and was daring her new governess to try to break it down. But Marion, with a patience that Eppie had never suspected her sister possessed, chipped away at it day by day, making the most of every flicker of interest she saw in her new pupil's eyes. While Charlotte worked diligently at her own lessons, Marion set herself to find different ways of attracting Lydia's attention and interest.

Sometimes, she suddenly called a halt to the schoolwork and announced that it was too nice a day to waste time indoors. Instead, they went out into the garden to play games or watch the bees in their busy comings and goings, or went into the town, or down to the shore. Without Lydia noticing it, each of these outings turned into a lesson and each step forward the girl took was rewarded with a warm smile and a quiet, almost casual word of praise.

Marion professed an innocent ignorance in the few subjects that Lydia felt comfortable with, finding ways of allowing the girl to turn the tables and teach her teacher. Within two weeks of Marion's arrival Lydia had begun to lose her nervous aggression, and to learn to approach lessons with, as Marion had intended, an open mind instead of a fear that she would fail and be judged ignorant.

Once she had begun to break through the girl's defences, Marion found some time to consider her own situation. There were moments, in those first few weeks after she and Charlotte had arrived in Portsoy, when she wished that she had never accepted the post of governess to Lydia Geddes. Ever since child-hood she had thirsted for knowledge; before she was old enough to attend the infant school her father had taught her the alphabet and basic arithmetic. While other little girls dressed their dolls and wheeled them out in their perambulators Marion gathered hers into a class, with herself as the teacher.

She had always known that she would follow in her father's footsteps, and had been impatient with Eppie when her younger sister, well able to teach had she wished to, chose marriage instead. Proudly independent, Marion had never even consid-ered matrimony for herself – until the day she looked into Alexander Geddes's face, and put her hand in his.

Since then, she had scarcely been able to stop thinking of him. At the breakfast table when Marion, at his suggestion, sat opposite him, the urge to drink in the sight of his heavy-lidded dark eyes, his firm mouth that rarely smiled – but when it did, revealed a smile of intense charm – and his thick dark hair with its fine shading of grey over the temples was almost more than she could bear. She longed to smooth his hair back, to ease the melancholy look that came into his eyes when in repose, to coax his mouth into the smile that made her knees feel too weak to bear her weight.

In the small hours of the morning, lying awake with Char-lotte sleeping soundly by her side, she was keenly aware that he was only a matter of yards away, in his own room across the square hall.

She knew from what Eppie had told her, that Helen Geddes was determined to make sure that her son would not marry for a third time. It seemed to Marion that Mrs Geddes must be won over if there was to be any chance for her. When she accompa-nied Lydia to her grandmother's house shortly after her arrival in Portsoy, Marion dressed carefully in her best clothes – a full skirt of dove-grey silk and wool with a matching high-necked, short-sleeved jacket. Skirt and jacket were trimmed with dark brown braid, and pretty brown tortoiseshell buttons ran down the front of the bodice. Her bonnet was of the same grey, with a pale blue lining and ribbons.

'I should go in to see your grandmother with you,' she said as they waited at the door.

'She'll not let you stay,' Lydia said mournfully.

'Even so, I think it only right that she should meet your new governess, if only for a moment,' Marion said, and once they were inside the house she followed Lydia upstairs to the parlour, ignoring the maid's doubtful, 'Mrs Geddes'll want tae see Miss Lydia on her own...'

'Who's this?' Helen Geddes looked Marion up and down. 'I don't recall inviting anyone except my granddaughter to visit me.'

'I am Lydia's new governess, Mrs Geddes. How do you do?'

'Indeed? You may come back for Lydia in one and a half hours,' the woman said coldly. 'No sooner and no later.'

'Yes, ma'am,' Marion said meekly, and left without protest. As she wandered about the town she felt that she had made progress, even though it was very little. At least Helen Geddes had seen her.

She had made more progress than she first thought. When Lydia came down from the parlour later she said, 'Grandmother wants to see you. I have to wait here.'

Marion allowed herself a small triumphant smile as she went upstairs and tapped on the door; by the time she had entered and half curtseyed to Mrs Geddes it had been replaced by an eyes-lowered meekness.

She was not invited to sit down, so had to stand, hands clasped primly at her waist, while she was interrogated as to where she came from, her family background, her qualifications – and her intentions as to Lydia's education.

'Mr Geddes wishes Lydia to be educated to the standard of other girls her age who attend the local girls' school, but of course, I will also see to it that she learns social skills,' she told the older woman sweetly. 'I have an excellent book on etiquette for young ladies in my possession, and I intend to make good use of it.'

'I understand from my granddaughter that you are sister to my son's housekeeper.'

'That is true, Mrs Geddes.'

'And that the woman's daughter is also staying in Portsoy for the summer.' There was no mistaking the contemptuous note in Helen Geddes's voice. Marion drew in a deep, slow breath before saying calmly, 'Charlotte is an exceptionally clever child, and would be of considerable assistance to Lydia.'

'I cannot hide from you, Miss McNaught, my concern over this situation. In fact, I cannot think why my son is doing this. Your niece may well be a perfectly respectable girl, but you must admit that she is not the type of child that my granddaughter should be mixing with.'

Eppie was quite right when she said that Helen Geddes only thought of herself. It must be terrible, Marion thought, to be so self-centred, and so stupid. Aloud, she said, 'I believe that Charlotte will be of benefit to Lydia – and they will only be together for the summer.'

'Hmmm.' Helen Geddes surveyed the new governess in silence for a long moment. The young woman was neatly dressed and well spoken; she knew her place, seemed sensible enough, and also seemed to be aware of the great responsibility Alexander had entrusted her with. He could, his mother thought grudgingly, have found worse.

'My son is a busy man, and not always aware of what is going on within his own household,' she said at last. 'I trust that should there be anything I ought to know, you will inform me?'

'Of course,' Marion agreed meekly. 'Men have so much on their minds, and at times they do not understand the responsibility of raising sensitive young ladies such as your granddaughter. I'm grateful, Mrs Geddes, to know that if in need, I can turn to you for advice.'

As she and Lydia walked home, she exulted inwardly. She had met the woman she already regarded as the one person, apart from Alexander Geddes himself, who was most likely to stand in the way of her hopes for a future life with him. She had met the enemy and it was an enemy she was determined to best.

* * *

It was obvious within ten minutes of Charlotte's first visit to the dance studio that she had no sense of rhythm at all. Watching her daughter's determined attempts to obey the teacher's entreaties to 'Just follow the music, lass – let it carry you along with it...' Eppie's heart ached for her.

In another corner of the studio, Lydia was floating across the floor, scarcely seeming to touch the wooden boards, her face lit up with the pleasure of the moment. She had no problem in following the music and letting it carry her along; every now and again, when the old piano produced a sudden rippling flurry of notes, Lydia twirled and spun as though attached to the music by an invisible, silken thread.

When Marion touched her arm and suggested in a whisper that they go out for some fresh air, Eppie agreed at once, glad to be free of the pain of watching Charlotte's failed attempts to dance.

'We have half an hour before we need to collect the girls,' Marion said as they emerged into the daylight.

'I'm going to call on Barbary. The bairn's due any time now and I like to keep an eye on her. It's at times like this that I wish I still lived next door.' Eppie had thought that as time passed, her friend would have picked up the threads of her life again, but Barbary had become more withdrawn. She roused herself only to attend to her children, but other than that she seemed to have lost her former zest for life.

'My poor Charlotte...' she went on as they set off for the row of cottages where Barbary lived '...perhaps I should withdraw her from the class, for it's clear that she'll never be a dancer.'

'Nonsense, of course she must keep going to the class. It will be good for her, and good for Lydia. She struggles in the schoolroom while Charlotte's way ahead of her. Lydia needs to realise that while she may be behind Charlotte academically, she is ahead when it comes to something else – even if it is only the ability to dance. It will encourage her and develop her confidence.'

Eppie stopped short and glared at her sister. 'Did you know that Charlotte couldn't dance to save her life when you suggested that she join the class?'

'Of course not – well, perhaps I had an inkling of an idea,' Marion admitted airily. 'The school had that little concert last year, as you know.'

'The one where Charlotte did a reading.'

'Exactly – she was given something that she could do well.'

'Because she wasn't good enough for the little dance troupe. Marion, you knew! How could you let her be humiliated like this?'

'Don't be so...' for once, Marion had to fumble for the right word and could only think of '...maternal. Charlotte will benefit from the dance classes too,' she said in her most firm, school-teacher voice. 'Knowing one's shortcomings is character-building.'

'Sometimes I wonder if you're putting Lydia before your own niece.'

'Charlotte has had the benefit of my teaching, and Father's, all her life. Lydia has not. She has a lot of catching up to do. And Mr Geddes is paying me handsomely to raise his daughter's education to the necessary standard for her age,' Marion was saying haughtily as they reached Barbary's cottage.

Nearing the cottage, they could hear wee Thomas crying, a monotonous sobbing as though he had been crying for some time. Without stopping to announce her arrival by rapping lightly on the door, Eppie went straight in.

She saw the two older children first, huddled together and staring across the small kitchen. Following their gaze, Eppie saw Barbary sitting on a low nursing chair, her arms wrapped about her swollen belly. Uncombed black hair straggled about her face, which was red and gleaming with sweat.

'Barbary?'

A guttural, animal-like groan was the woman's only answer. One of the children whimpered, and then came another whimper, this time from Marion.

Eppie was at her friend's side in an instant. She put an arm about the woman's shoulders, and Barbary reached up to catch her free hand in a hot, tight grip.

'It's all right,' Eppie said as much to Barbary as to the frightened children. 'Your mam's all right – it's just time for the new wee bairn tae come tae live with you. Marion, take them to the hoosie across the road – and the wee one as well and ask Agnes tae come over quick. Tell her the bairn's on its way.' And then, as Marion just stood and stared at Barbary, one hand at her mouth, she said sharply, 'Marion!'

Her sister stood as though rooted to the ground. A faint moan could be heard from behind the clenched fist held to her lips.

'I'll take them over myself,' Eppie said. 'You help Barbary on to the bed and I'll be back right away.'

'No! I'll take them.' Marion was suddenly galvanised into action. She scooped the baby from his crib and took wee Martha's hand. 'Come on now. Then I'll have to go and fetch the girls,' she said as she manoeuvred herself and the children out of the door.

'There's plenty of time before then, and plenty to be done, so come straight back with Agnes.' Eppie turned her attention to Barbary. 'Let's get you tae your bed – you'll be more comfortable there.'

'It's dead,' Barbary said flatly, making no move. 'My bairn's dead.'

'Of course it's not dead!'

'Aye, it is. Tolly told me.' Barbary gasped as a bout of pain struck her. Her entire body clenched and her fingers tightened so cruelly on Eppie's hand that she had to bite her lip to hold back her own cry of pain.

'He's that lonely without us, Eppie,' Barbary panted when the paroxysm had eased. 'He needs the bairn for company.'

A chill ran down Eppie's spine but she managed to keep her voice even as she said, 'And all your bairn needs right now is tae be birthed. Can ye stand up?'

'Tolly'll look after it until I can go to them,' Barbary assured her, making no effort to move. Just then, to Eppie's relief, the door opened. But Marion was on her own, her eyes large with fear in an ashen face.

'Agnes is with a friend. Her grandson's been sent to fetch her. I have to go to the girls...'

'Not until you've helped me to get Barbary onto the bed, and fetched a basin of hot water and a clean cloth.' As she spoke, Eppie worked at releasing her aching hand from her friend's grip. 'Come here, Marion,' she ordered as her sister began to back out of the door. 'If you dare tae run away and leave me, I promise ye I'll pull out every hair from your head when this is over!'

The childhood threat they used to use on each other worked, and at last Marion did as she was bid. Together, they managed to settle Barbary on the bed, where she sprawled like a beached whale, her skirt twisted about her white thighs.

'Pull her skirt down and help her tae look decent,' Eppie ordered, unwilling to trust Marion with the kettleful of steaming hot water. She was filling the basin when Marion gave a sudden cry and backed away from the bed, both hands now clapped to her mouth.

'Blood,' her muffled voice wailed. 'She's – she's...' Then she ran to the back door, wrenched it open, and stumbled outside.

As Eppie heard her start to retch out in the yard, the street door opened and, to her relief, Agnes came bustling in.

* * *

On her way to fetch Charlotte and Lydia, Marion forced herself to take slow, deep breaths, filling her lungs to their full capacity each time. Just before she reached the dance studio it started to rain, and she paused at the door and looked up at the grey sky, then halted again in the passageway in order to dry herself with a handkerchief. By the time she reached the girls she had regained some of her composure.

'Where's my mother?' Charlotte wanted to know.

'She's with Barbary. She'll come home later.'

'Is Barbary having her bairn?'

'What bairn?' Lydia wanted to know.

'Have you not noticed?' Charlotte asked in amazement.

'Noticed what?'

Marion broke into a light sweat. This was no time for Lydia to start learning about the facts of life. 'Come along,' she said firmly, hustling the two of them along the passageway and out of the door. 'It's started to rain and we'll have to get home before it gets worse, for I forgot to bring my umbrella.'

As the three of them hurried to Shorehead, she kept the conversation fixed on the dance lesson. To her relief, Charlotte was happy to turn her own efforts to dance into an amusing story, and Lydia was more than ready to listen.

'If Barbary's having her baby,' Charlotte said as they went into the house, 'that means that Mother could be out all night. She won't be here to make dinner.'

'Why will she be out all night?' Lydia asked.

'I'm capable of making the supper,' Marion said swiftly.

'I'll help you,' Charlotte volunteered. 'We both will.'

* * *

Eppie had still not arrived back by the time the rest of the household sat down to supper. As they ate, Lydia proudly told her father all about her own part in cooking it. 'Charlotte helped,' she conceded, 'and Miss McNaught told us both what to do.'

'And an excellent business you all made of it.' His smile swept across all three of them. When the meal was over and the two girls had helped Marion to clear the table before going to bed, he invited her to take tea with him in the library.

'Lydia seems more settled now, and more at ease than I have ever seen her,' he said as she poured out the tea, concentrating hard on the task in an effort to prevent her hands from trembling. 'I am most grateful to you, Miss McNaught.'

'She's a pleasant child, and intelligent. It's just a case of finding ways to stimulate her interest. Children can't be made to do things against their wills – that is,' Marion corrected herself, 'they can, but they will never give their best if there is no enthusiasm or willingness to succeed.'

'Lydia can be difficult sometimes. I blame myself – I should have found more time for her instead of leaving her in her grandmother's company so much.'

'It's not easy for a man to be mother as well as father to a child,' Marion ventured. 'Especially to a daughter.'

'It's kind of you to try to reassure me, but—' He broke off, then said after a pause, 'I thought that I had done a better job of raising my son, but it seems that I failed him as well as Lydia.'

Marion's fingers itched to smooth away the lines on his forehead and about his mouth, but she could do nothing other than say, feebly, 'I wonder when Eppie will be back.'

'Bairns make their own decisions as to when they will enter the world. It's only natural that Eppie will want to stay with her friend after what the poor woman has been through recently,' he said easily, then: 'Talking of Eppie, that's another reason for me to feel grateful to you. If you had not agreed to come to Portsoy for the summer Eppie would have left us, and I would have been hard put to find someone to take her place.'

'Eppie was going to leave your employment? Why would she do such a thing?'

He looked over at her, surprised. 'I thought she would have told you about my proposal of marriage.'

Marion had just lifted her cup from its saucer; she jumped so violently that the saucer almost went flying one way and the cup the other. Hurriedly, she managed to reunite them and set them back down on the desk.

'I see that she did not. I should have known – Eppie has always been the soul of discretion.'

'You proposed marriage to my sister? And she turned you down?' Marion heard a strange, faraway ringing noise in her ears. She could scarcely believe that her own sister had been offered the very thing that she herself longed for and, even worse, had rejected the offer.

'She rapped my knuckles severely, and she was quite right. I proposed to her in a fit of despair, thinking that it was the only way to stop the malicious gossips who had realised that once my mother moved to her own house, Eppie and I were alone together here, apart from Lydia. She was determined to silence them by leaving, while I was bent on trying to find a way of stopping her. You see, Miss McNaught, what foolish creatures men can be?' He smiled, inviting her to share his amusement, but she could only stare at him.

'In any case,' he went on, 'things have turned out even better than I could ever have hoped. Now you are here, and Eppie is staying – and she has her daughter close by, while my own daughter is receiving the best education she has known to date.'

The clock chimed the hour and Marion suddenly realised that her mouth was gaping open in shock. She shut it so firmly that she heard her teeth click together and a stab of pain ran along her jawline. 'If you will forgive me, I must go to bed now,' she said, getting to her feet and then, as he rose from his own chair and she turned towards the door, her skirt brushed against a pile of papers balanced on top of his desk, sending them fluttering to the floor.

'How clumsy – forgive me!' she almost sobbed as they both knelt to gather up the mess.

'The fault is mine – please don't feel upset, Miss McNaught,' he said, misunderstanding the cause of her agitation. 'The Board of Trade is to meet soon to look into the loss of the fishing vessel that widowed Eppie's friend and made the bairn being born tonight fatherless. And I've been so busy with other matters that I haven't yet found the time to sort out the paperwork and find a way to present my own contribution to the inquiry.'

'I could help you, if you wish,' Marion said without thinking. 'I could put the papers in order and make note of the particular points you should know.'

'You would do that?' The smile broke out again. 'My dear Miss McNaught, I would be eternally grateful!'

She smiled back, still slightly shaky, but beginning – now that the subject had moved on to business matters – to regain her natural confidence. 'Why don't I make a fresh pot of tea?' she suggested. 'And we can make a start tonight.'

18

Eppie returned to the house in the early hours of the morning – so early that the streets were empty and she walked through them and past darkened house windows without meeting a soul. A dog crossed her path, nose to the ground as it eagerly snuffled up an intriguing story of scents from the cobbles and flagstones. Now and again a cat slid by soundlessly, one of them stopping to look back at her, its knowing golden eyes the only spots of colour in the gloom.

Before going into the house she walked further, to the edge of the inner harbour. Most of the boats were out at the fishing and even the farlins, normally busy with fisher lassies gutting and packing herring, were silent and empty. It was a still night and the few boats left in the harbour rocked almost imperceptibly, the tops of their masts swaying against the star-scattered sky. She could hear the muted sound of the sea beyond the outer harbour walls, hurling itself against the black rocks thrusting up above the surface.

She drew in a deep breath of salt-laden air and stretched her arms high above her head. It had been a long night, and a hard one for poor Barbary. But now the delivery was over and when Eppie finally left the cottage her friend was in a deep, healing sleep, her long black hair spread over the pillow, with her new little son, also asleep, nestled in the crook of one arm and Agnes watching over them both.

'Poor souls,' she had murmured just before Eppie left. 'Mebbe the wee one'll help tae ease her loss.'

Eppie knew from her own bitter experience that nothing could fill the aching gap left by the premature death of an adored husband. Standing on the harbour wall, looking out to where the unseen sea kept trying and failing to bury the sharp, hungry rocks, she suddenly felt closer to Murdo than she had in many a year. She lingered for a while, talking to him with the silent voice in her head, until the early-morning chill began to burrow through her flesh to her bones. Finally, she turned to make her way back to the Geddes house.

She was halfway there when a sudden scuttering sound made her jump. She halted, then gasped and stepped back as a large rat ran across the ground in front of her, its body almost brushing against her shoes. It paused and eyed her, crouching low, with its belly pushed against the stone. It opened its mouth to hiss at her, and the moonlight gleamed white on sharp teeth. She stamped her foot hard on the ground and it melted into the darkness, dragging its long reptilian tail after it.

Suddenly, the silent harbour did not seem to be such a pleasant place to linger; Eppie hurried the rest of the way home and in another minute she was in her small bedroom by the kitchen.

When she lit the lamp and began to undress she realised that there were spots of blood from the birth on her blouse. She changed into fresh clothes and took the soiled ones to the kitchen, where she put them into a basin of cold water to soak.

With the energetic use of a poker she roused the range fire from its glowing slumber and made herself a cup of tea.

Then, deciding that there was little point in going to bed now, she fetched flour, eggs and lard from the larder and set to work on the day's baking.

* * *

Two floors above her, Alexander Geddes slept soundly, a slight smile on his face. He had finally bested his mother, had retained his housekeeper – and at last he had acquired the right governess for Lydia: an intelligent, sensible young woman who was even willing to help him with the mountain of paperwork required for the Board of Trade inquiry. At last, his home had become a pleasant place to return to at the end of a busy day.

In her pretty bedroom, Lydia, too, smiled in her sleep. She was dancing better than she had ever danced before – swirling and swooping, so light and so fast that she skimmed above the ground, covering mile after mile of space, her body and her mind free of all worries and duties.

Charlotte was not even dreaming. She slept deeply, unaware that beside her, her aunt stretched her toes luxuriously to the very foot of the bed and hugged herself in glee. She had found a way to be of help to Alexander Geddes, a way that would allow her to work alongside him.

Even the shock of hearing about his proposal to Eppie, and the greater shock of hearing that her sister had actually turned him down, could not dampen her happiness. She should be grateful to Eppie, she reasoned as the clock in the hall below struck four, since her sister's refusal meant that he was still free.

* * *

'How is your friend?' Alexander Geddes asked as Eppie laid a neat bundle of letters, just delivered, by his plate at breakfast.

'She had a wee lad last night. They're both fine.' She fetched the silver letter knife from a sideboard drawer and put it close to his hand.

'Can I see him?' Charlotte asked at once, and Lydia chimed in with: 'I want to see him too!'

'Next week, perhaps,' Marion told them both firmly. 'You must wait until he and his mother are rested and able to receive visitors. In the meantime—' she glanced at the clock on the wall '—you have five minutes to finish your breakfast, and another ten minutes to prepare for your lessons. I will expect to see both of you in the schoolroom at nine o'clock exactly.'

'Poor woman,' Geddes said as he slit open the first letter, 'left on her own with another mouth to feed. If there's anything she and her family needs, let me know. If you want to give them any food, no need to ask, just take it.'

'Thank you, Mr Geddes, that's very generous of you.'

'There's no generosity in sharing something you've plenty of – mind that, Lydia,' he added to his daughter. 'Remember it when you're a grown woman.' Then, as his eyes ran over the page he had taken from the envelope he gave a sudden exasperated grunt.

'Is there something amiss?' Lydia asked at once.

'The Glasgow man who owns the bulk of the marble quarry is sending someone to Portsoy within the next two weeks to "discuss improvements to the site".' He quoted the last few words in a mocking, angry voice. 'I've already been warned that it would happen, but I had hoped that it would not be for months yet. It's the last thing I need just now, when I'm trying to get justice for the families of the men on the *Grace-Ellen*. Eppie, you'd best get a room ready since we don't know when he might descend on us.'

'The back bedroom, Mr Geddes?'

Lydia had been eating her porridge, seemingly uninterested in the conversation, but now her head came up suddenly and her spoon clattered into the bowl, sending a few drops of milk bouncing onto the tablecloth. 'That's Duncan's room!'

'It used to be your brother's room, but now it must be made available for anyone who needs it,' her father told her sharply.

'But you can't let anyone else sleep in Duncan's room!'

'Lydia, how many years has it been since your brother last used it? Five, by my reckoning. Five years, and not a word from him. I doubt if giving this man from Glasgow the use of it over the next week or so is going to inconvenience Duncan.'

'He'll come back – I know that he'll come back!' Her face was red and she was close to tears.

'That's enough, Lydia.' Her father pushed his chair back and got to his feet. 'I am quite sure that this conversation is making our guests and Eppie feel uncomfortable. Eppie, you may prepare the back bedroom for our visitor, if you please.'

When he had gone, Marion reached out to touch Lydia's shoulder. 'My dear, from what your father says, it's unlikely that your brother will come home soon...'

'But he will come back one day,' the girl insisted, her voice wobbling and a tear beginning to tremble on her lashes, 'and it could be any day at all. He hasn't forgotten me – I know he hasn't!'

'Of course he hasn't,' Marion began, while Eppie moved towards the child, her arms opening to hold her. But before she got to the table Charlotte was on her feet and taking Lydia's hand in hers.

'Come on, Lydia,' she said, 'let's tell the bees. It's the best thing to do.'

Left alone in the room, the sisters looked at each other in silence for a moment before Marion asked, 'Do you think he'll come back?'

'I thought he'd have done it by now.' Eppie began to stack used dishes on the tray she had brought in with her. 'He thought the world of Lydia and I'm surprised he's left her on her own for so long. I'm sure his father's longing to see him too, only he's too proud to say so. Poor wee Lydia thinks that she's the only one who misses the lad.'

'Men are hopeless at dealing with emotions,' Marion said, as though she knew all about it. She gathered up the letters. 'I'll take these in to Mr Geddes – some of them will probably be about the inquiry into the loss of the fishing boat.'

'Are you sure it's right to go into the library? He might want to be on his own.'

'I'm quite sure.' Marion pulled her shoulders back and shot a triumphant smile at her sister. 'As a matter of fact, he asked me last night if I would help him with his preparations for the Board of Trade inquiry. I thought you should know, since there should be no secrets between sisters. At least,' she added, 'as far as I am concerned.'

'When have I ever kept a secret from you?' Eppie asked, stung by the cool note in Marion's voice and the accusation in her gaze.

Her sister gave a little toss of her head. 'You never told me that Mr Geddes had asked you to be his wife. He told me about it last night,' she added, as Eppie felt hot colour flood her throat and face. And then, unable to resist, she burst out with: 'And you refused the man, without even discussing it with me! Why did you turn him down when you and Charlotte could have been settled comfortably for life?'

'Because I'd never marry for such a reason – surely you know that. And I didn't tell you because I knew that if I did, you'd try to talk me into accepting him just to make my life more comfortable.' Eppie's hands flew about busily, gathering the last of the plates and cutlery. 'And that wouldn't have been fair on him *or* me.'

'What about Charlotte – and Lydia? They'd both have had a mother and a father.'

'They're well looked after, and loved. In any case, even if I had said yes to the man his mother would have found a way to put a stop to any such idea. You know what she's like – she'd move heaven and earth to prevent him marrying again, especially someone from our class,' Eppie retorted, before picking up the laden tray and escaping to her kitchen.

Left on her own, Marion picked up the neat bundle of letters and made her way thoughtfully to the library. Having met Helen Geddes, she fully agreed with what Eppie had said.

But there were ways and means. And if it came to a battle of wills, as in the end it must, then Marion McNaught intended to be the winner.

* * *

Over the next two weeks, Alexander Geddes and Marion spent most of their spare time in the library, preparing for the investigation into the sinking of the *Grace-Ellen*. Although Eppie noticed a sparkle in her sister's eye and a new spring in her step, she assumed that the change was brought about by Marion's pleasure in discovering that her quick mind was of good use outside the schoolroom as well as within it.

Eppie herself was fully occupied with her household duties and caring for Barbary, who was now up and about after the birth of her baby. She ate little and her clothes hung loose on a body that had once been strong and agile. For the first few days of his life, Jeemsie, her new little son, had wailed pathetically, beating his tiny fists in frustration against his mother's empty breast.

'The bairn's goin' tae waste away for want o' milk,' Eppie fretted while Barbary rocked to and fro, the screaming child cradled against her. 'You must eat more, Barbary!'

'The weans need the food more than I do,' her friend said, fixing her with empty eyes. 'I've enough tae dae me.'

'But not tae dae wee Jeemsie,' Agnes said, and went out, to return ten minutes later. 'Eppie, Myra Beaton two doors up's got a new bairn no' much older than Jeemsie, and she says she's got more than enough milk tae satisfy the both o' them. Take the wee one up tae her house.'

In another ten minutes Jeemsie was suckling greedily, almost choking himself in his efforts to take in as much desperately needed nourishment as he could before being deprived again. Eventually he fell asleep, his little belly as tight as a drum and a thin trickle of milk glistening at the corner of his rosebud mouth.

From then on, either Eppie or Agnes took him to Myra's cottage every few hours, since Barbary could not be relied on to remember her duties, even when she heard the child crying with hunger.

One problem solved, Eppie thought with relief as she tucked him into his little crib, but what of Barbary herself? Nothing, not even Jeemsie's birth, seemed to shake her free of her grieving for Tolly. As she straightened up from the crib, Eppie's eye was caught by a photographic likeness on the wall facing her:

Barbary, strong and handsome, sitting in a chair with newborn Thomas in her arms, while George and Martha crowded at her knee, the two of them staring with wide, bewildered eyes at the camera. Tolly, his likeness caught for all eternity, stood behind his wife, one hand on her shoulder, beaming and proud of his lusty, good-looking family.

He had died only months after the photograph had been taken by a travelling photographer who moved from village to village seeking, and always finding, work. Eppie had a very similar photograph among her possessions: herself, with small Charlotte in her arms, standing beside Murdo, who was holding the baby's hand and, like Tolly, grinning proudly into the lens.

So many of the cottages in this village, and no doubt in every other village along the coast, had similar portraits hung on their walls, or standing on mantelshelves or chests of drawers. So many men, Eppie thought, captured forever in sepia shades on card – so many men claimed by the sea, never to grow old; caught in a moment of time that had passed on, leaving them behind.

* * *

When the date of the inquiry arrived, Alexander asked Marion if she would be willing to attend it with him. 'I realise that you will have to take time from your duties towards the two girls, but I would appreciate your company.'

'Of course,' she said demurely, while her heart leaped for joy. 'If that is your wish, Mr Geddes.'

'The hearing may last for longer than one day, so I will book two rooms at a hotel just in case.'

'Very good, Mr Geddes,' she said, and then, startled by a sudden and unexpected warmth spreading from her throat to her cheeks, she picked up a letter and took it over to the window on the pretence that it had to be read in a better light. She had never blushed in her life before and she found the experience profoundly disturbing.

She spent some time going through her meagre wardrobe in search of an outfit that was businesslike, but at the same time, flattering. Finally she settled for her dove-grey skirt and jacket to travel in and to wear in court, and for the evening, just in case they were required to stay overnight – her pulse quickened at the very thought – a green and yellow silk dress in large black-edged checks with sloping shoulders, a wide skirt and long cream muslin sleeves beneath short pagoda oversleeves.

She carried the clothes down to the kitchen, where she spread them out on the table, after carefully covering it with a clean sheet, and examined them inch by inch to make certain that there were no stains or marks. Then she started working with the flat irons that had been heating on the range.

'Do you think they'll do?' she asked her sister, who had been watching, first with surprise and then with carefully hidden amusement.

Eppie stroked a fingertip over the silk gown. 'I think you could safely be introduced to Queen Victoria herself. It's only an inquiry you're going to, not a banquet.'

'But if the inquiry lasts more than the one day we'll have to spend the night in a hotel. I need something to change into for the evening.' Much to her own vexation, Marion flushed. 'I don't want to let Mr Geddes down.'

It was only when she saw the rush of colour come to her sister's cheekbones that the truth dawned on Eppie. 'You'd never let him down,' she said earnestly, her amusement gone. 'You always look respectable – and grand too. Mr Geddes would never have asked you to accompany him to Aberdeen if he didn't care for the thought of being seen in public with you.'

Marion's smile was radiant. 'You think so?'

'Of course I do,' Eppie told her firmly, and then, as Marion carefully gathered up the newly ironed clothes, she added, 'Marion...'

'Yes?' Marion asked just as Eppie realised that what she was about to say could so easily be misunderstood.

'Nothing,' she said. 'I can't remember what was in my mind.' And Marion tutted at her, before bearing her clothes back upstairs.

Eppie had always looked up to Marion, the older sister, the clever one, the calm, self-possessed woman who had dedicated her entire life to the education of other women's children. Had anyone asked her, before Marion came to Portsoy, as to the right man for her sister, she would have said at once that any man in the kingdom would be proud to take Marion as his wife.

But 'any man in the kingdom' did not include her employer. Eppie was convinced that Alexander Geddes had no wish to marry again. When he had asked her to be his wife, it had only been said in a desperate attempt to retain the housekeeper he and his daughter were both used to and comfortable with. Even if Marion did manage to find her way into his heart, his mother would make certain that nothing came of it.

Although they had grown up together, Eppie had never really got to know Marion well. While Eppie played with her friends, Marion had stayed at home, reading, writing, studying and learning; but in the few weeks since she and Charlotte had come to Portsoy Eppie had come to know her better. She was proud of Marion's obvious devotion to her work and to her young pupils, and her calm yet confident manner had brought a new serenity to a household that until recently had been dominated by Helen Geddes's sharp-tongued, self-centred intolerance. Eppie had come to love Marion where before she had merely admired and respected her, and she did not want to see her sister dealt a hurt that could well cripple her emotionally for the rest of her life.

But the damage was done – she could tell that Marion was truly and deeply in love, and if Alexander Geddes did not return her feelings, then she was doomed to suffer – and there was nothing that Eppie could do about it.

19

Alexander Geddes and Marion left early on the morning of the investigation, taking with them in the coach that he had hired for her comfort a large box filled with papers.

Lydia and Charlotte, delighted to have a free day from the schoolroom, started to make plans even before the coach was out of sight.

'Can we go out on our own, for once?' Lydia begged Eppie. 'We're not bairns to be taken all over the place.'

'Your father...'

'My father's in Aberdeen for the day, and if you let us go out on our own we promise not to tell him, don't we, Charlotte?'

Charlotte nodded agreement. 'You know that I can go all around Fordyce on my own, Mam – and Lydia's right, we're not bairns.'

They were certainly not bairns, Eppie thought, looking at the two of them as they stood before her in the kitchen. In fact, she realised with sudden shock, Charlotte's eyes were on a level with her own and Lydia was only half a head smaller than Charlotte.

'I'll think about it,' she said and then, as both pairs of eyes lit up, 'but if I say yes you'll have to look out for each other, and keep in mind that if you do anything daft it'll be sure to get to Mr Geddes's ears, and then I'll be dismissed from my post.'

'We won't be daft, we promise!' Lydia said at once, horrified by the prospect of losing both Eppie and Charlotte, while Charlotte chimed in with: 'I'll look after her, Mam!'

'I can look after myself – and you into the bargain,' Lydia said huffily.

'You'll look out for each other,' Eppie cut in before they could start arguing. 'But before you go out, Charlotte, you can help me to put the hoose to rights.'

'I'll help as well.' Lydia was not going to be left out of anything.

'Then the two of you can start by making Lydia's bed and tidying her room. After that you can see to your bedroom, Charlotte.'

She furnished the two of them with dusters and brushes and when they had scampered upstairs she started work in the library. Since all the papers that Alexander Geddes had been working on had gone to Aberdeen with him, she was finally able to give his big desk a good polish, something she had been longing to do for weeks.

* * *

Upstairs, Charlotte taught Lydia to make a bed properly and then the two of them put all the toys and books in order and dusted the deep windowsill and every other surface they could find. Then they moved into the room shared by Charlotte and her aunt, where Lydia got the chance to show off her new bed making skills.

'You learn fast,' Charlotte said approvingly, and Lydia only just managed to hide her pleasure at the compliment by snatching up a duster and whisking it briskly over the top of the chest of drawers.

Since Marion was a very neat person and Charlotte had been well taught by her aunt, there was little to do once the beds were made. When everything had been put to rights the two girls hovered by the door, making sure that nothing had been overlooked.

'It's a very small room, isn't it?' Lydia said thoughtfully. 'Not nearly as big as mine, and yet there's two of you sleeping in here.'

'You should see my room at Fordyce, it's more like a cupboard. But I don't mind,' Charlotte added swiftly. 'I like it because the window looks out on the back garden, and the bee skeps. In the summer evenings when I'm supposed to be in bed I can sit there and watch the bees coming and going.'

'I'd like to see your room. I've never been to Fordyce.'

'Have you not? It's very pretty.'

'Prettier than Portsoy?'

'Different,' Charlotte said diplomatically. 'My gran and granda live in a cottage that's much smaller than this house, but it's got a pretty garden. And there's the castle not far from our house.'

'A real castle?'

'It's quite wee,' Charlotte admitted, 'but it's still a real castle.'

'Does a princess live in it?'

'No, but one of the four ladies who looked after Mary, Queen of Scots, lived there once...'

Lydia's eyes rounded. 'Did Queen Mary visit her there?'

'She was dead by then, poor woman.'

'I'd like to see your castle. We could go there today,' Lydia suggested. 'You'd like to see your grandparents, wouldn't you?'

Then, making for the door: 'Let's go and tell Eppie that that's where we want to go.'

* * *

'I'm not sure,' Eppie said when the two girls ran her to ground in the schoolroom. 'Your father might not like it, Lydia.'

'I don't see why not – and we don't even need to tell him. He won't be back until late, and we'll be home long before then. And it means that you'll be with us all day,' Lydia pointed out slyly, 'so you wouldn't have to worry about us getting up to mischief on our own.'

'Please, Mam,' Charlotte begged. 'I'd like to see Gran and Granda, and so would you.'

'Well, if you're sure, go and get ready,' Eppie conceded and the two girls fled upstairs, shrieking with pleasure.

* * *

It was a pleasant day for a walk, and they had time to dawdle along, which was just as well since Lydia, unused to walking distances, had to pause several times to catch her breath. When they finally entered the outskirts of the village the girl was charmed by the narrow, quiet streets and the neat cottages, each with its colourful, well-tended garden.

She insisted on a slight detour to see the castle, a small, neat structure cheek by jowl with the surrounding houses but taller than they were, with its crow-stepped gables and a corner tower proudly proclaiming its superior status.

At last they turned their backs on Fordyce Castle and crossed the road to enter the lane where the McNaught house stood. As always, Eppie felt her steps quicken and her spirits begin to rise as she neared the house where she had spent her happy childhood, and where she still felt safe and contented even when life was at its hardest.

As they neared it, Lydia paused and stared, entranced. 'It's like a picture hanging on a wall!' she said, and both Eppie and Charlotte glowed with pride. The front garden was small, but thanks to Annie McNaught's love of colour and fragrance and her husband's fondness for balancing his sedentary job as a teacher with an enthusiasm for manual work and fresh air, every inch of earth was rich with colour. Hazy blue drifts of fragrant lavender blended with white and red and pink daisies, clumps of scarlet poppies, morning glory, marigolds, red hot pokers, and lupins in white, creamy yellow, deep red, sky blue and purple. Hollyhocks were staked out along part of the low grey stone wall separating the garden from the lane, and a stand of huge yellow sunflowers stood at one corner of the house, their brilliant petals almost brushing the slate roof. A rainbow of red, white, pink, peach and orange was thrown over the soft grey stone walls by climbing roses massing around the windows and the blue-painted front door. The air was fragrant with mingled scents, and the contented humming of bees collecting pollen from the flowers was soft on the ear.

As they stood at the gate, allowing Lydia time to drink in the riot of living colour before her, the door opened and Annie McNaught hurried down the short path. 'Eppie? Charlotte? I didnae ken ye were comin' today. And ye've brought us a visitor too. Come in, m'quine, intae the shade and rest yourself. It's a hot day for a long walk.'

Lydia, suddenly shy, would have hung back and taken refuge by Eppie's side, but before she could do so she found herself being bustled along the short flagged path to the door. Sprays of Solomon's seal, curving down onto the path, seemed to her confused mind to fall back before her feet like the waves of the Red Sea, allowing access to the door and then through it, surrounded by the perfume of dozens of roses that brushed against her hair and her shoulders as she went into the cool, shady interior.

As though by magic, glasses of lemonade and a plate of shortbread appeared on the kitchen table. Charlotte plunged out of the back door and returned almost at once with Peter McNaught, who had been working in the back garden. He washed his hands at the sink before shaking hands with Lydia and bidding her welcome, in his gentle, almost musical voice, to his home.

Suddenly, her nerves melted away and she felt as though she had been a member of the McNaught family for her entire life. They looked on, smiling indulgently, as Charlotte showed her friend her tiny bedroom and took her out into the back garden to introduce her to the bees. Annie handed a bowl to each of them as they went out, and after visiting the skeps they picked plump gooseberries for the meal that Eppie and Annie McNaught were preparing.

When the bowls were filled, Charlotte picked another gooseberry and bit into it. 'Try one, they're good.'

'Will your grandfather not be angry?'

'Only if we eat too many and spoil our appetites. Once when I was a little girl I ate a whole lot of them before they were ripe and got a bellyache. But they're ready for eating now. Go on,' Charlotte urged, and Lydia pulled a large berry, pale green and almost as translucent as marble, from the bush and bit into it. It was one of the most delicious things she had ever tasted – pleasantly sweet, and fresh as a summer drink.

As the two of them settled down on a bench at the back door to top and tail the gooseberries Lydia thought of her own grandmother, with her straight back and thin mouth and hard blue eyes. And she envied Charlotte with all her heart.

Dinner consisted of fish that Eppie had brought from Portsoy, served with potatoes, carrots and peas fresh from the back garden. They finished the meal off with a gooseberry crumble and cream. Afterwards, Lydia would have liked to return to the back garden and lie on the soft grass, listening to the bees as they gathered honey from the bushes close by their hives, but to her disappointment Eppie decided that it was time to return to Portsoy.

'We've got a long walk ahead of us, and I want these two in their beds before Mr Geddes comes back.'

'Aye, best be on your way, lass,' her father agreed. 'There's bad weather comin' in across the water.'

Lydia, her skin glowing from a day spent in the sun, found it hard to believe him, but just as they entered Portsoy, Eppie carrying a basket of fresh-picked fruit and vegetables from the McNaught garden and Lydia's ears ringing with Mrs McNaught's final: 'Now that ye've found yer way here, m'quine, haste ye back,' ringing in her ears, the sky ahead of them began to darken and a stiff breeze played around their skirts.

By the time they reached the house they could hear the sea booming against the harbour walls and they were scarcely indoors before rain began to pepper the windows.

The lamps had to be lit earlier than usual and, as the girls went to bed, both too full to eat anything else, rain streamed down the windowpanes. Eppie, snug in her kitchen, could hear the wind howling around the house walls as though trying to find its way in.

She doubted that Alexander Geddes and Marion would be back tonight, but just in case, she set the makings of a fire in the dining room fireplace, ready to crackle into life should the travellers return. Then she set the table for two before making sure that a hot meal could be prepared at short notice. Her work done, she settled herself by the kitchen range with her knitting wires flickering in her hands and the ball of wool in her lap shrinking fast.

The storm, by the sound of it, was getting worse; as the clock ticked the minutes away Eppie yawned, laid her knitting aside, and had just decided that her employer and her sister must be snugly ensconced in an Aberdeen hotel and that it would be safe for her to go to bed when someone began to wield the front door knocker vigorously.

She hurried up the stairs, tutting in exasperation as the knocker continued to bang hard against its metal plate. She could well understand her employer's anxiety to get indoors and out of the storm, but surely, she thought to herself as she ran along the hall, Mr Geddes knew that she would get there as quickly as she could – and he also knew that the two girls would be in bed and asleep at that hour of the night. The racket he was making would waken them.

As she fumbled with the big key it suddenly occurred to her that he might be in a temper because the inquiry had resulted in bad news. Please God, let that not be true; for women like Barbary, left on their own with children to feed, were dependent on receiving some compensation for the loss of their menfolk.

She had no sooner unlocked the door and put a hand to the latch than it shot up from beneath her fingers and the door flew open, almost knocking her down. She skipped back just in time as a man surged into the hall on a gust of wind and a shower of icy rain.

'Are ye deaf, wumman?' he growled from behind the thick scarf that muffled the lower half of his face. 'This is no night for a man tae have tae staun' ootside!'

Eppie's heart missed a beat, and almost leaped into her mouth. This was not Mr Geddes. The voice was deep and rough, with an accent alien to the Moray Firth; a wide-brimmed hat had been jammed down over his head and the eyes glaring down at her – all she could see between scarf and hat brim – were much lighter than her employer's. This man was not as tall as Alexander Geddes, but considerably broader in the shoulder.

'Who are you?'

'A veesitor, that's who I am, come a long way in this foul weather an' expectin' a ceevil greetin' an' a good hot meal. God save us, where's the boy got tae noo?'

He swung the door open, letting in more of the gale and another handful of rain, and went back out onto the top step to lean over the rail and shout into the turbulent darkness. One or two of the paintings on the walls shifted uneasily in the blast of wind whistling along the hall, and Eppie could see rain darkening the rug by the door. She looked around for a weapon with which to defend herself and her two charges if necessary, but all she could see was the brass gong that Helen Geddes had insisted on being used to summon the family to their meals. Eppie snatched up the stick, which was padded but better than nothing at all, and seeing that the man was clear of the door, she threw herself against it in the hope of being able to shut and lock it before he realised what she was up to. That done, she would run back downstairs and out through the kitchen door to seek help.

But luck was against her. He turned just as the door began to swing shut, and reached out a long arm. Once again, she was tossed back, this time against the wall.

'Mam?' Charlotte's voice quavered from above, and Eppie, the breath almost knocked out of her, looked up to see two small faces smudged against the darkness of the stair head.

'Go to your rooms and close the doors,' she shouted, just as another man, not nearly as burly as the first, surged in from the wild night. The house was being invaded, she thought, terror beginning to overcome her.

The man with the rough, frightening voice followed his companion in and slammed the door shut, then as both men removed their hats and began to unwind the scarves from their faces there came a piercing scream from above.

'Duncan!' Lydia Geddes flew down the stairs, her bare feet scarcely touching them, her long nightdress flying out behind her, her face radiant. 'Duncan – you've come home!'

And while Eppie, the stranger and Charlotte, clinging to the banisters at the top of the stairs, watched in bewilderment, the girl launched herself into her brother's arms, heedless of the rain saturating his coat and dripping steadily onto the floor.

20

Marion was torn between excitement and compassion as she listened intently to the evidence given at the Board of Trade inquiry into the sinking of the Portsoy fishing vessel, the *Grace-Ellen*. Excitement because she had never been at an inquiry before and found the solemnity and formality of it absorbing, and compassion because, as she had to keep reminding herself, she was listening to the story of how a well-built and well-maintained fishing vessel had ended up on the seabed, no longer a boat, but a coffin for eight strong, brave men, every one of them someone's son, brother, husband, or father.

The list of names alone, with its occasional repetition of surnames, was enough to make her heart twist and set her eyes prickling with sudden tears, for among the crew were two brothers from one family, two cousins from another and a lad on his first voyage.

Alexander Geddes sat so close to her that their sleeves brushed together; she could tell, by the way his breath caught in his throat as the names of the dead were read out, slowly and clearly, that he too, was suffering. Unlike her, he had known every single one of those men, and in all probability he knew their bereaved mothers and wives or sweethearts as well.

His name was called first, as the major shareholder of the *Grace-Ellen*, and representative of the two minor shareholders, who were not present. One of them, she knew, was related to the dead skipper, and had taken to his bed when the sinking was confirmed. It was believed by all who knew him that he would never recover from the blow.

As his name was called, Marion saw that his hand tensed on the papers he held, and heard him take a long, deep breath before he rose to take his place on the witness stand, where he waited, seemingly calm and composed, stacking his papers neatly on the shelf before him and then bowing slightly to the officers of the court.

He produced a copy of the fishing boat's registration and then, his voice calm and unemotional, gave details of her build and her exemplary past history. He described the fishing gear on board and the lights she would have been showing when the accident occurred, and assured the lawyer representing the owners of the other ship that the *Grace-Ellen*'s skipper was a competent, experienced man who would have made certain on the fatal night that everything was in order and nothing overlooked.

'Apart from being one of the most respected skippers on the Moray Firth, and a man I would trust with my very life, sir,' he said clearly, 'I can vouch with confidence that he would not have shirked his duties by one inch on that last voyage, since the crew in his care included his own cousin and that cousin's son, a lad of only fifteen years, aboard the vessel for the first time. If I may give more details of the crew...?'

He glanced at the sheriff, and then, on receiving a nod, proceeded to read out the list that Marion had helped to make up. This time, each name was followed by details of the dead man's dependents – wives, children, and parents. In some cases, the man had been the breadwinner for three generations of his family.

Although his voice was steady and lacking in any form of emotion, there was something in the sombre way he spoke that brought the human tragedy home to Marion. When he had finished, the court was silent for several seconds. The sheriff, Admiralty officers, lawyers and Geddes himself stood with heads bowed in silent homage, while the only sound that Marion heard from the rows of seats behind her was a woman's muffled, hurriedly suppressed sob, and then a very faint ripple of sorrow that seemed to pass through the listeners like a summer breeze drifting across a cornfield. She herself had to swallow hard and blink her eyes several times to hold back the tears that threatened to spill down her cheeks.

Geddes was asked a few questions and then allowed to step down. As he settled himself by her side she could tell that he was trembling slightly and she yearned, but did not dare, to reach out a hand and place it on his.

As soon as he left the stand, the sense of mourning for the dead that the reading of the list had created was swept aside by the brisk way in which the next witness, the master of the ship that had run the *Grace-Ellen* down, was called to give his own evidence. Marion felt a wave of indignation at the sudden change of tone, but as the inquiry proceeded and witness after witness was called, she came to realise that to the sheriff who presided over the hearing, the Admiralty's three nautical assessors who sat with him and the advocates hired to represent the owners of the two vessels involved in the night-time collision, the details were little more than hard facts to be discussed, questioned and considered.

It was almost as though, to them, the incident was a story, a thing of fiction and imagination, she thought, then she realised that this inquiry was by no means their first, or their last. It was their task to ascertain facts and to apportion blame, should there be any, fairly and justly. They could not afford to dwell on the tragic, human side of every case they were asked to consider.

The master of the other vessel, a larger boat than the *Grace-Ellen*, told the sheriff that at one point, although he had seen nothing, he had the feeling that another boat had passed close to his own, moving swiftly through the darkness. Not long after that his own vessel shivered slightly, as though it had brushed against something. He thought then that he saw a light on the sea and heard a voice call out, but nobody else on board his ship saw or heard anything. The storm was coming up fast and the wind had been too strong for him to risk ordering the ship's boat out, lest it be blown into the night and lost; in any case, there seemed little sense in such an action since they had no reason to suspect that there had been a collision of any importance at that time.

Other members of the crew told of feeling 'a shock' and a momentary halt in the movement of their vessel while those on deck ordered more lights to be brought in order to scan the sea around them. But by then the waves were mounting and their ship was being tossed about; there was nothing to be seen other than the waves rushing at them out of the dark, each one higher than the last, and nothing to be heard other than the roar of the storm.

Men from some of the other vessels that had been fishing in the vicinity reported seeing the *Grace-Ellen* bring her nets in as the storm began to make itself felt, then leaving the fishing grounds. They themselves were too busy, hauling in their own nets and battening down the hatches before running for home, to notice anything else.

The skipper of the *Homefaring* was the final witness; he told of fishing near to the *Grace-Ellen* and seeing the other boat haul in her nets before turning home, her lamps lit and in good order. He had returned to harbour, fully expecting to see the other vessel already berthed there, and had then taken his own boat back out into the storm in search of her, thinking that she might have lost her mast and be in need of help. But there had been no sighting of her, and since his own boat and its exhausted crew were sailing into danger, they had no choice but to turn back to Portsoy.

It was a long and tiring day and although she had done little more than sit and listen, apart from the short break allowed for lunch, Marion was exhausted by the time the Board of Inquiry gave its verdict. The master of the Aberdeen vessel was chastised for not ensuring that a better watch system had been in place and for deciding against putting the ship's boat out, when lives might have been saved. His certificate was suspended for nine months, and a claim for damages was made on behalf of the dependents of the crew of the *Grace-Ellen*.

Marion had been so involved in the rising drama being acted out in the meeting room that she had not heard the wind beginning to moan around the building and rain beating against the windows. But it seemed fitting, when she, Alexander Geddes and his lawyer finally stepped outside, to find that although it was only late afternoon on a July day, darkness was already falling. The sky above was black with heavy storm clouds and she gasped as the wind plucked at her skirts and hurled raindrops in her face.

Geddes had made arrangements for the three of them to dine at the nearby hotel where he had booked rooms in case the inquiry ran for longer than a day. The food was good, but Marion, who had been looking forward to dining in a hotel for the first time in her life, discovered that she had lost her appetite.

She picked at her food while Alexander Geddes and the lawyer mulled over the evidence they had heard that day, and agreed that the court's decision had been just.

'At least the dependants will get some money,' Geddes said, 'though that's little consolation for the terrible loss they've suffered.'

'It's the way it goes for folk who make their living from the sea,' the lawyer opined, then flinched visibly when Geddes turned on him and snapped, 'Mebbe so, but that doesn't make it any easier for the poor souls, or for the women and children and parents they leave behind!'

Then Geddes glanced at the two shocked faces before him and lifted his shoulders in a tired shrug. 'I beg your pardon; it was unfair of me to lose my temper like that. But I knew those men – they worked for me. I can't just dismiss them.'

'Of course not,' the lawyer said uncomfortably. 'Your sensitivity does you credit.'

'Sensitivity,' Geddes pointed out drily, 'costs nothing, especially not lives.'

The conversation round the table became somewhat strained after that, and it was no surprise to Marion when the lawyer excused himself as soon as the meal was over, pleading the need to get home before the storm became any worse. He left the small, comfortable dining room, only to return almost at once.

'The weather is much worse – I would advise you not to set out for Portsoy tonight. You said that you had reserved rooms? I think you should make use of them.'

Alexander Geddes accompanied him to the door and came back brushing raindrops from his coat sleeves. 'It's not a night to venture out, as he says. I've told the hotelier that we'll stay here for the night. He will take our luggage to our rooms and arrange accommodation for the coachman. I regret the inconvenience, Miss McNaught, but I'd rather stay here than expect you to undertake a very uncomfortable journey home in this weather.'

'It's not in the least inconvenient,' Marion said primly, while at the same time she exulted secretly over the adventure she was having. And then, seeing the shadows beneath his eyes and the slight slump of his usually straight shoulders: 'I think I will go to my room now.'

'No, stay,' he said at once, and then, as though embarrassed by his own words: 'I mean – there's a fire burning in the parlour and I thought we might have a cup of coffee before retiring.'

'Of course.' She rose swiftly to her feet, glad to know that the adventure was to be prolonged. 'I would like that – after all that has happened today I'm sure that my mind is too active to let me sleep.'

The parlour was quiet and the log fire comforting. They settled down close to it and Geddes ordered coffee and two small brandies.

'I believe we both need the brandy,' he said almost apologetically as the waiter bustled off. 'It has not been an easy day.'

'It must have been very difficult, having to give evidence.'

'And just as difficult spending an entire day listening to such a harrowing story.'

'At least there will be some financial compensation for you and the other owners of the boat – as well as the families of the crew,' she ventured.

'All the money in the world can't make up for the loss of one life before its natural God-given span is over,' he said, the shadows returning to his features. 'My share of the compensation will be added to the money paid out to the dependents. That lad on his first voyage – he was younger than my own son by almost five years. I know from my own experience that it's hard to lose contact with a child, but as least I have the certainty of knowing that my son is safe and well.'

The coffee arrived and Marion poured it out. 'It must be very hard for you, even so.'

'I wonder, every time I think of him, where I went wrong, that he should have decided to go as he did.' He sipped at his drink and then went on, 'But that's dishonest – I know very well where I went wrong. I tried to force him into a future that he didn't want, just because it was his mother's wish. Perhaps I should have given more thought to the living rather than the dead. I should have remembered what it was like to be led along a path that is not of one's own making.'

'It happened to you?'

'In a way. My father died when I was young and it seemed only natural that I should take up the reins of his business interests when I was old enough. Did that not happen to you, Miss McNaught? I understand that your father is a schoolteacher.'

'He is, but it was what I wanted – what I have always wanted. My parents never sought to influence me, or Eppie.' Even as she said the words Marion realised that although her parents had left their daughters to choose their own destinies, she herself had tried to guide Eppie along the same path she had taken.

She took a small mouthful of brandy, her very first taste of the fiery spirit, and after managing to suppress a desire to cough she allowed its spreading warmth to ease the guilt. At least Eppie had gone her own way and had dealt bravely with the results of her own decision.

'My mother, unfortunately, has never been one to let other

folk find their own way in life,' Alexander Geddes was saying. 'I am well aware that she chose my first wife, Duncan's mother, for me – not that I fault her for that, for we were contented enough throughout the eight years we had together. But it was when I met Lydia's mother...' his face suddenly softened and he smiled across at her; a smile that brimmed over with good memories, and gave her a heart-stopping glimpse of a younger, happy Alexander Geddes '...that I knew what true joy feels like. My mother was displeased, but we had a very happy marriage. I wish Celia could have lived – a girl needs her mother as she grows older. Don't you agree, Miss McNaught?'

'Yes, I do. But I'm sure that you have done your best to make it up to Lydia for her loss.'

'Your sister has been a good influence on the girl, and I see an improvement in her since you and Charlotte came to the house.'

'I like Lydia; she has a clever and enquiring mind, and she can be very charming and lovable when she wants to be.'

'When she wants to be,' he agreed with a wry twist of his mouth.

'Young folk of her age can only learn about the world by stretching their boundaries. They look to us to tell them when they are going too far, even though they resent us for it. I know how to handle Lydia – you have no need to worry about that, Mr Geddes.'

'I can assure you that I have no worries as far as you and your sister are concerned, Miss McNaught. I have every faith in both of you and consider myself fortunate to have met you.'

Marion hugged the words in her mind as she lay in bed later that night. The thought of leaving his house in September and returning to the life that she had considered to be complete until she met him, was quite unbearable. She must do something before it was too late.

* * *

While her sister was sipping brandy in the Aberdeen hotel, Eppie was saying in Portsoy, 'You might have sent word ahead that you were coming.'

'Mr Ramsay had already sent word that I'd be here sometime soon. I didnae think that I needed tae let Geddes know the time tae the very minute.' The man's voice was once again muffled, but with food this time, not the heavy scarves that he had used to protect his face from the wind and rain on his journey to Portsoy. 'Anyway, I believe in surprisin' folk. That way ye see matters as they are, wi' no chance tae hide the truth.'

He was at the kitchen table, demolishing a heaped plateful of food. The girls had been ordered back to bed, but Lydia, clinging to her brother like a limpet to a rock, had refused to leave him. Finally, Duncan had taken her upstairs while his companion, divesting himself of his coat and hat, made himself comfortable in the kitchen, ignoring Eppie's suggestion that he would be better upstairs.

'She's gone to sleep, at last.' Duncan came into the kitchen. 'Eppie, I'm starving!'

'You always were, as I mind,' she said drily as she opened the oven and withdrew the food she had been keeping hot for him.

'I'm still a growing lad,' he teased, and then, a more serious note coming into his voice as he dug his fork into the food: 'Eppie, I'm pleased to see that you're still here. Has Lydia not grown into a beautiful young lady? I've missed her such a lot!'

'And she's missed you, every day. You should have kept in contact with her, Duncan.'

'I wanted to, but my father was so angry with me for ending my studies and going off to Glasgow that I thought it better for Lydia if I just stayed silent. How is he, Eppie?'

'He's well. You know that your grandmother's got a house of her own now?'

'And your sister is Lydia's new governess and your daughter's staying here as well. Yes, Lydia told me all of it. D'you think that he'll welcome me, or throw me out by the scruff of my neck?'

'Jist let him try – he'll have me tae reckon wi',' the older man growled.

'This is between me and my father, Foy,' Duncan told him. 'I'll deal with it. Well, Eppie?'

She recalled the angry exchange she had overheard between her employer and his mother, shortly after Duncan ran away. Helen Geddes had said that her son should follow the boy and march him home. But Alexander Geddes had said, *'He's made his mind up... if he wants to come back to beg my forgiveness he will have it, but the move must come from him.'*

Now Duncan was back, and soon he and his father would come face to face.

'I think he's missed you. I think he'll be pleased tae see you back.'

'I hope so,' he said, and returned to his food. Eppie, with nothing else to do, picked up her knitting and sat down by the range, studying the boy with quick sidelong glances.

When he left Portsoy he had been fifteen years of age, with a childish chubbiness still covering his bones, but in the five years that had passed since then, he had become startlingly like his father in many ways – and yet unlike him in others.

He had Alexander Geddes's lean build, heavy-lidded eyes and longish nose. His hair was the same dark shade although tonight, still damp with rain, it erupted over his head in a mass of curls. But his eyes were lighter than his father's – a warm brown, sparkling with life and quick to smile. And when he glanced up, caught her eye and grinned at her from his seat at the table, his mouth lifted easily at the corners, as though smiles came easily to him. In that respect, he was not like his father at all.

'Why have you come back now, with no warning?'

'By God, Eppie, I'd forgotten what a grand cook ye are.' Five years of working as a quarryman had altered his speech. 'There was warning,' he went on thickly through a mouthful of food, 'a letter sent tae say that folk were coming from Glasgow tae have a look at the marble quarry. But me and Foy here didnae know just when we'd be free tae travel and it was all arranged at the last minute. Lydia said Father's in Aberdeen.'

'Aye, he and my sister are at a hearing to find out the truth behind the loss of the *Grace-Ellen*.'

'The *Grace-Ellen*'s gone?' Duncan's head came up swiftly and he stared at her with horror in his eyes. 'I mind her well – I've been out on her. What happened?'

She told him as briefly as possible, then said, 'There's more tea in the pot if you want it. I'd best go and get your bed ready.'

She left him with his silent companion to get over the shock of her news and when she returned to the kitchen both men were sitting by the range, smoking pipes.

'Duncan's bed's too narrow for two folk,' she said to the man who had come with him, 'but there's a truckle bed in the attic we can fetch down...'

'No need, I'll sleep here.' He patted the arms of the chair he sat in.

'It's no' very comfortable, Mr...' she recalled the name Duncan had given him '...Mr Foy.'

'I've slept in far worse places, I can tell ye. A pillow an' a blanket'll do me fine. An' it's no' "Mister Foy", just "Foy",' the man said.

Duncan knocked out his pipe and yawned, stretching his arms high above his head. 'Nobody calls him Mister, Eppie. It's just Foy, as he says. I think I'll away to my bed, if it's ready.'

When he had gone, Eppie fetched a pillow and some blankets; when she brought them back to the kitchen Foy took them from her when she would have made up a bed for him in the chair.

'I can manage. I'm used tae seein' tae mysel'. Off ye go tae yer ain bed,' he said, and shooed her from the kitchen as though she were a hen being chased back to the house.

In her own room, she opened the small window for a moment. The storm was at its height; wind gusted in, bringing with it a handful of icy rain, and she could hear the sea booming against the harbour walls. It sounded like a huge chorus of voices, every one clamouring to be allowed into the light and warmth of the houses on the shore.

She shivered, closing the window and latching it securely against the night, and the voices, before going to bed. She lay awake for a while, listening to the muffled sounds of the storm and thinking of Duncan, who had left as a boy and returned as a man, bringing with him a stranger, a man with only one name who spoke in a harsh, jarring West of Scotland dialect totally alien to the soft, musical tongue of the people he had come amongst.

And she wondered, before sleep finally claimed her, how Alexander Geddes would react to his son's return.

21

The storm blew itself out in the early hours of the morning, and Eppie awoke to a blessedly silent morning.

She dressed swiftly and went out of her small bedroom, only to reel back, hand to her throat in sudden panic, at the sound of an animal-like grunt from the kitchen. Then she remembered that Foy, the stranger who had arrived the previous evening with Duncan, was sleeping there.

He was still sprawled over her armchair by the range, his head tipped right back and his mouth gaping open, with loud snores ripping at regular intervals through the air. One knobbly bare foot was propped on the kitchen chair he had pulled over to face the armchair, while the other lolled on the floor. He looked uncomfortable, but even so, his sleep was deep.

Averting her eyes, Eppie let herself out of the back door and walked down to the edge of the harbour to breathe in the fresh, salt-laden air.

The boats had come in early the night before, fleeing before the oncoming bad weather, still high in the water, their holds not more than half filled. Since fish could not be left unattended for long, the fisher lassies would have had to work into the stormy night, those at the farlins gutting and packing beneath makeshift tarpaulin shelters, and those in the smokehouse splitting the fish open and stringing them on poles before hanging them over the fires.

At rest now within the safety of the harbour, the boats shifted gently, brushing against each other now and again like a herd of animals crowding together for comfort. Beyond the outer harbour she could hear the sea, calm now, whispering around the sharp-toothed rocks where, last night, it had foamed and crashed and whirled in a thousand impatient eddies.

The first sparkle of sunlight was already tossing bright lights over the water on the horizon, and although the sky above was still a soft pearl grey, as yet untouched by the rising sun, far out to sea it had already begun to turn blue – like a swathe of material scrubbed clean by the storm's violence and then rinsed by the final rain, but still holding a small drift of white cloud, like soapsuds, here and there. Peace had returned to the coast, and the fishermen who relied on the dangerous waters for their livelihood were safe again – until the next time.

Eppie closed her eyes and sent up a brief prayer that the next time would not come too soon, and then as she turned to walk back to the house she was sharply reminded of the drama waiting to unfold within its sturdy grey stone walls. What sort of welcome would Duncan get from his father, after their years apart, and what would Mr Geddes make of the strange man who had come to Portsoy with his son?

Foy was still snoring, but when she began to rattle the poker between the bars to clear the ashes and rouse the fire in readiness for the day's work, the snores stopped suddenly and he seemed to jump from sleep to waking, bounding out of the chair and stretching his hands far above his head.

'Good mornin' tae ye.' He yawned mightily and then clawed his hands busily through his tousled hair, for all the world as though he were trawling the thick tangle in search of head lice. 'Where can I get a wash?'

'You can wash here, at the sink, if you'll just give me five minutes tae start the breakfast.'

'D'ye no' have a tap outside?'

'There's the wash-house...'

'That'll do. Out the back, is it?'

She nodded to the door in a corner of the kitchen. 'Through there. Not that one!' she said hurriedly as he snatched up the cloth she used for drying the dishes. 'Here...'

He waited with ill-concealed impatience while she looked out a clean towel and then said scornfully as she handed it to him, 'Ye're awful pernickety.'

She bit back the sharp retort that sprang to her lips and said instead, 'You'll want hot water.'

'I'm no' that fussy. Cold water never hurt nob'dy.' He swung through the door, throwing it open and then letting it bang shut behind him.

When he returned some fifteen minutes later, fresh and vigorous and ready for the day, his clothes, which had been crushed and creased after a night's sleep, were miraculously straightened and tidied, and his hair, still wet, was tamed down into a dark-chestnut helmet fitting snugly over his skull.

'When d'ye expect Geddes back?' He slung the damp towel over the back of a chair.

'When I see him.' Eppie rescued the towel and spread it over the metal rail in front of the range. 'The inquiry might still be going on, or mebbe it only lasted the one day but they decided to wait out the storm before travelling back.'

'They?'

'My sister Marion's with him. She's governess to the two girls for the summer,' Eppie explained as he raised shaggy eyebrows. 'And she's been helping him with the papers for the inquiry.'

'Is that a fact?' He sniffed the air, then came over to the range to eye the pots and pans simmering there. 'When'll the food be ready?'

'Whenever you are. I've set the table upstairs. No doubt you'll find Duncan there.'

'Nae need tae eat upstairs – here'll be fine.' He began to draw one of the chairs out from beneath the table.

'In this house,' Eppie said shortly, 'we eat in the dining room. If you want food, that's where ye'll have tae go for it.'

He surveyed her for a long, thoughtful moment before saying, almost admiringly, 'There's no' much o' ye, wumman, but what there is, is awfu' nebby.'

Eppie gasped at the sheer effrontery of the man. 'D'ye want your food on the table upstairs, or thrown about yer ears?' she asked, and this time his craggy face cracked into a grin.

'Since ye put it that way, it'll have tae be upstairs.' He crossed to the table and picked up the loaded tray waiting there.

'I can see tae that.'

'If I must eat upstairs I might as well take it for ye,' he said, and left the kitchen.

* * *

During breakfast Lydia, who had seated herself opposite her brother, bombarded him with so many questions that on several occasions Eppie had to order her to get on with her meal and leave Duncan to do likewise. During one of the enforced silences she noticed that Foy, seemingly concentrating on shovelling food into his mouth for all the world as though he hadn't eaten for days, was watching the girl from beneath his shaggy eyebrows. When he had emptied his plate and wiped it clean with a hunk of bread, he sat upright, gave a satisfied sigh, then said to Lydia, 'Lassie, ye're the spit o' yer mother.'

Charlotte had remained silent through breakfast, lifting her gaze from her plate only to throw an occasional nervous look at Foy, but Lydia did not seem to find the man in the least frightening. 'Did you know her?' she asked eagerly.

He pushed his empty teacup towards Eppie, who filled it for the third time. 'Aye, I kenned her well when she wasnae much older than you are now. Jist as bonny as yersel', and jist as lively.'

'You never told me that you'd known my stepmother,' Duncan said, and Foy grinned at him. 'It's never wise tae tell folk everythin',' he said enigmatically and commenced to spoon sugar generously into his tea.

'Tell me about her,' Lydia commanded.

'Mebbe I will – another time.'

The scowl that had once been part of Lydia's everyday expression but was now rare twisted her pretty face. 'I want to hear all about her now!'

'Ye'll have tae want,' Foy said calmly.

'There'll be plenty of time later for talk,' Duncan cut in. 'We're going to be here for a wee while and I've got a lot to tell you myself – and to ask. D'you still have the bees?'

'Of course, and Charlotte and I talk to them every day. That's why you're here,' Lydia said. 'I asked them every day to tell you to come back home. But you're not here to stay, are you?'

'No. I've got work to do in Glasgow. But I'll be here for a while,' he repeated reassuringly.

'How do I know that you'll not go away again without telling me?' Lydia argued.

'I give you my word that I'll never do that again.' He reached out to cover her hand with his own.

When he had eaten and drunk his fill, Foy went down to the harbour with his pipe while the girls were sent upstairs to tidy their rooms and make their beds. Duncan helped Eppie clear the table and carry the used dishes down to the kitchen.

'Mind you,' he said, leaning against the table to watch her at her work, 'the length of time I stay here depends on my father.'

'You mean that you'd be willing to settle here again if he wanted you to?'

'Not that – at least, not right now, for I'm well contented in Glasgow and I like the work I'm doing there. But Foy and me are expecting to be here for a week at least, probably longer. We've got grand plans for the marble quarry, Eppie.' His voice suddenly filled with enthusiasm and when she glanced up she saw that his brown eyes sparkled. 'Foy's been in the Americas studying the way they quarry marble and we're going to use their system here, in Portsoy. We'll erect a shed on the land above the quarry, and install a crane to raise the blocks when they're cut, and a steam engine to shape them...'

'You've not changed, have you? Still full of ideas – and you ken fine that I don't understand the half of it!'

He laughed. 'You see and hear and understand more than you let on, Eppie Watt,' he teased, and then, suddenly serious: 'I was so glad to see that you're still here. You've done wonders with Lydia – she's growing up to be a fine young lady.'

'That's none of my doing. And I like working here. Your father's a good man to work for.'

He dug a hand into his pocket. 'There's another reason why I'm pleased you're still here,' he said.

Eppie stared at the hand he held out to her. 'What's this?'

'The money you loaned me when I last saw you.'

She shook her head. 'I wasn't looking for it back. It was a gift.'

'It was a loan, and it was given in kindness and friendship. I've never forgotten how good you were to me. Take it, Eppie,' he insisted, and then, as she reluctantly did as she was bid: 'What happened to make my grandmother leave the house?'

'It's just that your father thought she'd be more comfortable in a place of her own. And a bonny house it is too. You'll see it when you visit with her.'

'You're not telling me that she left here without a murmur?'

'It's not my place to tell you anything about your family.'

'Mebbe not, but tell me this, Eppie, for the sake of the friendship we always had between us – d'you think my father'll put me out when he finds me here?'

She turned from the sink to look straight at him, and saw that his young face was troubled. 'I doubt it. He's missed you, Duncan.'

'I missed him, and Lydia, and you, but I had to do what I did. Just think, if I hadn't run away I'd be a physician now, as miserable as sin and probably killing off my poor innocent patients in error. I'm glad that he didn't try to force me back to my studies.'

'Your grandmother wanted him to – and if you tell a living soul that I told you this I'll deny every word, for I wasn't supposed to overhear. But your father said that you were the one who had to decide to come back. And you have. I'm glad of that, lad, for Lydia's sake more than anyone else's.'

'I'm not home to stay, mind, just on business to do with the quarry.'

'Even so, it'll bring the family back together,' she said as Foy stamped in.

'Ready, lad? It's time we went tae have a look at this wee quarry. We'll be back at noon for some food.' He tossed the final sentence at Eppie as casually as if he were tossing a chewed and discarded bone to a stray dog.

'I'm more than ready,' Duncan said, and a moment later Eppie, seething at the man's impertinence, was alone. She went upstairs just as Lydia came hurrying down from her bedroom with Charlotte on her heels.

'Where's Duncan?'

'Gone to the quarry with Foy – and you're not to go there,' Eppie said sharply. 'They've work to do and you'll only get under their feet and mebbe end up getting hurt. Quarries are dangerous places.'

'Duncan will look after me.'

'Your brother's got more on his mind than looking out for you. The two of you can take a basket and a list and go round the shops for me. I'm too busy to do it myself. I'll write the list.' The truth was that she was anxious to be in the house should Alexander Geddes and Marion return, so that she could break the news of his son's arrival as gently as possible.

The prospect of being entrusted to do the day's shopping had its appeal, and ten minutes later the two girls had gone into the village, leaving Eppie alone in the house.

While awaiting her employer, she had to resolve the problem of where Foy should sleep that night – certainly not in her kitchen. As far as she was concerned he could sleep on the harbour wall, but when all was said and done he was her employer's guest, and had to be treated as such. She looked into Duncan's small bedroom and saw that if his bed was moved over against the wall there was just enough room for another narrow cot. Access to the loft was by a narrow flight of steep wooden stairs tucked into a corner of the upper hall; she fetched a lit candle and with some difficulty managed to get the stiff door to open.

The space below the roof was dark and stuffy, and the exposed rafters meant that she had to stoop all the time. Once or twice she thought she heard a scuttering noise in a corner, and stamped her feet loudly to deter whatever made the noise from showing itself.

The few items stored in the loft were stacked neatly and it did not take long to find a wooden cot that might not be very comfortable, but would surely be better than the chair in the kitchen.

Duncan and Foy could fetch it down later, she decided, and climbed back down the stairs after latching the loft door firmly, just in case there were any unwelcome residents that, once disturbed, might take it into their sharp-teethed, furry heads to find their way down into the living quarters.

She looked out blankets and sheets and a pillow, then got to work on her usual morning duties. When the girls arrived back, they helped her to unpack the basket and put everything away, and then she sent them into the garden. Duncan and Foy arrived back sooner than she had expected, but disappeared at once into Alexander Geddes's library, only emerging when summoned for their midday meal.

'You've had a good morning?' Eppie hazarded as she ladled stew on to their plates.

'A grand morning,' Duncan said enthusiastically. 'It was good to see the quarry again. It's doing well.'

'But it could do better.' Foy dug a serving spoon deep into the big bowl of potatoes Eppie had set on the table. 'And it will.'

'I'd a look in the loft this morning – there's a bed up there that'll do you, and space for it in Duncan's room, if the two of you could bring it down after you've eaten.'

'No need,' Foy said easily, tearing a hunk of bread from the loaf she had put out, and dipping it into his gravy. 'I've arranged tae lodge at the quarry foreman's house while I'm in Portsoy.'

Eppie, catching the bright-eyed way the two girls watched him biting off a mouthful of dripping bread, gave a slight cough to catch their attention, then delivered an intense stare. She had no wish to see them copying the man's uncouth eating habits. 'Oh, but Mr Geddes would want you to lodge here, surely,' she said, when Lydia and Charlotte had both lowered their eyes hurriedly to their own plates.

'I doubt that, and I'd be more comfortable elsewhere.'

'More comfortable? This is the most comfortable house in Portsoy!'

'There's comfort,' Foy said enigmatically, 'and there's comfort.' And then he devoted all his attention to his food.

As soon as the meal was over he and Duncan returned to the library while the girls were sent off to their dance class, delighted to be unaccompanied for once.

Eppie took a tray of used dishes to the kitchen and was returning for another load when her sister swept in through the front door, which she had left on the latch.

'There you are, Eppie!' There was high colour in her face, and her eyes were bright. 'We're back, and it's been such an adventure…!'

'Where's Mr Geddes?' Eppie interrupted. There was no time to waste in idle chatter.

'I'm here,' he said from the open doorway. 'What's the matter?' And then, his voice sharp with anxiety: 'Is it Lydia?'

'She's fine, Mr Geddes, but—'

Eppie stopped in mid-sentence as his gaze suddenly swept past her, fixing on the library door. She turned and saw Foy standing there, feet apart and thumbs hooked into his waistcoat pocket, looking as much at home as though he, and not the new arrival, owned the place.

'So ye're back, Geddes?' he said amiably.

There was nothing amiable about Alexander Geddes. Even before he spoke Eppie was aware of tension and antagonism filling the hallway. She heard her employer draw his breath in with an audible hissing sound, then he said coldly, 'Foy. What the devil are you doing in my house?'

'Sent frae Glasgow on business. Did ye no' get word that I was comin' north tae discuss the future o' the quarry with ye?' Foy's rough voice was still relaxed, with perhaps just a slight undercurrent of amusement at the other man's reaction.

'I got word, but if they'd told me that you were the one they were thinking of sending I'd have made sure they changed their minds.'

'Mebbe that's why they didnae mention me. Surely ye know that I'm the best quarryman they've got – always was, an' always will be. I've no' come empty-handed, though,' Foy went on when Geddes would have spoken. 'I brought a wee gift, tae sweeten yer mood.'

He stepped aside to reveal Duncan, who had come to stand in the doorway at his back.

'Hello, Father.' His voice was quiet, with just a slight catch in the throat. 'I hope you're pleased to see me, after all these years.'

22

'Duncan.' For a long moment it seemed that that was all Alexander Geddes had to say; then, clearing his throat, he added, 'So you've come home again – at last.'

'Better late than never – eh, Geddes?' Foy said.

To her astonishment, Eppie saw her employer throw a look of sheer hatred at the man. Then, almost at once, it was gone as he turned back to Duncan and held out his hand. 'Welcome home.'

Duncan's face cleared and he bounded forwards to shake the proffered hand enthusiastically. 'I'm glad to be back, sir, even though it's only for a week or so.'

'A week or so?' Geddes asked, but Foy's voice was louder than his as the man said, 'Are ye no' goin' tae introduce me tae yer lady friend, Geddes?'

Again, contempt swept over Geddes's face; for a moment Eppie thought that he was going to offer a sharp reproof, but his voice was calm when he said, 'Miss McNaught, I would like you to meet my son, Duncan Geddes, and this...' he waved a hand at the other man, almost as though dismissing him '...is Foy. Miss McNaught is my daughter's governess.'

Foy looked Marion over with open approval. 'So ye're a governess, Miss McNaught?'

'A teacher, Mr Foy, from Fordyce.' Marion offered her hand. Her colour had been high when she first hurried into the house, but now Eppie saw, by its deepening from pink to rose, that far from disturbing the fastidious Marion, the open admiration in Foy's eyes and in his voice pleased and excited her.

'It's no' Mr, it's just Foy.'

'Really?' Marion said, intrigued and apparently oblivious to the fact that he still held her gloved hand in his.

'Eppie, we've not eaten since we broke our fast early this morning,' Alexander Geddes cut into what looked like becoming a conversation. 'I'm sure that Miss McNaught must be as hungry as I am.' And then, glancing towards the stairs: 'Where are the lassies?'

'At their dancing class, Mr Geddes. I've got food waiting, for I thought you'd be back any minute. I can have it on the table in ten minutes.'

'I'll help you, Eppie,' Marion said, and followed her sister through the door at the back of the hall, leaving the three men on their own. 'Who is that strange man?' she asked as soon as they were safe from being overheard. 'And what sort of a name is that – Foy?'

'You know as much as I do. He arrived last night with Duncan – they're here to see what can be done with the quarry. Duncan's been staying in Glasgow with his stepmother's family, the Ramsays, these past five years. He seems to be awful fond of that Foy, for all that Mr Geddes doesn't care for the man at all,' Eppie said uneasily. Her employer's antagonism towards Foy had been tangible enough to thicken the air in the hallway.

'He's – I don't know – different, somehow. He has a way of looking at folk...' Marion's voice trailed away and Eppie looked up to see a flush on her sister's face, and a gleam in her normally serious eyes.

'Aye, he does – and not in a way that I like,' she said briskly. 'To my mind, a man like that could be dangerous.'

'Sometimes,' Marion said, 'danger can be exciting.'

'And more often it can just be dangerous,' Effie said drily. 'There's something worrying about the way Mr Geddes looked and sounded when he found Foy here. Did you not notice it yourself?'

'I can't say that I did.'

'Never mind him – what about the inquiry? Did the families of the men from the *Grace-Ellen* get justice?'

'As much as they could, seeing they'll never get their menfolk back. The master of the other vessel was blamed for not having enough men on watch and for not putting out his ship's boat to see if he could find survivors. And he's lost his certificate for nine months. Mr Geddes and the other owners have made a claim for damages in the name of the crew's dependents.'

'So Barbary'll get some money to help feed and clothe the bairns. That's something, at least. Mebbe,' Eppie said without much hope, 'it'll help her to put her grief behind her, and look to the future.'

'It was such an adventure, Eppie. We would have been back late last night, but the storm was so severe that Mr Geddes decided it was safer to stay in the hotel.'

'What was it like?' Eppie had never before known anyone who had stayed in a hotel.

'Like a big house – very grand, and my room was nearly the size of our cottage. We dined in a very large room with a lot of tables, and waiters – that's what it must be like for folk who live in grand houses, with footmen serving their food to them. Mr Geddes's lawyer dined with us. I would have gone to bed after he left, but Mr Geddes asked me to take a cup of coffee with him in the parlour. And I took a glass of brandy with it as well.'

'Marion McNaught!' The family were not against drink as such, but they rarely had the opportunity to taste anything other than the elderflower wine that Annie McNaught made each year.

'It was only a very small glass.'

'What did it taste like?'

'It had a real sting to it. I had trouble in keeping a cough back, and tears came to my eyes with the first sip. But then I had a lovely warm feeling all down here...' Marion put the flat of her hand against her bosom '...and down into my stomach. The next sip was easier, and the next again. And we talked until I could scarce keep my eyes open.'

'What about?' Eppie could not imagine her employer, a man who never spoke for the pleasure of hearing his own voice, talking far into the night with her own sister, of all people.

'Oh – this and that,' Marion said vaguely. For some reason, she wanted to keep the memory of the previous evening as her own secret, to be taken out when she was alone and played over and over, word for word. 'Lydia's schooling, and what was said at the inquiry.'

She was unaware that the splash of vivid colour over her cheekbones, the sparkle in her eyes and the quickened lilt in her voice were giving her innermost thoughts away.

'Marion,' Eppie said hesitantly, 'Mr Geddes has buried two wives. He's never going to seek a third.'

'I don't know what you're talking ab...' her sister began hotly, and then, as Eppie said nothing, but eyed her steadily, she gave a flounce, rather than a shrug, of her shoulders. 'Mebbe a third wife's what the man needs – someone with no intention of going to an early grave. Someone who's determined to stay by his side for the rest of his life. D'you not think the man deserves happiness?'

'Of course I do.'

'Well, I can tell you that he's not happy with the life he has now. There are too many cares on his shoulders, and Lydia's one of them. It's hard for a man to raise a lassie on his own. If I can find a way to help him, I'll do it. I just want to make him happy, Eppie,' she suddenly pleaded as her sister continued to look at her levelly. 'You surely know that I care for the man and I'd never want to do anything to hurt him.'

'I know that. It's you I'm fretting for. Mr Geddes isn't what you'd call free tae make up his own mind, Marion. There's his mother to deal with first.'

'She approves of me – I've made sure of that.' Marion gave her sister a conspiratorial smile. 'I've never lost a battle yet, once I've set my mind to winning it.'

Then she picked up one of the two trays Eppie had been loading and marched from the kitchen, her head held high.

* * *

The two girls hurried home after their dancing class ended, for Lydia could not wait to return to Duncan. When she burst into the house, Charlotte at her back, Eppie was clearing the empty dishes from the dining room table and the three men – Alexander Geddes, Duncan and Foy – were in the hall.

'Father, you're home – wasn't it a surprise to find Duncan here?' Eppie heard Lydia say, so excited that she almost sang the words.

'Indeed it was,' her father agreed just as Eppie took the full tray from the dining room. She saw with relief that he was smiling down at his daughter, clearly as pleased to see Duncan home as Lydia was.

'We've so much to talk about – where are you going?' the girl asked, suddenly noticing that the men were in their outdoor clothes.

'To the quarry.'

'Now? But I've just got home! And I have so many questions to ask Duncan!'

'You'll have plenty of time to ask them later.'

The little group was blocking the way to the kitchen, so Eppie had no option but to wait, balancing the tray against her hip. Charlotte and Foy, she noted, were both in the background, unnoticed and forgotten. Her daughter was watching the Geddes family with a shy half-smile on her lips, while Foy seemed unable to take his eyes from Lydia's pretty, animated face. He stood by the library's open door, and every now and again, Eppie noticed, he glanced into the room and then looked back at Lydia.

'Can I come with you?'

'Of course not. We have business to discuss and the quarry is a dangerous place for young ladies.'

Lydia's lower lip began to push forwards. 'But I haven't seen Duncan for years!'

'And you heard your father say that you would have plenty of time to speak to him later,' Marion's voice cut in from the school-room door. 'Since you have both missed lessons for two days, I think that we should spend the rest of the afternoon with our books.'

Charlotte looked relieved, and so did Alexander.

'Miss McNaught is quite right,' he told his daughter firmly. 'Upstairs now, and change to your indoor clothes, then come back down to the schoolroom.' Then, as Lydia, shoulders drooping, did as she was told, with Charlotte at her heels as always, Alexander suddenly noticed Eppie.

'Eppie, about accommodation for... for our guest...'

'No need, Geddes,' Foy said easily. 'I've arranged tae lodge with ye foreman an' his family while I'm here.'

It seemed to Eppie that her employer's relief at the news was as obvious as his strange dislike of the man from Glasgow.

Later, when the men had gone out and Marion and the two girls were shut in the schoolroom, she glanced in through the open library door, as she had seen Foy do, when she happened to pass it on her way upstairs.

He had been staring at the portrait of Celia Geddes, and comparing her to Lydia, who looked so like her mother.

* * *

Foy marched into the kitchen by the back door some thirty minutes later, demanding tea. 'My throat's dry,' he announced and Eppie, busy packing a basket of food for Barbary and her young family, nodded at the tea kettle, puffing steam on the range.

'It's there if you want it.' She was determined not to run after this man who had, for some unknown reason, upset Mr Geddes, even though he had brought Duncan home. To her surprise he nodded, as though he had expected to be told to wait on himself.

She watched as he took two cups from the dresser and poured tea into them both, then sought out and found milk and sugar.

'For a man, ye've a good idea of the way a kitchen's run,' she said, curiosity overcoming her. 'D'ye have a wife and family of your own in Glasgow?'

He gave her a sidelong glance from eyes more of a deep golden shade than ordinary hazel. 'I'm no' the marryin' sort, but I've been around a few kitchens in my time.'

He slid the second cup across the table to her and as she took it she saw that his broad hands were covered with the silvery gashes left by long-healed scars, and that the knuckles were unusually large and very knobbly.

'Every quarryman's got scars like these,' he said easily, following the direction of her glance. 'And there was a time—' he ran the tip of a finger along the knuckles of the other hand '—when I'd tae earn my keep by bare-knuckle boxin'.'

'That's a heathenish thing tae do!'

'It put food in my belly and taught me that the world's a hard place an' we a' need tae learn tae look out for ourselves.'

'So Duncan's hands'll get cut like yours?' She thought of the boy's hands, graceful and long-fingered like his father's.

'Mebbe they will, but it'll dae him no harm.'

'His father wanted him tae become a physician and use his hands tae heal, not tae tear rock open. It was what his mother wanted too.'

'But not what the boy wanted. He's goin' tae be a grand quarryman, and he's got brains, tae. And what harm will it do if he picks up some scars along the way? Our hands are the best tools we have, and it's only natural that folk's hands tell their own story.'

With a sudden movement Foy caught hold of one of Eppie's hands in a warm, rough grasp. Startled, she tried to pull away but he held on, turning her hand over and running a fingertip over her palm. 'Ye've got some scars yersel', lassie.'

'That's from workin' with the herrin'.'

'Ye see?' He released her hand and picked up his mug. 'The only folk wi' smooth white hands are the employers and the nobility. We all come intae the world wi' soft hands, but maist o' us end up takin' the scars o' our labours tae the grave. They're our medals – an' damn the credit we get for carryin' them.' Then, eyeing the basket she was packing, 'What are ye doin'?'

'Taking some food tae a friend who's got bairns tae feed and a man lost at sea some months back. I've got Mr Geddes's permission,' she added swiftly. 'I'd no' do this without it.'

'I'll carry it for ye.'

'Should you no' be at the quarry?'

'Duncan's there wi' his faither and I'm leavin' it tae him tae tell Geddes aboot the plans we have for the place. The lad's learnin' well and it's time he took on some authority. I'll go with you tae yer friend's house,' he finished, picking up the basket and marching out of the back door, leaving her with no option but to follow, which she did with poor grace.

'Have ye known Duncan since he ran – since he left Portsoy?' she asked as they walked to Barbary's cottage.

'It was me that found him sleepin' in the stables at the back o' the house one mornin'.' He gave a bark of laughter at the memory. 'I couldnae unnerstaun' it, for the laddie was well enough dressed an' no' like the usual beggars ye come across on the Glasgow streets. So I nudges him awake with my foot an' he opens his eyes and looks up at me an' he says for all the world as if he's come tae the front door and I was the butler that had opened it, "Tell Mr Ramsay that Duncan Geddes has come to call on him."' He mimicked Duncan's educated accent. 'An' him wi' straw stickin' oot his hair and a smudge o' horse shit on the shoulder o' his fine jacket.'

'Why was he sleeping in the stables?'

'He'd arrived in Glasgow in the middle o' the night and didnae like tae waken any'b'dy. So I made him tidy himsel' up an' took him tae the hoose. An' after a good long talk wi' the lad,

Mr Ramsay took him in and handed him over tae me. "The lad thinks he can make a good quarryman, so let's see what you think of it," he says. "If he's right we can make good use of him."'

A stout woman with a basket looped over her arm came towards them, taking up the full width of the footpath. They both had to step into the roadway to let her pass, and as they returned to the pavement Foy resumed his story. 'I worked him hard, for there was nae sense in molly-coddlin' him, an' lettin' him think that he was somethin' he could never be. But he stuck at it wi' never a word o' complaint, and one day he's goin' tae be as good as me.'

'Modest, you mean?' Eppie asked.

'There ye go again wi' that sharp tongue. It's fortunate that I like my women tae have minds o' their ain,' he said, and then, before she could retaliate: 'Quarry work's what the lad always wanted, and it's what he does best. The boy's got a good brain in his noddle and laddies like him dinnae take kindly tae bein' told what tae dae wi' their ain lives. He'd never have made a decent physician – his heart wouldnae have been in it. His father was wrong tae try tae force him tae go against his own wishes. But that's Alexander Geddes for ye – he aye thought that money could buy anythin' – and more often than not,' he added, his voice suddenly grim, 'he was proved right. But no' with Duncan, thank God.'

'You speak as if you've had dealings with Mr Geddes before,' she said, and then glanced up at him, conscious of his swift sidelong glance. But he had already returned to looking at the road ahead.

'Aye, mebbe,' he said, 'but that's for me tae know an' you tae wonder aboot.'

'Does Mr Ramsay not work in the quarry himself – or is he too grand?'

'He did. He was a braw worker, and no' afraid tae pull his weight along wi' the rest o' us. Him an' me learned the trade thegither, but ten year ago he got caught in a bad rock fall an' lost the use o' his legs. When his faither died no' long after that, Mr Ramsay set me up as his quarry master.'

'Does he have any family?'

'He and his wife had three bairns, but they were all lassies, and none o' them lived tae make auld bones. They've been an unlucky fam'ly a'thegither, an' they deserved better, for they're the best folk that ever walked the earth.'

'It would be Mr Ramsay's sister, then, who married Mr Geddes? You're right about their bad luck, for she died young herself.'

'Aye.' The word fell to the ground at their feet as though it were a piece of slate and Foy seemed to close himself down; it was just as though he had slammed and bolted a door, shutting himself in and leaving her alone on the outside.

Barbary was in her usual rocking chair by the range, with the baby asleep on her lap. The back door was open and the other three children were in the backyard, contentedly making mud pies with earth from the neglected vegetable bed, and water from the kettle, which sat on the flagged path beside them.

Barbary scarcely seemed to notice Eppie, who set the basket on the table and hurried out to rescue the dented kettle. Five-year-old George beamed up at her.

'We're makin' biscuits for our mammy's tea,' he announced proudly, slapping a fistful of mud between his hands to flatten it. He was wearing an old short-sleeved smock; dirty water oozed down his bare little arms and the front of the smock was soaked and filthy. Martha was in an even worse state, with mud tangled in her dark hair and smeared over her round face. Wee Thomas was sitting on the path, making swirling patterns in the soft mud with wide sweeps of his hands.

'Are ye hungry?' Eppie asked them, and when they all nodded vigorously: 'I've brought better things for ye tae eat than these pies. Come on inside and wash yer hands, then I'll put the dinner on the table.'

In the kitchen, Foy was crouched by Barbary's chair, talking quietly. She was smiling at him, but all her attention seemed to be focused on a large pink shell that she held to one ear. Tolly had brought it back from the previous autumn's fishing at Lowestoft, having bought it from a man who had travelled the world.

Deftly, Eppie washed the three children and put them into clean clothes, then she sat George and Martha at the table and put plates of food before them while she took Thomas on her knee. As she spooned food into his willing little mouth, she told Barbary about the Board of Trade's decision, finishing with: 'And so you and the bairns'll have some money comin' soon. That'll make a difference, will it no'?'

Barbary nodded and smiled, but Eppie was not sure that she had taken in a word of what had been said to her. She turned to glance at Foy, but he had gone. Then she saw him out in the backyard, shovelling the mud from the path and sweeping the dirty water into the vegetable bed.

Thomas fell asleep almost as soon as he was fed, and Eppie laid him down in his cot before taking the baby, now wakening, from his mother's arms.

'Go and eat your dinner, Barbary, while I take wee Jeemsie along the road,' she urged, and the young woman obedient as a child, laid the shell down on the table by her place before spooning food into her mouth, her eyes fixed on the opposite wall as though watching something that nobody else could see.

Now that he had a wet nurse to feed him, the baby was thriving. Eppie changed his napkin and then handed him over to his foster mother. When she returned to the cottage, Foy had found an old hoe and was working on the vegetable bed. After settling George and Martha down on the floor with their few toys, she tidied the place and put the provisions she had brought into the larder. Barbary had eaten most of her food and was listening to the shell again, a slight smile on her face.

Eppie touched her friend's arm; although Barbary ate everything put before her, her once-round arm was so thin that Eppie could feel the skin loose on the bone. 'Barbary, did ye hear what I said, about Mr Geddes gettin' the court tae send money tae help you and the bairns and the other folk that lost their men?'

'Aye, I heard.'

'It means that you'll no' have tae worry about money, no' for a good whiley anyway.'

'Aye. He's a good man, Mr Geddes,' Barbary said, and then held the shell out. 'Listen tae that, Eppie...'

Eppie took the pretty thing and put its pink and white whorled opening to her ear to listen to the soft continuous roar of the sea. Barbary had loved the shell from the moment Tolly had put it into her hands, and she had often encouraged the children to play with it, laughing at the wonder on their little faces when they heard the shell's murmuring.

'D'ye hear it?' Barbary was saying now, her eyes, sunk into their sockets, holding Eppie's gaze.

'Aye, I hear it. I hear the sea.' Eppie had always marvelled at the way the shell, on dry land and far from the warm tropical seas that had given birth to it, could still carry the sound of the ocean.

'But can ye hear *them*?' Barbary said. 'Can ye, Eppie?'

'Them?'

'Them,' Barbary insisted. 'Can ye no' hear the voices, callin' tae ye?'

'Just the sea, Barbary. There's no voices – there's just the sea.'

'Of course there's voices.' Barbary snatched the shell back and clamped it to her ear, her face knotted with anxiety. Then it smoothed into a contented smile. 'It's all right – they're still there. Still talkin' in the shell.'

All at once Eppie remembered the previous night, when she had opened the window of her small room before going to bed, and had then shut it hurriedly because she fancied that within the crash of the waves being hurled across the firth she could hear the multitude of men the sea had taken in its time, asking, pleading, demanding to be allowed back to the dry, warm lamplit homes they had been forced to desert against their wills.

She drew back, then jumped and only just suppressed a squeal of fright as the street door opened and Jeemsie's wet nurse carried him in, fed and contented.

The woman stayed to chat for a moment, and not long after she had left, Foy came in from the backyard, dusting earth from his hands.

'She's in a pitiful way, yer friend,' he said as they made their way back to the Geddes house. 'She's taken the loss o' her man badly.'

'She'll be all right, once Mr Geddes gets the claim for payment settled,' Eppie assured him. 'She'll be able tae look tae the future then.'

But deep down, she did not believe her own words. It seemed to her that Barbary was slipping away from her, out of her grasp, and unless something could be done to help her, she would one day slip out of reach entirely.

* * *

Duncan Geddes hesitated before the house where his grandmother now lived, conscious of a sudden dryness in his throat. He had turned down his father's offer to accompany him, for he was a man now and this was something that he had to do on his own. It was his duty, he told himself sternly, setting one hand on the latch of the gate. And any man worth his salt had to do his duty, especially where elderly female relatives were concerned.

In any case, his grandmother already knew that he was back in Portsoy, so there was no chance of completing the business he and Foy had come on and then creeping back to Glasgow without seeing her.

His thoughts carried him through the gate and up the flagged garden path to the front door. Almost as soon as he had used the polished brass door knocker he heard a faint scurrying sound from within – the sound, he thought wryly, either of rodents behind the wainscoting of a room, or of a maidservant who had been trained to within an inch of her life, and lived in terror of her employer's anger – and then the door opened to reveal the servant herself, neat as a new pin in her snowy cap and apron, and trying hard to conceal her breathlessness.

'Aye, sir?'

'Duncan Geddes, come to call on my grandmother.'

The maid looked at him with sudden interest, mixed with curiosity. It was a look he had come to know well since returning to his birthplace. In fact, he had been stopped several times on his way to his grandmother's by folk anxious to greet him and to find out what he had been up to during the five years of his absence.

'If ye'll come away in, sir, I'll see if the mistress is at home.' The woman reversed with practised skill, drawing the door with her in order to widen his access. When she had closed the door she took his hat. 'If ye'll just bide here for a wee minute,' she said, and hurried upstairs.

Duncan waited in the large entrance hall, looking about him with interest. The hall was furnished like an anteroom, with a large rug covering most of the polished floor, flock paper on the walls, brocade curtains at the windows on either side of the front door and chairs with tapestry seats and backs grouped about a small table. The house was very comfortably furnished – no doubt at his father's expense. He guessed that his grandmother had struck a hard bargain before agreeing to move here.

The maid came scurrying back down. 'This way, sir,' she said, and set off on a second trip upstairs. By the time Duncan joined her in the upper hall she was tapping on one of the doors.

His stomach clenched as a familiar voice snapped something from inside the room. For a moment, he was a little boy again, summoned to his grandmother's parlour to answer for some real or imagined wrongdoing.

The maid opened the door. 'Mr Duncan Geddes, ma'am,' she said, and Duncan resisted an urge to smooth his hands over his hair and check that his shoes were polished before following her into the parlour where Helen Geddes awaited him sitting in a high-backed chair by the window, her wrinkled hands gripping the carved wooden armrests.

'Well, Duncan—' her voice was as strong and as harsh as ever '—so you've decided to come back to Portsoy at last? You may kiss me,' she added as he hesitated in the middle of the room, unsure as to what to do next.

As he approached obediently she tilted her head to one side, graciously, offering her cheek to his lips. Her skin was very soft and wrinkled, making him feel that if he was not careful to keep the kiss light, his mouth could easily sink right into her face. She smelled of lavender water, and he saw, as he straightened up, that although she had aged a great deal in the past five years, her pure white hair was still thick and her eyes of the vivid blue he remembered. Looking at her with a man's eyes rather than a boy's, he realised with a shock that his grandmother must have been a very beautiful woman in her youth.

'You may sit there.' She indicated a chair opposite her own, where the light from the window would fall on his face. He sat and waited as her sharp eyes studied his features, then his clothing.

'You're a man now.'

'Twenty years of age, Grandmother.'

'You did a terrible thing, running off the way you did without a word of explanation, then staying away for all those years.'

Nothing had changed, Duncan thought wryly. Here he was, being chastised for his behaviour. But at least this time, he was a man, and well able to speak up for himself.

'I had to leave, Grandmother, because I was being forced into a profession that wasn't right for me.'

'That's nonsense! Laddies don't know anything about the world; it was the responsibility of me and your father to make sure that you got the best education and the best chance in life. You could have been a physician or a banker or you could have gone into your father's business so that you could take over from him, but instead you chose to be a common workman!'

'A quarryman, Grandmother. It's an honourable calling, and a family business. I work for my Uncle Ramsay.'

'The Ramsays are no kin to you!'

'No,' Duncan admitted, 'but as far as Uncle Ramsay's concerned, close enough, since Lydia is his niece, and my half-sister. He has no sons of his own.'

'So he's making you his heir?'

'I don't know about that. As you say, we're not blood kin. But he's a fair man and I think I can always be sure of a position in one of his quarries when he's gone.'

'You're daft to be so trusting,' Helen Geddes snapped, and then: 'Let me see your hands.'

Almost of their own volition, his hands shot forwards for inspection, turning over when she raised an eyebrow in mute command. He found himself glancing down at his own finger-nails and was relieved to note that they were neatly cut, and scrubbed clean.

'They're not the hands of a gentleman. A common work-man,' she repeated, settling back against the high, rigid back-board of her chair.

'An honourable calling,' Duncan said again, obstinately, 'and one that I chose for myself. I'm here to use my knowledge to help my father. Foy and I have great plans for the Portsoy quarry, and my father will profit by our ideas.'

'Who did you say?'

'Foy's my uncle's quarry master. He's taught me everything I know about quarrying,' Duncan said with pride.

'Is it Mr Foy you mean, or is that the man's Christian name? I've never heard the like.'

'Just Foy. It's what he prefers to be called.'

'It's a heathenish name – no doubt for a heathenish man.'

'I can assure you, Grandmother, that Foy is not a heathen. He's travelled the world to learn his trade. And my education wasn't neglected just because I left Aberdeen for Glasgow. Uncle Ramsay sent me to college to learn the history and theory of quarrying, as well as geology and something of architecture and lapidary. I've got all sort of plans for the quarry here in Portsoy...'

He was so caught up in his explanation about introducing a steam engine and a crane to lift the larger blocks of marble to the new workshop, which he and Foy intended to build on the high ground above the quarry, that he didn't notice Helen's eyes glazing over. She suffered his enthusiasm for a few minutes, and was just about to cut him short with a sharp remark when Maisie brought in the tea tray.

'So, how are you, Grandmother?' Duncan enquired politely, nibbling at the corner of a sandwich so small and thin that he could have eaten it in one gulp and scarcely noticed.

'Older. Frail and alone.'

'You're not alone – you have servants, and friends, and Lydia tells me that she visits every week.'

'Lydia! What d'you think of your sister, Duncan?'

'I think that she is growing fast, and soon she will be a very beautiful young woman, the image of her mother.'

'She's spoiled. Your father indulges her too much – he and that housekeeper of his! She's got her own companion now – the housekeeper's daughter, of all people. The moment he managed to push me out of his home – and mine for all those years – and into this place—' Helen Geddes looked around the elegant, beautifully furnished parlour as though it were nothing more than a hovel '—your father took the housekeeper's daughter into his house – of all people!'

'She seems a pleasant, well-raised lassie.'

'Hmmm! Just you wait – one day Lydia will inherit your father's share of the quarry, and money from his estate besides, and that's when the "pleasant lassie" from Fordyce will show her true colours. She'll make herself indispensable to my grand-daughter – your sister, Duncan – and not be content until she's fattened herself on poor Lydia's wealth.'

Duncan was beginning to find it hard to remain civil in the face of such vindictiveness. 'I doubt that very much. Eppie's a kind, honest woman and I'm sure that she would never raise her daughter to be avaricious.'

'You're like your father – far too trusting.'

'And the governess, Miss McNaught, seems to be making a good fist of Lydia's education.'

'Alexander will find the entire family running riot over his home if he is not careful. You must speak to him about it, since he seems determined to ignore anything I have to say.'

'As I understand it, my father was anxious to find a good governess for Lydia, and from the way she speaks of Miss McNaught and Charlotte, Lydia is enjoying their company.'

It would seem, Helen Geddes thought, that she was not going to find the ally she had hoped for in Duncan. 'The governess seems to be a sensible young woman – I'll grant you that,' she conceded with poor grace. 'She's taken to visiting me regularly to report on Lydia's progress and very respectful and well spoken she is. That's because of her education, of course.'

She leaned forwards in her chair, her blue eyes fixed on her grandson's face. 'You see how important a good education is, Duncan? Two sisters raised in the same cottage in Fordyce and both, presumably, given the same education. Yet what a differ-ence between them. One makes full use of it and comes as near as anyone with her background can to being a lady, while the other spurns the chances offered to her and marries a fisher-man. Now she's a mere servant.'

The scone Duncan was eating was still warm from the oven, and as light as a feather, but all at once it seemed to lie in his mouth like a lead ball, and he had to take several sips of tea before he could swallow it.

He could scarcely bear to wait for the next ten minutes to pass, and when they did, and he was free to make his farewells and leave the house, he drew in great gasping lungfuls of salt air, blowing it out hard several times in order to flush out the poisons and prejudices he had been subjected to while in Helen Geddes's presence.

How his father could have borne to have that woman in his house for all those years he could not understand. As he strode down into the village, swinging his arms vigorously as he went, he was furious with Alexander for having exposed his children to her vindictive, snobbish narrow-mindedness; then, as the good sea air did its work, cleansing mind and body of the atmosphere in his grandmother's house, he found himself admiring his father for having finally found the courage to regain his own home, and for introducing Eppie and her sister into it. They would surely be the saving of Lydia!

He was still walking quickly and as he passed a baker's shop he almost bumped into a girl as she stepped out from its doorway.

'I beg your pardon.' He put one hand to her elbow to steady her while the other went up to tip his hat. 'My fault entirely, I wasn't looking where I was going.' And then, as she glanced up at him: 'Miss Charlotte – I am doubly sorry. Please excuse my clumsiness.'

She clutched her large basket against her body as though using it to prevent him from getting too close. 'It's perfectly all right, Mr Geddes; I got a wee fright, that's all.'

'You've been sent out to do the shopping?' And then, when she nodded: 'Have you much more to do?'

'It's all done.'

'Then we can walk back to the house together.' Duncan felt himself in need of some pleasant company. 'I'll carry your basket.'

Charlotte looked up at him with such horror that he laughed out loud, then had to hurry to assure her that he was not laughing at her. 'Well, not entirely. For a moment you looked as though you thought I might bite you. But I have just had tea with my grandmother and I am so full that I couldn't even manage a nibble.'

He had already decided that she was a very quiet, serious girl, but the unexpectedness of his comment brought a fleeting smile, which she hurried to bring under control.

'I can carry the basket easily; it's not heavy. And I'm sure that you have other places to go – the quarry, perhaps? Please don't feel that you have to walk to the house with me.'

'I would enjoy your company,' he said firmly, taking the basket. And then, as they set out: 'That pendant you always wear, with the Portsoy marble – I remember helping Eppie to choose it, not long before I left Portsoy. It was for your birthday, I believe.'

A hand flew to her throat. 'It's my favourite possession,' she said, flattered that he had noticed it and delighted to hear that he'd had a hand in the choosing of it.

'I'm glad to hear that you are so pleased with it.'

A passer-by stopped Duncan before they had gone far to welcome him back to Portsoy, and to ask about his future plans. Charlotte hesitated and her hand moved towards the basket he carried, as though to take it and walk on alone, but he gave her such a pleading look that her hand fell back to her side and she waited until he was free again.

'They must have all told each other that I'm back home, and what my plans are, over and over again, for I've told so many people,' he said, 'and yet they all seem to want to hear it from my own lips. I'm tired of repeating myself.'

'They're just pleased to see you after all this time,' she said reasonably.

'I suppose so. Do you have to go back to the house right away?'

'Not at once.'

'Come out to the headland with me for a wee while. I've been cooped up in my grandmother's house for the past hour and I need to look at the sea and breathe in its salt air and talk to someone sensible.'

24

Charlotte had done her best to let Lydia have Duncan all to herself since his visit was to be short. Now the prospect of being on her own with him, and even worse, of being expected to talk sensibly about goodness knows what, alarmed her.

'You don't have to listen,' Duncan was saying now, almost as though he could read her thoughts. 'A nod now and again would do.'

He grinned down at her, and she found herself smiling back at him, and following him as he turned away from the harbour.

It was a fresh day with a strong breeze. They found a grassy spot not far from the quarry, and Duncan insisted on putting his coat down for Charlotte to sit on. She need not have concerned herself about having to make conversation because he immediately launched into a description of the plans that he and Foy had for the quarry, and although she scarcely understood a word of it, she found herself caught up in his enthusiasm.

She watched his brown eyes come alive and his long arms and work-roughened hands sweep and circle through the air as he spoke. Occasionally, one hand paused in its outlining of some piece of machinery or the shape of a building to sweep a tumble of wind-blown dark hair from his eyes.

The words poured from him and filled the air around Charlotte, and she found herself being affected by his sheer exuberance. One day, she told herself as she listened, she wanted to care as much about something as he did about quarrying. One day, she wanted to have her own dream to follow.

Then a church bell sounded the hour and the spell was broken. 'My mother will be wondering where I am – I must go.'

He helped her to her feet, shook his jacket out and put it on, and then picked up the basket. 'I apologise for talking so much, but I must persuade my father to agree to our plans, and I believe that I was using you for practice. It was unfair of me.'

'I found it all very interesting, though I didn't understand much of it.'

'When I next come back to Portsoy I'll take you to the quarry, if you like, and explain things to you properly.'

'I'd like that very much.'

'Then we'll make a point of it. And now,' he said as they began to walk back to the harbour, 'tell me something about yourself. Are you enjoying your stay in Portsoy?'

'Oh yes, it's exciting to live in such a large house when I've always been used to a cottage.'

'How do you get on with my sister? She can be overbearing at times.'

'It was difficult at first,' Charlotte acknowledged, 'but I think that it was just as hard for Lydia to share things with me when she's not been used to it before.'

'You wouldn't have been used to it before either, but I suspect that you managed it better than Lydia.'

'It was harder for her,' Charlotte said in a matter-of-fact tone.

'She has so much more than I have, which means that she had much more to share.'

'Ah.' Duncan estimated that the serene and sensible girl hurrying along by his side was probably Lydia's age – some twelve years old. But she seemed so much older and wiser.

'She dances beautifully,' Charlotte was saying. 'We both go to classes, but Lydia's so much more graceful than me. It's as though she's being lifted up and carried along by the music. I feel so clumsy beside her.'

'I can't dance either. I went to a ball once, and I made a complete fool of myself. My partner and I were hand in hand and she had to sink into a curtsey, then I had to draw her to her feet. Unfortunately all I managed to do was to pull off a pretty ring she was wearing, and the poor girl was sent tumbling back to the floor.'

'How dreadful!' They had reached the kitchen door of the house and Charlotte looked up at him, her eyes wide. 'What did you do?'

'I laughed and the young lady never spoke to me again,' he said cheerfully, then: 'Have you tried ice-skating?'

'No.'

'It's easier to be graceful on the ice. I must come to Portsoy in the winter, and teach you to skate on Loch Soy when it's frozen,' he announced.

They both went indoors smiling, Duncan because thanks to his young companion he had been cleansed of the memory of his grandmother's vindictive nature, and Charlotte wallowing in the glow of her first taste of hero worship. The pendant, with its chip of red marble, had become even more precious to her than before.

* * *

Although he was lodging with a family in Seafield Terrace, Foy spent most of his time in the Geddes house. He ate some of his meals in the dining room with the family, though more often he preferred to eat on his own in the kitchen.

He spent most of what spare time he had in the kitchen, watching Eppie at her work. Sometimes he was silent, and to her surprise she found that it was a comfortable silence with no awkwardness to it. When he was in a talkative mood he wanted to know about Portsoy and the folk who lived in it, and something of her own life. She answered his questions easily, for there was nothing about her past that required being kept secret.

But she soon discovered that her attempts to find out more about his background were met with evasion and skilful changes of subject. He was willing to talk only about Glasgow, his work and his employer and friend, Edward Ramsay, Lydia's uncle and Duncan's patron.

'He dotes on that lad. The man had no kin tae speak of until Duncan came intae his life, and ye can be sure that the boy's been well cared for and well educated – his father should be pleased about that, since it seems to be the only thing he wanted for the boy.'

As always, she was quick to defend her employer. 'It's natural for Mr Geddes to want the best for his children. That's a father's duty.'

'Faither's duty!' he snarled, and spat through the cast-iron bars and into the hot fire. The gob of saliva did not entirely pass through the gap between the bars, and some sizzled on the hot metal. Eppie, who had done her best to stop him from the disgusting habit, tutted loudly and glared at Foy, who avoided her eye as he went on, 'Mebbe faithers should mind that it's human bein's they're raisin', no' possessions. There's more decent folk crippled for life by ambitious faithers than I've had hot dinners.'

'You sound as if you know a lot about it. Are you a father yourself?'

'Me?' He gave an abrupt laugh. 'I made up my mind years back that I'd no' let mysel' be guilty o' ruinin' some poor bairn's life. Anyway, I dinnae believe in marriage.'

'I'm sure that the womenfolk of Glasgow would be pleased tae know that.'

'Oh, there's plenty weemen can appreciate a man withoot tryin' tae turn him intae a husband,' he said slyly, giving her a sidelong glance. But if he had hoped to shock her, he was disappointed, for she kept on with her darning, and only said, 'We'll have a cup of tea in a minute, before you go off tae your lodgings.'

Since doors were rarely locked and barred at night in Portsoy, she sometimes found him sitting at the kitchen table early in the morning, eating food foraged from the pantry. On those days, the range had been cleared of the night's ashes and was burning brightly, ready for the day's work. When he arrived early on the next washing day, she went into the wash-house to find that the boiler was hot and the fire she had lit below it the night before to give herself a good start in the morning had been replenished.

He returned to the house later that day, more restless than usual. He walked about the kitchen, peering out of the window then going to the range to fidget with the pots and pans before strolling to the table, where Eppie was trying to make pastry, to pick at a piece of dough.

'Put that down – what's amiss with ye?' she asked, exasperated. 'If ye cannae settle, go outside and let me get on with my work.'

'Duncan's upstairs wi' Geddes, showin' him the plans we have for the quarry. I'm feart that the man'll give him a difficult time.'

'Why should he? He's happy to have the lad back home; I can see it in his face every minute of the day. He'll want to please Duncan.'

'It's no' Duncan that's the problem, it's me.'

'What d'you mean?'

'Nothin'. Just get on with yer work an' stop naggin' at me,' he said roughly. Colour flooded into her face and she had just opened her mouth to order him out of her kitchen when the inner door was thrown open and Duncan stormed in, his own face flushed and his eyes bright.

'He'll have none of it!' He glared at Eppie, and then at Foy. 'He says the quarry's fine as it is and he'd not listen to a word I said!' He threw a fistful of papers on to the table, heedless of the baking preparations. A cloud of flour billowed up, some of it going over his brown jacket. He ignored it.

'Mebbe ye didnae explain it right,' Foy said, and the young man rounded on him.

'I explained it fine! It's him – he's as thrawn as ever he was. No wonder I left home when I did. I should never have come back!' His voice broke and he made for the back door, dashing an arm across his eyes as he went.

'Duncan—' Foy put a restraining hand on his arm and was thrown off so violently that he fell back against the table. By the time he had steadied himself Duncan had gone, slamming the door hard behind him.

'Go after him!'

'No,' Foy said. 'Leave him tae calm down. He'll no' want an audience at the moment.'

'But he might do something daft!' Eppie had visions of

Duncan walking blindly into the harbour, or even throwing himself in.

'He's got more sense than that. He just needs tae be left tae his own company for a while.' Foy glanced up at the ceiling, his face darkening. 'That man has tae learn how tae deal with his own blood kin,' he said savagely, and made for the inner door.

'Wait – wait until you've all had time to draw breath...' But the door closed on the final word, and Eppie was alone.

She caught her apron up, twisting the material around both hands as she always did in times of stress or uncertainty, looking first at the back door, and then at the inner door. Then, unsure of what to do, she rescued the pages that Duncan had flung down and brushed flour from them.

They were covered with detailed sketches of machinery and buildings, with notes and measurements written neatly alongside. Even after five years she recognised Duncan's tidy hand. Foy was probably right – angry as he was, Duncan was too sensible to do anything rash. But Foy was another matter...

Eppie put the papers down on the dresser, out of harm's way, and hurried upstairs. As she gained the upper hall she heard the men's voices behind the library door; they were both talking quickly and angrily, but at least they were talking and not fighting. Not as yet. For some reason she could not understand there was bad feeling between the two of them, and who knew where an argument might lead?

Once or twice Eppie had overheard things not meant for her ears, but each time it had been by accident. Never before had she deliberately eavesdropped, but now she pressed her ear against the door, determined that if the talking gave way to violence, she would do all she could to stop it, even if it meant running out into the street to fetch help.

'...what's best for this quarry,' Alexander Geddes was saying. 'It's small and it works well as it is.'

'It could be extended,' Foy replied. 'This area's rich wi' the stuff. There's serpentine below ground right back tae the Hill o' Fordyce, an' south nearly tae Knock Hill. How can ye ever hope tae bring out the most o' it without the help o' steam engines an' cranes?'

'I'll not see the countryside plundered and ravaged just to make Edward Ramsay wealthy.'

'Ye'd become wealthy yersel',' Foy pointed out. 'An' if *we* dinnae dae it, someone else will.'

'Let them, when their time comes. For now, I'll not agree to your proposals.'

'They're more than proposals, Geddes. Mr Ramsay holds a greater share in the quarry than you dae, and I've a wee share an' a'. Ye could be outvoted.'

'I'll put up a fight if it comes to that. As things stand at the moment, I'm the man who's in charge of mining this quarry, and for that reason alone, if no other, I've got the right to be heard.'

There was a brief pause, then Foy said slowly, 'Duncan's fair upset by yer stubbornness. The lad's worked hard on these plans and he's done a grand job. It's hit him hard, his own faither turnin' doon his ideas without even givin' him the courtesy o' considerin' them first.'

'Duncan's a man now – he has to learn to accept disappointment. God knows,' Geddes said bitterly, 'that we all have to live with it.'

'You an' me ken that mair than most, Alexander. If ye ask me, ye're treatin' the boy hard because ye're angry wi' him for runnin' off tae Glasgow and meetin' up wi' Edward Ramsay. The lad doesnae ken it yet, but Ramsay's plannin' tae leave what he has tae Duncan. Your son's goin' tae dae well for himsel',

Geddes, but what does that matter tae you? Ye're angry wi' Duncan and eaten up with envy at me an' Ramsay, because we like the lad, and he likes the baith o' us. Ye've no' got the common sense tae know that nob'dy'll take your place in the boy's life. Duncan's loyal, an' ye're no' man enough tae see that.'

This time the silence lasted so long that Eppie began to grow uneasy. Then, at last, Alexander Geddes said levelly, 'Why would I punish Duncan for the past by refusing a plan that would benefit the quarry? I've no quarrel with him.'

'But ye have wi' me.'

'If I have, it's because you've managed to draw my son under your influence, and you've done it deliberately, to punish me for taking Celia from you.'

'Well now!' Foy's voice was triumphant. 'Ye've faced up tae the truth o' the matter at last, Geddes. Though I cannae see why you should have any grievance against me, since you're the one who got her.'

'She made the choice. I didn't influence her.'

'Ye didnae need tae. If you'd no' set eyes on her, she might have chosen me – oh aye, Geddes, there was a time when her an' me were as close as that. But then you had tae come intae her life, and why would a lassie like Celia Ramsay choose tae marry wi' a quarryman when she could have a fine gentleman like yoursel', Geddes, wi' yer big hoose an' yer genteel ways?'

'Why indeed? But even though you knew that she wanted me you did your damnedest to come between us. D'you think I didn't know about your pathetic attempts to turn her and her father against me?'

'Mebbe if I'd had your fine education, *Mister* Geddes, I could have done better.'

'Whoever she chose, it's all in the past,' Geddes said sharply. 'Neither of us has her now.'

'But you've got yer memories, an' yer bonny wee daughter who's the image o' her mother. It fair stopped my heart when I first caught sight of Lydia. It was like seein' Celia brought back tae life.'

'Don't speak my daughter's name, Foy!'

'Ye've got the lassie – surely ye cannae deny me sayin' her name now and again?' Foy's voice was suddenly taunting. 'If things had been different Celia might have ended up with me And mebbe she'd be alive today if I'd had the right tae look after her as she—'

There was a sudden exclamation and Foy's words ended in a strange gurgling sound. Something crashed over inside the room and Eppie, throwing caution to the winds, turned the door handle and burst into the room to see Foy on the floor, and her employer kneeling over him, his hands at the other man's throat.

'Mr Geddes!'

He looked up, startled by the intrusion, and for a moment she didn't recognise his face, distorted as it was by sheer naked hatred. His normally pale skin was dark red and his heavy-lidded eyes wide and glaring. Hair flopped over his forehead and his lips were drawn back to reveal clenched teeth.

'Mr Geddes!' she said again, this time in little more than an appalled whisper. Her hands flew to her mouth and for a split second she felt more frightened than she had ever been in her life. Then the primal rage ebbed from his eyes as Foy's arms came up and then swung apart, breaking the other man's hold.

'Eppie? Is there something wrong?' Marion called nervously from the hall. 'Mr Geddes?'

'Get her out o' the way,' Foy hissed, pushing Alexander Geddes aside and scrambling to his feet. 'Go on now, we're fine!'

Eppie backed out and closed the door before turning to

where Marion stood in the open doorway of the schoolroom, Lydia and Charlotte peering round her shoulders.

'Is Mr Geddes ill? I thought I heard someone fall to the floor.'

'It's nothing – Foy's in the library with him, and he fell over a chair. I was dusting out here,' said Eppie, hoping that her sister wouldn't notice that her hands were empty, 'and I thought the same as you. But it's nothing.'

'That man's so clumsy,' Marion tutted, then whisked round on her pupils. 'And who gave you two permission to stop your work? Back to the table, if you please.' She shooed them into the room and closed the door while Eppie, shaken by what she had heard and then witnessed, hovered in the hall for a moment, uncertain as to what to do next.

There was silence from the other side of the library door, then someone spoke, low-voiced. It seemed to Eppie that the speaker was moving towards the door, so she hurried to the rear of the hall and had only just closed the door at the top of the kitchen stairs when she heard the library door open.

She rushed back to the kitchen and got there just in time to be busy with the range when Foy came in. To her surprise he was grinning broadly.

'How can you look so pleased with yourself after what I've just seen?' she asked, outraged.

He winked at her. 'I never thought tae see the day I'd get Alexander Geddes tae behave like a man instead of a mammy's boy!' he crowed, and then, suddenly suspicious: 'Here – were you listenin' outside that door? Did you hear what we were sayin'?'

'If I had been listenin', I know it would just have been about the quarry – what else would you two ever want tae talk about?' she said tartly, banging a pot down on the cast-iron range. 'Of course I wasn't listenin' – I'd just come up to speak to Marion when I heard the stramash from the library. I told her you'd fallen over a chair.'

'An' so I did, though it was him that knocked me against it. I'll away an' see if I can find Duncan,' he said, and went out, whistling to himself.

Eppie went to the sink to splash cold water on her face and wrists, shocked at the sins she had committed in the past hour. She had deliberately listened at the library door and then lied to Marion – and to Foy. The wonder of it was that they had both believed her. She was not entirely surprised about Marion, but she would not have expected to get away with lying to Foy. She must be good at it, she thought, concerned. It wasn't as if she had ever had the chance or the inclination to practise.

She had no sooner dried her face and hands than Alexander Geddes came down to the kitchen.

'Eppie—'

'Marion and the girls heard a noise from the library,' she cut in swiftly. 'I told them that Foy had fallen over a chair. I was on my way to speak to her about something—' another lie! '—when I heard the noise as I was passing the library door. I'm sorry I didn't stop to knock, but I thought you might have hurt yourself.'

'Oh.' He hesitated, then said, 'I must apologise for losing my temper as I did, Eppie. I can assure you that it will never happen again.'

'I know that, Mr Geddes.'

'D'you know where Duncan is?'

'He went out a while ago. He was – a bit upset. Foy's gone to look for him.'

'I see. Thank you, Eppie,' he said, and went back upstairs while Eppie, her mind whirling with what she had heard at the library door, got on with her work.

At last she knew why there was such enmity between Foy and her employer, and the reason why Alexander Geddes, normally the most self-controlled of men, had behaved so badly, attacking a guest under his own roof.

A shiver ran down her spine as she thought of what might have happened had she not burst in when she did. Her fear was not for Foy, but for her employer. If Foy had chosen to retaliate – or had been given time to retaliate – he might have injured Alexander Geddes seriously, or even killed him. The man's burly body and big, scarred hands singled him out as someone well used to facing up to foes.

She recalled him at her kitchen table, telling her that he had once earned his keep as a bare-knuckle fighter. A man who could thrive in such a barbaric world would be able to kill the likes of Alexander Geddes without even meaning to.

25

Neither Duncan nor Foy returned to the house for supper. Since Helen Geddes had moved to a home of her own, meals had become a time for conversation and the members of the household were encouraged to take turns to say grace. Foy viewed the custom with some amusement and when he was first invited to contribute he had said smoothly, 'Ach, I wouldnae know how tae start. The way I see it, I work hard for my ain food, so I'm no' minded tae thank anyone else for providin' it for me.' But this evening, though it was Marion's turn, Alexander Geddes asked briefly for a blessing before picking up his soup spoon.

'But Duncan's not here yet,' Lydia pointed out. 'And Foy usually eats with us too.'

'I see no reason why the rest of us should go hungry because of them,' her father said curtly. 'If they choose to come late to the table they'll still be fed.'

The rest of the meal was eaten in silence. Lydia and Charlotte, subdued and clearly aware that something was wrong, glanced at each other occasionally, but at nobody else. Geddes, at the head of the table, concentrated on his food and scarcely lifted his eyes beyond his plate, while Marion, as always, watched her two charges in order to catch and quash any lapses of etiquette.

When supper was finished Marion sent the girls out into the back garden to play before bedtime while she helped Eppie to clear the table and take the dishes back to the kitchen.

'What was going on earlier?' she asked as soon as they got there.

'What d'ye mean?'

'You know very well what I mean. In the library, when I was in the schoolroom with the girls.'

'I told you – Foy fell over a chair, clumsy creature that he is and took it and himself to the floor. I got a fright myself at the noise of it.'

'Eppie Watt, I could tell by the look on your face when you came out of the library that there was more to it than that.'

'I've told you all I know myself,' Eppie fibbed desperately. It was not her place to talk about her employer's private life.

'I still say there's more to it than that. Those two men can't bear the sight of each other and we don't know why. D'you think it's all to do with Duncan?' Marion wondered aloud. 'He's awful fond of Foy, and I could understand his father feeling as if his own nose is being put out of joint.'

'I thought you disapproved of gossiping,' Eppie reminded her, and it was Marion's turn to flush.

'I wasn't – I just wondered,' she said, and then, with a toss of her head, 'I'd best get back to the schoolroom. I've not set tomorrow's lessons yet.'

The kitchen was blessedly peaceful, though Eppie kept expecting Foy to come barging in through the back door as he so often did. She even hoped that he would – as long, she told herself, as he brought Duncan with him. There was enough food keeping warm on the range for both of them.

She looked around for the soup tureen, then realised that she must have left it on the sideboard in the dining room. She went back upstairs to fetch it and was passing the library door, which was ajar, when Alexander Geddes called from within, 'Is that you, Eppie?'

'Aye, Mr Geddes.'

He was sitting at his desk, papers spread before him and a half-filled glass and an empty decanter by his elbow. 'Would you bring another bottle of port up from the cellar?'

'Aye, sir.' Another journey, Eppie thought as she carried the tureen downstairs, then went to fetch the port. It was little wonder that once age began to creep up on her, Jean Gilbert had had to give up her work. In Jean's time Helen Geddes had been living in the house, and her continuous demands for attention must have kept poor Jean running up and down stairs all day.

Still intent on the papers before him, her employer waved a hand vaguely towards a corner of the desk when she took the port into the library. Putting the bottle down carefully to make sure that it did not cover any of the papers, she noticed that they looked very like the sketches Duncan had thrown down as he stormed out of the kitchen. Geddes was making swift notes on a clean sheet of paper.

'Is Duncan back yet?'

'No, sir.'

He grunted, then said, 'Thank you, Eppie, that will be all.'

As she turned to go her eyes went to the portrait hanging over the fireplace. Celia Geddes's green eyes seemed to be filled with life, and the slight but unmistakable curve of her full mouth hinted, as it always did to Eppie, of a smile about to illuminate her beautiful face.

It was no wonder that both Alexander Geddes and Foy had fallen in love with the woman, Eppie thought as she went back downstairs. The wonder, to her mind, was that Celia Ramsay, as she had been then, would ever have considered marrying an uncouth man like Foy.

But at the same time, she had to admit there was something about the man that caught her own interest. He was nothing like Murdo, and yet... She cleared the silly thoughts from her mind by making herself check the pantry shelves to find out if anything needed replenishing.

* * *

When the girls were in bed and the next day's lessons prepared, Marion came to the kitchen and took a cup of tea with Eppie before announcing that she was off to her bed. She was on her way towards the door when it opened and Alexander Geddes came in, dressed in his outdoor clothes.

'Miss McNaught.' He smiled down at her. 'I take it from the silence upstairs that the girls are both in their beds.'

'Yes, Mr Geddes. They've done well today and we've caught up with the lessons missed while I was in Aberdeen. I'm just off to my own bed.'

'Is Duncan not back yet, Eppie?'

'Not yet, sir, but I'm sure he won't be long.'

'I'm going out for some fresh air. No need for you to wait up.'

'I wonder if he might want a companion on his walk?' Marion said when he had gone. 'I should have asked him.'

'He might want to be on his own, and anyway, you told him that you were just off to your bed.'

'So I did. I wonder why I said that?' Marion said, vexed. 'Now

I'll have to do it – and I quite fancied a wee breath of fresh air myself.'

* * *

Rain was falling when Alexander Geddes stepped out of the house; a soft but persistent summer drizzle that seemed, from the state of the streets and pavements, to have been falling for some time. He turned up the collar of his coat and decided that Duncan was probably up at the quarry.

The sky was heavy with clouds and there was no starlight or moonlight to illuminate his way. Not that he needed any light, for he knew this place so well that he could even have found his way in dense fog – and had done so, on occasion. Duncan knew it well too, he recalled, staring out across the darkness that was the Moray Firth. The fishing fleet had set out some time earlier, and now they were well over the horizon, with not even a speck of light from the masthead lanterns of the few stragglers to be seen.

Duncan loved this place, and the quarry. He cared enough about the quarry to spend hours working on the well-drawn plans he had brought to the library that afternoon – and what had his father done? Dismissed them out of hand, and all because – Alexander found it hard to admit the truth to himself – of his intense dislike of Foy.

As he struggled up the hill he also admitted to himself that he should have seen Duncan's plans as an opportunity for father and son to work together; instead, he had only seen the plans as Foy's way of taking over the quarry that Alexander had come to look on as his sole property. One day, he now knew from what Foy had told him, it would be part of Duncan's inheritance, which was exactly what Alexander would have wanted for him.

And surely, as the future major shareholder, the lad had the right to think of the quarry's well-being?

He had arrived on the headland and was standing on the area that Duncan – and Foy, a small voice in his head added, before he ordered it to be silent – had earmarked for a workshop where the men could shape the blocks of marble under cover and with no worry about the tides that regularly covered most of the beach they worked on.

The great blocks of marble would be lifted from the quarry, not by manpower as happened now, but by a steam-driven crane, which would also power the machinery used to work on the marble blocks. A shed to house the steam engine would also be built up here.

It all made sense, Alexander admitted, and despised himself for having crushed Duncan's enthusiasm without stopping to think of his feelings. It was, he realised bitterly, the sort of thing his mother would have done.

'I thought I might find ye here. Ye shouldnae be staunin' sae near tae the edge.'

The harsh, flat voice left him in no doubt as to who was behind him. Geddes turned slowly, taking his time, moving his feet carefully but confidently on the wet grass only inches from the drop to the quarry below. Night had come on since he had left the house and now Foy was almost lost against a background of wasteland and lowering sky.

'Why should that worry you? D'you find the temptation to push me over the edge too much to bear?'

'Dinnae be daft, man, what wid I want tae dae a thing like that for? Anyway, I'm no' thinkin' o' you, but o' the folk that'd miss ye. Duncan for one, an' that bonny wee daughter o' yours, and the wee schoolteacher that can scarce take her eyes from ye.'

For a moment Alexander's attention was diverted. 'Miss

McNaught? You don't know what you're talking about!' he snapped.

'It seems that I ken more than you dae.' Foy's rusty chuckle rang out. 'Yer blind, man, tae the folk round ye – even yer ain son!'

'I doubt if Duncan would miss me much,' Alexander's bitterness returned. 'He managed to get through five years without me – but then, he had you instead.'

'Dinnae tell me yer still frettin' aboot that? You didnae see him, or hear him. There was scarce a day that you an' Lydia didnae get a mention from him, an' Duncan's no man enough yet tae be able tae veil his eyes. Oh, he missed ye – every bit as much, I'd say, as you missed him – but he left here because he wanted tae prove tae ye that he was his own man an' he could make his own way in the world. And what did ye dae when the time was ripe and he came back wi' the proof? Ye turned him doon without even givin' him the chance tae talk his ideas ower wi' ye.'

'*His* ideas?' Alexander deliberately put emphasis on the first word. 'No, Foy – you used him to get me to do what you want for this quarry.'

'For God's sake!' There was such a flare of sudden anger in the Glaswegian's voice that Alexander braced his body and clenched his fists, preparing for an attack. 'D'ye really think that those drawin's are mine? I'm a labourer, no' a planner. I dae the manual work, and mebbe I'm far travelled and I ken mair about quarries an' how tae get the best out o' them and out o' the men that work them than you'll ever pack intae that arrogant noddle o' yours, but how could I come up wi' the ideas that Duncan has? That takes scholarly learnin' and I never got any' o' that. But you did, an' mebbe it's time ye started tae make yer heid work for ye.'

'You're telling me that these plans are all Duncan's work?'

'One day he'll be able tae come up wi' ideas that are just as good as these, mebbe even better, but the lad's ower young yet for that. It was him and Edward Ramsay that worked it oot atween them, then wi' Edward's guidance, Duncan drew up the plans.'

'I thought...'

'Ye didnae think, ye jumped tae conclusions. You decided that I had Duncan in my pocket, did ye no'?' Foy said with disgust. 'You think I'm some sort o' puppet master that just pulls on the strings and makes the boy dance tae my tune. D'ye know somethin', Geddes? I'm staunin' here, in the rain and the dark, wonderin' why the hell this Lord God ye worship sae religiously every Sunday mornin', an' thank for every bite o' food ye put intae yer mooth, ever saw fit tae bless ye wi' a son like Duncan. Can ye no' unnerstaun' that he's his own man now, like you and me are? He doesnae belong tae me, or tae you for all that he's yer blood kin. He doesnae belong tae anyone. He's his own person, and if you cannae grasp that, an' grasp it soon, he'll be off again an' this time, ye'll no' see him back.'

His voice stopped and he turned his head to the side and spat his anger and exasperation out onto the grass. For a moment there was silence apart from the soft hiss of rain falling steadily, and the sound, far below, of the incoming tide rattling on the stony beach, each wave clutching at the stones with white foaming fingers as the sea dragged it back, then giving way to the next wave, which gained a little more ground before being pulled, in its turn, back to the firth's maternal bosom.

Then Foy said, 'Onywey, I just came lookin' for ye tae tell ye that the lad's back at yer hoose. He had his supper wi' me at the hoose where I'm bidin'.'

'He's come home?'

'Aye. It's where he belongs, is it no'? It aye the place he'll come back tae, if ye can find the sense tae speak tae him man tae man tomorrow aboot those plans o' his – and Edward Ramsay's. I'm no' sayin' ye should agree tae them just because o' what I've telt ye, but ye should at least hear the lad out, an' think o' what's best for the quarry. Guidnight tae ye,' said Foy, and began to walk down towards the town.

'Wait...' Geddes called after him. He started forwards and one foot landed awkwardly on a clump of wet grass and skidded back, throwing him off balance. He tried to swing his weight to the other foot, only to realise, too late, that it was nearer the edge than he had thought. Despite strenuous efforts, he lost his balance entirely, and cartwheeled clumsily over the edge.

Foy, hurrying downhill, heard a faint cry followed by another, the second more prolonged. He stopped short.

'Geddes?'

There was no reply. He hurried back to the spot, as closely as he could estimate in the darkening night, where he had left Alexander Geddes, calling the man's name. There was silence at first, and then his ears caught a faint sound that might have been the call of some nocturnal bird, or perhaps the scream of a rabbit startled by the sudden agonising snap of a fox's jaws.

He threw himself down on the grass and started squirming his body towards the edge of the cliff, fingers clawing at tussocks of grass and using them to drag himself along. Then there were no more tussocks, only space. He eased himself forwards slowly until his head was clear of the ground and surrounded by nothing but air. He drew in a deep breath and bellowed, 'Geddes!'

He thought, again, that he could hear a faint cry in answer. It could have come from the void that he knew, but could not see, below, or from somewhere out on the water.

'I'm comin'!' he bawled, and began to ease himself back over the solid ground. When he judged himself to be safe, he scrambled to his feet and ran, cursing as he went, towards the town.

* * *

Eppie was damping down the range for the night when the street door flew open and Foy lunged into the kitchen as though all the fiends of hell were after him. His clothes, face and hands were muddy, and he was labouring to draw breath into his lungs.

'Dear heavens, what's happened? Did ye get yersel' intae a fight? Sit down at the table, man, and let me have a look at ye.' She took his arm, the sleeve soaking wet, and tried to draw him towards the table, but he fought her off, still whooping and wheezing as he tried to get his breath. For a moment they wrestled in the middle of the kitchen before Foy found his voice.

'It's no' me that needs – help, it's Geddes...'

Her hands flew to her mouth and she stared at him over her fingers. 'What have ye done tae him?'

'He went... over the cliff at the... quarry. Where's Duncan?'

'Gone tae his bed.'

'Tell him what's... happened and fetch... him doon. I havenae got the breath yet... for those stairs!'

When Eppie burst in with the news Duncan, who had been reading, shot from the bed with one movement and was reaching for his clothes before she had finished talking.

'Tell Foy to wait in the kitchen for me. You rouse some of the quarrymen,' he ordered, and she fled, bumping into Marion who was standing in the hallway, a robe clutched about her shoulders.

Her face drained of colour when Eppie told her what had happened. 'I'm going with Duncan!'

'You're needed here,' Eppie said as Charlotte's frightened face peeped round Marion's arm and Lydia's bedroom door opened. 'Foy's in the kitchen waiting for Duncan. You don't know where any of the quarrymen live so I'll have to rouse them. Put a hot brick in Mr Geddes's bed and make sure there's plenty of hot water, for he'll be cold when we get him home. And see to the lassies,' she added as both girls began to babble questions.

Duncan overtook her when she was halfway down the stairs and arrived in the kitchen before her. When she got there he was questioning Foy, who had recovered his breath.

'You're certain you heard him?'

'I think so, though it could have been anythin'. I don't know my way down tae the quarry in the dark, but you do, lad.'

'So do the men who work there. Eppie, rouse as many as you can and tell them we'll need lanterns and ropes and mebbe canvas in case he's hurt himself and can't climb up. Foy and me are going to the harbour to find a boat.'

'A boat?' Foy yelped.

'Aye, a boat. The tide'll be comin' in now, and if he's hurt and he's gone all the way down,' Duncan said, his young face suddenly ageing as fear drew the skin taut over the bones beneath it, 'then he could drown before anyone manages to get down to him.'

'I don't know how tae work a boat!'

'But I do.' Duncan hauled the door open and hustled the other two out into the rain. 'Run, Eppie,' he ordered, and set off at a fast pace towards the harbour himself, hauling Foy along with him.

* * *

Eppie raced round the streets, heedless of the shawl slipping from her head and the rain soaking her hair so that it came loose and hung round her face in dripping strands. The first quarryman she roused said as soon as she had gasped her message, 'You go along that way, m'quine, an' I'll go the other way. Tell them tae bring ropes an' make for the top o' the quarry as quick as they can.' Already, he was hopping about as he struggled into the trousers he had brought to the door with him. In a fishing community a sudden violent knocking at the door in the night could mean only one thing – someone was in danger, usually on the seas, and so the menfolk kept their clothes near to hand when they retired.

When she had roused two more men one of them woke his two sons and sent them out to continue raising the alarm. 'You go on home, m'quine, and get yoursel' warm. We'll get him, never fear,' he said. 'We'll have him home afore ye know it.'

Home – but dead or alive? Eppie didn't voice the words, for nobody could tell her the answer as yet. She hurried off obediently, but instead of returning to the Geddes house she made for the headland. She might be needed at the quarry, she told herself as she ran, and in any case she couldn't face returning to the house, and to Marion's anxious questioning. If her employer were injured, she could at least tear up her petticoats and use the material as bandaging.

How could he not be injured? The quarry, small though it was, had had its share of injury and death over the years. She had seen it in daylight, with its terraces of jagged rocks that had been split open and made to give up the beautiful marble they had nursed over the eons, like infants in their wombs. No human could fall from the top of the quarry and hope to miss those sharp outcrops, as hard as iron and as merciless as the black heart of the devil himself.

She thought of Lydia and Duncan and Marion – how would Marion bear it if anything happened to the first man she had ever cared for? – and began to murmur prayers as she ran.

A group of men had already gathered on the headland; someone held Eppie back as she tried to thrust her way to the forefront. 'Na, m'quine, you stay back. There's one over the edge already,' he said, 'an' we dinnae want you tae go as weel.'

'Have they found him yet?'

'No' yet. Roddy Finlay's taken a lantern an' gone doon on the end o' a rope, looking for him. Roddy's all right,' the man told her, 'he's got a good head on his shoulders, and no fear o' heights. I've seen him dancin' his way along the cliff here tae amuse the rest o' us, and never once has the man slipped.'

'What about the doctor?' Eppie suddenly remembered. 'I never went tae his hoose...'

'He's been told. One o' the boats seemingly had tae come back in wi' a crewman who got hurt. The doctor's seein' tae him, and comin' here as quick as he...'

He stopped as a faint shout was heard from below. He, and the men in front of Eppie, pressed forwards, all falling silent to allow one of their number to be heard as he shouted through cupped hands to the man on the end of the rope. Eppie only just heard a second faint call, and then the group gave a collective groan that made her blood run cold.

'They've found him? Is he...?' She couldn't bring herself to say the word.

'Roddy's seen him, but the man's tumbled a' the way doon to the beach and the tide's comin' in. We'll have tae find a way tae get doon there quickly – an' that's no' easy.'

Rain ran into Eppie's eyes as she tilted her head back to look up into her companion's face, dimly lit by the lantern he held. Although she could not make out his expression she could tell by the tone of his voice that he, and no doubt the others, held out little hope for Alexander Geddes. 'They're sendin' down more ropes, and another two men,' he went on, passing the information to her as he received it, 'and they're makin' a canvas sling, but...'

'Duncan and Foy went to look for a boat. Duncan knew about the tide.'

'They might be our best chance,' the man said. And then, looking out towards the sea, 'Though God help them, for it'll no' be an easy task.'

26

Duncan had expected to have to do the rowing himself, but the skipper of the fishing boat that had been forced to return to harbour with an injured crewman was still on board. As soon as he grasped what was happening the man said, 'We'll take our wee boat and you and me, m'loon, can take an oar each.'

When they cleared the outer harbour the sea was suddenly choppy, and Duncan, who had not rowed a boat in years, was grateful for the help of the man who was with him. Foy crouched in the bows with a lantern and a coil of rope from the fishing boat.

'We'll have tae row out tae sea first,' the fisherman said, 'then we'll bear roond tae the quarry once we're clear o' the worst o' the rocks.'

His advice was sound; although it seemed to Duncan, desperate to find his father, that they wasted too much time rowing away from Portsoy. When the boat began to curve round towards land they had clear water, though as they neared the shore they began to meet submerged rocks. Occasionally, if the rock was below the surface and Foy didn't notice it, they brushed against it and then, as the fisherman coaxed the boat on, it gave out a grating sound that set Duncan's teeth on edge and convinced him that they were going to founder before reaching the quarry. He could hear Foy cursing non-stop, and agreed heartily with everything the man was saying.

His arms began to ache, and it was a relief when Foy shouted that they were almost at the quarry. 'Look – there's lights up on the headland! They've brought lanterns.'

Duncan blinked the rain from his eyes and stared into the darkness, eventually making out tiny glimmers, like a collection of fireflies dancing up in the sky.

They took the boat in, bumping against more rocks and sliding away from them noisily, until they could make out the sound of waves rattling through pebbles on the beach. Under orders from the fisherman they eased the boat between two rocks looming from the water and wedged the oars against them in a bid to keep the boat as still as possible.

The skipper had brought a loudhailer with him, and although the men on the headland only had the use of their cupped hands, the sea was quiet enough in the sheltered little bay for those below to make out the gist of their shouts, and to gather that Alexander Geddes had fallen all the way down to the beach and was lying motionless across a rock, half in and half out of the water. It was almost impossible for the men on land to get down to him, though they were doing their best.

'And the tide's still coming in – we've got to get him out before he drowns, or gets washed out to sea!' Duncan said urgently.

'An' we'll dae just that, m'loon,' the fisherman assured him calmly. Then, to Foy: 'Haud the lantern high, man, so's we can see – there he is, see? Lyin' across that rock.'

Duncan's heart, which had been racing after the strenuous

row from the harbour, almost stopped as he spotted the limp figure sprawled over a large rock and looking like a rag doll tossed away by a bad-tempered giant child. The incoming waves were washing over it.

'Can ye no' get ony closer?' Foy roared from the bows.

'No' unless ye want tae join him,' the fisherman responded. 'We'll rip the bottom from this boat if we try it.'

'Then I'll jist have tae go in an' get him. Take a haud o' that.' The Glaswegian handed the lantern to the fisherman before picking up the coil of rope. Swiftly, he found the end and knotted it securely around his waist, then located the other end and tied it to the thwart, tugging on it with all his might to make sure that it would hold.

'I'm coming with you.' Duncan began to rise, but even as Foy barked 'No!' the fisherman put a hand on his arm and pushed him back to his seat.

'We're both needed tae keep her steady. If we slip out frae between these rocks there's little chance o' gettin' the man on board.'

'Foy!'

'Do as yer told, lad. I'm stronger than you are an' I can manage on my lone,' Foy said, and then, to the fisherman: 'Mind an' keep the boat steady till we get back.'

'We'll do our best.'

'Ye'll have tae dae better than that,' Foy said, and then he was overboard and waist deep in water. The incoming waves helped him to move forwards, though once or twice Duncan caught his breath as he saw the man being thrown against the rocks scattered between him and the motionless figure several yards away. When the waves that had helped him to move forwards hurried back to the sea, they tried to draw him along with them, which meant that he was thrown against the same rocks for a second time.

'He'll never make it!'

'If he doesnae,' his companion said grimly, 'nob'dy else can.'

The rope Foy had tied to the thwart tightened as it ran out, pulling the boat further in between the rocks. Wood grated uneasily against pitiless stone as a wave larger than the others came rushing by, lashing the rocks and dashing cold spray over the two men.

Duncan peered ahead, afraid that the rope had not been long enough, then saw that Foy had reached his father.

With a strength that borrowed something from the desperation of the situation, the Glaswegian lifted Alexander Geddes clear of the rock and gripped him close, as though in a loving embrace.

'I'll try tae hold us steady,' the fisherman shouted above the noise of the waves. 'You take the rope and pull with a' yer might, m'loon. He'll never make it withoot help.'

He wedged his booted feet against Duncan's oar in an attempt to keep it steady against the rock as Duncan scrambled forwards, wrapped the rope around his arm and began to pull. Foy, he saw, was keeping his back to them in an attempt to protect his burden from the worst of the waves and the rocks.

Once the slack had come in and the rope was taut between the boat and the two men in the water Duncan felt as though he were trying to drag the headland itself towards the boat. It seemed as if he was doing no good at all, but when he was forced to pause for a second to catch his breath he saw that Foy was nearer than he had been before.

Hours, months and even years seemed to have passed before the man's hand reached out and gripped the boat. 'Now,' the fisherman shouted, hauling his oar in and lunging forwards, 'pull – it's the only way!'

Freed from the brake formed by the oars, the boat bucked, then dipped ominously at the bows as Duncan and the fisherman both went forwards. Water poured in, but Foy, with a final superhuman effort, took advantage of the dip to turn and half lift, half throw the man in his arms up and over the gunwale. Duncan tumbled backwards into the well of the boat as the dead weight that was his father landed on top of him; the bows dipped even further as the fisherman leaned precariously over the side and thrust an arm towards Foy. His own arm came up out of the water and the two men connected, hands grasping elbows.

The fisherman pulled with all the skill and strength developed from hauling in nets loaded with fish, and Foy's boots grazed Duncan's shins as he landed in the boat. For a moment the four of them were caught up in a wet tangle while the boat, taking advantage of a sea-going wave, backed away from the rocks where it had been wedged. It started to swing around, out of control, then the fisherman was grabbing at one of the oars and yelling at Duncan, 'Get tae yer oar, man! We need tae control the boat afore the rocks take us!'

Somehow, Duncan managed to struggle back to his seat and grasp the other oar. Between them the two men got the boat under control and turned towards the open sea while Foy, coughing and spitting seawater, pulled himself up into the bows, clutching Alexander Geddes around the waist to keep the unconscious man's head clear of the water swilling round in the bottom of the boat.

* * *

While the doctor tended Alexander Geddes upstairs, Eppie saw to Foy, now wrapped in blankets while his wet clothes steamed on the dryer before the kitchen range.

'It's no' ointments an' tea I need, wumman, it's whisky,' he grated at her through clenched teeth. He was shivering so hard that the chair he sat on rattled faintly against the stone floor.

'Try tae hold still, Foy – and what sort of daft name's that?' she snapped, a reaction to the events of the evening bringing on a sudden bout of irritation. 'Ye must have a Christian name – why don't ye use it like other folks do?'

'Mebbe I have, an' mebbe I havenae,' he shot back at her. 'If I dinnae choose tae use it, then that's my business.' Then, pushing her hands away as she tried to wash out a gash in his shoulder: 'For God's sake will ye fetch me a *drink*?' And then: 'Aboot time!' as Duncan came in with a bottle in one hand and a filled glass in the other.

Scorning the proffered glass, Foy seized the bottle and tipped it up to drink greedily.

'For goodness' sake!' Eppie said, scandalised, then as he gulped whisky down as though it were water: 'Duncan...!'

He grinned down at the quarryman. 'Leave him be, Eppie, he deserves the whole bottle – the whole cellar full – for what he did tonight. I'll have this.' And he drank deeply from the glass.

When Foy finally set the bottle down it was just over half full, but his eyes, which had been dull with exhaustion, were brighter and his voice, when he said, 'By God, I needed that!' was stronger. 'Any word o'the man upstairs, lad?'

'Not yet. But at least he's alive, thanks to you.'

'Ach, dinnae be daft,' Foy said, and took another swig from the bottle.

'What about the girls?' Eppie asked. Lydia had gone into hysterics when she saw her father's limp body being carried into the house, and Charlotte had been hard put not to join her, while tears had poured down Marion's ashen cheeks.

'In Lydia's room. She's calmed down and I said that Charlotte could stay with her tonight. She needs the company.'

'I'll go to them later – once I've seen tae you,' Eppie added to Foy.

'I'm fine!'

'Look at you...' She pulled at the blanket covering his upper body to reveal a muscular torso well decorated with dark bruises and abrasions. When he yelped and tried to gather the blanket back, she handed it to Duncan and went on scathingly, 'For goodness' sake, ye daft loon, d'ye think I've never seen a man before?'

'Ye've never seen this yin.'

'I doubt if you're any different from the rest. Sit still now.' The sea had washed any blood away, and she was glad to see that his injuries were all superficial. She dipped clean rags in a mixture of water and vinegar and ran them across the torn skin; he didn't say a word, or even draw in a sharp breath, but she could tell by the very slight tensing of muscles beneath her fingers that the treatment stung. His skin, surprisingly smooth to the touch, was still cold.

'There,' she said at last, taking the blanket back from Duncan and putting it gently about the man's shoulders. 'That'll dae ye, though you're goin' tae be stiff tomorrow, an' black an' blue for a whiley.'

'It'll no' be the first time, or the last,' he grunted, taking another deep drink from the bottle.

'And I don't know why we're botherin' tae dry your clothes,' she said, looking at the rags steaming on the wooden clothes horse, 'because they've been ripped tae shreds.'

'Nothin' that a good seamstress couldnae put right, surely.'

'If ye're thinkin' that I'll mend these for you, you're wrong. They're no' worth the trouble.'

'I cannae afford tae throw good clothin' away just like that!'

'I'll go to your lodgings and fetch dry clothes for you,' Duncan decided. 'And I'm sure my father'll be happy to buy all the new clothes you need to show his gratitude for what you did tonight.'

Foy screwed his face into a scowl. 'God save me from gratitude – I've no time for it.'

'Aye ye have, if it takes the form of some good new clothes,' Eppie said, and then stepped back, wafting one hand before her face. 'The smell of whisky from your breath's makin' me feel light-headed.'

'Me an' all, an' it's just what I need,' Foy told her with the first grin she had seen on his face since Duncan had helped him into the kitchen, staggering with fatigue, and with seawater pouring off him. 'On ye go, Duncan, an' fetch those dry clothes so's I can get back tae my lodgin's.'

'He'll go later, for you're staying here tonight,' Eppie said firmly. 'For one thing, you're needing a good sleep, and for another, you're so full of whisky that you'd probably fall into the harbour if you tried tae find your way home tonight. Ye don't want another wettin', dae ye?'

To her surprise, he didn't argue. 'I could do with some food in my belly,' he said. 'A' that seawater's left me famished!'

'Duncan, mebbe you could look in on the lassies again while I get food ready for the two of you.'

'I might get word of my father too,' Duncan was saying when the doctor came into the kitchen.

'He's gashed his head and sprained an ankle, and he's going to be bruised and sore for a few days,' he announced cheerfully, 'but the man's lucky, it could be a lot worse.'

'Can I see him?' Duncan asked at once.

'He's sleeping, but there's no reason why you shouldnae go up. Miss – McNaught, is it? – is sitting with him. Give him a bowl of soup when he wakens, and bland foods for the next twenty-four hours,' the doctor said to Eppie. 'What he needs more than anything else is to rest and be warm. We want to avoid a chill if we can. Now then...'

He advanced on Foy, who scowled at the man as he submitted to an examination of his cuts and bruises.

'Aye, you've been well looked after,' the doctor said, and then, glancing at the whisky bottle, which was almost empty, 'in every way.'

'Would you like a cup of tea?' Eppie asked.

He shook his white head. 'Don't trouble yourself, m'dear. But if you'd be so kind as to fetch another tumbler I'll have something from that bottle before I go off to my bed.'

An hour later the household finally began to settle down for the night. Duncan fetched a set of clothing for Foy and then retired to his room, and Eppie saw Foy settled in her room before putting the kitchen to rights and going upstairs. When she opened the door of Lydia's room she saw that the two girls were fast asleep, Charlotte's golden brown curls and Lydia's black curls mingling on the pillow.

Alexander Geddes had roused and taken the soup recommended by the doctor, then immediately fallen asleep again. A lamp burned in the room, shaded from the bed, but giving enough light to illuminate his face, and Marion, a blanket over her knees and a shawl about her shoulders, was sitting in a chair by his bedside.

'I'll have tae share your room tonight,' Eppie whispered. 'Foy's in mine, and I've let Charlotte sleep in Lydia's room tonight, for company.'

Marion nodded briefly without raising her eyes from the face on the pillow. 'On you go then. I'll stay here.'

'All night? Marion, you need your sleep, and the doctor says he's going to be fine.'

'Even so, I'll not leave him on his lone.' Marion glanced up briefly, and the lamplight made the tears in her eyes sparkle like precious gems. 'Just think, Eppie – he could have been killed!'

'But he wasn't killed. He's all right.'

'No thanks to that Foy!'

'Foy saved him! Duncan says that he might have drowned or been carried out to sea if the man hadn't gone into the water after him.'

'Mebbe so, but who put him there in the first place?' Marion's voice was hard and cold. 'From what I've heard there was nobody else but Foy there when Mr Geddes fell down into the quarry. And you know as well as I do that they detest each other. They must have been quarrelling, Eppie, and Foy pushed the poor man over!'

'That's nonsense,' Eppie began, her voice rising, and then, remembering that her employer might well hear them although he seemed to be asleep, she lowered her voice to a whisper. 'Foy wouldn't do that – and if he had, would he have risked his own life tae save the man?'

'He might, to cover up what he had done.'

'You're havering!'

'We'll see – when Mr Geddes wakens tomorrow. Oh, Eppie —' Marion's voice broke '—look at the man – he's so pale.'

'He'll be grand after a good night's sleep. Come to bed, Marion – we can leave the door open so you'll hear him if he calls out in the night.'

But her sister settled more firmly into the chair, gathering her warm shawl more closely about her shoulders. 'I'm not leaving him,' she insisted, and Eppie, bone-weary after all that had gone on, left her to her vigil.

* * *

She woke at her usual time in the morning to find that she was still alone. There wasn't a sound from the other bedrooms, and when she silently opened the door of Alexander Geddes's room and peered in, she saw that patient and nurse were both sound asleep.

Foy was sitting at the kitchen table, eating a sandwich made up of two thick slices of bread stuck together by what looked like a good half inch of butter topped with honey, and drinking a mug of strong black tea.

'About time,' he said, spraying crumbs. 'My stomach thinks my throat's been cut.'

'Since you're so good at helping yourself,' she said drily, looking at the massive sandwich clutched in his hands, 'you should just have gone on and fried half a dozen eggs and a side of bacon.'

'You're better at that than I am.' He got up to fetch another mug, moving stiffly. 'Ye'll have a cup o' tea while ye're workin'?'

'Aye, I will. How d'you feel this morning?'

'Ach, I'm fine.' He winced slightly as he turned from the dresser, mug in hand, then added as he caught her eye, 'It'll ease off once I get tae the quarry.'

'You're going to the quarry this morning?'

'Of course. The man upstairs isnae goin' tae be able to for a week or mebbe more, so Duncan an' me'll have tae see tae things for him – as far as the quarry's concerned, at any rate.'

'Foy,' Eppie said carefully as she stirred the oatmeal she had left soaking overnight, and added a generous handful of salt before putting it on the range, 'what happened last night?'

'Ye ken whit happened. Geddes lost his footin', an' fell frae the top o' the quarry intae the sea.'

'Before that – how did you know he'd gone over the edge? Were you there?'

'O' course I was. How else would I have known he'd fallen? I went up tae have a look at the place, and Geddes was a'ready there, so I telt him that Duncan was back home. I'd jist started back tae the village when I heard him call oot, an' when I turned, he was gone. Lucky I was there, else he'd have lain there until—'

He stopped suddenly, staring at her. 'Are you thinkin' that I might have pushed the man?'

'No, I just... there's no' much love between the two of you. Last night I came into the library and saw you...'

'Don't be daft, wumman,' he said. 'It was him that went for me then, no' the other way around.'

'He might have tried again, later.'

'Well he didnae, so ye can just put that sort o' nonsense out o' yer heid,' he said as Duncan came in, yawning and stretching, and ready for his breakfast.

27

Helen Geddes swept past Eppie as soon as the door was opened, demanding to see her son at once. 'Where is he?' Her tone was heavy with accusation, as though she suspected Eppie of hiding him from her.

'In his bedroom, and he's mebbe asleep. The doctor said to let him rest,' Eppie went on, hurrying up the stairs behind the woman, 'but he's had a good breakfast and he's not hurt bad.'

'I'll be the judge of that,' Helen snapped over her shoulder, then threw open the door of her son's bedroom. 'Alexander?'

If he had been asleep, he certainly would not be now, Eppie thought. But when she reached the door she saw that her employer was awake and propped up on several pillows. Marion, who had been standing by the bed, gave a slight bob of her head when Helen came in.

'Miss McNaught. What are you doing here?'

'Being of assistance to me. Good morning, Mother,' Geddes said as Marion stepped back, out of the woman's line of sight.

'Alexander, are you all right? What on earth has been going on?' Helen sat down by the bed and studied him closely. 'What a thing to have to hear from the servants! Why did you not send word to me at once?'

'I'd other things on my mind,' he told her drily. 'Eppie, could you bring some tea for Mrs Geddes?'

'Aye, sir, at once.' She closed the door thankfully and went back to her kitchen, shooing the girls in front of her as they appeared from the schoolroom. 'Away out to the garden and play.'

'Was that my grandmother I heard?'

'Aye, Lydia, she's come to see how your father is.'

'Are we not supposed to have lessons?' Charlotte asked. 'We've been waiting for Aunt Marion.'

'I think she's too busy looking after Mr Geddes to see to your lessons today. Out you go, now. I've got tea to make for Mrs Geddes.'

The girls fled, delighted at being allowed to miss a morning's work.

* * *

In the bedroom, Helen Geddes was saying, 'And what were you doing out on the headland at that time of night? Alone with that grim-faced Glasgow man too. I've seen him going about the town and I'd not trust him anywhere near my house. There's some folk saying that he attacked you.'

'That's nonsense!' He was still pale and drawn, but his voice was strong when he said angrily, 'It was entirely my own fault – I slipped on the wet grass and went over the edge. It's fortunate for me that Foy was there, for he raised the alarm and then went out in a boat with Duncan to get me.'

'What were the two of you doing there at that time of night?'

'Talking over Duncan's plans for the quarry – and if you hear any more nonsense about an attack, or a fight, I'd be grateful if you would put a stop to it at once.'

'It would never have happened if I'd still been living here. Perhaps I should move back in, at least until you're recovered. You look as though you have a slight fever.'

'The doctor has assured me that I have no fever, and there's no need for you to move in.'

'But you're my only son. I should be looking after you.'

'Eppie looks after Lydia and me very well. In any case, the house is full with Duncan back home. You'd not be comfortable.'

'I'm sure that Miss McNaught and her niece would be willing to return to Fordyce, given the circumstances.' She seemed to have forgotten that Marion was standing quietly in a corner.

'But I don't wish to see Miss McNaught and Charlotte return to Fordyce until they have to. Lydia needs her tuition if she is to go to school in September, and Miss McNaught has also been assisting me with my work.'

'Indeed?' Helen was saying as Eppie came in with a tray.

Helen stayed for some time, and when the bedroom door closed behind her back Alexander gave a long, weary sigh and felt his body relax into the mattress.

'Would you like some beef tea?' Marion came over to tidy the bedclothes. Her hand brushed against his for a moment; it felt deliciously cool.

He smiled at her gratefully. Throughout his mother's fussing he had been aware of the neat, still figure in the corner. 'Later, perhaps.'

She nodded. 'I think you should sleep now. You look tired.'

'My mother tends to have that effect on me. But there's more work that I should see to – letters...'

'After you've rested. There's plenty of time and I can help, later.' She settled his pillows into a more comfortable position and then drew the curtains against the morning sunlight. 'There, that's better.' And then, on her way to the door: 'Mr Geddes, Charlotte and I could return to Fordyce if you felt that you would like to have your mother near until you've regained your strength. Lydia's done very well this summer, and I'm quite sure that she's ready for school.'

'But Miss McNaught, I want you to stay,' he said, and she turned and gave him a dazzling smile that gave her normally serious face such unexpected beauty that it almost took his breath away.

For some time after she had left the room Alexander Geddes lay in his bed, his eyes closed and that radiant smile glowing on the inside of his lids. Earlier, when he told his mother that he did not wish Marion McNaught and her niece to leave his house until the agreed time, the words had been spoken automatically, but he now recalled Foy saying, as they faced each other on the headland above the quarry, *'the wee schoolteacher that can scarce take her eyes from ye,'* and his own instant denial. He ran the words over again in his mind. After a difficult start, Lydia now enjoyed Charlotte's company and he enjoyed Marion's. He liked to see her sitting at his table, neat and composed, keeping a watchful eye on the two girls, or working in his library, her smooth forehead taking on a puzzled little frown as she sought to grasp the sense of the paper she was studying – and then the sudden flash of satisfaction as the solution came to her. He liked to wake in the mornings and know that she was in the house.

He puzzled over this new and strange realisation for a few minutes and then, deciding that his mother could be right when she said that he had a slight fever, he put the matter from his mind and let sleep creep over him.

His last thought was that before the day was out, he would

summon Duncan to his room, and ask the lad to talk him through the plans he had drawn up for the quarry.

* * *

Marion leaned back against the bedroom door for a moment after she had closed it quietly behind her, the smile still lighting up her face. He wanted her to stay – he didn't want her to go!

Humming to herself, she almost danced down the stairs to the lower floor.

* * *

Alexander Geddes made a swift recovery but his ankle, badly twisted, kept him confined to his room for a few days. Marion ran between the library and his bedroom, fetching papers and books as he needed them and writing letters at his dictation while Charlotte and Lydia rejoiced in their new-found freedom and made full use of it.

Eppie was kept busy providing tea for the visitors who came and went – the doctor, business friends, and Helen Geddes, who visited her son daily.

The invalid found his limitations frustrating, and despite Marion's concern and his mother's protests, he was soon out and about with the aid of two strong walking sticks. He had made use of his enforced idleness to spend time with Duncan, and by the time his son was due to leave for Glasgow the two of them had come to know and understand each other, not as father and son, but as adults. Alexander had gone through the plans carefully, and with Marion's help had worked out the financial costs and possible benefits. Although he had not committed himself to an agreement, he was at least prepared to give the proposals long and serious thought.

* * *

Once Alexander Geddes was up and about again, Marion returned to her duties in the schoolroom and life for the household went back to normal. To Eppie's relief, Barbary seemed to be in better spirits and she began to take more of an interest in her appearance, and in her children and the cottage.

She was still fascinated by the pretty pink shell that her husband had given to her, and as often as not Eppie would find her friend sitting in her fireside chair or on the bench in the backyard, watching the children at play and rocking wee Jeemsie's cradle with one foot, with the shell on her lap or held to her ear while she listened intently, a slight smile on her lips.

'I've fairly let the hoosie go,' she said on one of Eppie's visits. 'Tolly would be angered at me if he could see it. Will ye help me tae set it tae rights properly for him?'

'If you want, though it looks fine tae me.'

'My Tolly's aye been particular.' Barbary bent to the cradle to chuck the baby under the chin. 'And I've sat around the place long enough. I want tae give it a good turnin' out.'

Charlotte volunteered her help, and so, to Eppie's surprise, did Lydia. The three of them advanced on the cottage one sunny morning and soon the place had been put to rights; the range was black-leaded, the steps at the front and back of the cottage scrubbed and whitened, curtains and bedding washed, the rugs beaten, pots and pans hung up in order of size and the few pieces of furniture polished with beeswax from the Geddes bees.

The pretty gold-edged plates that Tolly McGeoch had brought back for his wife from his annual fishing trips to

Lowestoft and Yarmouth were all washed and put back into the corner cupboard, and when Foy found out what was afoot he offered to paint the front and back doors and the window frames.

When it had all been done, Barbary looked around her home with a sigh of satisfaction. 'That's better! He's a nice man, that one with the strange way o' speakin'.'

'Foy? He's no' frightened o' hard work,' Eppie acknowledged.

Foy, for his part, was pleased to see Barbary start to take an interest in herself and her surroundings again.

'She's a bonny lass, an' too young tae mourn for the rest o' her life. She needs a man tae help her raise they bairns o' hers. Women wi' wee ones tae raise need menfolk aboot the place.'

'We don't always have a choice, and if we lose our menfolk we just have tae manage. Most of us do,' she said drily.

'Mebbe, but it's no' natural,' said Foy. Then, cocking his head to one side and surveying her thoughtfully, 'Would ye never conseeder a second marriage yersel'?'

'Mebbe – if the right man came along.'

'An' what sort o' man would that be?'

'For a start,' Eppie said, enjoying the slight flirtation, 'I'd have tae know his full name. I've no time for men with only the one name.'

'Weemen are the nosiest creatures on this earth, apart from cats.'

'Everyone's got a first name, even you.'

'I've heard tell,' Foy said, 'o' a tribe o' heathens that live in the jungles o' Africa. Awfu' superstitious they are, an' they believe that anyone who gets a hold o' their names gets a hold o' their minds, and if that happens, they cannae be independent any more. I've aye thought that they have the right way o' it.'

'Mebbe they've just got somethin' tae hide – like you.'

'Wumman, ye're like yer own rock cakes,' Foy said. 'Soft and tasty on the inside but awfu' crusty on the outside.'

* * *

Because of Alexander Geddes's accident Duncan and Foy had remained in Portsoy longer than originally planned. When the day of their departure finally arrived Lydia wept and clung to her brother, begging him to stay.

'I must go back to my duties,' he told her gently. 'But we'll write to each other, and I'll be back in the spring.'

'You didn't write to me last time, and you didn't come back for years and years!'

'It's different now. I promise,' he said, his eyes meeting Charlotte's over his sister's shoulder. He smiled and she smiled back, hoping that when he did return to Portsoy she would see him. The new school term was coming closer and soon, all too soon, she and her aunt would be going home to Fordyce. Although she was close to her grandparents, Charlotte had loved being able to see her mother whenever she wanted, and now looked upon Lydia as her best friend. She would miss them both dreadfully.

In the library, Alexander Geddes said to Foy, 'Duncan's to come back to Portsoy in the spring, to reach a decision about the machinery, and the sheds – you'll be returning with him?'

'If Mr Ramsay hasnae got some other work for me. But yer lad's learnin' fast and I've no doubt that he could deal wi' things on his lone.'

'You'll always be welcome in this house, Foy.' Geddes held a hand out to the other man. 'I'll not forget that you saved my life.'

'Och, that? I didnae dae it for you; ye could hae drowned for all that I cared,' Foy said gruffly, taking the proffered hand. 'I did it for Celia. Mebbe I still feel that she chose the wrong man, but

I have tae admit that she cared for ye, and I know that ye made her happy. That's why I had tae get ye off that rock afore the tide got ye.'

'I never thought it was just for me,' Alexander Geddes told him, straight-faced.

* * *

'I'll mebbe see ye next year,' Foy said in the kitchen, ten minutes later.

'I'll see that the pantry's well stocked then, since ye've eaten poor Mr Geddes out o' hoose an' home while ye were here.'

'If ye werenae such a good cook I might no' have eaten so much.' He picked up the canvas bag that held all his possessions and slung it over his shoulder. 'That's me away then.'

When he had gone and she got her kitchen back to herself again, it took a while to get used to the silence, and the peace.

And, at times, the sense of loneliness.

* * *

A few days after Duncan and Foy returned to Glasgow, Alexander Geddes called Eppie and Marion into the library to hear his offer to pay Charlotte's fees if Eppie agreed to let the girl stay on in Portsoy and accompany his daughter to the girls' school in Durn Street when the new term started.

'I know from what Marion says that she's an exceptionally clever lass, and if you agree, Eppie, it'll mean that she'll be near to you.'

At first Eppie was uncomfortable with the idea of her employer paying Charlotte's school fees, but to her surprise Marion was in favour of the idea.

'Charlotte's already getting a good education in Fordyce,' Eppie pointed out when the sisters had retired to the kitchen to discuss the offer.

'I know that, but she'll do just as well in this new school. And she'll be with you all the time,' said Marion, who was glowing inwardly. He had called her by her first name, and although neither he nor Eppie seemed to have noticed it, it was all that Marion could think of. Another reason for leaving Charlotte in Portsoy was that she would have more reason to visit the house once the new term started and she had to go back to Fordyce.

'What would Mother and Father say?'

'I think they'd want what Charlotte wants. We'll ask them – but first,' Marion advised, 'we should speak to Charlotte herself.'

Charlotte – and Lydia – were delighted, and as Annie and Peter McNaught had no objections, the matter was settled.

* * *

On the day Marion took both girls to Elgin to buy their school uniforms, Alexander Geddes – restless and unable for some unknown reason to concentrate on anything – returned home in the middle of the morning. He was standing in the hall, wondering what to do next, when Eppie appeared in the library doorway, a duster in one hand.

'It's yourself, Mr Geddes. Have you forgotten something? It's not your ankle bothering you again, is it?'

'No, it's fine.' His ankle was almost completely healed now, though he still walked with a slight limp. 'I just thought I'd get some paperwork done while the place is quiet,' he said vaguely.

'I'll be out of here in just a minute or two.'

'There's no hurry,' Alexander said, and wandered into the schoolroom. He looked around the place, at the books neatly stacked on the bookshelf, and at a tidy pile of papers on the desk that Marion McNaught used. A book lay on top of them; he picked it up and saw that it was a book on French grammar. When he opened it he was surrounded by the delicate scent of the eau de cologne she wore. It was almost as though she were standing beside him, the top of her head, with the dark brown hair drawn neatly into a small bun at the nape of her neck, reaching halfway between his elbow and shoulder.

'That's the library done now,' Eppie said from the doorway, and Geddes closed the book and put it down hurriedly, strangely guilty at being seen with it in his hands.

'Did your sister say when she and the lassies are expected back?'

'Sometime in the afternoon, I think. Will you be wanting something to eat at midday?'

'No – maybe – I'm not sure,' he said, and went to the library.

Eppie looked after him, puzzled. He was missing Duncan, she thought as she started to put the schoolroom to rights. It was understandable, given the long years the lad had been away from home. But this time was different, for Duncan would come back, again and again.

And perhaps Foy would come with him.

28

Eppie, on her way to Barbary's cottage, could sense a hint of autumn in the air already – a slight mellowness, as though Mother Nature were slowly, reluctantly drawing summer to a close. In two weeks' time Charlotte and Lydia would be at school, and Marion back in her usual classroom in Fordyce.

Once autumn had taken hold the local fishing boats would be scrubbed, overhauled, painted and made ready to follow the herring shoals on the long journey down the coast to Scarborough, Yarmouth and Lowestoft. The gutting crews would travel south by train and the few fishermen left in the town would put away their nets and turn to line fishing for haddock and codling.

'Nessie Jamieson came by yesterday tae ask me if I'd go on her crew for the Yarm'th fishin',' Barbary said when Eppie mentioned the coming English season.

'Are ye thinkin' o' it?'

Barbary smiled the slow, placid smile she had recently adopted. It was nothing like her former joyous smiles, but it was an improvement. At last, she was beginning to adapt to life without Tolly. 'Agnes said she'd move in here wi' the bairns

while I was gone, but I dinnae think so. I've things tae do here.'
Her hand strayed to the pink shell, always close by her.

'Mebbe next year, when wee Jeemsie's older.'

'Aye, mebbe next year. Things'll be more settled next year,'
Barbary agreed. She held the shell to her ear, her eyes half
closed as she listened to its voice murmuring to her. The baby
was tucked into the crook of her free arm, and after a moment
she put the shell to his tiny ear. 'D'ye hear, my bonny wee loon?'

Jeemsie, half asleep, opened the dark blue eyes that were just
like his father's, and gazed into Barbary's face. Then he smiled
up at her.

'He can hear it,' she said, satisfied, and put the shell back
down on the hearth.

There was something about the shell, and Barbary's fascination with it, that made Eppie uneasy, but it seemed to bring
comfort to her friend, and so she said nothing, other than to
Marion.

'If it gives her comfort, then I see no harm in it,' her sister
said.

'It does, but it's almost as if she can't do without it. It's never
far from her hand, and she keeps getting the bairns tae listen
tae it.'

'Children like that sort of thing. Stop fussing about the
woman, Eppie,' Marion said irritably. 'She's old enough to do as
she pleases, surely.'

Marion had more important things on her mind than
whether or not Barbary McGeoch was putting her ear to shells
too frequently. It was almost time for her to return to Fordyce,
and the thought of having to leave Alexander Geddes was
almost more than she could bear.

She had tried reasoning with herself and she had tried
speaking to herself sharply, but it was no use. Common sense,

her greatest ally and comfort since childhood, had deserted her at first sight of the man, and there was little she could do about it other than feel utter misery at the prospect of having to return to the home and the career that, until he came into her life, had been all that she wanted.

Dripping silent tears into her pillow at night, terrified in case she wakened Charlotte, she began to realise why Eppie had turned down the idea of becoming a teacher in order to marry the man she loved.

Over the summer Marion had worked hard to win Helen Geddes's approval, and she had succeeded – but what was the point of that, she asked herself miserably, if she could not find some way of making Helen's son fall in love with her? Eppie was probably right when she said that the man was still enraptured by Lydia's mother, and that for him, there would never be another woman.

Once or twice since their conversation in the Aberdeen hotel, Marion had fancied that he looked at her with a new interest; once or twice she believed that she'd detected a warmth in her voice and in his eyes – but she knew that it was all in her overactive imagination. He saw her as nothing more than his daughter's governess and, from time to time, a useful assistant in his own work. Soon she would leave his house and he would forget all about her.

These thoughts were running through her head while she sat at the desk in the library, writing a report as he dictated it to her. He paused to consult a document and as she waited, Marion found her gaze lifting, as it always did, against her own will, to the portrait above the fireplace. Celia Geddes smiled down on her kindly, graciously, secure in the knowledge that a Plain Jane such as Marion McNaught could never take her place in Alexander's heart.

Working with him in the library had at first been a joy and, she thought, a step forward; but because of that portrait it had turned into a torment. A lump came into Marion's throat and when she swallowed hard to dislodge it, it immediately turned into tears pressing against the backs of her eyes. Before she could blink them away they were trembling on the edge of her lower lids. She was so busy trying to banish them that when Alexander Geddes started dictating again she didn't hear him.

He was pacing the room as he spoke, and it wasn't until he had delivered another two sentences that he reached the window, turned to pace back towards the desk, and noticed that she was not writing.

'Miss McNaught? Miss McNaught,' he said again as she paid no heed. 'Is something wrong? Do you feel unwell?'

She raised her head and the light from the window caught her tears, still poised to fall, and made them sparkle.

'Miss McNaught?' he said again, alarmed. She made no reply, but simply stared at him, her neat little mouth trembling. One tear slowly spilled from each blue eye to course down her pale cheeks, and as he watched, something inside Alexander Geddes seemed to break open, releasing a surge of emotions that he had not known for a long time – not for all the years of his daughter's life.

'Miss McNaught…' he said yet again, and then, since it seemed much more natural and right: 'Marion…'

* * *

How it had happened, Alexander Geddes was uncertain; all he knew was that it had, and he was very happy about it. He had never thought, in the long lonely years after his beloved Celia's death, that he would ever find another woman to take her place, and yet here he was, on his way to his mother's house to announce his forthcoming marriage.

As he walked up the path towards the front door a sudden, familiar sense of panic began to cloud his vision. He swallowed hard – and then a gloved hand brushed against his palm, and as his own fingers automatically curled around it, he knew that he *could* face his mother; could face anyone and anything, with her by his side – Miss McNaught, now Marion, and soon, as soon as possible, the third and final Mrs Alexander Geddes.

He smiled down at her as they reached the doorstep, and seized the door knocker, banging it hard against its polished plate. 'Good morning, Maisie,' he said cheerfully to the maid, 'I trust that my mother is at home?'

'Yes, sir, but she's expectin' some of her friends to call in half an hour's time.'

'Our business won't take as long as that,' Alexander assured her. 'We'll announce ourselves – and don't bother with tea.'

Helen Geddes was at her usual early-morning task of checking every surface in her parlour for dust and shifting ornaments very slightly to prove to herself that the maid had not put them back where they should be.

'Alexander, this is unexpected.' Her eyes went from him to Marion by his side. 'Maisie should have announced you.'

'I'm your son – I...' he had been going to say, *'I paid for this house,'* then amended the sentence to: 'Surely I don't need to be announced.'

'Perhaps not – but on the other hand, you haven't come alone.' She tipped her head, bird-like, to receive his dutiful kiss. Once it had been delivered she went on, 'I take it that as Miss McNaught is with you, you've called on a matter concerning Lydia.'

'It has nothing to do with Lydia. She's in the best of health and looking forward to starting school next week. Sit down, Mother. I have news for you.'

'I can't think of any news that requires the presence of Lydia's governess,' Helen said, and then, as her son said nothing, but stood smiling at her, she moved to her usual chair and folded her hands in her lap. 'Very well, give me your news. I am expecting friends to call.'

'So Maisie told us.' Alexander ushered Marion to the sofa and seated himself beside her. 'We won't keep you long. I just wanted you to know that I am soon to be married – to Marion.' He took Marion's hand in his.

Helen sat absolutely still, her face suddenly as hard and as cold as marble hewed from the quarry.

'Married?' she said at last, in a harsh croak. 'To Miss McNaught?' And then, beginning to recover her voice: 'Don't be ridiculous, Alexander, you can't possibly marry this woman.'

'I can, Mother, and I will.'

'But you'll be the laughing stock of the village!'

'I doubt it, but if they want to laugh, let them, I say.' Alexander Geddes had not known such a sense of freedom, well-being and sheer joy in years. His entire body tingled with vitality; he felt intoxicated although he had not had a drop to drink.

'Think what the shame will do to your children!'

'Lydia and Duncan both like Marion very much. I believe that they will both be delighted to accept her as their new stepmother.'

Helen stared at her son, at a loss for words. He had changed, and in a way that made her uneasy. He was more confident than ever before, and younger, and – she sought for the word – defiant. It was almost as though he cared nothing for her opinion.

'I forbid it,' she said at last, and even to her own ears, the words sounded feeble. 'Alexander, I will not allow this marriage to go ahead!'

To her horror, he laughed. 'My dear mother, I'm far too old to be forbidden to do anything I choose to do. Marion's father is a schoolteacher, highly regarded in Fordyce, as is Marion herself. Her brain—' he turned to smile fondly at her '—is as sharp and as fine as any man's, and I intend to make her my wife as soon as it can be arranged. We wanted to tell you before we tell anyone else, including Lydia, but we are not looking for your blessing.'

'Although,' Marion spoke for the first time, 'we would like to have it. I would like to have it. Mrs Geddes...' she rose from the sofa and moved to a chair close to Helen's '...I think highly of you, and I have enjoyed our talks together in the past. I would dearly like to know that our decision to marry will have your blessing. It would,' she went on smoothly, her pale blue eyes holding Helen's sapphire glare without flinching, 'be so much easier for all of us if we were to face the world as a united family instead of allowing the people of Portsoy to see us at logger-heads. I know that you dislike malicious gossip as much as I do. We are alike in that – and in caring deeply for Alexander. We both want him to be happy, do we not?'

She had lain awake the night before, rehearsing her speech. While her mouth formed the words, her gaze delivered its own message, from one woman to another.

All at once Helen Geddes realised that she had finally met her match. Alexander's first wife had been her personal choice, and hers to mould in her own image; his second wife, aware that she would not have been Helen's choice of daughter-in-law, had been anxious to placate and please. But this one had somehow, without Helen noticing what was happening, taken over Alexander's heart and she obviously fully intended to keep it. This one would not be denied, and any attempt to fight her would alert the village gossips, many of them Helen's own friends. Alexander and his future wife might not care about being laughing stocks, but Helen did, and Marion McNaught knew it.

'We would indeed like your blessing, Mother, if you could find it in your heart to be pleased for us,' Alexander added, rising to put a hand – a possessive, husbandly hand – on Marion's shoulder. She turned slightly to smile up at him, and then turned back to Helen. Again, their eyes locked, while Alexander, totally unaware of the brief, silent war that had just been waged in front of him, waited without great concern for his mother's answer.

Helen suddenly felt old and feeble. She had finally met her match and the time had come to hand over the reins to a younger and much more able woman. She had no option but to force her lips into a semblance of a smile and give her blessing.

* * *

'But you can't marry Mr Geddes!' Eppie said, horrified.

'What's to stop us? I'm a spinster and he's a widower.'

'But he's my employer! And yours!'

'Mine only for another week until the school year starts. As for your position,' Marion said, 'there's no reason why that can't continue, at least for the time being. If you're unhappy about it then I shall find someone else, for I don't know much about running a house. In any case, I'll be assisting Alexander with his business interests. I've discovered that I enjoy that sort of thing.'

'Mrs Geddes won't allow it,' Eppie insisted, and Marion gave her a sweet smile.

'On the contrary, we've just come back from visiting her, and she's given us her blessing. It'll be all over the place in no time, since she was preparing to entertain some of her gossipy old friends. We're about to tell Lydia, and then we're off to Fordyce to tell Mother and Father.'

'You're really going to marry him?'

'I'm really, truly, going to marry Alexander Geddes and oh, Eppie, I'm so happy!' Marion's voice started to shake as tears sprang to her eyes. 'I had never once considered marriage, and yet the moment I set eyes on him I knew that without him my life could not be complete. I can't thank you enough – if it hadn't been for you we might never have met each other.'

She swooped across the kitchen and caught Eppie up in a tight hug. 'I promise you that I intend to live until I reach a hundred, at least, and I mean to make him happy, every single day that we spend together!'

* * *

Lydia greeted the news with shrieks of joy and immediately demanded a new dress for the wedding. 'Just think,' she said to Charlotte as the two of them got ready to travel to Fordyce with her father and her future stepmother to break the news, 'this means that we'll be sisters.'

'Sort of sisters, since I'm Aunt Marion's niece. And now,' Charlotte said, awed by the thought, 'your father will become my Uncle Alexander!'

'Sisters,' Lydia insisted firmly. 'We both need a sister. Have we got time to go and tell the bees before the carriage arrives?'

29

Winter was settling in. The sea, cold and grey, raged against the harbour wall, while the chilly, damp air kept most of the towns-folk indoors, only venturing out when they had to.

With most of the boats down in England, the harbour was almost completely empty. The entire town felt lonely, Eppie thought as she hurried to Barbary's house, a filled basket over her arm. It would not waken until the day when the first sighting of a cluster of red sails on the horizon hailed the return of the Portsoy fleet. On that day, and on every day thereafter until all the boats and their crews were home, the town would suddenly come alive, whatever the weather. Doors would be thrown open and men, women and children would flock down to the harbour to welcome the fishermen home. Every seaman's kist – the wooden trunk that held all their possessions – and every fisher lassie's box would be crammed with gifts brought from the south, some to be given out on arrival, some to be kept for the New Year celebrations.

The entire town would be in festive mood; even those, like Eppie, whose men would never return, joined in the pleasure of those fortunate families who were complete again now that their menfolk – and the women who had gone with them to gut and pack the herring – were home again, where they belonged.

But for Barbary, still in the first year of widowhood, it would be a difficult time. Eppie recalled her own secret pain, carefully hidden behind bright smiles, the first time she had watched her neighbours greet their men when the boats came home. But with each year that passed, as Barbary would have to find out for herself, the pain eased, little by little. Nearing the cottage, Eppie resolved to make a point of spending as much time as possible with her friend when the fishing fleet started to return.

She could afford to give Barbary more of her time now that Charlotte and Lydia were both at school. Charlotte, used to being in a classroom, loved her new school and was doing well, but it had been difficult for Lydia at first; moving from a small schoolroom within her own home to a classroom shared with more than twenty other girls.

She had reacted by retreating to her old ways and becoming irritable and arrogant, but forewarned by Marion, Eppie had managed to coax her out of her black moods and there was no doubt at all that having Charlotte in the classroom with her, the only person she knew and trusted, had helped the girl settle in, albeit reluctantly. With time, Marion assured Alexander and Eppie, Lydia would even begin to like school.

Marion herself, busy with her own work and with preparations for her wedding in the spring, visited Portsoy as often as she could – in order to keep an eye on Charlotte, she said, although Eppie was convinced that Alexander Geddes was the real reason. The two of them were like a pair of young lovers, glowing at the very sight of each other.

Once she came to accept the fact that it was impossible to stop the marriage, Helen Geddes decided to behave as though she had been the one to choose Marion as her third daughter-in-law. Marion and Alexander, caught up in the wonder of finding each other, were happy to let her have her pretences. A truce of sorts had been established.

On reaching Barbary's cottage Eppie bustled through the door, glad to get out of the cutting wind, and into the warmth. The fire burned brightly in the range, and the place was spotless. George, Martha and Thomas, playing contentedly on the rug before the fire, looked up and beamed at Eppie.

'Where's your mammy?'

'Gone out. I'm lookin' after the bairns,' said George importantly. He already considered himself as the man of his family.

'Gone tae the shops?' It wasn't like Barbary to leave her children on their own, but perhaps she was only going to be away for a few minutes. Martha had recently recovered from a bad chest cold, and Barbary had probably decided against taking the child out on a cold day.

'Not tae the shops,' George said. He beamed at Eppie, a wide, delighted grin. 'She's gone tae fetch my daddy.'

'What?' Eppie wasn't sure that she had heard right.

'Gone tae get my daddy. That's what she said. If we're very good and don't touch anythin' while she's away, Daddy'll come home with her.'

'Daddy,' Martha confirmed, her smile as wide and as happy as George's, while Thomas, scrambling to his feet and toddling over to Eppie, his fat little arms held up to her, echoed, 'Dadda!'

She put down her basket and lifted the toddler, using his solid, warm little body as an anchor. A chill began to steal over her. She suddenly noticed that the three children, like the room itself, were spotlessly clean, and that they were all dressed in their best clothes, instead of the smocks they usually wore.

'How did she know that your daddy was coming home?' She

tried to speak naturally, though to her own ears her voice sounded far away and as though it belonged to someone else.

'He telt her,' George explained, 'in the shell. He spoke tae her and he telt her he wanted to come back hame. So she's gone tae fetch him.'

'She's pretty,' Martha added. 'A pretty dress, and a pretty shawl, and red flowers in her hair.'

Eppie's gaze flew to the window where Barbary always kept a bunch of bright-red paper poppies. Barbary loved the big splashy flowers and sometimes, to amuse herself and the children, she would wind them through her thick black hair. Tolly, Eppie recalled with mounting horror, loved to see his wife wearing poppies in her hair. Now, the jug was empty of flowers.

'He told her in the shell,' George had said. The pink shell too, was gone from its usual place on the hearth. Then Eppie realised that the shell and the flowers were not the only things missing. The crib was empty, the blankets pulled back carelessly, the pillow still bearing the imprint of a small round head.

'Jeemsie – where's wee Jeemsie?'

'He was cryin', so Mammy took him with her,' George said placidly, intent on the wooden train he was running over the rug.

The children were confused, Eppie tried to convince herself. They had got mixed up. Barbary had had to go to the shops, and because the baby was crying she had taken him with her. They would be back at any minute. But she knew that Barbary would not have put on her best clothes and woven red poppies through her hair just to go to the shops. Something terrible had happened, or was going to happen, to her and her baby.

Swallowing back the terror that threatened to engulf her, she put Thomas back down on the rug.

'You two look after Thomas while I go to fetch Mammy and Jeemsie,' she said.

'An' Daddy,' Martha said, smiling her father's sweet smile.

'I'll not be a minute,' Eppie assured them, and almost fled from the house. She didn't know what to do or where to go; she only knew that she needed to fetch help. Remembering that Alexander Geddes had been going to the salmon bothy that afternoon she was on the point of turning towards the harbour when her name was called.

Spinning round, praying that the call had come from Barbary hurrying home with a parcel in one hand and wee Jeemsie snugly wrapped in her shawl, she saw Jeemsie's wet nurse coming along the footpath. To Eppie's relief, Jeemsie himself was in the woman's arms.

'Barbary handed the bairn in tae me a while back,' the woman said, puzzled, when they met. 'He was girnin' and she said he was hungry, but he's scarce taken a suck. He jist wanted a wee bit o' a cuddle – did ye no', my wee loon?' she added to the baby, who was busy chewing at his fingers.

'Did Barbary say where she was going?'

'No' a word, but she was a' dressed up and lookin' excited, as if she was expectin' visitors.'

'D'ye think ye could stay with the bairns for a wee whiley?' Eppie begged. 'I have tae find her.'

'Aye, I can stay for a bit. Ye dinnae think somethin's wrong, dae ye?'

'I dinnae ken, but I don't want the bairns tae worry. I'll try tae find her,' Eppie said, and ran.

The salmon bothy was a three-storey building on the opposite side of the harbour from the marble quarry, in the old part of Portsoy known as Seatown. Portsoy salmon were caught by means of large open-mouthed nets set on poles to catch the fish as the incoming tides brought them to the shore. Once caught, they were washed, then weighed and packed in ice at the bothy before being taken to Aberdeen, and from there to be sold in Edinburgh and London. Salmon fishing was one of the local businesses that Alexander Geddes was involved in.

As Eppie turned into the harbour she caught sight of a splash of colour on the grey, rain-washed stones. She knew what it was before she reached it – a scarlet poppy made from paper.

Alexander Geddes was standing outside the bothy talking to another man when she got there. As soon as they caught sight of her, running, and with her shawl blown half off one shoulder, both men immediately came to meet her. 'What's amiss?'

'It's my friend Barbary, Mr Geddes.' Eppie paused to suck air into her labouring lungs. 'She's left her bairns alone, dressed in their best, and she told them that she's gone to fetch Tolly – her man that went down with the *Grace-Ellen*,' she explained urgently. 'She says he told her that he's coming back home from the sea. She gone to meet him.'

It sounded far-fetched, but both men had lived by the sea all their lives, and they knew all about the terrible things that loss and grief could do to folk.

'Is there somewhere she used to go to watch for his boat coming in?' Geddes asked swiftly.

'Up there...' Eppie pointed across the harbour to the head-land opposite. 'At The Breeks – there's a path down tae a ledge where ye can see the boats comin' over the horizon.' She pulled her shawl off and tied it about her head and shoulders, knotting the ends to make sure they could not come loose.

'I'll go there now – you gather some of the men together and send them after us,' Geddes told his companion. 'Send some of them along the shore.' He glanced out to sea. 'The tide's ebbing, so they should be able to get along below the headland. You go back to the children, Eppie.'

'Someone's with them. I'll come wi' you – Barbary knows me.'

He didn't waste time arguing with her, but set off, with Eppie, having had a moment to gain her breath, puffing after him.

As they climbed to the top of the headland they became more exposed to the wind, which seized on its new playthings with delight, buffeting them with increasing violence. Eppie gripped her shawl but the wind made several bids for Geddes's tall hat. He pulled it down over his ears as firmly as he could, but it was lifted up and carried away.

He caught her arm and dragged her along with him, his support helping her to stay upright when her feet stumbled over loose stones or clumps of grass. At last they were above The Breeks, a double-pinnacled rock formation that looked like a pair of trousers, upside down and sticking out of the water.

'There's the path,' Eppie gasped, 'the one that leads down to the ledge. And look...' She pulled away from him and went towards the edge of the headland.

'Eppie!' he thundered at her as she stooped and turned to him, holding out a limp, sodden paper poppy. He caught hold of her wrist again, pulling her back towards safety.

'I thought you were going over there!'

'It's one of the poppies the bairns said she put in her hair before she went out. She's down there, watchin' for Tolly, or mebbe she's hurt an' needin' help!'

'If she's there at all the men going along the shore will see her. If we try to go down in this wind we'll be plucked off and sent down onto the rocks. We'd be no help to her if that happened.'

The wind whipped his dark hair around his face as he

turned and looked down the way they had come; following his gaze, Eppie saw two men below, on their way up.

'Wait here and don't move.' Cautiously, Geddes moved towards the edge. As he neared it, he knelt down and then lay almost flat on the wet grass before starting to worm his way towards the edge. She watched, her heart in her mouth, as he looked down, then he began to wriggle backwards to safety.

The men who had been on their way up arrived in time to help him to his feet. 'I can see the men coming along the shore; they're almost below us now,' he said, the wind snatching the words from his mouth and hurling them out to sea. 'There's nobody on the ledge, but I think I saw something – a wee splash of scarlet. A neckerchief, mebbe.'

'A poppy,' Eppie said dully. 'A paper poppy.'

And as she said the last word they heard a hoarse cry from the men down below...

* * *

It was said, among the fishermen, that what the sea wanted, it took, and what it took should not be claimed back. Many of them, should they happen to find a body among the thrashing, glittering herring their nets brought up, returned it to the deep with a swift prayer rather than anger the sea by taking it ashore.

The sea had not wanted Barbary McGeoch, and so as the tide went out it abandoned her after first tucking her body behind a small rocky outcrop where a dip in the shingle formed a natural open-ended pool. When the men on the shore found her she was floating placidly and easily just below the surface of the salt water. It was the bright glow of the few poppies still entangled in her long black hair that led them to her.

* * *

Alexander Geddes paid for the funeral, and when Barbary had been laid to rest, old Agnes McBrayne and her daughter, with help from Eppie and wee Jeemsie's wet nurse, took it in turns to look after the bewildered children.

Although most folk in the community had large families, Barbary had been the only child of parents in their early forties when she was born, while none of Tolly's four siblings had survived beyond their first few years. Both sets of parents were dead, and the only living relative who could be found was an elderly aunt of Tolly's who lived on her own in Buckhaven, further along the firth.

Alexander wrote to her, and received a scrawled reply informing him that Mrs Macready would visit Portsoy on the following Wednesday afternoon to see the children.

Eppie and Agnes were both there when the woman arrived. She was grey-haired, grey-faced and angular, and she inspected the children, all dressed in their best, closely, as she sipped at her cup of tea.

'I'm a widow woman,' she said in a voice that sounded rusty and in need of oiling, 'and I didnae even ken Bartholomew, for his faither an' me never got on, even as bairns. I havenae set eyes on the loon since he was a bairn,' she continued as Eppie and Agnes, after a puzzled glance at each other, came to realise at the same time that by 'Bartholomew' she meant Tolly. 'I live in two rooms and I'm no' wealthy.'

'There's the compensation money in the bank,' Eppie offered. 'Mr Geddes saw to it that the families of all the crew members on Tolly's – Bartholomew's – boat got compensation after the accident.'

'That wid help,' the woman conceded and then, when she

had finished her tea and taken a second cup, she said, 'I'll take the two eldest, for they're of an age tae be useful about the house. But I cannae be doin' wi' the wee ones. I dinnae like children and I thank the good Lord that me an' my man were never burdened wi' any.'

Eppie looked at the children. Jeemsie, rosy from sleep, was propped on cushions in his cot, chewing at a mutton bone to ease the teething pains in his gums, while the other three, unusually subdued, were watching the adults' faces closely. Young though they were, they seemed to sense that their futures were under discussion, and they were trying hard to follow the conversation passing to and fro above their innocent little heads. She glanced across the room at Agnes and saw her own horror mirrored in the older woman's face.

'They're a family,' she said. 'They've lost their father, and now their mother, and they've only got each other. They have tae stay together.'

'The only thing they need,' said the woman, 'is tae be fed an' housed an' clothed, an' I can dae that for the two eldest. I'll dae my Christian duty by them, ye need have no worries aboot that. The other two are comely enough – mebbe local folk'll be willin' tae take them in. Or there's an orphanage in Aberdeen. Now...' she dusted down her skirt and rose to her feet '...I have tae be on my way. If ye'll gather up the older ones' clothes I'll take them wi' me. As for the money set aside for them, mebbe Mr Geddes that wrote tae me about Bartholomew and his wife'll send it on tae me.'

George took one step back, and then another, bringing him up against Eppie's thigh. He grabbed a handful of her skirt and twisted it tightly in his fist, looking up at her with his brow wrinkled and his dark eyes apprehensive. She smiled down at him and he immediately beamed back at her, the wonder and unease replaced by utter trust.

'No,' she said. 'No. The children are going to stay together. Mr Geddes owns this cottage and he has already said that it can continue to be their home. We thought that you might like to come and live here, with them.'

'Me? Live in Portsoy?' The woman looked almost affronted. 'I'm Buckhaven born and bred. I'd no' be content anywhere else.'

'The bairns are Portsoy born and bred,' Agnes pointed out in her gentle voice. 'They've got friends here and Geordie's doin' well at the school. They dinnae ken anywhere else.'

'Bairns can get used tae anywhere,' Mrs Macready said scathingly. 'Their brains arenae right grown yet – they havenae got the sense tae ken where they are and they're too young as yet tae get attached tae any place.'

'They're staying here,' Eppie said firmly.

'An' who's tae look after them? I'm the only blood kin they've got an' I'm no' goin' tae bide here, money or no money.'

'They don't need blood kin, just folk that care for them,' Agnes told her, and Eppie added, 'We'll manage. We'll think of something.'

'And now,' Agnes said when the woman had gone and the children, aware that they were freed from some threat but not knowing just what it had been, were playing happily, 'we'll have tae think o' somethin'. They're grand wee bairns, Eppie, but my rheumatism's no' gettin' any better and wi' the winter comin' on it'll be all I can manage tae help my own daughter wi' her wee ones.'

'I know that. Don't fret yourself, Agnes,' Eppie said, her mind already made up. 'I'm going tae move in here as soon as Mr Geddes finds another housekeeper. I'm goin' tae take Barbary's place.'

'Are you sure about this?' Alexander Geddes asked.

'I'm certain. It'll be a lot easier to find a new housekeeper for you than someone to look after those bairns. And after missing out on years of my own daughter's growing, I'll enjoy being with Barbary's bairns.'

'I'll find another housekeeper, Alexander, since it's my responsibility now,' Marion said. It was the day after George and Martha had been saved from an unhappy life in Buckhaven with Mrs Macready. 'You'll want to move into the cottage as soon as you can, Eppie?'

Eppie smiled gratefully at her sister. 'I do.'

'Then I'll start looking for a suitable woman at once. Since Eppie wants to move as soon as she can, Alexander, and I must be here to settle the new housekeeper in, would it not be advantageous for us to marry sooner than we had planned? Next month, say, instead of in the spring?'

His face lit up. 'An excellent idea – if you think that you can make arrangements in such a short time.'

'I shall speak to the school tomorrow; I'm sure that they will agree to let me leave earlier, given the circumstances. And as we're both agreed on a quiet wedding there's little to arrange. You'll help me, won't you, Eppie? And,' she added sweetly to her intended, 'I shall visit your mother later today to explain our new plans, and ask for her help as well. I'm sure that she will be happy to do all she can for us.'

It was strange, but delightful, Marion thought, how fate worked out at times. Now that she had finally won Alexander she could not wait to become his wife, and spring had seemed so far away.

* * *

Although it was only mid-March there were already days, scattered in among the winter's final blustering attempts at intimidation, when spring seemed to be just around the corner, and this was one of them.

Eppie had spent the morning washing the curtains and beating months of dust from the rugs, with some hindering help from the children. She had been in the cottage for almost three months, following Marion and Alexander Geddes's wedding on Hogmanay, the last day of 1870. By then, the new housekeeper, a cheerful, capable woman, had been installed in what used to be Eppie's kitchen.

It wasn't until she moved into the cottage, with its small cosy rooms and the knowledge that neighbours were just through the wall on either side, that she realised how much she had missed it. Marion was in her element as mistress of the Geddes house with its large, lofty rooms, but places like that were not for Eppie.

At first, she had thought to augment the money that had been banked for the children by returning to her former work at the farlins, but Alexander Geddes had taken it upon himself to act as unofficial guardian to the orphaned family and insisted on paying a regular amount of money into the bank account that had been set up for Tolly's compensation money, enough to support Eppie and the children without the need for her to work.

As the cottage was small and also noisy because of the four children, it had been agreed that Charlotte could best continue her studying if she remained at Shorehead. As she and Eppie could still see each other every day, the arrangement suited them both well enough.

Eppie's new little family was thriving, and she was even beginning to think of returning to the farlins, if not that year then the next, if she could find someone to keep an eye on the children while she was at work. She appreciated her new brother-in-law's determination to make life as easy for her as possible, but she was independent, and liked to feel that she was earning her own keep.

There was just one thing missing in her life now, and at the moment she could not quite put a finger on the cause of the restlessness she felt when the children were in bed and she sat alone by the fire at nights.

The feeling was strong that day, and after putting the beaten rugs back on the floor and making sure that the curtains were pegged securely on the line and unlikely to be pulled down by the wind, she gave the children their midday meal and then started putting them into their outdoor clothes.

'We'll go for a walk along the shore,' she announced. A long walk and a good blow would tire them out, and perhaps settle her.

The children jiggled around excitedly, and it took some time to push arms into sleeves and feet into boots. But at last they were ready, and she picked Jeemsie up and ordered the other three to stay close to her until they were past the harbour.

Then she opened the door, just in time to see a familiar figure come striding along the footpath. He turned in at the gate and then halted at sight of Eppie in the open doorway, the baby in her arms and the other three children clustered about her skirts.

They looked at each other, and as Eppie's stomach tangled itself into a knot she knew what had caused the restlessness, and what was missing from her life. At the same time she felt a slight sinking of her spirits. Did she really want another bout of sparring and arguing, to be followed by another parting?

Foy had swung his canvas bag from his shoulder, and as she looked at him, pleasure and dread chasing each other around in her head, he let the bag fall to the ground and then raised both arms in the air before dropping them to his sides in a submissive gesture.

'My name,' he said, 'is Ludovic.'

* * *

MORE FROM EVELYN HOOD

Another book from Evelyn Hood, *A Fisher Girl's Destiny*, is available to order now here:

https://mybook.to/FisherGirlBackAd

BIBLIOGRAPHY

Old Cullen and Portsoy by Alan Cooper. Published 2001 by Stenlake Publishing, 54–58 Mill Square, Catrine, Ayrshire.

Mither o' the Meal Kist, a Pictorial History of Fordyce by Christine Urquhart. Printed by W Peters & Son, Ltd., 16 High Street, Turiff.

Portsoy, Onwards From My Youth by Mrs M. A. (Bunty) Williams. Produced 2001 with assistance from the Banff Partnership Ltd.

Portsoy Manuscript of 1843. Produced 1993 by Portsoy Old Harbour Tercentenary Committee (with thanks to Texaco Oil Company for their assistance)

BIBLIOGRAPHY

ACKNOWLEDGEMENTS

Although this book is set in the beautiful Moray Firth village of Portsoy, the characters and their actions all come from my imagination.

Only three historical facts have been echoed in the book. Fordyce graveyard is indeed the resting place of one of Mary Queen of Scots' ladies-in-waiting, the famous 'four Marys'; the story of the *Grace-Ellen* is based on the tragedy of the Portsoy fishing vessel *Annie*, lost in January 1887 (*Banffshire Journal, 25th January, 1887*); and Duncan Geddes's plans for the marble quarry were borrowed from similar plans by the real lessees of the quarry, Messrs McDonald, London (*Banffshire Reporter, Friday, October 13th, 1876*), which never came to fruition.

My thanks to the following people for their invaluable assistance in researching for the book – Moira Stewart, Portsoy Librarian; Christine Urquhart of Fordyce; John Watson, who patiently explained the workings of a nineteenth-century marble quarry; Finlay Pirie, who gave me permission to use his research material; Jean Forsyth; Betty Welsh; Irene McKay and Tom Burnett-Stewart, the owner of the Portsoy marble and craft shop.

My thanks also go to the Past Portsoy website.

Evelyn Hood

ABOUT THE AUTHOR

Evelyn Hood is a *Sunday Times* bestselling author best known for her Scottish family sagas set in her hometown of Paisley, and the 'Prior's Ford' series set in the modern-day Scottish borders. Throughout her distinguished career, she published more than 40 novels, numerous short stories, plays, pantomimes, and musicals. Evelyn Hood passed away in Ayrshire in 2023, but the legacy of her writing continues, inspiring a generation of saga writers and touching reader's hearts worldwide.

Sign up to Evelyn Hood's mailing list for news, competitions and updates on future books.

ALSO BY EVELYN HOOD

Standalone Novels

A Widow's Hope

A Fisher Girl's Destiny

The Paisley Women Series

Hidden Family Secrets

Bonds of Friendship

The Defiant Seamstress

The Housekeeper's Promise

Sixpence Stories

Introducing Sixpence Stories!

Discover page-turning historical novels from your favourite authors, meet new friends and be transported back in time.

Join our book club Facebook group

https://bit.ly/SixpenceGroup

Sign up to our newsletter

https://bit.ly/SixpenceNews

Boldwood

Boldwood Books is an award-winning fiction publishing company seeking out the best stories from around the world.

Find out more at www.boldwoodbooks.com

Join our reader community for brilliant books, competitions and offers!

Follow us
@BoldwoodBooks
@TheBoldBookClub

Sign up to our weekly deals newsletter

https://bit.ly/BoldwoodBNewsletter